CW01337856

Praise for
The Knox Trilogy

'This is no dour Calvinist slog. Instead it's a page-turner from beginning to end, fusing wider themes like the Reformation with the intensely personal story of Elisabeth Hepburn as she struggles against oppressors who include her godson John Knox.' -- *Scottish Field*

'The author deftly tackles a very complicated, emotionally charged subject and brings it to life with historical and emotional accuracy.' -- ***The Historical Novel Society***

'Historically convincing, full of action and excitement ...This book creates a dramatic narrative against a background of Scotland in political and religious turmoil.' -- **Lexie Conyngham, Author,** *Death in a Scarlet Gown, Murray of Letho Series*

'The brutal, earthy world of the 16th century seems real and immediate, laced with saving humour. The thrilling narrative is evocative and descriptive.' -- **Ann McMillan**, *Honorary President of the Dorothy Dunnett Society*

'Essential reading for anyone with an interest in this period of Scotland's history, and for anyone who wants to know just how good historical fiction can be.' -- *Undiscovered Scotland*

'A story told in a language that pulses with real characters living their lives in the moment, surrounded as they were by religious and political turmoil... Marie Macpherson has brought them to vivid fictional life.' -- **Tom Murray, Author, Poet and Playwright,** *Sins of the Father, The Skull; Sons of War; Soldiers Tale; I am Flodden*

THE SECOND BLAST
OF THE TRUMPET

THE SECOND BLAST OF THE TRUMPET

The Knox Trilogy
BOOK TWO

To Michael

Marie Macpherson

Very best wishes

Marie Macpherson

KNOX ROBINSON
PUBLISHING
London & Atlanta

KNOX ROBINSON PUBLISHING

34 New House
67-68 Hatton Garden
London, EC1N 8JY
&
3103 Briarcliff RD NE 98414
Atlanta, Georgia 30345

First published in Great Britain and the United States in 2016 by Knox Robinson Publishing

A CIP catalogue record for this book is available from the British Library.

ISBN HC 978-1-910282-51-9

ISBN PB 978-1-910282-10-6

Printed in the United States of America and the United Kingdom

www.knoxrobinsonpublishing.com

To the memory of my mother and father

There arose my father's prayer, in holy evening's calm

How sweet was then my mother's voice, in the martyr's psalm

Now a' are gane! We meet nae mair meath the rowan tree

But hallowed thoughts around thee twine o' hame and infancy

Oh, rowan tree.

Lady Carolina Nairne

Contents

CAST OF CHARACTERS

★ Denotes fictional characters

HOUSE OF HEPBURN

Elisabeth Hepburn	Prioress of St Mary's Abbey, Haddington; godmother of John Knox
Joanna Hepburn	half-sister of Elisabeth; widow of Lord Seton; co-founder & abbess of St Catherine's Convent, Edinburgh
Sir David Lindsay	poet and playwright
Patrick Hepburn	3rd Earl of Bothwell, dubbed the Fair Earl; married & divorced Agnes Sinclair; nephew of Elisabeth Hepburn; father of James
Agnes Sinclair	divorced wife of Patrick Hepburn, 3rd Earl of Bothwell; dubbed Lady Morham
James Hepburn	son of Patrick, 3rd Earl of Bothwell & Agnes Sinclair; Master of Hailes, later 4th Earl of Bothwell
Jean Hepburn	sister of James Hepburn, 4th Earl of Bothwell
Harry Cockburn	groom at St Mary's Abbey, Haddington
★Sister Agnes	French nun at St Mary's Abbey, Haddington
★Isabelle Hepburn	(formerly Campbell) orphan adopted by Elisabeth Hepburn

SCOTTISH COURT

Marie de Guise	Queen Regent; mother of Mary Queen of Scots; widow of James V
Henri Cleutin	Seigneur d'Oisel; French ambassador
James Hamilton	(Errant Arran) 2nd Earl of Arran, later 1st Duke of Châtelherault
John Hamilton	Archbishop of St Andrews; half-brother of James Hamilton
James Hamilton	3rd Earl of Arran; son of Châtelherault; Captain of the Scot Guards
James Beaton	Archbishop of Glasgow; nephew of Cardinal David Beaton

John Row	Papal Nuncio
James Balfour	
of Pittendreich	former galley slave; lawyer

English Court

John Dudley	Earl of Warwick; Duke of Northumberland
Guildford Dudley	son of John Dudley; later husband of Lady Jane Grey
Mary Dudley	daughter of John Dudley; wife of Henry Sidney
Edward VI	King of England; son of Henry VIII & Jane Seymour
Thomas Cranmer	Archbishop of Canterbury
Richard Cox	Canon of Windsor; Chancellor of Oxford University
Matthew Stewart	4th Earl of Lennox; husband of Margaret Douglas; father of Henry, Lord Darnley
Margaret Douglas	Countess of Lennox; wife of Matthew Stewart; mother of Henry, Lord Darnley; daughter of Margaret Tudor & Archibald Douglas, 6th Earl of Angus
Henry Stewart	Lord Darnley; son of Matthew Stewart & Margaret Douglas
Jane Grey	daughter of Henry Grey, 1st Duke of Suffolk & Lady Frances Brandon; granddaughter of Mary Tudor, Henry VIII's sister
William Cecil	Secretary of State

Reformers

John Knox	godson of Elisabeth Hepburn; married Marjory Bowes
William Knox	older brother of John; merchant & skipper of the *Saltire*
Elizabeth Bowes	wife of Richard Bowes; mother of Marjory; mother-in-law of John Knox
Richard Bowes	captain & warden of Norham Castle; husband of Elizabeth
Marjory Bowes	daughter of Elizabeth & Richard; wife of John Knox
Amy Bowes	sister of Marjory
Mary and Beth Bowes	twin sisters of Marjory
Robert Bowes	brother of Richard; uncle of Marjory
Robert Stewart	archer; galley slave; Scots Guard
*Jamie Campbell	servant of John Knox; brother of Isabelle Hepburn

LONDON

Anna Locke	née Vaughan; poet & translator; wife of Henry Locke
Henry Locke	mercer; husband of Anna
Thomas Locke	mercer; brother of Henry
Rose Hickman	sister of Henry Locke; wife of Anthony Hickman
Anthony Hickman	mercer & merchant adventurer
Elizabeth Hill	sister of Henry Locke; wife of Richard Hill

FRANCE AND SWITZERLAND

John Wedderburn	Scots merchant in Dieppe
Heinrich Bullinger	Swiss reformer
John Calvin	French theologian
Antoine Calvin	brother of John Calvin
Anne Le Fert	Annette; wife of Antoine Calvin
Catherine Jacquemin	ward of Calvin; married William Whittingham
Judith Stordeur	stepdaughter of John Calvin; daughter of Idelette Stordeur
William Whittingham	pastor at Frankfurt; married Catherine Jacquemin
Christopher Goodman	English pastor
Walter Milne	Scots reformer; former Roman Catholic priest
Marta Milne	wife of Walter Milne
Miles Coverdale	English Protestant; translator of the Great Bible
Elizabeth Macheson	Scots wife of Miles Coverdale

SCOTTISH LORDS OF THE CONGREGATION

Henry Balnaves of Halhill	
Alexander Cunningham 4th Earl of Glencairn	
John Erskine of Dun	
John Willock	Protestant minister
William Keith	4th Earl Marischal
William Kirkcaldy of the Grange	Castilian; Scots Guard
William Maitland of Lethington	
James Stewart	natural son of James V & Margaret Erskine; half-brother of Mary Queen of Scots

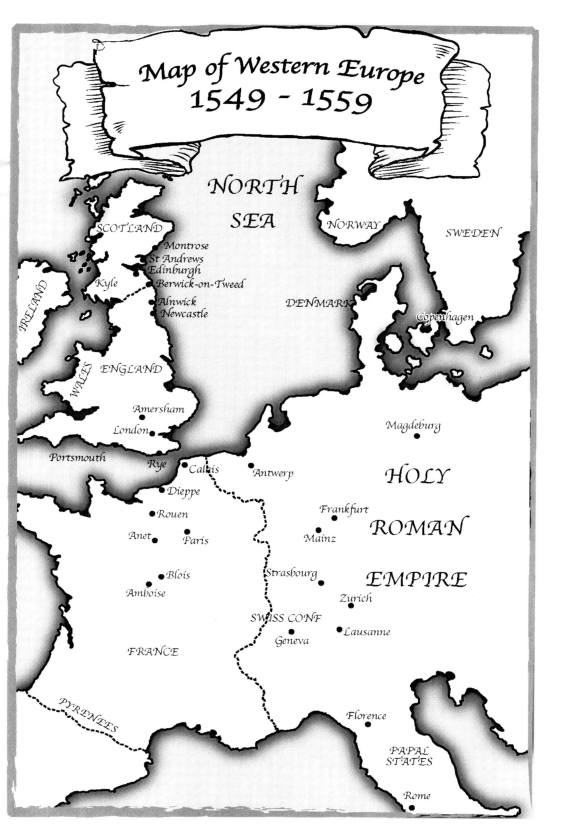

PART ONE

I

At Liberty at Last

> Ah! Freedom is a noble thing!
> *The Bruce*
> John Barbour, 14th Century

Dieppe, Northern France, Spring 1549

'Look o'er yonder, master prophet! There it is!'

Above the clamour of screeching gulls, ropes clacking against masts and ship carpenters hammering and banging at timbers, Robert Stewart's strident voice rang out. Knox raised his head and squinted upwards. There was no mistaking the pennant fluttering in the coastal breeze – the white diagonal cross of St Andrew set against a sky blue background. They had found William's boat.

Knox tried to quicken his pace but, hampered by feet clad in tattered cloths tied with hempen laces, he could only shuffle along. Forbye, the muscles in his legs, though strong and sinewy from hauling at the oars in the galleys, were unused to walking.

'Come along, master prophet,' Stewart chided. 'Let's foot it out together.'

Knox groaned inwardly. Despite his pleas, the mercenary had refused to drop the undeserved title. Now Stewart hooked a brawny arm through his and together they staggered along the quay like a couple of drunken mariners on shore leave. Only their red felt caps betrayed them as galley slaves.

Behind them, James Balfour slunk along in their wake, slewing from side to side to dodge puddles of bilge water and pools of tar. Every so often he stooped to rub his ankles still raw from the recently released shackles.

'I'm sick to my stomach with the sea,' he grumbled, sniffing the air like a cur, 'with the stench of slimy seaweed bunging up my nostrils and the salt stinging my eyes. I'll be glad to be back home on dry land, breathing fresh Fife air.'

'You're aye snivelling and whining,' Stewart snapped. 'You should be jumping for joy now you're free.'

'I should never have been chained to an oar in the first place,' Balfour retorted.

Paying no heed to their squabble, Knox leant against a capstan and examined the boat tied up at the quay. After nineteen months as a galley slave encountering all manner of shipping on the seaboard, Knox had learnt to identify vessels. With its name emblazoned on the hull in white letters *The Saltire* was not a humble fishing coracle as he'd expected but a square-rigged, single-masted, broad-beamed coble. His brother William must be doing well to afford such a stout trading vessel.

Stewart tugged Knox's arm. 'Come on, master, let's clamber aboard.'

'Haud on a wee.' Knox pulled off his red cap and flung it into the sea.

Stewart followed his lead and within an eye-blink a screech of seagulls had swooped down to snatch up their symbols of slavery. 'And may thon foul flying rats choke on them.'

As Stewart held out a hand to help Knox onto the gangplank, Balfour shoved in front of them. 'Watch where you're going,' he barked. 'The prophet takes precedence.'

'To hell with the prophet,' Balfour mumbled.

'Steek your gab, you cheeky wee cur, or I'll shut it for you.' With a well-aimed elbow in the ribs, Stewart toppled him into the sea.

As Balfour thrashed about in the murky water, a voice from the boat boomed, 'Fish out the flounder, Jamie.'

A young lad jumped from the deck and flung out a rope to drag Balfour onto the quay. Sodden and shivering and dripping with fronds of rotting sea wrack, the salvaged wretch muttered curses under his breath.

'That'll teach you to curse the prophet, Blasphemous Balfour,' Stewart scoffed.

Balfour lunged at his tormentor but his rescuer grabbed his arms and twisted them behind his back. As Stewart clenched a fist to punch Balfour's chin, the skipper leapt between them and whacked his arm down. Grabbing Stewart by the scruff of the neck he growled, 'There's no fighting on my watch, or I'll throw you both in the brine. Now make your peace.'

Once the two rivals had shaken hands and promised no more blows, Skipper William Knox greeted his brother with a hearty slap on the back and clamped an arm round the young seaman's hefty shoulders. 'Johnnie, do you mind this braw lad?'

Knox peered at him. At eighteen-years-old, Jamie Campbell was no longer the shilpit wee orphan he'd rescued but a brawny, bearded mariner. 'Aye, that I do. He's grown to be a fine lad.'

'In truth. And lofty enough for a seaman. O'er lang and he'd keel over in the wind. Now, my bonnie lads, you'll be welcome aboard once you've been deloused. You'll be ridden with wee beasties and I'll no risk your fleas crawling all over my precious cargo.'

Careful to keep the two rivals at arms' length, Jamie led them to a shed where they stripped off their ragged brown tunics and canvas breeches. A quick douse in a tub of salt water followed by a rub down with a hessian cloth soused away most of the lice and fleas that had feasted on their scratchy skin.

Back on board the *Saltire*, Skipper Will showed them their berths for the voyage – a heap of sheep fleeces.

'At least it's no a pile of reeking herring,' Knox said.

The skipper laughed. 'Nay, I've bigger fish to land. Shearlings are now my stock-in-trade. They're worth more than their weight in salted salmon.'

'So, you've cast off the nets of the apostles.'

Will laughed. 'Aye, I've traded up from fishing to freight. We not only ferry fleeces from England and wool from Flanders but any kind of cargo: goods and chattels, letters and messages, pedlars and passengers. Forbye, a sea voyage is faster and safer than an overland passage.'

'Not always,' a listless voice said. A figure swathed in a fur-lined cloak crawled out of the cuddy: he slowly uncurled, rubbing the small of his back as he stretched.

'If you will sail in the depths of winter and in a foreign vessel, Sir David!' Will turned to his brother. 'Our ambassador was shipwrecked off the Danish coast and marooned in Esbjerg for months with the survivors of the Scottish embassy.'

Sir David Lindsay's crumpled face creased into a smile. 'Until this skeily skipper came to my rescue.'

'Since you named this vessel the *Saltire,* it should bring you better luck,' William quipped.

'May it bring good fortune to us all.' Lindsay stepped forward and held out his arms. 'It's good to see you, John. There's been a wheen of water under the bridge since we last met.' For a few moments they remained locked in an embrace before breaking apart. 'If nothing else, your time in the galleys has given you powerful shoulders,' Lindsay remarked. 'And you'll need them to bear the burden I have in mind for you.'

'If it's what I have in mind, too, then I'm ready,' Knox replied. A gleam of hope in his deep blue eyes lit up his weather-beaten face.

When the boat left harbour on the evening tide, Knox edged his way to the stern. 'I pray that's the last I shall ever see of Dieppe,' he murmured to himself as the French coast dipped beneath the horizon. 'I'm longing for my first sight of Scotland and St Andrews where I shall preach my first sermon. Give me the strength, dear Lord, to bring your true word to my people.'

'This new order you keep havering about – what does it mean?' a gruff voice asked.

Roused from his reverie, Knox swivelled round. Throughout their long months of captivity, the mercenary Stewart had mocked the so-called heretics for their thrawn tenacity to their faith but now, for some reason, he was taking Knox's side. Had he had a change of heart?

'Almighty God has entrusted me with a mission to bring the reformed faith to Scotland,' he explained. 'To pull our compatriots from the puddle of papistry and put an end to idolatry.'

Stewart's face wrinkled. 'Aye, well you've lost me there, master prophet.'

'The pope in Rome is our avowed enemy. Thon Antichrist and whore of

Babylon holds more gold than the legendary Croesus yet he's bleeding the poor folk of Scotland dry. And pardoners, thon bloodsucking leeches, are filling the Vatican's coffers to build a vast basilica. The apostle Peter would be black affronted at their avarice. I am called upon to slay the Beast.'

In words the archer might understand, Knox paraphrased Psalm XXI. 'Though they intend evil against us and have devised a plot, they will not succeed. For we will make them turn their backs; we will aim with our bowstrings at their faces.'

Stewart grinned. 'I'm the very man to do the hitting for I'm a champion archer.' He held up two fingers. 'In spite of all thon rowing, they're still intact. I brought doon the doo with one shot the most times at Kilwinning Abbey.'

'You must be knacky indeed.' While taking refuge in Kyle, Knox had witnessed the annual shoot at the abbey where archers competed to bring down a wooden pigeon flown from the top of the tower.

'Words cannot be your only barbs,' Stewart said. 'You'll need bowmen like me, proven in battle.' Straightening up, he showed off brawny shoulder muscles, honed after months of hard graft in the galleys. He then drew the string of an imaginary bow to the worn cleft in his chin and closed one eye. 'My pulling arm is still strong but I'll need to sharpen my eye. Then I'll be fit to serve in this reformation. Only say the word, master prophet and I'll leap to defend you and fight for your faith.'

'But you're a mercenary – I cannot pay you.' Knox took his passion with a skillet of salt for Stewart was a blustering braggart. He doubted religious zeal had spurred the Ayrshire archer to offer his services to the Castilians during the St Andrews siege but the rich rewards to be gained from King Harry of England. The seasoned mercenary had taken captivity in his stride, confident that a skilled archer would attract a good ransom and soon be set free.

However true his aim or however quickly he emptied his quiver, the archer was tarred with the same brush as the Castilians – and no one was willing to redeem a heretic. Since Stewart's only allegiance was to the highest bidder, Knox was sure he would soon be seeking more lucrative employment.

Stewart waggled his head and rubbed his thumb with his fingertips. 'I can wait for my rewards.' Madness gleamed in his eyes and his lips curled into a leer. 'Once we've purloined the Vatican treasure kist there will be prizes aplenty for all, master prophet.'

Back on deck, Knox bedded down on a fleece and lay brooding. How could he shake off the errant archer?

Cocooned in his blanket, Lindsay wriggled over to him. 'Your two companions, your bench-mates at the oars – tell me about them, John. As far as I mind young James Balfour seemed eager enough when he joined the Castilians.'

Knox sighed. 'Aye, and he saved my life when I was left for dead in the stinking bowels of the boat. But towards the end, he became dour and sour as bitterness nibbled away his soul. He's sorely aggrieved at being unfairly punished for being in the wrong place at the wrong time. Balfour seems to be losing hope and faith.'

'He's only a lad of what – twenty years? Doubtless he's regretting his decision to join our cause but what about thon mercenary? He seems an unlikely soul mate.'

Knox groaned. 'In truth! I may have lost Blasphemous Balfour but I've gained an ally in the Ayrshire archer. Robert Stewart clings to me like a louse but only for the gold he can loot from the Vatican.'

Lindsay chortled. 'So Mammon, not God, drives your money-grubbing mercenary? Not a true soldier of Christ then.'

'Nay, but how am I to rid myself of this self-appointed bodyguard?'

'Never fash, John, I ken how to make use of his military skills. Trust me.'

Knox was sinking into sleep when Lindsay whispered in his ear. 'Listen, John, this may not please you, but I want you to ken your godmother had a hand in your release. Being lowly born *and* a heretic, you'd never have been freed at all without her intercession. But one of the concessions in the Treaty of Haddington was to free the Castilians, including the galley slaves, otherwise you'd have been left to wither away at the oar. Dame Elisabeth bent the ear of Marie de Guise to put in a word for you as her godson. Whatever anyone else may say, it was these two women who requested your release.'

Knox stiffened. In captivity he'd forsworn the mass and pitched the idolatrous icon of *Notre Dame* over the side of the galley – to signal he'd jettisoned his former life. Born again, he'd been baptised not only in the blood of the martyr, George Wishart, but in his own blood, sweat, and tears from toiling at the oars.

'That may be true,' Knox replied, his voice gruff, 'and I'm grateful. But she must ken I can never return to the papist church.'

'I know that, John. But as your godmother, Lisbeth, I mean Dame Elisabeth, fears for your life. She loves you – as a son. Aye keep that in mind.'

Knox turned over and fell into a fitful sleep disturbed by dreadful dreams. He was back in the galleys, pulling at the oars, jerking awake every time a whiplash stung his back. The manacles burned weals on his wrists and ankles, his arms grew heavier and his body screamed out for rest. The icon of Our Lady loomed before him but with the benign face of Dame Elisabeth reciting the ballad of True Thomas:

> And if ye dare to kiss my lips,
> Sure of your body I will be.'

He yearned to rest his head on her maternal lap, to bide awhile and be beguiled by her tales. Rocking back and forth, back and forth, he lay listening to her gentle voice:

'And see not ye that braid braid road,
That leadeth down by the skerry fell?
It's ill's the man that doth thereon gang,
For it leadeth him straight to the gates o hell.'

Saying this, her divine features warped into the crude grimace of the Black Madonna. Knox woke with a jolt and lay for a while disconcerted. The *Saltire* was no longer moving forward but swaying gently from side to side. They must have docked somewhere to unload a cargo. He had snuggled down again when a lantern shone in his face.

'Liven up, Johnnie my lad,' William tugged his blanket. 'We're about to land.'

Knox yawned and stretched his arms. 'That must have been the shortest voyage to Scotland ever – or else I've slept the sleep of the dead.'

'You're no in Scotland. We've just skipped across the *Manche* to Rye, one of the Channel ports. This is where you and Sir David step ashore.'

Lindsay wriggled out of his cocoon and scrambled to his feet. 'Aye, and make our way to London.'

'London?' Knox was fully awake now. 'Why?'

'You'll find out soon enough, John. I have plans for you, mind.'

Roused by their voices, Stewart stumbled towards them. 'You'll need me to look out for you, master prophet. I'm coming with you. And you, too, my sulky wee kelpie.' He gave the sleeping Balfour a hefty kick. 'Bestir your blighted bones – or else you'll get another dousing with a bucket of cold water.'

Balfour grunted and pulled up his blanket. 'I'm staying put.'

Stewart knelt down on one knee and yanked back the blanket. 'They'll burn more than your arse if you go back to Scotland. They'll crucify a blasphemer.'

'I'll take my chance.'

'The devil take you, Blasphemous Balfour. A cowardly knave if ever I saw one,' Stewart rasped and spat in his face. Getting to his feet, he put a hand on Knox's shoulder. 'Never fash, master prophet, I'll no let you down.'

Knox shot a worried glance at Lindsay who shrugged and mouthed, 'Keep tryst.'

II

The Siege of Haddington

Dies irae! Dies illa
Confutatis maledictis,
Latin Hymn, 13th Century

St Mary's Abbey, Haddington, March 1549

Strangers shall possess your houses, chase you from your habitations and set upon you with sword and fire. Pestilence and famine shall afflict you. And the walls of this rose-red kirk by the Tyne will be open to the skies.

'George Wishart's words have come back to haunt us. His curses have come true.'

Despite long years as prioress of St Mary's Abbey, Elisabeth Hepburn could not slough off the weird feeling, thon eerie sense of foreboding overshadowing her life. Ever since the Protestant preacher had railed against the ungrateful folk of Haddington in his final sermon at St Mary's Kirk, the town had suffered sword, fire and famine. Was churlish Haddington being chastised for spurning the reformer's message? Had his sacrifice at the stake aroused divine wrath?

'Wishart was a heretic who deserved to die.' Sister Agnes's Lenten grey face, distorted into a mask of hatred, was disturbing. Grasping the pestle with two bony hands, she pounded the dried hemlock seeds in the mortar as if crushing the charred bones of the profane preacher.

'Cardinal Beaton is the martyr, murdered by those heathens in St Andrews,' she said. 'Now we've lost our champion of the true faith, we must stand firm against the faithless foe. How dare the English infidels try to inflict their false doctrines on us! How dare they bully us into wedding our Catholic queen to their Protestant king! Let us give thanks she's now safely in France.' The sister's skeletal hands trembled as she signed herself with the cross.

No doubt Sister Agnes was right, Elisabeth thought. Furious that the Treaty of Haddington had snatched Mary, Queen of Scots from under their noses and betrothed her to the French Dauphin, the English were wreaking their revenge. The invading army had driven the townsfolk from their homes and cannon fire had destroyed the roof and bell-tower of St Mary's Church. Before the grain could be harvested, the River Tyne had broken its banks, swamping the fields and rotting the crops. Now, after a long winter of want, the spectre of the plague was stalking them.

'The pest is already raging through the besieged town, scything down the weakened English troops,' Elisabeth said.

'That's divine retribution for what they have inflicted on us.' Sister Agnes tilted the ground hemlock seeds into a mash of bran and powdered puffballs. Spread on a poultice, the paste helped to clot blood and heal wounds. As she stirred the mixture, her bony hands quivered from weakness or wrath or both.

'That may be true,' the prioress replied, 'but the townsfolk are shovelling the plague-stricken soldiers out into the streets along with the rotting corpses. I fear the miasma from the burial pits may taint the air and spread the scourge. Some of the women may already be smitten. They've been whinging about weeping sores and chancres breaking out all over the body. The masks don't seem to be fending off disease.'

To protect the women from infection while tending the wounded soldiers, Sister Agnes had designed a muslin mask. Stuffed with a mixture of dried lavender, mint and sage, it stifled the stench of decaying flesh but did not seem to ward off this mysterious malady.

While Sister Agnes ladled her mixture into pots, Elisabeth untied a posy of herbs drying on a rafter, scattering the crumbling sprigs all over the floor. 'These herbs have been left drying too long. They've lost their smeddum – like us all. Perhaps we should try more pungent spices – camphor or cloves. What about a sponge soaked in vinegar?'

Sister Agnes looked doubtful. 'It's not the plague, of that I'm sure. They have no fever, nor any black swellings under the armpit or the groin, *Deo Gratias*. And I doubt so many can be afflicted with leprosy.'

Elisabeth shuddered. 'Then might it be the grandgore – the pox?'

Sister Agnes shook her head. 'Nay, the pox forms pus-filled blisters that scab and leave the skin pockmarked. These sores are more like warts and, worst of all, they infest the groin.'

Elisabeth heaved a sigh. Whatever it was, the lesions were proving difficult to heal. Calendula ointment would soothe the infected sores but they had run out of marigold petals and, more seriously, honey. The bees had abandoned the besieged convent, leaving them with no honey for healing wounds and sweetening and preserving fruit, and no beeswax for ointments and candles. Elisabeth sniffed a bowl of lard: it smelt sour but was better than nothing.

'We'll have to wait till Skipper Will brings more supplies,' Sister Agnes said. 'The *Saltire* is due any day.'

Would he have any news of John, Elisabeth wondered but did not say, for it brought to mind a recurring nightmare. At the start of the siege, slaves from the French galleys moored in Aberlady Bay had been commandeered to help build fortifications. Herded up to Haddington, the captives were put to work digging trenches, all the while under fire from the English troops. At dusk, the mutilated bodies of both dead and dying were flung onto carts, to be buried indiscriminately in pits outside the town.

That her godson might be amongst those dumped alive into the pit had preyed on Elisabeth's mind. In the nightmare, she scrabbled among piles of rotting corpses, fighting off carrion crow that were picking the flesh off bones and pecking out eyes. And always the leering skull taunting her with its grisly grin.

She dared not mention this to Sister Agnes. The devout Catholic nun believed John Knox had been bewitched by Wishart's evil spell and would be damned to hellfire. Nor did she dare reveal her nightmare featuring Agnes's other *bête-noir*.

When Davie Lindsay was dispatched on a diplomatic mission to the Danish court, Elisabeth fretted he might be tempted to bide with King Christian III, a Lutheran who shared his reformist ideas. That she may never see Davie again haunted her, a fear intensified by news of a shipwreck that had taken the lives of many members of the Scottish embassy. Her Davie drowned! It could not be. Sweat broke out on her brow: she closed her eyes.

'Are you unwell?' Agnes asked.

'Nay, just wabbit and worn out. No worse than we all are.' As she gripped the edge of the countertop an ear-shattering blast shook the walls of the apothecary. By the time they had taken shelter under the counter, the bombardment was over.

Elisabeth scrambled to her feet. 'That was swift. The English must be running out of cannonballs,' she said.

'Not fast enough,' Agnes replied. 'For we cannot afford to lose any more bottles.' Still on her knees she carefully swept up shards of glass from bottles smashed to smithereens on the flagstones. After a moment, she leant back on her haunches. 'Where is Isabelle?'

'Never fash, Agnes, the soldiers will make sure their little pet comes to no harm.'

'I pray it is so. They've taken *la petite soeur* to their hearts for she's braver than a Celt, they say.'

'That is praise indeed. Thon rough highlanders might be warriors *sans pareil*, but the blast of cannon fire fills the Celts with such terror they cover their ears and throw themselves on their bellies.' Elisabeth chuckled at the thought.

'It's not cannon fire that worries me. Isabelle is growing up quickly: she'll soon be nearing womanhood. She's too trusting with all these lone men far from home. As for those highlanders ...' The French sister didn't know what to make of those wild men with their bows and targes, wielding a hefty two-handed sword and winding a length of coarse woollen plaid round their waists to cover their nakedness.

'The Celts would never harm Isabelle,' Elisabeth said, for they loved to hear her laugh, lightsome and blithe, like the lilting of a linnet. Being a natural mimic with an ear for languages, their *gealbhonn-lin* had picked up some of the Gaelic and her attempts at rolling the sounds round her tongue sent them into paroxysms of laughter.

'Perhaps we should have sent her away.' Sister Agnes's brow creased with concern.

Elisabeth puffed out her cheeks. 'How could we have known the siege would drag on for so long?'

They both gave a start when the door banged open and Isabelle came rushing in.

'Did you hear thon blast? That'll make the Celts skirl! It fairly made my head dirl and my belly rumble.' Her bright eyes darted around the apothecary.

After a woeful harvest, food was scarce. Elisabeth and Sister Agnes had sacrificed their rations to satisfy the twelve-year-old girl's appetite but she was still always ravenous. When Agnes nodded in the direction of a barrel, the lid weighted down by a stone, Isabelle screwed up her nose in disgust. 'Yeugh! Thon creepie crawlies give me the cold creeps.'

'You eat cockles and whelks, don't you? These are no different,' Sister Agnes said. 'Since beggars cannot be choosers, we must be grateful for any food in times of famine. In France, when food is scarce, we savour *les escargots*.'

'At least it's better than rats,' Elisabeth said.

When their supplies were cut off at Aberlady, the English had slaughtered and devoured their horses and were now surviving on rats, mice – any living creature that moved.

'Then toss these nasty wee beasties over to them,' Isabelle said.

Sister Agnes lifted the lid and picked out a snail. As she fingered the slimy edge of the opening, the creature poked out from its shell, its tiny antler horns waving in mid-air. Isabelle shrank back. Once they were fattened up, the French sister boiled them up into a brose. Alive. 'Soft, so still growing,' she judged and put it back.

'Thank goodness,' Isabelle said. 'They make me puke.'

'Then it will have to be a bannock, dipped in rancid lard.' As Isabelle pounced greedily on the fusty oaten bannock, Elisabeth clasped the girl's wrist. 'Hardly enough to put meat on those skinny bones.'

Abandoned as orphans, Isabelle and her brother Jamie had scavenged for food until rescued by Knox who brought them to the abbey. It grieved Elisabeth that her goddaughter had to suffer the gnawing pangs of hunger yet again.

Isabelle wiped the crumbs from her lips with the back of her hand. 'There's a wheen of whingers waiting outside this evening. Have they all got the French boils on their behouchies?'

Sister Agnes whirled round. 'Where did you hear that?' Her thin, bloodless lips squeezed tightly together.

'Och, the soldiers are aye snickering about it. Our lads taunt the Italians by crying it the Italian itch or the Neapolitan nip, and they pester the Spaniards by saying it's the Spanish scabies. But they all say the fushionless French are plagued with the plooks.' She giggled and threw Sister Agnes a furtive glance. 'They say swyving is the cause.' Her eyes loomed large as she waited for the nun's reaction.

Sister Agnes scowled. 'Keep away from the soldiers, Isabelle. Do you hear?'

'But I'm their talisman, their lucky charm,' Isabelle trilled and, pinching another bannock, dashed out.

'Out of the mouths of bairns, Agnes. Our lass may be right.' Elisabeth heaved a rueful sigh. For the worst affected were the camp followers attending the foreign mercenaries who rewarded the women with food, wine and fripperies in return for their care. Nursing was not the only service on offer.

When the camp followers queued outside the apothecary, Sister Agnes waggled a finger and refused to dispense any remedies until they agreed to withhold their favours. This new scourge must be stopped.

But a scraggy thrawn-faced woman carrying a babe in a shawl draped round one shoulder merely scoffed. 'Och, Sister, we're no holy nuns. We've no taken a vow of chastity. Forbye, we maun put food in our bairns' mouths.' She turned to the prioress. 'If you were a mother would you leave your wee mites kyte-clung with hunger?'

Elisabeth could sympathise. Sister Agnes's warnings were as straw in the wind to these poverty-stricken women who had too much to lose from well-paid mercenaries who had too much to give. At her nod, Sister Agnes grudgingly dispensed the ointments.

While they tidied up the apothecary, the woman's words preyed on Elisabeth's mind. Perhaps she should send Isabelle out of harm's way. To Morham, in the foothills of the Lammermuirs, to live with Agnes Sinclair, Patrick Hepburn's discarded wife, who had offered to take her as a steadying influence on her unruly twelve-year-old daughter, Jean. Before she could decide, Isabelle poked her head round door.

'Skipper Will's here! And Jamie's with him!' she yelled and ran off to catch up with her brother.

Now an experienced seaman who knew every cove and cranny along the coastlines from Bergen to Bilbao, William Knox was their lifeline. During the siege, when the English had blockaded the main ports on the Firth of Forth, this skeily skipper had found a way to smuggle in provisions from France. More importantly, Elisabeth never lost hope he might hear news of Knox, imprisoned in the French galleys. *Nil desperandum.*

Elisabeth gripped his arm and whispered. 'Any news of John? I've heard the prisoners held in France are to be released.'

'Aye, he's free,' Will replied but his dour face made her fearful.

'What? Is he here? Have you brought him home?'

'Nay, it's still too dangerous. I dropped him and Sir Davie off at the port of Rye.'

'Sir Davie Lindsay, too? He's alive and well?'

'Well enough – when last seen.'

'Thanks be to the Blessed Virgin!' As Elisabeth crossed herself, her fingers pressed the king's ring close to her heart. She gripped the skipper's sleeve.

'I beg you, Will, please if you can. Bring them home safely. Both my bonnie lads.'

III

New Beginnings

Gem of all joy, jasper of jocunditie,
Most mighty carbuncle of virtue and valour;
Empress of towns, exalt in honour
In Honour of the City of London
William Dunbar, 15th–16th Century

Cheapside, London, Spring, 1549

The early morning mist swirling around their skiff stifled any sounds and blurred any sights of the countryside, but it failed to staunch the foul reek rising from the mighty River Thames. Lindsay wrinkled his nose.

'Hardly the *sweet paradise precelling in pleasure* William Dunbar waxed poetic about. *London, thou art the flower of Cities all! With beryl streams, pleasant and preclare.*'

'O'er liberal use of poetic licence,' Knox scoffed. 'Our great makar could never have set foot in this city nor been borne along in the arms of auld Father Thames. Why, it's nothing more than a cesspit full of keech!' He pinched his nose and pointed to lumps of raw sewage floating along the surface of the murky river.

'Oh, but he did,' Lindsay replied. 'James IV dispatched Dunbar to London to negotiate his marriage with Margaret Tudor. He wrote the eulogy to impress her father but clearly failed for Henry VII provided a measly dowry. We had such high hopes that grafting the Scottish thistle to the English rose and signing the Treaty of Perpetual Peace would end all conflict between the two kingdoms but alas, no.'

As they sailed along the Thames, the morning haze gradually lifted to unveil the sovereign city. When the arches of London Bridge – more like a street than a bridge with row upon row of high buildings – hove into view, Knox grimaced at a row of spiked heads on the southern gatehouse.

'Thon grisly tradition began with William Wallace,' Lindsay said. 'Traitor to the English but hero to the Scots. Since then countless martyrs and traitors have had their severed heads boiled and dipped in tar before being stuck up there as a warning.'

'Have no fear, Master Knox. I'll make sure your head never rolls,' Stewart said.

The church bells of nearby St Mary-le-Bow were pealing six o'clock when the skiff dropped them off at Cheapside.

'Here we are. The sign of the Padlock where we'll be biding with the Lockes, as it happens,' Lindsay quipped. 'Mercer Henry Locke has kindly offered us hospitality. He has a winsome wife who writes poetry, forbye.'

At the door of a black timber-framed house a stout young man offered a robust handshake before ushering them into the parlour. His wife, Anna, greeted Lindsay with a welcoming smile but looked askance at the two scruffy men dressed in skimpy mariner's tunics. After a whispered consultation, her husband directed Stewart to the servants' quarters while she led Knox to a bedchamber.

'Please make use of these garments.' Pointing to a pile of clothes on top of a chest, she blinked back tears. 'They belonged to my dearly departed father. He passed away a few months ago.'

'I'm sorry for your loss,' Knox replied before attempting to raise a smile on her bonny face. 'Better buskit in dead man's weeds than barefoot and freezing to death.' But his cheeriness faded when a maid brought in a steaming bowl and a razor. 'That I shall never do again. My beard shall grow to show the world I'm no longer one of Baal's shaven sort.'

Mrs Locke arched her eyebrows, two skeins of black silk above dove grey eyes that radiated intelligence. 'I understand. A sign that you have cast off the papist church and no longer worship false gods.'

'That's very wise of you. You must be well versed in scripture.'

Her lips curled into a smile. 'Not only the Bible. I may be a mere woman but I've also studied Dr Calvin's writings. I plan to translate his works into English so that the faithful here can benefit from his teaching.'

'A most worthy task,' Knox replied, even more in awe of her learning.

Downstairs in the hall, Lindsay gave his newly acquired attire a nod. 'Well enough bruikit to meet some kenspeckle folk.'

In the parlour, a group of men were gathered round a table, deep in discussion. One of them broke away and extended a hand. 'Here's the man himself.'

It took Knox a moment to recognise Sir Henry Balnaves who'd also been taken captive at St Andrews. No backbreaking galleys for this nobleman and ambassador who'd become fleshy and flabby serving his sentence in the relative comfort of Rouen palace. As Balnaves shook him firmly by the hand, Knox cast a glance round the room.

'What of the other prisoners? Have they also been released?' Knox was concerned for those lads incarcerated for their part in Cardinal Beaton's murder. William Kirkcaldy of the Grange had written from Mont St Michel asking whether they might, with a safe conscience, break their prison. Knowing those young hotheads would have no scruples about killing lowly prison guards, Knox had worded his reply carefully. As long as they used no unlawful means, they could take advantage of any God-given opportunity.

'Nay, not released, but they are at large,' Balnaves replied. 'When the guards got drunk during the Twelfth Night revels they stole the keys and slipped out.'

'So they escaped without shedding blood?' Knox asked.

A slight man with the sallow complexion of a scribe and the sharp snout of a shrew sidled forward to answer, 'As far as we know.'

'If he doesn't ken then nobody does,' Balnaves said with a grin. 'Meet our saviour, the man who negotiated our release. William Cecil, secretary to the Duke of Somerset.'

Clad from head to toe in clerical black Cecil tucked his hands in his sleeves and gave a low bow. 'At your service.'

'Never be fooled by his humble façade,' Balnaves said, 'for it hides a canny mind. The wily secretary convinced the French that as an English adviser I was an English subject, not a Scot. Therefore I was being held illegally. How's that for cunning?' He chuckled. 'Then, when I sang your praises, he leant on the French to set you free. By what means, only he kens.' He gave Cecil a conspiratorial wink. 'You have him to thank, Mr Knox.'

Knox glanced at Lindsay who shrugged as if to say, *What did I tell you?*

'Now you'll see what mettle our man is made of, Master Cecil,' Balnaves went on. 'While I was languishing in luxury, this miserable wretch was lying in irons in the middle of the Loire.' He slapped Knox on the back. 'Yet, despite his calloused hands he took the trouble to edit my treatise on justification by faith.' He pointed to the manuscript rolled out on the table.

'Do not be making a martyr out of me, Sir Henry, I bid you,' Knox said quietly.

'Indeed not! You are no martyr but a veritable hero.'

'It cheered me to know I wasn't a lone voice crying in the wilderness. Forbye, for the sake of the unlearned reader, I had to make this lawyer's long-winded ramblings comprehensible.'

Balnaves chuckled good-heartedly. 'So, Secretary Cecil, now you see why Mr Knox should be our champion to lead the reformed church and defeat the Antichrist in Rome.'

Excitement stirred in Knox's breast. 'It shall please me greatly to return to Scotland. Throughout the long dark months, thon dream kept me going.'

When the others exchanged troubled glances, Lindsay steered Knox aside. 'You cannot go back, John. By the terms of your release you're free to live in any country,' he paused, 'but Scotland. Forbye, John Hamilton, Archbishop of St Andrews, is keeping close watch on all reformist sympathisers. It isn't safe for you to return – not yet.'

'I'll take the risk. For one thing, no one will recognise me now. Not behind this.' Knox tweaked his neatly trimmed beard. 'For another, I'll use my mother's name.'

Lindsay winced. 'What do you mean?'

'Sinclair. I shall call myself John Sinclair.'

Momentarily confused, Lindsay quickly recovered his wits. 'As soon as you open your mouth, John, your vehement voice will give you away.'

'I must go back. God is calling me! The spark of hope that I would return one day and light the beacon of the true faith in my homeland has kept me alive.'

'I could not help but overhear, Mr Knox,' said Cecil who'd sneaked up on them. 'For the foreseeable future, you will not be greeted as a prophet in your own land. However, you would be most welcome here in England. My lord Somerset, guardian and protector of King Edward, will guarantee your safety – and of course your salary.' Cecil held out a drawstring pouch and a parchment.

'What's this?' Knox asked.

'By a new statute, only those granted a licence by the Privy Council are to be allowed to preach. On the recommendation of your friends, the king has appointed you chaplain. This is the first payment of your stipend. Five pounds.'

Knox examined the coins closely. 'Not five pounds Scots, I see, but sterling?'

'Of course, for you won't be needing Scots money where you're going.'

'Where will that be? London?'

'However deep and meaningful your sermons may be, a southern congregation will toil to understand your Scots accent, so, no, not London. Your ministry will be most welcome in the north where the newly reformed church is in dire need of preachers.' He paused. 'St Mary's is to be your parish – in Berwick-upon-Tweed.'

Bowing to divine will, Knox accepted the mission and, after a pleasant few days receiving the Lockes's warm hospitality, prepared to leave for the north. He had just stepped out of the Padlock when someone grabbed his arm. When Robert Stewart's face leered down at him, Knox's heart sank. He thought he'd cast off the pest.

'I ken you'll be greatly grieved, master prophet, but I'll no be coming with you. God has other plans for me and I must obey his will.'

When Knox looked bewildered, the archer went on, 'Did you no say God has already decided our fate? Even afore we were born?'

'Aye, the Lord God Almighty kens everything – past, present and future.'

'As my auld grannie used to say: we maun dree our weird. What's for us will no go by us – that's what you're saying, is it no?' As Stewart's face crinkled, the grime-engrained lines widened and whitened into a demonic grin. 'For I've my ain mission to fulfil, master prophet I'm to ...' his words skittered to a halt. 'Better steek my gab for I'm sworn to secrecy.'

Whatever the archer's mission was, Knox silently gave thanks they were parting ways. Following Stewart's shifty eyes to where Lindsay, Balnaves and Cecil were in deep conversation he was overcome with the uncanny premonition, the weird feeling as Betsy Learmont the spaewife had called it, that he'd not seen the last of Robert Stewart.

IV

The Wild Frontier

Berwick- upon-Tweed
Is the Devil's ain neuk
Traditional Legend

Berwick-upon-Tweed, Spring, 1549

There is better order among the Tartars than in this town. No man can have anything unstolen; the price of victuals is excessive; the sick soldiers from Haddington are shut out of houses and die of want in the streets. The whole picture is one of social disorder.

Knox gripped the wooden rail of the ship and gulped down mouthfuls of salty sea spray to quell the brash rising in his throat. Toiling at the oars for nineteen months in the galleys had severely taxed his health and a diet of maggot-ridden gruel had ravaged his guts. He'd been hoping to recover his strength in Berwick, not have to endure yet more labours, but the description of the border town Lindsay read out was not only making him sick to the stomach but striking fear into his very soul.

He groaned. 'Why then in God's name are you sending me to the Devil's ain toun? From what you say, there's truth in the auld legend. When Satan tempted Christ with all the kingdoms of the earth, he hid Berwick beneath his thumb to keep as his ain wee neuk.'

Lindsay laughed. 'Then you'll be the one to wrest it from under Satan's thumb.' He tapped the parchment. 'For, as John Brende, Master of the Musters in Berwick, writes: *It will require a stern disciplinarian in the pulpit as well as a stirring preacher to work out a moral and social reform.* Put simply, that preacher is you, John.'

Knox hunched forward to hug his aching belly. 'My stomach isn't strong enough for such a task.'

'But your heart is. You've been tested and come through. After thon Sodom and Gomorrah of St Andrews you can cope with the boorach that is Berwick. *Cometh the hour, cometh the man*, John. Dame Fortune is leading you a merry dance where you follow in John Rough's footsteps as you did once before in St Andrews. Whatever his qualities, Pastor Rough is not the man to control this carnaptious congregation.'

'Such faith you have in me.' For Knox was not so sure. St Andrews had only been under siege for months whereas the border town had been fought over for centuries. During the long and bloody wars between the two kingdoms, the English and the Scots had passed Berwick back and forth like a bartered bride, changing hands so many times even the townsfolk forgot which realm they were in.

Forbye, in this divided town, Knox was not only a Scot who had to deliver his message to the auld enemy, the English, but a Protestant among papists, for the reformation had made little headway in the northern counties. He'd need all his strength and courage to bring some kind of harmony between divided loyalties.

'Here, take this. I swear by it.' Lindsay handed him a phial. 'It may not be a panacea, but it calms the pounding heart.'

Knox took the tincture gladly, thankful to Lindsay for sensing his doubts. It had calmed his fears before in St Andrews and he welcomed it even more now. If Brende's warnings were anything to go by, he'd need the laudanum. He flinched feeling a firm hand on his shoulder.

'I cannot leave you alone in thon god-forsaken place, Johnnie,' his brother Will said. 'You'll need a pair of strong arms to help you to fend off the reivers and a pair of keen eyes to watch your back.'

A shiver ran through Knox. Surely not Stewart? He thought he'd seen the back of him.

Popping two fingers into the corners of his mouth, Will gave a shrill whistle. 'Here's your bonnie fighter.'

Bowed under the weight of a hempen sack, Jamie Campbell tacked his way across the deck and dropped his sea bag at Knox's feet.

'Forbye, he has the homing instinct of a rookety doo. You could leave him in a mist in the middle of a moor and he'd find his way home.'

'Aye, with the help of these.' Jamie pointed to the string around his neck on which dangled a lodestone to use as a compass, and a sunstone, an ice crystal to detect the position of the sun on a cloudy day.

More importantly, Skipper Will explained, Jamie had been initiated into the secret order of the Free Fishers of the Forth. This fraternity of merchant seamen and fishermen had established a trustworthy network, not only to transport goods but to deliver documents, letters, messages, news. On their travels they kept their eyes and ears open to glean interesting titbits, using secret codes to pass them on.

'Any time, any place, a whisper in the street, a word at the harbour-side or a whistle on the links will bring a Free Fisher to your aid. But you need your own slogan, Johnnie. What's it to be?'

Without skipping a beat, Knox replied, 'Sinclair.'

William looked bemused for a moment before grinning. 'Our mother's name. Aye, that's one to remember. I'll put it about at our next meeting. Never fash, when Sinclair calls, the Free Fishers will answer. Forbye, Jamie's a trustworthy lad. He kens the ropes and will give you no grief.'

In the town of Berwick, Lindsay headed straight for Scots Gate, to St Mary's church where Knox would preach. He hirpled down the nave and halted at the plain, stone altar. A wistful look crossed his face. 'This chapel has a special place in my heart,' he confessed. 'After the carnage of Flodden, they brought the corpse of my beloved monarch, James IV, and laid him here. Headless, for the fiends had hacked his skull off as a trophy.' He broke off. 'I can scarcely believe it's thirty-six years since thon fateful day in 1513 when the flower of Scottish manhood was struck down.' His voice choked with emotion.

'The year I was born,' Knox said.

Lindsay shot him a quizzical look before nodding. '*Tempus fugit*, in truth. King James was like a son to me. But though I lost one son I gained another for you, too, are a son to me, John.' He gripped Knox's shoulders and gazed into his eyes. 'As you set out on your perilous voyage, my thoughts and prayers will be with you always.'

'Your words touch my heart, Sir David, and I shall always keep them in mind.' Knox paused. 'I give you my word that, whatever battles I face in life, I shall keep *my* head. Here's my hand on it.'

'That's the spirit, John.' Lindsay's grey eyes glistened as he pulled Knox into an embrace. Wiping away a tear, he took up his staff and thudded it on the flagstones. 'Now let's see what's afoot in Berwick.'

On the way to their lodging, they had to dodge fishwives with creels, trudging back and forth to the harbour, and rowdy rabbles of soldiers roaming the narrow cobbled wynds. Glancing upwards, Knox was alarmed to see armed guards parading the parapets of Berwick Castle, headquarters of the English Warden of the Eastern Marches. Hemmed in by high walls, flanking towers and deep ditches, he felt a prisoner. Had he been released from the galleys only to be incarcerated in this garrison town? Beyond the twenty-two-feet high ramparts lay Scotland where he'd been planning to launch his own campaign. So near and yet so far.

When they stopped to give way to a convoy of carts carrying injured soldiers in tattered bandages, Lindsay muttered, 'More spoils of war.'

'Master,' a voice cried. Knox turned to see Jamie running at full tilt towards them. 'Thon soldiers are from Haddington,' he gasped, 'survivors of the plague that's still raging. My sister Isabelle is there! What if she's caught the pest? What if she's dead?'

'Never fash, Jamie lad,' Lindsay said. 'Skipper Will would have told us if anything untoward had happened. As far as I ken they're all hale and hearty at the abbey. Including the prioress.' When Knox looked away, he took his arm. 'Whatever you may feel about Dame Elisabeth,' his tone was low but stern, 'she is your godmother and worries about your welfare.'

Before Knox could reply, the door of a nearby tavern was flung open and two soldiers were hurled out into the gutter. They staggered to their feet and confronted each other drawing daggers from their belts.

'Dare to call me a feardie-gowk, you sassenach bastard,' the Scots soldier growled, 'and you'll end up in a gory bed.'

'Do you deny fleeing Pinkie?' the English northerner retorted. 'If not, then you're a cursed liar as well as a whoreson knave.'

Clearly the defeat at Pinkie Cleuch, where Somerset's troops had massacred the Scots army, was still a raw wound, but Knox was curious. He turned to the soldier beside him. 'Why is the Scotsman wearing the cross of St George?' he asked.

The soldier chafed at the red cross emblazoned on his tunic. 'Aye, there's the rub. After the rout at Pinkie, we had nae choice. We were forced at sword's point to serve the English king.' He hauched up a gob of phlegm and spat into the gutter. 'For thon English call us cowards and our ain countrymen cry us traitors. We're all at each other's thrapples. A Scotsman maun wear the red St George's cross on his breast but the blue and white sacred saltire of St Andrew is engraved on his heart and will be until his last dying breath.'

His words were drowned out by jeers and hoots from the bystanders egging on the two foes who began fighting with daggers drawn – to the death, Knox feared.

'It must be stopped,' he said but as he moved forward Lindsay grabbed his sleeve.

'Leave them to it, John. What if you're stabbed? What good would that do?'

A spine-chilling scream rang out. The crowd parted and a body fell to the ground. A crimson stream of blood flowed into the gutter, mingling with the sewage.

'Christ's blood! He's killed him!' someone shouted. 'Fetch the priest! He needs the last rites.'

The mob was bewildered: the Catholic priests had all been booted out of Berwick. What could be done for this dying man's soul?

Without thinking, Knox stepped forward but swiftly brought himself up short. What was he doing? He no longer believed in the so-called last rites, the final sacrament of Extreme Unction concocted by the Catholic Church. This send-off that supposedly paved the soul's path to heaven was nocht but a papist fraud. But the distraught onlookers clearly craved some kind of spiritual comfort for the mortally wounded man.

Kneeling down, Knox clasped his hands in prayer. A reverential hush descended over the crowd as he recited from the Book of Psalms. 'Remember not the sins of my youth nor my transgressions: according to thy mercy, remember thou me for thy goodness' sake, O Lord.' And when the wretch drew his last, blood-curdling breath, he ended with the words, 'Unto thee, O Lord, do I lift up my soul: O God, I trust in thee. Amen.'

'Amen,' the crowd intoned. Satisfied that due respect had been paid to the slain soldier his comrades carried away his corpse. Before the bystanders could drift away, Lindsay raised his staff.

'Tak tent! Behold your new minister. Preacher Knox will hold his first service at St Mary's on Sunday. Come and hear the true word of the Lord.'

Knox's jaw dropped in panic. He'd planned to spend the first few weeks gathering strength, getting to know the lie of the land – not preaching. Not yet – this was too soon.

Lindsay placed a steadying hand on his shoulder. 'Listen, John, the air in this town is so dour you could cut it with a cleaver. What you saw today only skims the surface of a cauldron seething with bitter bile. There's nocht to be gained by delay except dirt and long nails. Now's the time to reap what you've just sown.'

Knox was silent until they reached their lodging where he paced the floor, scratching the newly grown beard sprouting from his chin. 'Sunday's too soon, Sir David. Where do I begin? What do I say?' Though he'd written lengthy treatises during his captivity, he hadn't delivered a sermon before a congregation for a long time.

'You have the gift, John,' Lindsay assured him. 'Once you start, your speech will flow but do not aim above their heads like a proud Pharisee. Speak to them directly as brethren. Mind how you kept the rough soldiery in check at St Andrews? That should stand you in good stead here. Forbye, as a galley slave, you've served your time in the lowest rank and proved your mettle.

'These are your fellow warriors: heckle them if need be. Believe in yourself as a leader and they will follow for soldiers are trained to obey orders. Target your words to stir the hearts and stiffen their sinews with war cries, what the Gaels cry slogans. Use the Bible as your arsenal for it's crammed with calls to arms.'

Knox could hardly gainsay the gifted playwright and skilled director who knew how to capture an audience's attention. 'Aye, in truth. Let us *put on the whole armour of God, that ye may be able to stand against the wiles of the devil.*' He raised his arm high in the salute of a knight winning a bout. 'Throughout all the dreich, dreary days at the oars, the dream I would one day preach again kept me going.'

'It won't all be plain sailing,' Lindsay warned. 'Watch out for Cuthbert Tunstall. The powerful Bishop of Durham will be your greatest foe and one of the reasons why the Privy Council has sent you. They wish to rid the north of recalcitrant recusants such as Tunstall who's been lukewarm in putting into effect the new liturgy. The bishop showed his true colours by voting against Cranmer's Prayer Book yet he's been allowed to carry on his public duties. This former priest, indoctrinated in the credo of the one, true apostolic faith, has been unable to shake off the shackles of Rome. At his great age, old habits die hard. He may deny being a closet Catholic, but he's proving to be a reluctant Protestant. The Council of the North are concerned he's stirring up dissent among his congregation – if not outright revolt.'

Knox gritted his teeth. 'Then I shall be the one to blow him out of the water –

with a cannonade of truth.'

'Maybe so, but in Tunstall you'll be dealing with a shrewd statesman. I would advise the gloved hand of diplomacy rather than Mons Meg.'

'The bombard is the only weapon that will break through their besieged papist brains.'

'Still, I would be wary, John,' Lindsay warned. 'All it took for Joshua to bring the walls of Jericho tumbling down was a trumpet.'

V

The Lesser Shipwreck

> Greatly it doth perturb my mind
> Of dolent death the divers kind
> And how many ane man
> Upon the sea doth lose their lives.
>
> *The Monarch*
> Sir David Lindsay, 16th Century

St Mary's Abbey, 19 September 1549

All over the Lothian countryside the autumn air hung thick with smoke that stung their eyes. Standing at the top of the abbey bell tower, Elisabeth and Sister Agnes gave thanks the auld enemy had at last withdrawn from the gates of Haddington – but not before scorching everything in their path on the way to Edinburgh. In fond farewell, the defeated English had thrown blazing torches onto the turf roofs of farmhouses and cottages: flames were rising high from Lethington Tower, the home of the Maitlands.

Elisabeth dabbed at her smoke-sore eyes and coughed. 'At least the abbey has been spared.'

'Sadly there are no bells to ring out in celebration,' Sister Agnes said. 'The heathen English have plundered ours to make more guns.'

'Wishart's words are ringing true. Now, after flood, famine and pestilence, fire is the final scourge.'

'Not a curse but a blessing. The purifying flames will cleanse the town of disease and cremate the plague-ridden bodies.'

'And thanks to the Black Madonna – and Isabelle – you may have found a miracle cure for the scabby pox.'

When Isabelle had remarked on how soft her work-worn hands had become, Sister Agnes had examined them in wonder. No longer red and raw and criss-crossed with cuts and scrapes, the skin on her hands looked pink and healthy. The wet summer had brought a glut of slugs as destructive as a Biblical plague of locusts and, after days plucking them off kail leaves in the *potagerie*, it had been the devil's own task to clean off the sticky sludge. Since scrubbing had only irritated her skin, she'd left the slime to rub off in its own good time.

'Out of evil good may come,' Sister Agnes murmured. 'There must be some good reason why God put these beasties on this earth.'

The prioress laughed. 'You'll have your pick of patients, Agnes, but whether they'll be willing to smear slug slime on their nether parts remains to be seen.'

Elisabeth's laugh stretched into a deep yawn. Her limbs grew heavy and her eyelids drooped. The strain of the past year was catching up with her.

'Rest is the best remedy for you, dear prioress,' Sister Agnes said and ordered her to bed.

With a welcome breeze wafting in through the window, her chamber at least was cool but the bed curtains were closed. Strange, Elisabeth thought. To prevent mildew Sister Agnes insisted on bedding being aired and the bed curtains kept open during the day. She tugged them open and gasped.

Someone was sound asleep on top of her feather bed – draped in a fur-lined cloak. Joy and relief surged through her. Davie Lindsay was home and safe! He must have sneaked in through the secret tunnel from the chapel to her chamber. She fain would wake him, but his face looked so grey with exhaustion that she held back. Let him sleep.

But when he grew restless and his eyeglasses threatened to slide off, she removed them as gently as possible. He stirred, opened his eyes and rubbed the bridge of his nose. He squinted up at her, his expression vacant.

'Lisbeth? Is that you? Or am I dreaming?'

'Dame Remembrance?' She gave a wry smile, recalling one of their meetings in an earlier life – a life that now seemed centuries ago. 'No dream, Davie, but I jalouse you were having a nightmare.'

He smiled weakly. 'Aye, I was. Come, sit by me.'

Slipping off her shoes, she climbed up onto the bed. For a few moments they clung to each other, staying silent: words were unnecessary to express their deep, intense love developed over many long years. Their lips brushed tentatively at first before they kissed, not passionately but with poignant tenderness.

'It's good to have you back, Davie.'

'It's good to be back home and dry for I thought I'd cowped my creels at the bottom of the sea. The shipwreck still gives me nightmares.'

Elisabeth settled into the crook of his arm. 'Tell me about it.'

Shortly after leaving Copenhagen, a storm had arisen. Their ship had been tossed about on the high seas before foundering on rocks not far from the Danish coast. Fortunately, the water was shallow enough for the survivors to wade ashore. While Lindsay had only lost some parchments and scrolls – others had lost their lives.

His recent brush with death had clearly rattled him. Silver streaked his beard and crows' feet around the corners of his eyes had deepened.

'That's my last mission abroad,' he declared. 'Once I've given my report to Queen Marie I shall beg leave to retire from court. I'm nearing three score years and ten and auld age never comes itself, Lisbeth. My creaking bones are telling me I'm getting too old for diplomacy. Being drookit in the North Sea brine should have soused me like a herring, pickling me for posterity.' His grey eyes twinkled. 'But I fear it has only soured my sinews and rusted my reason. In truth I'm an auld larbar, Lisbeth. Fit only for my winding sheet.'

She prodded him in the ribs. 'Haud yer wheesht! There's life in the auld seadog yet.'

'There ends my tale of woe, and you? Nor have you had your troubles to seek.' Gently taking her hand he encircled her wrist with his thumb and forefinger. 'Why, my jaggy thistle, you're a rickle of bones.'

A fleeting smile flitted across her gaunt, lined face. 'The trials of Job were as nocht to what buffeted our convent, but we've lived to see another day.' Her flippant tone became sombre. 'But what of John? Have you any news of him? William said he'd been freed from the galleys.'

'Aye, that's true. He's now in Berwick.'

'Berwick!' A spark flashed in her ferny green eyes. 'He's on his way home at last!'

'Lisbeth, don't get your hopes up. He'll no be coming back to Scotland – at least not for a while. He's been appointed preacher at St Mary's Church.'

She pulled a puzzled face. 'Preacher not priest? Does that mean he's still dabbling in heresy? Surely they thrashed that nonsense out of him in the galleys? For sure as death, thon Lutheran rigmarole will send him to the stake.'

Lindsay stroked her cheek. 'John must follow his own path, Lisbeth. And he's safe in England.'

'Where Harry Coppernose murdered – how many wives – to get his wicked way? And how many other women's lives did he wreck? All those holy sisters hurled into the gutters when tore down nunneries and convents? Miserly Harry of England always had his snout in the trough – even cheating his own people by coating copper coins with silver.'

'Whatever happens in England need not happen here. Luther's teachings are spreading throughout Europe in a peaceful way and times are changing.'

'Not for the better. What will we do if the heretics ding doun St Mary's?'

'Never fash, Lisbeth. I would take care of you.'

'Where? At Garleton? Where the French have been using your precious books for kindling? It won't be fit for swine to bide in.'

Seeing the misery on Lindsay's face, Elisabeth wished she could swallow her barbs.

'If not Garleton, then I'll crawl away to the Mount near Cupar, my home in Fife.' He hesitated. 'And I want you to come with me.'

Elisabeth's mouth gaped open. The court had been Lindsay's life. Service to the monarch had always come before his love for her, but now that had come to an end, he was asking her to give up her life to follow him.

His grip tightened round her shoulder. 'It's not safe here, Lisbeth. You're at risk of the plague, of disease – of starving to death.'

Her mouth set firm. 'I've survived this far, Davie. The longer you live, the longer you live, as Betsy would say. Forbye, I cannot leave the abbey, I cannot abandon my sisters.'

When Lindsay broke into a rasping cough, Elisabeth gently rubbed his back. 'You're not well, Davie. Why not bide here? We'll look after you. You'll have peace to scrieve. In spite of everything life has thrown at us …' She fumbled in the neck of her habit, 'we made a promise at our handfasting to *Keep Tryst*. Do you mind this?'

Lindsay squinted at the king's ring dangling on the end of the ribbon. 'Aye, I do that.'

'As a true Hepburn I've always kept my trust. Whatever happens I shall remain steadfast. What about you, Davie Lindsay? Will you swear to *Endure Fort*?'

VI

The Sermon on Lord's Mount

When first mine eyes did view and mark
Thy fair beauty to behold,
And when mine ears listened to hark
The pleasant words that thou me told...
Song XIX
Thomas Wyatt, 16th Century

Berwick-on-Tweed, November 1549

When the Scots and English soldiers thronging into St Mary's took off their steel bonnets, unbuckled their swords and stacked them in the porch, Knox nodded in approval. Word had quickly spread about the plainspoken preacher and every week, more and more worshippers from the lower orders – servants and groomsmen, tenants and soldiers – came to hear his sermon, he thought wryly. The northern gentry who craved the quasi-Roman rites offered by Bishop Tunstall attended the services in the old parish church.

But not the two young ladies lurking behind a pillar that Knox glimpsed on his way to the pulpit. Their plush fur-lined cloaks marked them out as being of higher rank. A red velvet bonnet with a jaunty feather sat atop the flaxen hair of the taller lass while an old-fashioned gable hood framed her companion's face. A group of young English officers who had also spotted the two lasses were carving a way through the crowd towards them. While the older and bolder of the pair fluttered her eyelashes and flashed meaningful glances at the youths the other, more modest lass kept her eyes cast down and chewed her bottom lip. Knox smiled to himself: he doubted these young folk would be paying attention to his sermon.

Meanwhile the congregation of soldiers hung on his every word, waggling their heads at any mention of girded loins, breastplates of righteousness, shields of faith or helmets of salvation. At the end of the sermon they stood up to cheer and yell their war cries. The coy lass looked astonished that such sounds could be heard within hallowed walls.

After reciting the Lord's Prayer to quieten them, Knox invited the brethren to take communion. Catching sight of one of the girls being jostled in the crush, Knox took her arm and led her towards the trestle table set up in the middle of the nave. When one of his deacons handed her a chunk torn off a loaf, she looked bemused.

'Aye, this is not the unleavened wafer offered by Tunstall, but our baker's daily bread,' Knox explained.

When the dry crumbs caught the back of her throat, making her cough, Knox snatched up a goblet and wiped the rim. 'Here, have a wee drop of wine to wash down your bread.'

She took a sip but spluttered and nearly spat it out again.

'Too wersh for your taste? Too much like vinegar, perhaps? Bitter and sharp? We cannot afford the fine claret papist priests kept to themselves but at least the faithful all take part in our communion – coming together to share bread and wine in memory of Christ Our Lord's sacrifice. For in the supper of the Lord, all are equal participants.' He studied her intently as she chewed and swallowed. 'Not too pleasant on the tongue at first, for it needs getting used to.'

From a distance he'd judged her to be plain but close up her serene, solemn face was bonnie with light freckles speckling her nose and when she peeked at him from beneath dark feathery eyelashes her hazel-flecked eyes momentarily unsettled him. She reminded him of someone. Slight of frame, she looked like a timid wee bird – a wren or a dunnock. 'I haven't seen you here before. May I ask your name?'

She twiddled her thumbs and looked down. 'Marjory Bowes. I came here with my sister. Our maid, Molly, praises your sermons to the skies.'

'And did my sermon today meet your lofty expectations?'

She flushed. 'Aye, though I strained to understand your Scots tongue.'

'Too harsh for your ears, perhaps.'

She shoogled her head. 'Nay, I didn't mean that.'

'Will you be here next Sunday? Or any other day when I preach.' His lips quirked into a smile. 'My sermons are not just for the Sabbath.'

Again she shook her head. 'Our father forbids us to come. He's the warden of Norham Castle. He doesn't agree with these new-fangled doctrines.' Her voice wavered as the words came tumbling out. 'He says that Luther is the Antichrist, the devil in man's clothing, who eats worms, and drinks the blood of newborn babes.' She licked her lips and took a deep breath, 'And he says you use satanic powers and magic spells to quieten these wild beasts.'

Knox fought the urge to guffaw. 'For centuries the magician in Rome and his conjurers have been beguiling beholders with their joukery-pawkerie while casting a hex – *Hoc est Corpus meum*. He's the one to talk! Catholics are the cannibals – eating Christ's body and drinking his blood.'

When her cheeks flushed pink and she cast down her eyes, Knox felt ashamed for teasing her. She was only a young maiden – hardly older than sixteen years. What could she know of the evils of papist doctrine?

Marjory nodded. 'Please forgive me. I don't mean to offend you.'

'No offence taken,' Knox replied. Her words had given him an insight into the superstitious nonsense he still had to overcome.

'I bid you please don't tell our father we've been here. He'll be so angry.'

Knox pressed his lips between two fingers. 'My lips are sealed.'

Blushing, Marjory looked around. 'I must go in search of Amy.'

Knox guided her through the crowd to where an auburn-haired officer was whispering into Amy's ear. When Marjory dashed over to drag her brazen sister away, the officer ran a hand through his bronze locks and gave a sheepish grin.

'Preacher Knox, I'm only doing my duty by protecting this young lady from the wanton soldiery. Our captain keeps his beautiful daughter under lock and key. Who can blame him when there are such bare-faced blaggards about?'

Before he could reply, Knox felt a hand on his arm.

'Preacher Knox – a word if I may.'

He turned and squinted, not recognising the middle-aged man dressed in his Sunday finery at first. Expensive brocade breeches stretched tightly across his paunch and silken hose clung to his bulging calves. Mr Robson, master butcher and widower, clasped his plumed hat against his broad chest and bowed. By all accounts, the Robsons were the respectable branch of a border reiving family. They'd moved up the social ladder from lawless raiding and stealing cattle to legally butchering their brethren's loot.

He took Knox aside. 'I see the young lady has been set upon by a company of gallants,' he said with unconcealed contempt. 'Up to no good, I fear. Such a gullible young maiden may fall for false promises from the glib tongues of soldiers. We cannot permit her reputation to be besmirched. Especially not by the Earl of Warwick's son,' he added moving in more closely.

Catching a whiff of the butcher's meaty breath, Knox tried not to flinch as Robson whispered, 'I strongly advise you to go canny with the Dudleys. No doubt Sir John has sent young Guildford to spy out the lay of the land and find out what message you've been spreading. You have my word. The captain's daughters shall come to no harm in our company.'

The butcher beckoned to two great hulks of lads who came forward to stand squat and square beside him. He set his plumed bonnet on his balding head and crooked his arm.

'I'm sure these young ladies will be honoured,' Knox said.

Thanking him, Marjory gave a shy smile and lowered her eyes but flaxen haired Amy glared daggers at him.

VII

The Captain's Daughter

> This is a strange disease,
> To serve and never please.
> *Sonnet XLVII*
> Thomas Wyatt, 16th Century

Berwick-upon-Tweed, November 1549

Casting a scornful eye over the trio of Robsons trailing in their wake, Amy linked her arm through Marjory's and whispered, 'What do you think of him?'

Marjory didn't know what to make of him. Every time she thought about her encounter with the Scots preacher, her cheeks burned. How could she have said that? How could she accuse the godly preacher of being in league with the devil? And quailing from his piercing stare that penetrated her very soul, she'd prayed a great pit would open and swallow her up.

From the way he thrust forward his pointed beard and jabbed a threatening finger, the wiry preacher had seemed so intimidating in the pulpit. But mingling with his flock in the nave, the pastor had dropped the stern countenance and greeted everyone in a friendly manner. Unlike Bishop Tunstall who veered away from any contact with the common folk, lest he catch fleas or some disease.

At the communion table, Marjory had glimpsed a genial twinkle in Knox's lively eyes. Full fleshy lips nestled within the scary black beard and his face had broken into a smile more often than a frown. 'He has a way of explaining the scripture in simple language for the common folk to understand,' she replied at last.

Amy snorted. 'Not that old windbag spouting fire and brimstone – I meant the young officer, the earl's son, Guildford Dudley.' Her face took on a dreamy look. 'How unique! A name fit for the hero of a romance. No simple Tom, Dick or Fred – but Guildford! With gilded hair or Gillyflower, the flower of love.' Amy kept saying his name, letting it roll round her lips. 'So handsome in his green and white livery, his auburn hair glinting like gilded bronze in the candlelight. Not like that lump of lard, Robson the butcher.' She glanced over her shoulder and sneered. 'Look at him all trussed up. *A frog went to the mill door,*' she chanted. 'But he's more like a toad.'

'Hush, Amy, he'll hear you.'

'I don't care. I've set my heart on him, Marjory. Now that I've met Guildford, no other will do.'

Marjory bit her lip. 'It's not our place to choose whom we marry. Besides, he's far above our rank.'

Amy glowered. 'Tell me, what would you prefer? To be handed over like a plate of meat to one of these two brawny butcher lads or win the heart of an earl's son? I'll move heaven and earth for him, Marjory, I promise you.'

Marygate, Berwick-upon-Tweed

Once home, Marjory left Amy to daydream about her gallant Guildford and clattered upstairs, worried that her mother might have missed her. Hearing raised voices, she halted outside the bedchamber.

'No! Please, no, Richard. Don't take them away from me. Give me back my holy books. That's all I ask. I must have them.'

Hearing the click of the latch, Marjory leapt backwards. The door scraped open and her father elbowed his way out, encumbered by two heavy books tucked under his left armpit and her mother clinging leech-like to his right leg.

'These are heresy, Elizabeth.' He looked down with disdain on his distraught wife. 'I shall burn them. These two Toms – so-called churchmen – are both traitors. Cromwell, the harsh Hammer of the Monks, deserved the block and Cranmer's head will be the next to roll. Mark my words.'

Marjory didn't need to read the titles to know which books her father was confiscating – Thomas Cromwell's *Great Bible* and Thomas Cranmer's *Book of Common Prayer.*

'If you continue to read these travesties of the truth,' he shook his leg to try and free it, 'I shall have Bishop Tunstall drive out the devils that possess you. Exorcism may be the only cure to cleanse your accursed soul.'

Her mother let go her grip and fell back onto her haunches. Tears stained her cheeks but her eyes burned with defiance as she pointed a finger at her husband.

'Don't you dare bring that hypocrite into this house. Cuthbert Tunstall is a cowardly turncoat who conceals his beliefs beneath his episcopal cope. Never let him darken my door again.'

His mouth twisted into a sneer. 'Would you rather I called the physician to clear your head of your harmful beliefs?'

Elizabeth Bowes screwed up her eyes and hissed like a cornered wildcat. 'What choice are you offering me, Richard? The devil or the deep blue sea?'

'The Lord knows I've tried to put up with your ridiculous religious ravings but unless you give up these fanciful ideas and attend to your household duties as an obedient wife should, I have no option but to keep you under lock and key.' With a look of scorn scarring his face, Captain Bowes turned his back on her. 'Marjory, fetch Doctor Mordue.'

Even Marjory shuddered at this. While she was her father's pet, she took her

mother's side when it came to Dr Mordue. Swathed in a miasma of pungent smells
– bergamot oil, Stinking Gladdens, orris root – and bearing a medicine chest full of
amulets of dried blood, crushed toad, and venomous spider, he seemed more like
a magician than a physician. 'There's no need to call for Dr Mordue, papa. I shall
attend to mama.'

The captain tweaked her cheek and smiled. 'Thank you, my pet. I can always
depend on my sweet little Marjoram.'

When Marjory clattered back into the chamber to heave her mother back into
bed, Mrs Bowes screwed up her face. 'Why do you keep clomping about in clumsy
clogs like a common scullion? It makes my head ache.'

'So as keep my feet dry in the muddy streets, mama.'

'Must you wear them indoors? How I detest the wretched north – nought but
mud and mire and monotony – life here is as drab and dreary as the weather. It
plunges me deeper into melancholy.'

As Marjory plumped up her goose-feather pillows, Mrs Bowes grabbed her
arm. 'Don't ever call Mordue: that bloodsucking cleg is death on legs. I refuse to
be cupped: I'll have no leeches gorging on my blood. And please, no purging with
boiled onions. The very stench turns my stomach. As for sousing my tender parts in
vinegar – what does he think I am? A herring?' She pulled a doleful face.

'Besides, I have no need him. Not when I have you to look after me, Marjory.
Amy will turn heads – she's the one most like me. Her beauty will be her dowry but
you are too plain for matrimony.'

Marjory twitched her speckled nose and tried to ignore the jibe. Dabbing her
freckles with lemon juice might make her more marriageable, but what did that
matter as long as she was her father's pet. At times she begrudged the way her
mother clung to her with limpet-like dependence but she put up with it for his sake.

Hearing the clippety-clop of hooves on cobbles, Marjory crossed to the window.
The groomsman was leading out her father's horse. Papa was leaving. She drew out
the forbidden prayer book hidden beneath her mother's pillow. 'Mama, read this
while I fetch you a tisane.'

Downstairs in the hall where her father was pulling on his riding boots, she
asked cautiously, 'When will you be home, papa?'

'I don't know, my pet. When duty calls at Norham Castle I must answer. Another
border raid is expected. Those treacherous Scots reivers are brewing up something
nasty and I must be on hand to drive them back.'

With his silvery beard and newly trimmed moustache, the captain looked
especially handsome and when he kissed her on the cheek, the scent of ambergris
wafted from his pomaded hair. Marjory clung tightly to him, fearful she'd never see
him again, a fear that never left her. Her hazel eyes glistened with tears. 'God speed,

papa, and take care.'

Captain Bowes fastened his riding cloak and picked up his gauntlets. He gave her a playful pat on the cheek. 'Never fear, my precious pet, I shall.'

His foot was in the stirrup when she stopped him. 'Wait a minute, papa.' She ran back into the house and returned with his steel bonnet and sword. 'You can't face the foe unarmed, papa. You'll have need of these. In case those wild Scotch reivers ambush you.'

The captain harrumphed and his ruddy face turned a blotchy purple. 'You're right, my pet. How forgetful of me.' He dug his stirrups into his horse's flanks and galloped off.

'I shall pray for your safe return, papa,' she murmured keeping watch until he vanished like a wraith in the mist.

VIII

The Raising of Mrs Bowes

And her spirit came again, and she arose straightway
Luke VIII: 55

Berwick-upon-Tweed, December 1549

By the low winter light from the narrow window in her mother's bedchamber, Marjory struggled to thread her bronze needle but noticing it had bent again she stifled a groan, fearful of disturbing her mother's rest. She made a mental note to ask her sister Nan who often travelled to London to bring some needles from the cloth market. The Moorish craftsman in Cheapside was famed not only for forging swords from Toledo steel but producing high-quality sewing needles.

For now Marjory would have to make do with this bronze one that was barely sharp enough to pierce the fine lawn linen of the collar she was sewing – a surprise Yuletide gift for her father. The latest London fashion, worn by the Earl of Warwick, was a high-necked ruffled collar decorated with black work embroidery.

Since the intricate design of intertwining flowers and birds was beyond Marjory's needlework skills, she used simple cross-stitches. The stark contrast between the black stitching and white fabric was just as striking but laborious. Biting her bottom lip, Marjory forced the blunt tip through the cloth.

When Amy came in and crept up to her mother's bed, Marjory put a finger to her lips. 'Mama is sleeping.'

'Then I'll wake her up. I need to speak with her urgently,' Amy replied and nudged her sleeping form. 'Mama, Uncle Robert has invited us to spend Yuletide at Streatham Castle. Isn't that wonderful? The celebrations will be in grand style, with masques and dancing, feasting and hunting. Please will you come with us as chaperone?'

Mrs Bowes peeped out from the coverlet and blinked. A pained expression crossed her face. 'How can you ask such a thing? My health will not allow it,' she replied and turned away.

Amy pressed her lips in a sulky pout and confronted Marjory. 'Put that down,' she said, 'and speak to mama. You're the only one she'll listen to.'

Snatching the collar out of Marjory's hand, she yelped and dropped it back into her lap. Marjory gasped: little droplets of scarlet were seeping into the immaculate white linen.

Amy pulled a pitiful face. 'Why didn't you tell me your needle was still in there? Look, it's pricked my finger.'

'Because you never asked me.' Tears of frustration stung Marjory's eyes. How was she going to wash out the bloodstains without the black dye running?

'Stop fretting, Marjory. Give it to Molly. She'll know what to do.'

Marjory wiped her eyes. 'Will papa be going to Streatham?'

'I don't know, but who cares,' Amy snapped. 'While he's done nothing to introduce us to worthy suitors, Uncle Robert has invited the Earl of Warwick and his sons as guests of honour to thank them for quelling a rebellion in Norfolk. I must be there. I can't miss this chance of seeing Guildford – he may be my salvation. If mother won't come then you'll have to.'

'Marjory dear, bring me something for my migraine,' their mother moaned. 'I feel as if someone is stabbing red hot needles into my head.'

'Bronze or steel,' Amy muttered before forcing a smile. 'Please let me go, mama. Were you not young once? Surely we can make merry at Yuletide? Christmas is the season of good cheer. Life is flying past. My beauty will fade and I'll be an old biddy before my time.'

'What is there to celebrate? Your father will not be with us.' Her mother's lips twisted into an ugly pout.

'What?' Marjory yelped. The measuring spoon dropped from her hand and clattered onto the pewter tray.

Mrs Bowes clucked in annoyance and pulled the plaits of the muslin nightcap more tightly round her ears. 'The dedicated captain's devotion to duty demands that he spend Yuletide at Norham Castle.' Bitterness peppered her usual petulant tone. 'For the reivers take advantage of the long winter nights and make surprise raids under cover of darkness. Or so your father maintains.'

Marjory stood rooted to the spot. Her beloved papa wouldn't be with them for Yuletide? These were not good tidings. When would she give him the collar? Without her father present there would be no joy for her at Yuletide. She set her face hard.

'Why should we celebrate Christmas anyway? Preacher Knox says Christ's nativity should not be an excuse for indulging in excess. He says the Yule festivities are pagan and nothing more than a ploy for debauchery and depravity.'

While Amy's blue eyes flared wide in surprise at her sister's outburst, Mrs Bowes lifted her head from the bolster. 'In truth? That's a very strict attitude to take. Where did you hear this?'

Marjory's face reddened. She dared not admit disobeying her father. 'From Molly. She's been attending St Mary's where the new preacher is a miracle worker, so she says. His sermons have the power to redeem souls. Even the soldiers take heed for there are fewer brawls and fights. The prophet's smooth tongue can soothe the savage breasts of the uncouth reivers.'

Mrs Bowes raised herself onto her elbows. 'Prophet, you say? From what you say this Preacher Knox sounds like a man who knows the truth. Not a shilly-shallying charlatan like Tunstall.'

Amy hissed through sharp white teeth. 'Thank you, dear sister. A cloistered life might suit you, little nun, but I'm wilting here,' she said and flounced out.

'Then it is time to rise from my sick bed.' Mrs Bowes threw back the bedcovers and swung a pair of blue-veined, puffy legs onto the floor. 'I must gather strength in these old shrivelled shanks if I'm to attend the Christmas service at St Mary's.'

St Mary's Church, Berwick-upon-Tweed, Christmas Day, 1549

Christmas morning had attracted the habitual as well as the curious, Knox noted, with standing room only in the small church and a crowd crammed into the narrow porch. He was about to ascend the pulpit when a commotion broke out.

A groomsman carrying an upholstered chair was pushing through the rows of parishioners − much to their annoyance. 'Make way for the captain's wife,' he commanded.

Ignoring their black looks, a plump well-dressed matron hobbled behind on the arm of a young woman.

'Mama, remember the parable of the vineyard workers,' Knox heard Marjory whisper, '*So the last shall be first, and the last shall be first.*'

Mrs Bowes puckered her lips. 'That may be so, but also recollect that while *many are called but few are chosen.* The Lord has led me here today,' she retorted and ordered her groomsman to deposit the chair in front of the pulpit.

While her mother settled her ample form into her seat, Marjory unfolded her creepie stool and perched awkwardly beside her.

As soon as Knox mounted the pulpit, the nave fell silent. Welcoming newcomers, he took heed of Marjory's complaint. 'For the benefit of soudron lugs, I mean southerner's ears,' he said a knowing smile, 'I shall temper my Scots tongue. Today on the 25th of December the Roman Catholic Church celebrates the birth of Christmas but because I condemn such a feast, I'm accused of being a carnaptious curmudgeon. However, my reasons are plain and simple.

'Firstly, nowhere does the Bible mention the date of the Saviour's nativity and without such testimony I cannot condone it. Christmas is a papist fib − a prank conjured up by Pope Gregory in the early days of the Catholic Church when it was spreading its tentacles throughout the pagan world. So as not to affright the heathen lieges, he ordered his priests to convert the pagan winter feasts of Saturnalia and Yule with all their worst excesses − feasting, frivolity and fornication − into a celebration of Christ's nativity.

'Think on it, dear brethren. Christmas means the mass of Christ and, as we well know, the mass is a papist abomination. Not only is it idolatry, it is blasphemy. To mark Our Saviour's birth by eating of his flesh and drinking of his blood – is that not akin to cannibalism?'

Throughout his sermon Mrs Bowes gawped open-mouthed at Knox, her head bobbing in agreement. Marjory, however, kept her head bowed. When his sermon rose to a climax and a great cheer erupted, her mother laid a hand on her bosom and gazed at him in awe. Waiting until the cheers died down, Knox asked his flock to form orderly queues to take communion: because of the great number attending, the bread and wine would need to be rationed.

'Alas, I'm no miracle worker. I cannot turn water into wine and so our few loaves will have to suffice.'

Casting his eyes over the congregation, Knox sought out Marjory. 'Sister, did you not attend Our Lord's Table one Sunday? I've not seen you again. Did my sermon or the manner of my service offend you, perchance?'

She shook her head and cast her eyes down. 'Nay, not in the least. But your words pierced my mother's soul. She wishes to speak with you. She doesn't keep good health,' she gabbled. 'You may find her ...'

'I'm always ready to listen to seekers after truth,' Knox replied.

Half-rising from her chair, Mrs Bowes held out both hands. The middle-aged matron had a pleasing face, which, though lined and wrinkled, bore traces of former beauty.

'Preacher Knox, may I congratulate you on your uplifting service. Such purity of worship! Such clarity of expression! I said to myself here's a man who knows how to simplify complex matters. Why, I could feel the fog of confusion clearing from my mind as you spoke. Here is a true prophet indeed.'

A flush crept over his face at her flattery. 'Bless you for your kind words, sister. My heart rejoices whenever I succeed in shedding light on God's vision.'

Bidding her sit down, Knox pulled up the creepie stool beside her. She turned imploring eyes on him. 'Oh and you have, and I feel truly blessed that God has sent me here today. For you see, Master Knox, before you stands a tormented soul, sorely troubled by doubts.'

From the corner of his eye Knox spotted Marjory cringing.

'But no priest or bishop is able to comfort me in my hour of need,' her mother lamented. 'Whenever I've asked Bishop Tunstall to explain the new doctrines, he hums and haws. He still believes in purgatory and limbo and clings to the false doctrine that Christ is bodily present in the Eucharist. Can you imagine?'

'I sympathise with your plight and disappointment, sister. The papist church has failed its believers whereas I strive to reveal the true word of God to my flock. If I can give you any consolation, then only say the word.'

Mrs Bowes's eyes widened and her expression shifted from pitiful pleading to grim determination. 'Where to begin? I have so many questions.'

Marjory tapped her mother's shoulder. 'Mama, you mustn't overtire yourself.'

Mrs Bowes responded with a blank stare. 'I'm perfectly well, my dear. I'm not an invalid. But I can have no peace of mind until I know the answers.'

Marjory sucked in a breath. 'Then think of Master Knox. He needs to rest after such a long service.' Knox stroked his beard. Did he really look so tired? He put so much effort into his sermons that they did indeed sap his strength. But he rarely turned down requests for spiritual solace.

'A good meal will replenish both body and spirit, 'Mrs Bowes replied. 'Your sermon has infused me with renewed spirit, Master Knox. In return for being invited to your table, you must come to ours.'

Marjory tugged her mother's sleeve, 'What will papa say?' Uneasiness tinged her voice.

'Your papa is otherwise engaged, Marjory,' Mrs Bowes muttered. 'And the rest of the family have gone to stay with their uncle at Streatham. And we have food aplenty.' She turned to Knox. 'May we expect you at noon, Master Knox?'

'Alas, with no degree to my name, I'm no master but plain Mister Knox.'

'To me you are indeed a Master, and that's how I shall address you.'

Knox shrugged and cast a glance at Marjory. 'As long as I'm not called on to act as Lord of Misrule or Abbot of Unreason, I shall be honoured to accept your kind invitation.'

Wading through the slushy streets on his way to the Bowes's house in Marygate, Knox brushed off the drunken wassailers, mummers and guisers who accosted him. He may have convinced his flock to shun papist Christmas rites but long-held pagan traditions were harder to shed.

Arrayed in a festive red satin gown and pearl-studded hood, Mrs Bowes greeted him heartily. She grasped his hands. 'My, you're frozen,' she gasped and led him to the coal fire burning in the grate. Settling him into an upholstered chair, she handed him a cup of mulled cider seasoned with pungent spices.

'This is a cosy chamber.' He glanced round the parlour hoping to see Marjory.

Mrs Bowes harrumphed. 'This is a hovel compared to the house we had to leave behind in Aske. It had a tiled roof and timbered floors but here we have to make do with thatching over our heads and beaten earth beneath our feet. How Gracie cooks meals over an open fire never fails to astound me. Look what she has prepared for us today.'

Knox surveyed the table adorned with a roasted goose stuffed with apples and smothered in butter and saffron, fruit tarts and a selection of sweetmeats.

'Where is Marjory? I don't know what's wrong with that girl. She's been rather glum recently. I shall call her.'

As she took her place at table, Marjory responded to Knox's welcoming beam with a wan smile. Mrs Bowes, however, remained in a jaunty mood. After her guest had said Grace, she cut off a generous slice of goose and laid it on his plate.

'Forgive me if my poor appetite doesn't do justice to your rich feast but my stint in the galleys has ruined my digestion,' Knox said. 'Forbye, these soft white rolls spread with golden butter are luxury enough for me. A welcome change from my daily bread of a rough yeoman's loaf.'

Marjory squinted at him. 'What was it like as a galley slave? Was it dreadful? Were you lashed with the knout? Did you have to eat dry biscuits crawling with maggots?'

Knox chuckled. 'It wasn't only the biscuits that were maggot-ridden – my skin was mawkit and my hair crawling with lice. Forgive me, such details are too crude for your douce ears. Forbye, my infirmity is a scourge and bridle that chides me never to glory in the flesh.'

Mrs Bowes placed a hand on her bosom. 'I, too, have endured great suffering, dear brother. The agony of childbirth – fifteen times in as many years – and unbearable grief after losing three sons. While my body bears the scars of a mother's suffering, my heart aches with the sorrow of bereavement.' She sniffed back tears and turned pleading eyes on Knox. 'No physical pain can compare with the anguish of a tormented soul. Is that not so, dear brother?'

Knox raised his goblet. 'May I be of comfort to you, dear sister, and help you to put those dark days behind you. Let us drink to a bright new dawn for all of us.'

'Amen to that, dear brother,' Mrs Bowes replied.

A generous hostess, she kept Knox's goblet filled. He must be careful for he could feel his head spinning when he stood up to leave the table.

Seated by the hearth, he basked in the glow from the fire and female attention. It had been many years since he'd enjoyed home comforts and the gentle company of women. His very bones, toughened by the hard graft of the galleys, seemed to melt in their douce presence. He was luxuriating in their cosy companionship when the door banged open. Mrs Bowes frowned but Marjory leapt to her feet. Joy lit up her solemn face and her hazel eyes shone.

'Papa!' she cried and fell into her father's arms.

A light dusting of hoar frost sparkled on the captain's dark hair and icy flecks speckled the fur collar of his jerkin. The scent of male sweat mingling with leather and dank wool lingered in the stuffy parlour. Mrs Bowes clucked in disapproval at his mucky riding boots dripping slush on her woollen rug.

'Wait, papa. I have a present for you,' Marjory cried and rushed off.

The captain took his wife aside. 'And who, may I ask, is this strange man, Elizabeth? How dare you invite a male guest outwith the family without my permission.' The heat heightened the flush on his ruddy face.

'You were not there to give it, Richard. Besides, during the season of goodwill we're charged to open our doors to all,' Mrs Bowes said tartly. 'Furthermore, as our preacher, Master Knox may be considered family. A minister may call on his parishioners any time he pleases.'

Knox rose unsteadily to his feet and held out a hand but the captain kept a tight grip on his sword hilt. He glared at him. 'So you're the preacher who has my men in his thrall.'

'Aye, and I shall be pleased to see you at my church any day.'

'I don't need to heed your sermons to save my soul. Since it's the holy feast of Christmas, I shall overlook today's visit, Mr Knox. But from tomorrow you will not be welcome in my house.'

IX

A Wretched Soul

O God! I me confess
Ane sinful creature,
Full of all wretchitness
Fragile, vain, vile and pure.
The Gude and Godlie Ballatis,
Wedderburn Brothers, 16th Century

Scots Gate, Berwick-upon-Tweed, Spring, 1550

Mrs Bowes bustled into Knox's parlour with her Bible in one hand and a sheaf of notes in the other. Knox's banishment from her home in Marygate did not deter her from visiting him daily at his lodging in Scots Gate. Knox groaned inwardly. After a sleepless night, he could not summon the strength for one of her interrogations.

The devout matron was a demanding disciple but in her pursuit of truth she reminded him of an excited wee terrier nipping at his heels with her questions, grinding her teeth on a biblical conundrum like a dog with a bone. No doubt she'd brought something meaty to chew over today.

Trailing behind her Marjory lugged a heavy leather bag. 'I've brought some foodstuffs,' she said. 'May I take this to the kitchen?'

'Thank you, dear sister. Jamie keeps a paltry pantry.'

Mrs Bowes undid the buckle of her leather bound Bible. 'This was a closed book to me until you opened my eyes to the truth, Master Knox. Brought up in the Roman Catholic faith I was taught to say my rosary, pray to saints and gain indulgences to lessen my time in purgatory. All papal falsehoods: now I know the Bible is the only true path to God. However, I struggle to make sense of it.' She gazed at him with doleful eyes. 'I depend on you not only to put it in plain words but to allay the doubts that cloud my understanding.'

'I shall do what I can.' Knox was apprehensive. What knotty problem was she going to fling at him today? He rubbed his temples to stave off the skulking migraine.

Marjory popped her head round the door. 'Jamie says you haven't eaten yet, Master Knox.'

Knox nodded. 'My appetite is poor today and cooking is not one of Jamie's finest skills. He hasn't been able to tempt me with his oatmeal gruel. I had too much of that in the galleys.'

Glowering at her daughter, Mrs Bowes went on. 'Though you have pulled me out of the slough of despond, I continue to be assailed by dark thoughts, Master

Knox. I'm sorely buffeted by Satan. I fear eternal punishment for my former idolatry and other iniquities; I pray long hours but receive no comfort.' Her eyes brimmed with tears. 'Even though your teaching has rekindled my zest for this life, fear and dread of the next continue to torment me.'

Knox listened dutifully to her prattling but pain and weariness wilted him: his eyes glazed over as his migraine took hold. He slouched in his chair as if flattened by a battering ram or bombarded by the great gun, Mons Meg. He was grateful when Marjory came in bearing a tray.

'Mama, forgive me for interrupting but Master Knox must drink this feverfew to ease his headache,' she said.

While Knox swallowed the tisane she set down a plate of eggs scrambled with a generous dollop of creamy butter and a batch of soft white rolls. He gaped in surprise.

'Baps! How kind! You must have noticed how greedily I devoured these at Christmas.'

As Marjory held out a brimming goblet of wine, Mrs Bowes glanced up from her sheaf of notes and snatched the goblet.

'All this talking is making me parched,' she said before raising it to her lips.

When Marjory gave an exasperated shrug and left to fetch another one, her forbearance impressed Knox. 'You're fortunate to have such a caring daughter.'

Mrs Bowes patted her hood and simpered. 'Aye, I've done my best to instil the virtues of charity and mercy in all my girls.'

'Her kindness has breathed new life into me for I've been feeling rather poorly today. Disturbing news drove away sleep last night.'

Mrs Bowes leant forward. 'I'm sorry to hear, dear brother. What ails you?'

'Bishop Tunstall has denounced me to the Council of the North.'

Her claret-stained lips curled in disdain. 'What? That man is a hypocrite if not a downright heretic. Treacherous Tunstall treats our religion as some new fashion that will soon be as out of date as the ill-fated Anne Boleyn's French hood. He's a fence sitter – just like my wayward husband. What's his charge?'

'He's accused me of heresy for condemning the mass as idolatry. He's calling for the council to rescind my license to preach.'

'That snake in the grass, who seeks to restore papist practices, dares to accuse you of heresy? I'd like to wring his fat neck and see him squirm. Then send him to the devil where he belongs.'

Knox chortled. 'Doubtless he'd fain do the same with me. Nevertheless, the council are curious to hear my side of the story and have asked me to give a sermon justifying my censure at St Nicholas's Church in Newcastle.' His blue eyes flashed with mischief. 'Never fash, dear sister, I shall not flinch from this challenge. Rather

I relish the chance to defend my views before such an esteemed audience. Forbye, being Tinoterius, as I sometimes sign myself, I shall be on home ground.'

'How so dear brother?'

'Born by the banks of the Tyne in Haddington, I shall deliver my sermon in Newcastle on the Tyne.'

X

An Abomination

Newcastle-upon-Tyne, 4 April 1550

The nave of the large gothic church of St Nicholas was already filling up, Knox observed, not only with local people curious to hear the renegade Scotsman but many members of his Berwick congregation who had travelled south to show their support. The rood screen had been dismantled, allowing a view of the choir stalls where members of the Council of the North were to be seated.

From the front of the gallery with an uninterrupted view of the pulpit, Mrs Bowes gave Knox a cheery wave and then grimaced. Passing below, Captain Bowes halted briefly to finger the black and white collar adorning his neck and smiled up at Marjory. A pang of envy at the loving exchange between father and daughter pierced Knox. How blessed the captain was to be loved by such a caring creature.

At the back of the church, the captain gave the order for the grand procession to make its way up the aisle. When Knox had expressed disdain for such a pageant of papist pomp designed to overawe the faithful, Bishop Tunstall had waved away his concerns. Now as he paraded behind the ecclesiastics clad in black cassocks and white surplices, Tunstall stood out like a peacock amongst a murder of magpies. In full episcopal garb – a cope of richly embroidered brocade and matching mitre, a gold pectoral cross – the proud prelate wielded his bishop's crosier in his left hand blessing his right hand free to bless the congregation.

The nobility followed, headed by the Earl of Warwick flanked by his four sons. The eldest three were dark-haired and swarthy like their father whereas the youngest, auburn-haired, tawny-eyed Guildford was blessed with softer, finer features. All five men exuded strength and power but John Dudley, the most senior earl, cut the most impressive figure in his scarlet riding cloak.

When the procession passed underneath the gallery, something white fluttered downwards. Knox looked up to see Amy leaning across the edge of the balcony. Guildford stooped to pick up the fallen handkerchief and lightly pressed it to his lips before tucking into his sleeve. He then raised his head and winked at crimson-faced Amy. Young love knows neither reason nor boundaries, Knox thought. The grand procession had just reached the choir stalls when a rabble of rowdy ruffians straggled in through a side door. Knox braced himself, immediately on his guard, while Captain Bowes hastened to apprehend the brigands. After a few moments he handed Knox a note. Knox swiftly skimmed it before nodding in the direction of the gatecrashers. 'Let them stay,' he told Bowes. 'I will vouch for them. They are kin.'

Once in the pulpit Knox surveyed the combined force of the Council of the North. A mocking smile skimmed his lips as he introduced the topic of his sermon: *A Vindication of the Doctrine that the Mass is Idolatry.*

'How did the mystical last supper of Jesus Christ become the idolatry of the mass?' he began. 'Who decided that specially baked wafer-breads should be distributed with superfluous ceremonies? Fasting aforehand, invocation of saints, kneeling and bell ringing?

'Did Our Lord and his disciples clad themselves in costly garments at the last supper? Yet perverse priests disguised in vestments have deceived people with false teaching. Our Lord said nothing about playing pipes or singing, nor pattering upon beads or praying in a language the faithful cannot understand. At the Lord's Supper, the apostles partook of the bread and wine, but in the mass, the brethren get nothing at all to eat and drink. Banned from the altar, behind a rood screen, they are baffled by the priest's joukings and jerkings, noddings and crossings, turnings and upliftings.'

Ignoring the astonished gasps breaking out among the congregation, Knox soldiered on. 'Who burdened us with all these vain trifles that profane the sacrament?' He leant over the edge of the pulpit and wagged a finger. 'The devil, brethren, that's who. Satan has twisted the mass into a pagan sacrifice to take away the toothache, cure the lowping-ill from sheep or the lungsocht from kye and oxen. The evil one has turned prayers into magic spells, incantations for peace in time of war, for rain, for fair weather.'

He laid a hand on his breast and raised his eyes to heaven. 'Alas, my heart abhors such abominations! So I say unto you, all religious worship invented by the brain of man without God's commandments is idolatry. The mass is invented by the brain of man without any commandment of God, therefore it is idolatry.' His fist thudded the pulpit. 'The mass is an abomination, equivalent to the worship of serpents, bulls, or calves in ancient Israel.'

He scanned the row of councillors before fixing his eyes on Tunstall. 'Neither hatred nor favour to anyone stirs me to speak – only the obedience which I owe unto God. So that Our Lord Jesus Christ may suffer no more, nor die no more, I say unto you – shed his blood no more! Pardon my vehemence of spirit, my beloved brethren, but do it no more! Do not slay Christ, for you have no power to do this.'

As his final words gradually died away, a hush fell over the congregation. No one stirred, no one coughed: no one dared break the stunned silence that seemed to last for eternity.

Knox lingered a few moments in the pulpit not only to catch his breath but to let his words sink in – a technique learnt from David Lindsay. Descend too soon and his audience would start chattering and quickly forget his message.

Aghast, the council members shared looks of shock and horror. Only Dudley remained unruffled, one long leg crossed over the other, his expression inscrutable, while Bishop Tunstall could not hide his delight. He leant back in his episcopal throne with an insolent sneer on his face that said: *There I told you so. Now send him to the devil where he belongs.*

When the council retired to the vestry, the band of latecomers formed a cordon round the pulpit. Knox heard a startled cry: Mrs Bowes had risen in panic. Seconds later she was by his side, remonstrating with the ruffians.

'Do not dare lay a hand on Master Knox, or you shall have to answer to my husband – the guardian of Norham Castle.'

Knox put a hand on her arm. 'Do not fret, dear sister. These are my kinsmen, all trusty Hepburn men. Meet my liege lord – James, Master of Bothwell. It's chancy that he's in Newcastle today, to board my brother's ship for France.'

Hepburn bowed. 'Aye, Sir David Lindsay asked me to call on you, Mr Knox. He holds you in the highest regard. And I wish to assure you that I'm no traitor rogue like my father who handed over Preacher Wishart to be sacrificed. His deceit sticks in my craw,' he said, pinching his gullet.

'And his namesake, my pox-ridden uncle Patrick, is no better. Like all thon bloated clergy in the papist church, the bishop has no sense of loyalty to our country – only to Rome. Bishop of Moray he may be, but he's no man of God. I spit on a man who avows one thing and does another but I respect any man who speaks the truth. Not all men do. That's why I brought along my kinsmen to lend support lest any stramash flare up.'

Mrs Bowes laid a hand on Knox's sleeve. 'You've not only won over us frail women, Master Knox, but conquered the hearts of the reckless reivers – and their souls, too, by all signs.' The smile on her face froze as a harsh voice commanded,

'A word, if you please, Mr Knox.' Captain Bowes grasped the hilt of his sword. 'The council now demand your presence to hear their decision regarding your sermon.'

Mrs Bowes grabbed her husband's arm. 'What have they decided? Are they going to arrest him? Tell me, Richard.'

'Take hold of yourself, wife,' the captain snarled. 'Don't shame me in front of my men.'

The captain propelled Knox into the vestry where Dudley lay sprawled on the episcopal throne, buffing his fingernails on the velvet-upholstered arm.

'I'm here to represent King Edward,' he began, 'Our young monarch seeks a more radical form of religion and a clean break from St Peter's chains. I have reminded the council of His Majesty's wishes and, after brief deliberation they have agreed to vindicate your "vindication" sermon, Mr Knox.'

Knox relaxed. 'My heart rejoices to hear they favour the true word of God over idolatry and superstition.'

'Unfortunately, some of our older clergy do not,' Dudley replied. 'After a thorough interrogation, your accuser reveals a reluctance to ditch the old ways and has confessed to papist practices. As such, it is Bishop Tunstall who has been found guilty of heresy. Take him away, lads,' he called out.

Two of the earl's sons led Tunstall from an adjoining room and marched him away. With shackled wrists and lowered head, the once proud bishop seemed a broken man.

Dudley stretched his long limbs and stood, powerful legs apart, towering over Knox. 'Tunstall's departure leaves a vacancy here at St Nicholas's. On the king's authority, I'm offering you the post of chaplain for this northern see where the king wishes papistry to be stamped out. Will you accept?'

Knox hesitated. Such promotion was very tempting but it would mean leaving the barbarians he had tamed, the flock he had nurtured, his friends – Mrs Bowes and Marjory.

'Since it covers the whole bishopric of Durham with parishes as far north as Berwick, you will not be abandoning your present flock but increasing it.'

'Then I accept,' Knox replied.

XI

Letters from France

Our gentyl men are all degenerate;
There is nocht else but ilk man for him self,
That gars me go, thus banist like ane elf.
The Complaint of the Comoun Weill of Scotland
Sir David Lindsay, 16th Century

Edinburgh, July 1550

'How do you like my new abode, dear prioress?' Marie de Guise asked as she showed Elisabeth round her new town house. 'It even has its own oratory.'

Elisabeth nodded her approval. After the English had burned Holyrood Palace during their rough wooing, the queen mother had chosen to squat in its ruins but now, despite the signing of a peace treaty with the English, she'd been advised to take up quarters in the heavily-guarded castle. For who knew when the auld enemy would strike again? But the queen had always loathed that draughty fortress atop the rock and had commissioned this new residence in Nairne's Close at the top of the High Street.

'It's close enough to the castle should you need to seek sanctuary,' Elisabeth said and stepped up to admire the view from the long window that looked out over the Nor'Loch and across the Firth of Forth to Fife. ' And it will be cosy with these fireplaces large enough to roast an ox.'

The queen pointed to the oak panelled door. 'What do you think, my dear prioress? Do they capture our likenesses?'

Elisabeth squinted at the crudely carved heads. 'With his slouched bonnet, I jalouse it must be King James. But yours is ...' she broke off, 'not so deftly done.'

The queen chuckled. 'I think the prentice chiselled my features. Your honesty is like a beacon in this court full of dissemblers. Who can I trust apart from you, dear prioress?'

'Certainly not our faithless Scots lords.'

'So true, and I'm afraid my lord Bothwell has let us down again.' The queen handed her one of the letters spread out like a fan on the table.

Elisabeth's spirits sank. This was the straw that would cowp the cart. Not for the first time her nephew Patrick had betrayed the Hepburn motto, *Keep Tryst*. After divorcing his wife to woo the queen dowager, he was now threatening to make public her promise of marriage – unless he received 2,000 crowns he claimed the queen owed him.

Elisabeth seethed with anger. 'The Fair Earl is ill-named. Fickle, false and feckless would better describe one who keeps breaking his trust. Patrick is a greedy grasping scrounger with not one courteous bone in his spineless body.' She jabbed her finger at the letter. 'Yet he has a brass neck. He girns that if you have enough money to build a new house you can afford to pay him. How dare he chide Your Grace.'

'I never promised to marry him and I will not give in to bribery. Especially since he has declared his allegiance to the English King Edward. I have proof.' The queen drew another letter from the fan of missives.

'An instrument, dated at Westminster, 3rd September, 1549, sets forth that King Edward has taken the Earl of Bothwell under his protection and favour: *granting him a yearly rent of three thousand crowns, and the wages of a hundred horsemen for the defence of his person, and the annoyance of the enemy; and, if he should lose his lands in Scotland in the English King's service for the space of three years, promising to give him lands of equal value in England.*'

This treachery made even Elisabeth gasp. But there was more.

'He's written to Protector Somerset,' the queen went on, 'asking for his help in finding an English wife, preferably a Tudor princess – Lady Mary or Lady Elizabeth. In exchange, he promises to hand over the Hermitage, his stronghold in the borders.'

Elizabeth sucked in a breath. 'Then you have no remedy but to summon him on a charge of treason and exile him, madame.'

The queen sighed. 'Indeed, but Bothwell is not the only lord who threatens to transfer allegiance to the English. I would have to exile them all.'

'I'm ashamed of these assured Scots, so-called noblemen only too ready to sell their souls to the highest bidder. Forget their noble slogans, they abide by the measly motto: no silver, no service.'

The queen held her arms wide. 'My coffers are empty. I've hardly a groat left to pay their pensions and bonds. I've already paid out over twenty-five thousand francs, and given honours and titles to all, including the undeserving. King Henri has promised to send funds but so far not a bean has been forthcoming. I must do something to guarantee at least their service if not their loyalty otherwise I fear these insidious reformist doctrines will seduce our lords. What's a queen to do if she cannot rely on her nobles to protect her?'

Elisabeth sneered. 'Religion is not uppermost in their hearts or souls when English gold is on the table.' She, too, was concerned for Henry VIII's heir, ten-year-old Edward, was proving to be more zealous than his father in espousing evangelical beliefs.

'That's why I must go to France,' Queen Marie said, 'and I shall take these money-grubbing lords with me. Once they see the riches to be gleaned from the prosperous French court, they may be more tempted to stay loyal to their beloved homeland.'

'Who will bide here to run the country? Surely not Errant Arran?' Elisabeth snorted.

Strutting around with his new title, Châtelherault, the first duke to be created in Scotland, was getting above himself as usual. Despite his bumbling and dithering, Regent Hamilton was no fool when it came to feathering his own nest.

'It worries me he's plotting to unite Scotland with our auld enemy,' the queen replied, 'while I desire to strengthen the Auld Alliance for my daughter's sake.'

'You never ken with Twa-fangelt Arran. If he sniffed there was the slightest chance to reel in your royal daughter for his witless son, he would lowp over to the French side.'

Queen Marie crossed herself. 'Please God, no! That's why I shall leave behind my ambassador. Henri Cleutin, Monsieur d'Oisel will keep our unruly lords in line. Besides, they respect him.'

Elisabeth chortled. 'But not Errant Arran! His lang neb will be sorely out of joint when he hears you trust a lower rank Frenchman over a noble Scot.'

'D'Oisel is tactful enough to let the regent think he's in control while he holds the reins of my reign.'

'Arran is a slippery eel, madame. He may agree at first but once Queen Mary reaches the age of majority, he'll refuse to resign the regency. In which case you should secure it for yourself. As the dauphin's wife, Mary will have to bide in France and so will need a representative in Scotland. There's no one better than you to look after your daughter's interests here.' Elisabeth took a breath. 'That's if you mean to return. You may be tempted to live out your twilight years with your sister, Abbess Renée, at her convent in Rheims.'

The queen looked thoughtful. 'Who knows, *ma chère amie*? The future is so uncertain.' She pulled out a knotted string from her pocket and let it drop to the floor. 'François sent me this to show how much he has grown. Look! He's as tall as I am and not yet sixteen-years-old!'

Her sad eyes misted over. She hadn't seen François, Duc de Longueville, the surviving son of her first marriage, since leaving France twelve years ago. 'He's no longer the boy I left behind but on the threshold of manhood. His De Guise uncles tell me proudly that he will make a fine warrior, a leader of men – unlike …'

Her unspoken words hung in the air. Unlike the other François, for Elisabeth knew the dauphin's health was causing the queen mother grave concern. While King Henri was fulsome in his praise for *la petite reine écossaise*, he never mentioned her betrothed. Only Mary's governess, the outspoken Lady Fleming, had dared to tell the truth: the heir to the French throne was puny and sickly and no match for their bonnie Queen of Scots.

The question also lay unasked: what if François dies? Henri might consider another betrothal to the recently born Charles but not if his wife had her way. Lady Fleming had let slip that Catherine de Medici was not at all happy with the Scots bride for François, never mind Charles. To the Florentine merchant's daughter, Scotland was an uncultured, barbaric kingdom, too wee and too faraway from the powerful European courts ever to have any influence in the world.

'*La Belle Écossaise* seems to have some sway with King Henri.'

'Not surprising,' Elisabeth replied. For even though Jenny Stewart was a widow well past her fortieth year, the red-haired siren still had the glamour, that mysterious allure, to bewitch men. 'The king may have fallen under her spell but not his consort or his courtesan, I hear.'

Queen Marie nodded. 'When Catherine and Diane de Poitiers learnt that Montmorency, the Constable of France, had been acting as a decoy for Henri to enjoy Lady Fleming's favours in secret, they were furious.'

Elisabeth gave a girlish giggle. 'By the sound of it the French court is a den of *liaisons dangereuses:* there's a lot of slinking about on tiptoe.'

The queen regent's strained face relaxed into a brief smile before tightening again. 'Because of this, Diane is determined to banish Lady Fleming. She has chided Henri for dishonouring my daughter's reputation by carrying on an affair within her household.' She picked up another letter. 'Read this, my dear prioress. From the spurned paramour.'

A strong scent of rose oil wafted from the embossed writing paper. Elisabeth inhaled deeply. *Rosa gallica officinalis* revived memories of the warm southern climes: another place, another time, another life. The thought flitted through her mind: how pleasant it would be to return to *la douce France.*

Diane's letter was no *billet doux*, however, but a barrage of complaints about Lady Fleming. She was sticking stubbornly to her uncouth Scottish ways and making no effort to adapt to the French *modus vivendi*. Even worse, her broad Scots accent was ravaging their precious mother tongue and rendering it incomprehensible to sensitive Gallic ears.

Elisabeth sniggered quietly to herself. *Sacre bleu! Quelle horreur!* Being unable to communicate with the French physicians was risking the health of *la petite reine*. For that reason Diane was recommending Lady Fleming be removed from her post as governess to Queen Mary.

'Hmm, a knotty situation,' Elisabeth said.

'Indeed for Lady Fleming is still high in the king's favour and the constable has no wish to humiliate her. However, he suggests a French-speaking Scots doctor may be the solution.'

Elisabeth nodded. 'A physician to pour balm on their wounded pride? Very wise.'

'The College of Surgeons have recommended Dr William Bog. Having gained qualifications from Montpelier as well as Edinburgh, he's a fluent French speaker. But he'll require an apothecary assistant to accompany him.'

Elisabeth frowned. 'Why? The French court swarms with quacksalvers hired by Catherine de Medici to help her conceive.'

'And who may be complicit in plots to poison my daughter, so Montmorency has warned me. I need someone trustworthy to attend to her medication.' Queen Marie gazed at Elisabeth with pleading eyes. 'As my dearest friend, will you come with me?'

Elisabeth rubbed her brow at the crease where the starched wimple dug into her skin. How tempting to visit France once more – until she recalled Lindsay's haggard face. His health was poor and if anything should happen while she was away – it didn't bear thinking about. She could not leave Davie.

'I've no wish to offend you, madame, but I have too many responsibilities at the abbey.'

Veiling her disappointment, the queen gave a nod of understanding. 'Perhaps Sister Agnes may wish to come? It would be a homecoming for her.'

'Sister Agnes is no longer young and may be too frail to travel.' A sudden thought flew into Elisabeth's mind. 'But her assistant is not. Isabelle not only reads Latin and speaks French but is a skilled apothecary for her years. Sister Agnes has taught her well.'

Queen Marie clapped her hands. 'So be it. Now I must seek advice from Diane de Poitiers on mourning protocol at the French court. For wearing either black or white may cause offence to Madame Diane who has claimed both colours for her own.'

PART TWO

I

Sodom and Gomorrah

… and because their sin is very grievous ..
Genesis: XVIII: 20

Newcastle, September 1551

Bent double, Knox paced the floor, rubbing his back to relieve the devil's grip that squeezed his kidneys. Tripping over the hem of the grubby robe that swamped his slight figure, he pulled the cord more tightly at the waist.

When a tingling sensation in his bladder signalled the urgent need to pass water, he aimed his swollen pistle at the pisspot and groaned as gravel scraped its way down. Relieved, he lay down on the bed but became alarmed when his swelling did not go down. He must drive lustful thoughts from his mind but the more he tried to pray, the more he became aroused. The devil must indeed have him in his grip.

In the cloisters of St Andrews, the temptation to pleasure oneself was a constant source of worry for students sworn to celibacy. How could they avoid sinning when inflamed by carnal desire? Some souls wore hair shirts or rope girdles while others indulged in flagellation – though this was said to whip up desire rather than cool temptation.

Because an accumulation of semen could cause illness, involuntary nocturnal secretions were nature's way of rebalancing the humours and therefore forgivable, the postulants were told. Nevertheless, provoking such a release for pleasure was a grievous sin and must be confessed to gain absolution. So, too, was sexual congress with women but, torn between the demands of their faith and the demands of the flesh, most clerics broke the *lex continentiae*. How could they not when ecclesiastical ideals were so at odds with nature? God had created man to plant his seed and woman to bear his children.

As his thoughts drifted to Marjory, Knox stiffened with desire and longing. He flushed with shame that he could not control his vain imaginings. Nor should he sully her honour with immodest yearnings.

For Marjory was a pure soul, unselfish and caring. Her pale, forlorn face reflected a moral beauty that aroused his sympathy. Her clear hazel eyes mirrored an inner integrity and honesty, with none of the artifice of her more worldly-wise sister.

But passionate feelings smouldered beneath Marjory's quiet breast, he suspected. Witnessing the obvious love she harboured for her father made him envious. If only he could arouse a smidgeon of such emotion for himself. That was a vain hope for, unlike the handsome, vigorous captain, Knox was a physical wreck. His scarred auld carcase would disgust the sixteen-year-old maiden. This realisation dampened any desire: he became flaccid.

From the passageway he heard Jamie's raised voice. 'Master Knox is still abed. He's no well. He's no able for to see folk this morn.'

Knox keeked his head round the door. Though he was always telling his flock religion wasn't just for Sundays, he didn't feel fit for visitors today.

'Forgive me, Jamie, it sounds like English but I can't understand a word you're saying.' Mrs Bowes's matronly figure pushed past Jamie, squashing him against the wall. She lifted her skirts clear of the mud-ridden rushes strewn on the floor and steered a course along the hallway, clucking with disapproval. 'And sweep this floor, Jamie. Muck and dust will ruin Master Knox's lungs.'

Knox quickly closed the door again. There would be no stopping Mrs Bowes bent on invasion – but Marjory? He had no wish for her to see him in this state – with a straggly beard untrimmed for days and eyes red-rimmed from lack of sleep. He ran a comb through his beard and tucked his lank hair beneath the greasy nightcap. Straightening up he opened the door and forced a welcoming smile. 'It's you, dear sister. What a surprise.'

'How could I not rise from my sick bed and answer your clarion call, dear brother? After reading this, I had to come at once.' She waved his recent letter.

The pain of my head and stomach troubles me greatly: daily I find my body decay ...
Your messenger found me in bed, after a sore trouble and most dolorous night ...

'I'm here as your friend in woe who shares your pain. Your welfare is my abiding concern, dear brother. To be near you, I'm staying with my sister Anne and her husband in Alnwick. I'm at your beck and call whatever the hour of day or night.'

'Thank you, dear sister. That gives me great comfort but there's no need.'

Mrs Bowes clucked and wagged a finger. 'This tormented soul knows what you're going through. Being pastor to so many parishes is ruining your health. Never fear, I am here to be your help and support and protect you from those who tire you with their trivial troubles. You know that *I* would never disturb you with anything trifling.'

'Nay, I'm sure you'd never do that. The sufferings of Job – be they boils, the killing of his children, and the destruction of his household – will be as mild irritants, weak as the waft from a mild spring breeze compared to your woes, my dear sister.'

Satisfied, Mrs Bowes sat down. 'Just so, dear brother. I'm sorely tried but the Lord knows I bear my cares without complaint.' She clasped her hands and bowed her head piously, as if in the confessional: some papist habits were hard to discard.

Resting his chin on his hand, Knox listened to her pouring out her worries in a great torrent – how the devil was tormenting her with the most despicable sins, the most vile vices known to man and God. Knox listened with half an ear – until her references to Genesis grabbed his attention. Striving to compose his features into a stern mask, he said, 'Tell me, dear sister, do you have *any* inkling of the sins committed by the wretched inhabitants of Sodom and Gomorrah – those twin cities of the damned?'

Her lips twisted into a sulky pout. 'Only that they were the most abominable that can ever be imagined on this earth.'

'As evil as the worst excesses thon shavelings, tonsured monks, cooped up in any monastery are likely to luxuriate in. Idleness that provokes filthy, unnatural lusts, violence and injury to strangers and all kinds of abomination and *monstrous violations*,' he stressed the last words. 'I repeat – such lewdness and obscenity a gentlewoman like you could never imagine.'

Mrs Bowes screwed up her face and folded her arms. Clearly she distrusted his explanation. How far should he go to hammer home the point? In the galleys, Knox had witnessed slaves indulging in unnatural practices to relieve their carnal desires: men deprived of women were reduced to committing vulgar acts that surpassed the laws of decency or any moral code. To describe these to Mrs Bowes was unthinkable.

'Sodomy and bestiality are the most vile sins against God,' he said to end her interrogation.

But Mrs Bowes would not be put off so easily. 'To be absolutely certain I must know what these dreadful abominations are.'

Knox stood up and tightened the cord round his robe. 'May as well be hung for a sheep as a lamb,' he muttered and took a deep breath. 'Sodomy is how the devil copulates with his satanic followers,' he paused, 'both male and female, while bestiality is fornication with the devil in animal form.'

That made Mrs Bowes sit up and listen. Shifting forward to perch on the edge of the settle, she cocked her head to one side and fixed her eyes on him, her whole body taut with intense concentration.

'Witches take on the form of beasts and tempt the lustful to copulation in order to conceive a monstrous being – a devil's bird for Satan's evil use.' Knox paced the floor, rubbing his back with both hands: his voice took on the tone of a schoolmaster teaching an inquisitive pupil. 'To staunch these repulsive practices, King Harry passed the Buggery Act in 1533, the penalty for which is death by hanging.' He paused. 'So, my dear sister, unless Satan has seduced you, you cannot be guilty of the sins of Sodom and Gomorrah.'

She sat dumbstruck, silenced by the horror of his frank explanation, Knox assumed.

After a few seconds, she recovered her power of speech. 'That's as may be, but what about the sins mentioned in Ezekiel? Now those *do* worry me.'

While Knox ransacked his memory, she explained, 'Such as pride and arrogance when I consider myself to be one of God's elect. And I often lack pity towards the poor and needy: I'm guilty of not doing enough to help my fellow man.'

Knox sighed. Nothing daunted this woman: she refused to be outshone. 'If that troubles you, my dear sister, may I suggest you do more in the way of charitable works. As I've instructed the virtuous womenfolk of Edinburgh to do.'

'You correspond with other women?' she asked, clearly nettled. 'Well, I'm not like one of your worthy Scots hens only fit for doling out offerings to the poor. Besides, are you not guilty of such sins? Did you not confess that your heart was subject to foul lusts and that you lamented not killing them?'

Knox sucked in his breath. Mrs Bowes stored away his every utterance, like a squirrel hoarding nuts, digging them up to feed her false reasoning.

'Aye, I confess lustful longings often pierce my evil heart and carnal desires afflict this wicked carcase. That only proves that I, too, am a man of flesh and blood; that I, too, have my weaknesses. But in practice I am no adulterer.'

A triumphant smile lit up her face. 'There! So you, too, are vulnerable. You're as susceptible to temptations of the flesh as any man – or woman. Whenever I am seduced by wicked thoughts, did you not advise me to say: Begone, wretched devil? A man such as you should not be tormented by lustful thoughts. To that end, I mean to remove all temptation from your path.'

Now Knox was struck dumb. A thought flashed through his mind. Surely she wasn't about to offer herself to him? Had she left her husband to follow him? Nothing she did would astound him. Her eyes sparkled as she leant forward and mischievously tweaked his beard. A hot flush coloured his cheeks.

'Dearest brother, to free your mind from wicked thoughts and your soul from temptation, I mean to see your physical needs are satisfied.'

Like a fly snagged in a spider's web Knox wriggled in panic. 'That's most considerate of you, dear sister,' he stuttered, 'but there's no need.'

He followed her disapproving glance as she surveyed the room, taking in the books stacked higgledy-piggledy on shelves or the floor and papers and documents strewn across every available surface. She picked up a book and banged it down, sending a cloud of dust flying into the air.

'That does it,' she said. 'You may deny lust as one of your vices, but cleanliness is clearly not one of your virtues, dear brother.'

'I'll confess our hovel is gey stoory. Jamie does his best, but he's no housewife.'

'Exactly so,' Mrs Bowes proclaimed, a note of triumph in her voice. 'This house lacks a woman's touch. You're in need of a wife, dear brother. You must marry. And soon. Now that you receive a regular stipend, lack of funds can no longer serve as an excuse.'

Knox coughed to clear his throat but his voice was still hoarse. 'Who do you suppose would wish to wed an auld birkie like me?'

When she looked at him from underneath her eyelashes, like a bashful young maiden, a cold clamminess crept over his skin.

'You and I, dear brother, are kindred spirits – soul mates. If I were a few years younger and unwed I would gladly offer myself. But …' Her sigh was heavy with regret. 'That cannot be.'

Knox also sighed – but with relief.

'Instead, I have in mind my daughter. The one who is most like me.'

'You mean Amy?' he asked.

'Amy?' Mrs Bowes looked bewildered: her hand fluttered to her throat. She tilted her head and gave him a coy glance. 'Oh, I see what you mean.' She giggled like a girl. 'Amy may favour me in looks, but she's vain and selfish.' She waggled her head and tut-tutted. 'Nay, you need someone modest and selfless who will be a patient, devoted companion. Not as pretty as her sister, perhaps, but Marjory will serve you well.'

Knox sucked in a breath and let out a long low whistle.

'I know what you're thinking.' She patted the back of his hand. 'The captain may dig in his spurs and refuse his permission, but leave that to me.'

'Nay,' Knox replied, 'I was thinking that Marjory may not be willing.'

'Not willing? Why would she not be? Who else would woo her? Wait and see, dear brother. Marjory will be both thrilled and honoured to accept your proposal. A girl with any sense would be.'

II

God's Trumpeter

If when the watchman seeth the sword come upon the land,
he blow the trumpet and warn the people;
then whosoever heareth the sound of the trumpet and
taketh not the warning, his blood shall be upon his own head.
Ezekiel XXIII: 2–4

Newcastle, 1 November 1551

'Let Newcastle witness!' Knox bellowed and thumped his fist on the edge of the pulpit. The congregation of St Nicholas's flinched.

'Yestreen, on All Hallows' Eve, the sweating sickness that scythed down the degenerate of London struck Newcastle. Why has God visited such a plague on us, dear brethren?' He paused to wag a finger. 'To punish those who refuse to practise the virtues of their religion. Meanwhile, the devil and his cohorts have hatched a gleeful conspiracy to hinder the work of Christ's disciples. The powers of darkness have persuaded papist nobles to set one champion of Protestantism to destroy the other.

'Protector Somerset is the victim of the Earl of Warwick's reckless *coup d'etat.* However blameworthy his conduct in other respects, Somerset was a simple man, a zealous friend to the evangelical church whereas the greed for power drives his rival. By promoting himself to Duke of Northumberland and proclaiming himself Lord Protector of King Edward, he's also guilty of the sin of pride.' After a dramatic pause he thumped the edge of the pulpit. 'Mark my words. The death of Somerset will be the ruin of his adversary.'

Alnwick, Northumberland

'Look at you, brother, you're drenched. Come in before you catch consumption.' Mrs Bowes dragged the drookit Knox in through the door of her sister's house in Alnwick.

He took off his wet bonnet and gave it a shake. 'The storm has been stalking me all the way from Newcastle.'

'I pray it doesn't bring the sweating sickness. Come in here and take off your wet gear.' She led him into a side room and hung his cloak on a hook.

'A word in your ear before you meet my sister and her husband.' Mrs Bowes spoke in hushed tones. 'The bruit of your sermon has reached Alnwick, making them uneasy. Anne and Henry were sheep in Bishop Tunstall's fold but now he's gone, they'll have to bow down to the greater glory.

'I've been doing my best to prod them along with Bible readings but Henry fears your All Saints' Day sermon was too outspoken. Look, you're spattered in mud. Let me brush it off.' As she fussed with his collar, her lavender scent permeated his nostrils. A wave of nostalgia washed over him: he went weak at the knees. When their eyes locked time stood still – until the clomp of footsteps on the flagstones disturbed their fleeting moment of intimacy. Startled, Knox spun round, knocking the crockery off the large oak dresser and colliding with Mrs Bowes who broke into a girlish giggle. The footsteps halted before moving on.

The mood at the Wickcliffe's dinner table was tense: Henry wore a face that would curdle cream, Anne wriggled wormlike in her seat but worst of all, Marjory steadfastly avoided Knox's gaze. He felt crushed. Was he so repugnant to her?

'Your reputation goes before you, Preacher Knox,' Henry said, 'and not only from my good sister who constantly sings your praises. You're not afraid to speak your mind but in your recent sermon you scaled new heights of controversy, I hear.'

While Anne shrank at her husband's challenge, Mrs Bowes leaned forward eager to savour the spat.

'I sympathise with your concerns, dear brother,' Knox replied, 'but just because my Lord Dudley has might on his side, does not mean to say he is right. I only ever say the truth which many men fear to do.'

'The truth can be deceptive, Mr Knox. One man's truth is another man's lie.'

'That may be so in many cases but in the pulpit I utter God's truth as enshrined in the Bible.' He glanced towards Marjory, fearful that expressing himself too forcefully would repel the young lass. He sucked in a breath.

'You see, however much my legs may tremble as I mount the steps, once in the pulpit I feel the spirit of God move within me: I become a man transformed. As the Holy Spirit inflamed the apostles with tongues of fire at Pentecost, so he inspires me. When I preach I become an instrument in the hands of the Lord through which he sounds his word.' He gave a wry chuckle. 'So much so that some folk cry me God's trumpeter.'

Mrs Bowes clapped her hands with glee. 'Well said, brother. And God's trumpet shall sound around the nation.'

Marjory glanced up. She puckered her brow before lowering her eyes again.

'Perhaps, but your tune may not be pleasing to my lord Dudley's ears,' Henry replied. 'Once he hears of it, he may seek reprisals.'

Mrs Bowes threw down her napkin. 'Nonsense! Pastor Knox has nothing to fear from one of the ungodly. Why, as he warned, the Lord is already showing his displeasure with the sweating sickness.'

'In which case, perhaps, you should return to your family, dear sister,' Henry said.

'There's no need. Lucy is a very capable housekeeper and the younger children dote on her. She's a much better mother than I am. Amy and the older girls shall stay at Streatham till the danger passes.'

Anne nervously twisted the corner of her napkin. 'And your husband? Surely Richard must be missing you.'

Mrs Bowes harrumphed. 'I doubt it. He's too busy trying to quash the rebellious Scots. Not that he's having much success. Yet, through the power of his words and without a drop of blood being shed, Master Knox brought peace to Berwick within a matter of weeks.' She beamed Knox a proud smile.

Marjory pushed away her plate and begged leave to be excused. With dismay Knox watched her scurry away.

'Marjory does seem quite pale,' her aunt said. 'She hasn't touched her food. 'Do you think she may be stricken with the sweating sickness?' She twisted and untwisted her napkin. 'She may have caught it at St Nicholas's. Why, we may all be at risk of affliction.'

Upstairs, Marjory climbed onto the four-poster bed and drew the curtains to shut out the world. The food stuck in her craw: she couldn't swallow a morsel. Ever since her mother had suggested she wed Master Knox, panic and dread had knotted her stomach. What if he'd come to ask for her hand today? What would she say? If only her father were here. She longed to go back to Berwick and leave her mother to her preacher. Yawning deeply she dozed off, only to be roused by a voice booming in her ear.

'Marjory!' her mother shouted and shook her awake.

Marjory rubbed her eyes. 'Has he gone?'

'Aye, he's gone and full of concern for you. How could you be so rude? Leaving the table in such a sulk.'

'I felt unwell, mama. My belly aches. Perhaps I'm coming down with the sickness.'

Mrs Bowes placed a hand on her brow. 'Quite cool – no fever there.' She perched on the edge of the bed. 'I don't understand you, Marjory. Do you realise whom you are turning down? Any young lady with an iota of sense should be honoured to tie the knot with such a man. Master Knox is God's messenger, a prophet, but that's still not good enough for you, you churlish child.'

Marjory turned away. 'However wise a prophet he may be, he's as old as Methuselah.'

'Don't exaggerate. He's only thirty-seven,' her mother snapped. 'A difference of twenty years is nothing. In fact, it's preferable for a maiden to be married to a more mature man than to a young whippersnapper wet behind the ears. Master Knox is a man of experience and wisdom, respected by those who seek out his guidance. It will be a most beneficial match.'

'For whom,' Marjory muttered.

'With a man like that at your side every day and every night for spiritual and physical comfort, you would be fortunate indeed.' Mrs Bowes heaved a sigh full of longing.

Marjory eyed her mother suspiciously. Mrs Bowes would have Knox in a blink of an eye if she could, but since she couldn't she would substitute Marjory. As his wife, she would be housekeeper, cook, bedfellow and mother of his children while her mother remained his soul mate – or more. She would be Martha the drudge toiling in the kitchen to her Mary bathing his feet in oils while soaking up his words of wisdom. Would she be her mother's proxy? No, she would not. Whatever had been going on in the cloakroom, she wanted no part of it.

'In my day we had no choice,' Mrs Bowes moaned. 'Daughters obeyed their parents. We all did as we were told. Without question.' She scowled. 'You're such a selfish girl, Marjory. You must take after your father.'

III

A Restless Heart

> The fancy, which that I have servèd long,
> That hath always been enemy to mine ease,
> Seemèd of late to rue upon my wrong,
> And bade me fly the cause of my misease.
>
> *The Restless Heart*
> Henry Howard, Earl of Surrey, 16th Century

Norham Castle, November 1551

Neither the dark rainclouds gathering overhead nor the bitter wind tugging at her cloak discouraged Marjory from riding to Norham Castle. She'd had enough of her mother's nagging. She had to cut free or else she'd find herself standing by the preacher's side reciting marriage vows. She'd go and live with her father and tend to his needs. It must be a hard, lonely life in the remote English fortress high on the bank of the River Tweed with no home comforts.

No sooner had Marjory reined her palfrey to a halt at the edge of the moat than the heavy clouds burst, soaking her in the sudden downpour. The drawbridge was up and the portcullis firmly closed. When a guard on horseback brandishing a drawn sword emerged out of the mist, she became alarmed.

'I mean no harm,' she yelled. 'I am the captain's daughter.'

'The governor is out on patrol but you can wait in his chamber. We'll go in by the Sheep Gate,' he said, seizing her palfrey's reins.

Her father's quarters surprised Marjory who had imagined a bare soldier's billet not a comfortable, cosy chamber with tapestries lining the stone walls and animal furs covering the flagstones. She pulled up a stool by the hearth where a well-stoked fire burned in the grate. She took off her sopping cloak and hung it over the back of a chair to dry. Though she was shivering, beads of sweat broke out on her brow: her head throbbed and her throat felt raspy and sore. When a fit of uncontrollable sneezing racked her ribs, a girlish voice cried out, 'Is that you, my lord?'

A maidservant, Marjory assumed as she pulled back the tapestry separating the two rooms. A high four-poster bed draped in heavy brocade curtains dominated the darkened chamber. She glanced round the room but could see no one until the heap of blankets on the bed shifted and a tousle-haired girl poked her face out.

'What are you doing here?' Marjory spluttered.

The lass flashed an indignant look. 'I might ask you the same.' She drew back the coverlet to reveal an infant suckling at her bared breast. 'This is what *I'm* doing. But what are *you* doing, storming into the captain's chamber without a by-your-leave?'

'This is my father's bed!' Marjory blurted. 'Who are you?'

The lass uncoupled the babe from her breast, swaddled it in a cloth and propped it against a pillow. With nary a stich on, the hussy slipped out of bed and slid her feet into a pair of sheepskin slippers. She wrapped herself in a fur-trimmed gown, tying it loosely round her waist. Flaxen-haired and buxom – and brazen beyond belief – the girl could be no older than Marjory. An insolent smirk frolicked about her sensual lips.

'So, you are Dick's daughter? Now, which of my captain's crop are you?' She looked Marjory up and down. 'Let me guess. Nay, not Amy. You're too dark to be the golden-haired one and too young to be Lucy. You'll be Sweet Marjoram, I wager. The soft-hearted, sensible, sober one.'

Her words blasted the breath out of Marjory. Not only did her father keep a harlot but he shared secrets with this strumpet.

The girl stretched across the bed and picked up her bundle. 'Come and meet your baby brother. We've named him Richard – after his da. But we call him Little Dicken.' She snuffled her nose into the swaddling and warbled, 'Cuckoo! Cuckoo! You're the captain's wee cuckoo!'

When Little Dicken gurgled with glee, Marjory could stand no more. She hurtled down the turnpike stairs and into the courtyard. The rain had turned to sleet and the glacial wind made her shiver. In her haste she'd left her riding cloak drying in front of the fire. But she refused to go back for her father's whore to laugh at her again. Let the river rise and drown her – that would be a merciful release.

Berwick-upon-Tweed

The blurred faces slowly swam into focus, the vague, faraway voices gradually became distinct and vivid dreams gave way to reality. Marjory opened her eyes slowly and blinked against the light.

'Praise be to God.' Her mother leant over her with clasped hands. 'What made you ride off in such weather? Had the guard not found you, soaked to the skin and with a high fever, you might have perished. We feared you'd caught the dreaded sweat. Let's give thanks to the Lord you're back in the land of the living.'

Closing her ears to her mother's carping, Marjory rested her head against the bolster. She wished she'd died. Her father had a whore! Her father had sired a bastard son! Her father had been unfaithful – not only to her mother but to her! Her beloved papa loved someone else – that was most hurtful of all. She, his favourite daughter, his Sweet Marjoram, did not come first in his affections. It made her sick to the stomach.

'Come, now, eat something. You're all skin and bone − like a wretched wee wren. See what Molly has made to tempt you.' Mrs Bowes lifted the cloth from a tray piled with little sweet cakes and other treats but Marjory turned up her nose.

'Then you must drink something,' her mother urged and put a cup to her lips.

The highly spiced cordial that burnt Marjory's throat and brought tears to her eyes was strangely comforting for it lessened the ache in her heart. 'Why didn't you tell me about papa?'

'That's not for a daughter to know.' Mrs Bowes pulled up a chair. 'She should learn to esteem her father as head of the household so as to bestow similar respect on her husband. Whether they deserve it or not is another matter,' she added with a sneer. 'For the sake of family pride, a bride is also taught to turn a blind eye to her husband's philandering. At least your father has tried to be discreet in his liaisons. He keeps his whores out of the way − far from prying eyes so as not to shame me.' Mrs Bowes puckered her lips, as if sucking on a sour plum.

Marjory pushed herself up onto her elbows. 'Whores? There have been others?'

'It's in a man's nature to stray. Your father is a soldier, a hunter forever on the prowl. One woman is not enough to satisfy his needs. Certainly not one at my stage in life,' she said peevishly. 'Dried up and withered after bearing his children, I'm of no further use to him. Who knows how many other children he has sired on strumpets and trollops? It's a blessing not to know.'

The more her mother revealed, the further her father fell from his pedestal. Marjory sank back against the pillows. 'So why did you marry him?'

'I had no choice. He was chosen for me. Orphaned at an early age, my sister and I became the wards of Sir Ralph Bowes. When I was betrothed to his youngest son, I thought myself very fortunate indeed, for Richard was strong and brave and handsome. Then on my wedding day, I learnt Sir Ralph had bought our wardship.' She snorted.

'He'd adopted us not out of the kindness of his heart but because we were wealthy heiresses with land inherited from our father and grandfather. Since a woman cannot own property, it is passed on to her husband as a dowry. On our marriage, Richard was granted title to my grandfather's lands. In other words, your father married me for my money. I had no say in the matter. I was handed over like a package.'

'Did you love him, mama?'

Mrs Bowes's eyes took on a faraway look. 'I thought I did. But I was very young, just a silly girl − I knew nothing about love. I looked up to Richard, admired him and bore his children but we never had the kind of closeness I craved. I yearned for someone with whom to share my innermost thoughts and feelings − I longed for a soul mate. But your father and I were never kindred spirits.'

Her wistful mood shifted to one of frustration. 'He's a warrior in a man's world with no interest in grappling with divine truth. For him, religion is only useful as a weapon in the battle for power. As a soldier flings aside a sword to wield a dagger, he throws off one faith for another with nary a twinge of conscience.'

Placing a hand on her heart, she went on, 'Whereas Master Knox is a true soldier of Christ. He'll never toss aside the shield of truth for any reason. He understands that women also crave spiritual fulfilment; that we're not only a husband's possession, a vessel to be filled with their seed and bear their offspring. Master Knox is not a man of base, bestial needs. He sees beyond a woman's body into her very soul.' Her eyes misted up. 'Because of that, once he has plighted his troth, he'll never stray. You'll never suffer the hurt and shame I've had to endure all these years. Fortunate indeed is the woman to whom John Knox gives his heart – and soul. Consider this carefully, my dear child,' she said, gently stroking her hair. 'The Lord has blessed you with a wonderful chance. Do not throw it away.'

Tormented by the discovery of her father's infidelity, Marjory refused to leave her bed. Her mother's confession only added salt to wounds that could not be healed by marriage to a man she did not love. She envied the ease with which Amy had set her heart on Guildford.

'You need to restore the bloom to your pale cheeks,' Amy said and drew back the curtains. 'Time to come out of the gloom and into the sun – if you wish to hear my news,' she added with an impish smile.

Bored of being bedridden, Marjory followed her into the garden where Mary and Beth were sitting on a rug spread on the grass. Always together with arms linked and blonde heads locked together, MaryBeth, as the family called the twelve-year-old twins, formed a disconcerting two-headed mythical creature. Two halves of the same soul, her mother maintained, who had exited the womb clasping hands. Marjory envied the sisters' unbreakable bond, the closeness she had longed to share with her father. Propped up on their elbows, they listened enthralled by Amy's prattle.

'Guildford still adores me,' she chirruped. 'I feared his head would be turned at court in London. But with my love token pressed close to his heart, he'll never forget me. I have you to thank, dearest sister,' she said and pecked her on the cheek.

Marjory had used up the fine lawn remnants from her father's collar to sew Christmas gifts. On Amy's handkerchief she had embroidered a bleeding heart – a red heart-shaped flower with a dangling red droplet.

'When did you give it to him?'

'At your preacher's sermon in Newcastle. You didn't notice? Now Guildford is going to ask papa for my hand.' She clasped her hands to her breast. 'Imagine, I shall become a lord's wife.'

'Dearest Amy, though it pains me to dash your hopes, Guildford is the son of an earl who will expect a substantial dowry which papa cannot afford. I would curb your fondness for Guildford before it becomes a passion.'

Amy flashed her sister a black look. 'My Lord Dudley can be tender hearted. Nan tells me he consented to a love match for his son Robert – to a girl also named Amy. That's a good omen. At least I'm aiming higher than a provincial preacher.' She paused to examine her nails. 'Mama tells me Master Knox has been courting you. Will you marry him?'

Marjory shook her head vigorously. 'No, although mama thinks I should.'

Amy scoffed. 'Mama only does what is best for herself and she wants you to wed her preacher. If I were you, I'd send him off with his beard knotted and tucked under his chin. Imagine kissing those hairy lips.' She shuddered. 'The very thought. He's not only old he's poor. Nor does he keep good health. So what can he offer you? You don't want to end up an old man's nursemaid, do you?'

'Better to be an old man's darling than a young man's slave,' Marjory retorted.

IV

Black Humour

My heid did yak yester nicht …
So sair the magryme dois me menyie …
That scant I luik may on the licht.
On His Heid-Ake
William Dunbar 15th– 16th Century

Alnwick, Spring 1552

Mrs Bowes was in a black humour. Lying in the darkness of a shuttered room, she scolded Marjory for any little noise or shaft of light that shattered her repose. She shifted about the bed to get comfortable.

'This mattress is lumpy,' she whined. 'And Henry keeps asking when we're leaving. He frets that our prolonged stay is straining his wife's weak heart.' She gave a snort. 'That's just an excuse. Anne has always been a timid wee mouse. I'm the one who suffers bad health. His callousness has severely wounded me and brought on the black bile. He can't throw out an invalid.'

Marjory wrung a cloth in sweetly scented water to calm her mother's migraine. 'It's true what they say, mama. Guests are like fish: they go off after three days. Perhaps we've outstayed our welcome.'

'Everyone seems to be going off me. Everyone is stabbing me in the back.' Sighing as if all the woes of the world were pressing down on her rather than a goose feather quilt, Mrs Bowes twisted a corner of the linen sheet to dab her eyes. 'Even Master Knox, and I believed him to be my dearest friend.'

'He is, mama. He listens to your woes with great patience and understanding.'

'Not the other day. When I questioned him about predestination he became quite grumpy and cut me short. You know how sensitive I am to the slightest slight. He may think I didn't notice, but I saw him cringe. Something has changed. Why is he cooling towards me?'

'Master Knox has many parishes to serve with a numerous flock demanding his attention,' Marjory said. Not an excuse to console her mother for, while the sun may circle the earth, the world revolved around Elizabeth Bowes.

She squinted suspiciously at her daughter. 'Have you consented to marry him, is that it? Have you been plotting behind my back to elope and leave me here? Have you poisoned his mind against me?' She hauled herself up onto her elbows and shot green-eyed darts of jealousy at her daughter.

'Of course not, mama. Why would I do that?' Marjory became alarmed as her mother's black mood turned hostile.

'If he finds this old woman repulsive then I shall have nothing more to do with him. He's not the only preacher in the parish. I hear Bernard Gilpin has been posted to Durham and already commands a following: they call him the apostle of the north. It's a pity he's Tunstall's nephew, but no matter, we'll go and hear what he has to say.'

This unexpected change of her mother's heart flummoxed Marjory. 'Does that mean you no longer wish me to marry Master Knox?'

'Not if he spurns me. If he thinks he can have the daughter without the mother, he can think again. You and I are as inseparable as MaryBeth and always will be, Marjory. You shall remain a dutiful daughter to comfort your mother in her old age. As soon as I'm rid of this wretched migraine we shall pack up and go. In the meantime leave me to rest in peace.' She laid her head against the bolster and closed her eyes.

Dismissed, Marjory slammed the door shut and stood outside quivering with resentment. Was she condemned to be her mother's keeper forever with no life of her own? Forever prey to her mother's whims? She blinked back tears.

In the kitchen, the maid gawped in surprise as Marjory seized a cleaver and began cutting, chopping and slicing up a pile of peeled onions. Self-pity gave way to fury as stinging tears streamed down her cheeks. She was attacking a roast chicken when the maid answered a knock at the kitchen door.

'It's a lad — asking for you.' The maid gave her a knowing glance. 'I'd be careful with that cleaver if I were you. You don't want to be cutting off *his* onions.'

'It's the master,' Jamie blurted, holding his side and panting. 'He's very poorly. I thought he'd just caught a chill for he was shivering and feeling cold. But when I piled blankets on him, the sweat just poured off him. The fever is burning him up and he's havering. I'm at my wits' end, mistress: I dinnae ken what to do.'

Marjory wiped her smarting eyes. 'It sounds like the sweating sickness, Jamie. Is the fever still upon him?'

He wiped his nose with his sleeve and nodded.

'Thank God for that,' she replied, struggling to calm the quaver in her voice, 'for the next stage can be fatal. The sickness waxes swiftly and just as swiftly wanes, leaving the sufferer either cured or a corpse. Merry at dinner might be buried by supper. So they say.'

Jamie gnawed his lower lip. 'Should I fetch a doctor — or a priest then?'

'A priest is the last person Master Knox would wish to see and the physicians will be too busy tending their paying patients to bother with a poor parson. Nay, I shall come.'

After stuffing remedies into her leather bag, Marjory stirred a sleeping powder into a goblet of wine and handed it to the maid. 'Please give this to my mother as soon as she wakes up. I'll be back shortly.'

Newcastle

The sour stink in the bedchamber churned Marjory's stomach. She clamped a hand to her mouth to stop from gagging. Knox was tossing about in a jumble of blankets and tangled linen sheets: his linen cap and nightshirt were sodden with sweat – and worse she suspected from the stench. His laboured breathing came in short gasps and every so often he cried out in his delirium.

Her knees trembled. Having nursed her mother, Marjory thought she'd be able to cope but this illness was beyond her limited experience. Her patient needed far more care than a gentle hand swabbing a fevered brow with scented cloths. Panic-stricken, her impulse was to flee and leave Jamie to clear up his master's mess. No one would blame a young maiden for shirking such a task.

Jamie gazed at her with tearful eyes. 'Is he dying, mistress? Is there nothing we can do?'

His distress roused Marjory. How could she live with Knox's death on her conscience? 'Fetch warm water and clean linen, Jamie. We must try to make him comfortable.'

While Jamie heaved up the patient, Marjory slipped off his sark, striving to keep the lower part of his body covered with a sheet. As deftly as possible, she wiped his chest and arms with a cloth soaked in camomile water. Like Amy, she had assumed Knox to be old and decrepit, but his broad shoulders and sinewy muscles honed in the galleys belied this. Then when Jamie folded him over to let her swab his back, she gasped. The skin from the shoulders down to his waist was criss-crossed with long, serpentine weals left by multiple floggings. Tears sprang to her eyes as her fingers ran down the rough ridges. What torture he must have endured for his faith. Knox may no longer be in the first flush of youth but the wrinkles and weals were testament to physical toil and spiritual stress.

Leaving Jamie to wash his nether parts, Marjory rolled up the soiled bedding and rummaged for a clean nightshirt. As she pulled it over his head, Knox's eyelids flickered and for a second she caught a glimmer of recognition before they closed again. They propped him up against the bolster to ease his breathing and after a while, he seemed calmer. His delirium subsided and his skin had cooled. When he fell into a more peaceful slumber, Marjory heaved a grateful sigh.

'All we can do now is wait and watch, Jamie, and make sure he doesn't lapse into oblivion. That's a dangerous sign for he may never wake up again. You go and rest while I keep vigil.'

Marjory lit the stubby end of a candle and settled into a chair, pulling her cloak round her shoulders. She prayed, begging God to take care of Knox. Surely the Lord could not let his divine trumpeter perish. When the guttering candle sputtered and went out – she sat up with a start. Was this an omen that a life had been extinguished? Life was so fragile, so easily snuffed out. Nervously she put her ear to his mouth: mercifully he was still breathing.

Lying with his mouth open, a grey pallor lingering on cheeks sunken by sickness, the powerful preacher looked frail and forlorn and alone. Pity pierced her heart. Apart from Jamie, this man of God had no one on earth to share his burden. When her mother had forbidden her to marry Knox she had been overjoyed. Now recalling her mother's cruel jibe that she was too plain for matrimony, she considered her own future – sentenced forever to solitary spinsterhood.

What had she said to Amy? Better to be an old man's darling than a young man's slave – or even a mother's drudge. Prophetic words. The thought struck her. What if God had chosen her to be his helpmeet? Was sending her to Knox in his hour of need his way of revealing her fate?

She prayed for guidance through the long dark night until the early hours when his painful groans disturbed her vigil. She rose to see Knox tussling with the blankets in his struggle to get out of bed.

'Where's Jamie?' He seemed confused. 'I need to get to the privy. Quickly.'

'Jamie's fast asleep. I shall help you.' Marjory drew the chamber pot out from under the bed and held it up.

He focussed dazed eyes on her and flopped back onto the bed again. 'Nay, I cannot, not with you here,' he moaned but his twisted face betrayed his discomfort.

'You must. You cannot keep it in.' Marjory blushed at her boldness. 'I shall turn my head away.'

'Aye, better out than in, I jalouse,' Knox said.

After disposing of the contents of the chamber pot, she poured him a beaker of ale: drinking lots made recovery from the sweats more likely.

'Dearest sister, you're an angel of mercy,' he croaked gazing at her with eyes brimming with gratitude. 'In the depths of my delirium, I sensed your gentle presence pulling me back from the brink. Thank you for saving my life.'

Flustered by his kind words, Marjory busied herself with tidying the bedclothes. 'I have to go back to Alnwick now.'

'Oh!' He looked crestfallen. 'So soon? When will I see you again?'

'I don't know. We're going back to Berwick.'

'Berwick? Why?'

Marjory cast her eyes down. 'My mother is upset because she thinks you're tiring of her. That you're bored with her soul searching and losing patience with her.'

'When it comes to giving an ear to a parishioner's woes, I have the patience of a saint – even though my infirmities make me groan with pain. Doubtless the onset of the sickness made me crabbit. Once I explain that to your mother, she'll understand.'

Marjory's lips twitched slightly. 'My mother's pride has been greatly wounded. She may not forgive so easily.'

'I pray it isn't so. Your mother is that rare being, a seeker after a higher truth. She is the very mirror and glass wherein I behold myself. I pray that nothing can extinguish the affinity of spirit between us.'

Hearing him praise her mother, Marjory felt an unexpected jolt of jealousy. She jerked her head. 'That may be so, but the faith that is meant to give her comfort only seems to deepen her melancholy.'

When he fell silent, Marjory fretted. Had she displeased him?

'What about you, dear sister,' he murmured, 'does your faith gladden your heart and soul?'

The question flummoxed her. The theological doubts that tormented her mother swept over her: she only ever listened with half an ear to her tortuous wranglings. She twiddled her thumbs, pondering her answer. 'I believe that whatever God has decided for me will come to pass. I put myself in his hands.'

'Thon's a very good place to be, my dear sister.'

She looked up and caught his flicker of a smile. Now was the moment to take her courage, if not her fate, in both hands. 'And I believe that last night the Lord revealed my destiny.' She licked her dry lips. 'To be your wife and share your life.'

Knox's blue eyes sparkled with unshed tears. 'Do you really mean that, dearest Marjory? Do I dare to hope? I thought I was a fool for imagining a young lass would wish to be burdened with my auld carcase.' His tears spilled over and flowed down the deep furrows in his cheeks. Gripping hold of the sheet to wipe his face, his hands trembled.

Marjory felt a frisson whizzing through her: not a huge surge of love or passion but a thrilling sensation of power. She'd won Master Knox's heart! God's trumpeter who commanded the attention of hundreds loved her and not her mother. She felt elated, triumphant!

'So, will you give me hope?' His voice croaked with emotion.

'Not only hope, but love and trust.'

He gently kissed her outstretched hand. 'Aye, that's the Hepburn motto: *Keep Tryst.*'

V

Lennox Rising

> Howbeit Gude Counsell hastily be nocht heard
> By young princes, yet should they nocht be scared
>
> *Ane Satire of the Three Estates*
> Sir David Lindsay, 16th century

St Catherine's Convent, Edinburgh, 1552

The pungent aroma of incense mingling with the smoky smell from beeswax candles sent a heavy odour of sanctity wafting through the cloisters of St Catherine's convent. Order prevailed in this religious sanctuary. Situated on the outskirts of Edinburgh, it had escaped plague, fire and destruction by the English army – unlike St Mary's Abbey, Elisabeth thought ruefully. But she should not begrudge her sister's success. Abbess Joanna had worked tirelessly since her husband's death at Flodden to establish a safe house for women. No wonder Queen Marie had taken refuge here.

'How is Her Grace?'

'Still in deep mourning,' Joanna replied. 'Grief and strife have taken their toll on her. She believes Our Lord must wish her for one of his own since he has visited her with such sorrow. But she will recover – by the grace of God.'

Elisabeth sympathised. Death shadowed Marie de Guise. Swift and unforeseen, disease had scythed down two husbands and three sons. In France a poison plot had threatened her daughter's life and on the way to Dieppe, her son François, stricken by some mysterious sickness, had died in her arms – also a victim of poison?

'Her Grace has never had her sorrows to seek. Her faith must be sorely tried yet she displays great fortitude.'

'Her upbringing at the convent of Poor Clares stands her in good stead. She feels at home here,' Joanna said. 'The tranquillity of a nunnery gives her the peace to reflect and regain both physical and spiritual strength.'

In the sparse nun's cell, Elisabeth had expected to find the queen resting on a bed of straw and reading her precious *Book of Hours*, bequeathed by her pious grandmother. Instead, she was sitting up and playing cards – with a male visitor.

'*Carte blanche*,' the queen declared and slapped the cards down on the table. Nodding in the direction of her opponent, she asked Elisabeth, 'Are you acquainted with James Balfour of Pittendreich? He plays a practised hand – but not practised enough. He learnt piquet at the Sorbonne, he tells me.'

'When you should have been studying?' Elisabeth chortled. 'I'll wager, James Hepburn, my nephew, was in your company. All the Scots students at the Sorbonne stick together, I hear.'

Balfour looked sheepish and his face reddened. 'I left afore he came.'

'Master Balfour has recently qualified in ecclesiastical law and has come highly recommended by Archbishop Hamilton,' the queen said.

Elisabeth arched a fine eyebrow. 'Perhaps he may be able to tell us what the archbishop is doing to quash the reformists multiplying right under his nose in Fife.'

'As far as I'm aware he has appealed to the pope for help,' Balfour replied.

Elisabeth scoffed. 'Much good that will do. Scotland may be Rome's "special daughter" but so far our holy father has been deaf to our pleas.'

'It's a pity Cardinal Beaton was slain,' the queen said. 'He would have burned out heresy.'

'In truth. Someone must do something to staunch this fanaticism,' Elisabeth said with a snarl, 'before it spills out and taints the whole land. For my part I've twisted the pilliewinks on Sir David Lindsay's thumbs until he agreed to put on a performance of his satire. A play might go some way to rousing the clergy and dousing fanatic fervour. What is your considered opinion, Master Balfour?'

When Balfour stared at his feet, she went on, 'As a native of Fife, you'll be well acquent with Sir David.'

'Aye, well,' he stuttered, 'I've had the pleasure of making his acquaintance but with Your Grace's permission, I must be on my way.'

Elisabeth watched suspiciously as the grovelling lickspittle left the room backwards, bowing all the way.

'Archbishop Hamilton assures me Master Balfour has a very sharp legal mind,' the queen said.

Handing her a goblet of wine, Elisabeth gave a scornful snort. 'Nevertheless, I'd be wary, madame. There's something sleekit about him.'

'*Ma chère* prioress, I'm in dire need of such advisers. Since d'Oisel left for France, I have no one share my burden.' The queen sipped her drink and sighed. 'To that end I have written to my Lord Lennox. In return for his loyalty, I have offered to restore his lands and bestow treatment befitting his rank.'

Elisabeth spluttered over her wine. Bring back Matthew Stewart – her scorned suitor. No sooner had the slighted Lennox left Scotland in high dudgeon, then he'd promptly married Margaret Douglas. Henry VIII's wayward niece may have a tarnished reputation but with a strong claim to English throne, she was a considerable catch for Lennox.

His defection to the English court had given the regent the chance to declare his rival a traitor – and for once Elisabeth found herself agreeing with Errant Arran. With his royal connections, Lennox had become the champion of the English cause, making his intrigues in Scotland all the more threatening.

Elisabeth was dumbfounded. Why on earth had she done such a thing?

Sensing her discomfiture, the queen raised a hand. 'After we signed the Treaty of Haddington, Lennox made four promises: that he, his friends and retainers would preserve the Catholic faith in Scotland; that they would guard the Auld Alliance; that I would remain guardian of the queen and that he would punish all who supported the King of England.'

Elisabeth rolled her eyes. It was unlike Marie de Guise reared within a family of shrewd *politiques* to be so naïve. Had grief doited her wits, perhaps? Inviting Lennox back into the fold seemed most unwise.

'That was in 1548 – a wheen of water has passed beneath the Abbey Bridge since then. Do you have these in writing, madame? For promises made by Scots lords tend to be but false gifts.'

Again the queen dowager sighed. 'Since Lennox professes to be a Catholic, I am relying on him to support me against the regent.'

'Madame, you are at risk of handing power to Lennox on a platter. What if he crosses to Arran's side?'

'I'm sure my lord Lennox will abide by the chivalric code and come to the aid of a queen in distress.'

Elisabeth cleared her throat. 'Forgive me for saying, madame, but by reinstating Lennox you'll be bringing a cuckoo into our nest. Forbye, you run the risk of the Earl of Angus rallying support for his gude-son and snatching the regency for him.'

Elisabeth shuddered at the memory of Archie Douglas. So as to be free to wed Margaret Tudor, 'Anguish' had murdered his wife, her beloved sister Meg. With Tudor and Douglas blood mingling in her veins, his daughter was turning out to be a scheming minx, a mistress of intrigue.

'I detect the hand of Margaret Douglas in all this. She's Mary Tudor's best friend. Isabelle tells me the devout Catholic Countess of Lennox doesn't so much wear her faith on her sleeve – but round her waist. I would be wary of inviting her to Scotland.'

'I, too, noticed. The clasp of her girdle is a miniature missal, its gilded covers decorated with expensive rubies and emeralds. But her true precious jewel is her five-year-old son.'

Elisabeth chuckled. 'Isabelle told me about him.' To impress the queen mother, the lad had pranced around the room flinging his lanky legs in the air and squawking songs in halting French.

'He's a healthy lad with the face of an angel,' the queen said but as she continued, sadness tinged her voice. 'In France my own eyes confirmed Lady Fleming's reports about my daughter's intended.'

'Aye, that the dauphin is a stunted wee creature unlikely to reach manhood.'

The queen dipped her head. 'In which case, Mary will be free to marry. Henry Stewart is an obvious choice. Countess Lennox is hoping that should Mary Tudor die childless she will name him as her heir – which is very likely as he is Catholic.'

Elisabeth shook her head in disbelief. Henry Stewart on the English throne? The King of England to wed the Queen of Scots? Two Stewarts to unite the two kingdoms. Was that Margaret Douglas's game?

VI

Morality Play

Ane silken tongue, ane heart of crueltie,
Smites more sore than any shot of arrow
The Paddock and the Mouse
Robert Henryson, 15th Century

Edinburgh, May 1552

Abbess Joanna looked askance at her sister. 'A play? A pilgrimage for priests to purge their wicked souls and a pyre for the heretical heathens would be more fitting.'

'*Ane Satire of the Three Estates* is a morality play written to shame the corrupt both in our church and court' Elisabeth replied. 'Sir David needs two lasses for the parts of Verity and Chastity and I ken the very pair to take to Cupar. Jean and Isabelle will do very well.'

The abbess frowned. 'Not Jean, she's an unbridled lass.'

'Lady Morham has high hopes you'll be able to tame her wild spirit enough to become a suitable bride.'

Joanna sighed. 'When we can catch her. Sir Robert Lauder's widow has proposed her grandson as a possible match but Jean would rather run about the meadows chasing the sheep and kye. However, Isabelle is proving to be a stalwart sister. We greatly value her work in the apothecary: her experience in France has stood her in good stead. I fain would keep her at St Catherine's – if you don't mind.'

Taken aback, Elisabeth shook her head. 'Nay, dear sister, I cannot part with her. Isabelle is the future of St Mary's: I'm not getting any younger and there is no one else to follow in my footsteps as prioress. I only pray that's her wish too. I've greatly missed her. But before she takes her final vows, let her have some fun in Fife.'

Just as Elisabeth and the girls left the shelter of St Catherine's cloisters, a fresh breeze sprang up.

'I'm glad to be free of thon hen coop,' Jean cried with glee. 'Aunt Joanna is so strict. She shouldn't be forcing a nun's life on me. I've no wish to enter a convent.' She ripped off her veil and ran off across the meadows.

With an understanding smile, Elisabeth watched her go and took Isabelle's arm. 'What about you, Isabelle? Are you content to take your vows or has the splendour of the French court turned your head?'

Isabelle sneered. 'Nay, thon court is riddled with deceit. Fops in fancy costumes – all airs and graces but rotten underneath. When I let slip I had a cure for the pox they queued up for pots of slug slime to smear on their scabs.'

Elisabeth chuckled. 'Good for you. Moral standards have slipped even more since my visit. I hope you charged plenty.'

'Not me, Dr Bog, the queen's physician, pocketed the proceeds. Poor man, he was sent home in disgrace after Queen Mary's life was put at risk.'

'Aye, I heard about that – and even more wicked – it was one of her Scots Guards who tried to poison her. Thanks be to God he failed and died the death he deserved – hanged, drawn and quartered.'

Isabelle fell quiet before replying. 'If indeed it was Robert Stewart on the scaffold.'

When Elisabeth gave her an enquiring look, she seemed hesitant. 'I was there watching with Dr Bog but I'm no sure if Stewart was the gallows bird ...' Her voice trailed away and then she gave herself a shake. 'But let's hope wherever he is, he's gone for good.'

A shriek from Jean interrupted their conversation. 'Come and see this,' she cried and pointed to the convent's herd lad sunning himself against the sheepfold. 'Cammie, make as if you're blind.'

When the lad flipped up his eyelids and rolled his pupils underneath until only the whites were showing, Isabelle shuddered. 'Thon makes my flesh creep.'

The lad grinned. 'My ma learnt me the knack afore she died. She said I'd never have an empty belly for folk would think me blind and give me alms.'

When he held out his hand, Elisabeth gave him a stern look. 'I'd be wary of doing thon trick when the wind shifts, my lad, for your eyes will stick like that. Then you'll be doomed to play blind till the kye come home,' she said before pressing a coin into his palm,

'Maybe we should take him with us,' Jean said. 'He could feign a miracle at the Cupar fair! Will you come with us, Cammie?'

'Where's that?'

'Across the Forth in the Kingdom of Fife.'

He shook his head. 'Cupar sounds gey far away and I've my yowes and kye to tend.'

'Come, lasses, let's leave Cammie to his wool gathering,' Elisabeth said and led them back on the path to Edinburgh.

On the Pleasance, a washerwoman was struggling against the wind to lay her laundry on bushes. When the breeze whipped away some linen cloths, the girls raced to chase after them.

The washerwoman put her hands on her hips and arched her back. 'The air up here is pleasant enough, but it can be o'er breezy at times.'

Curious to see labourers coming and going through a gate in the Flodden Wall, Elisabeth questioned the washerwoman.

Screwing up her ruddy face she replied, 'When the English laidrons invaded they did a wheen of damage to the auld kirk of St Mary's in the Field. They're clearing away the auld Friars' Hospital to make way for a braw big hoose for twa-fangelt Arran. Now he's a Frenchified duke he's building himself a mansion. Three storeys would you believe! He has a high conceit of himself.'

'Is that who you work for?'

'Me? Naw. I launder for Master Balfour the lawyer. He lives in Old Provost's Lodging nearby.'

'Balfour? James Balfour by any chance?'

'Naw, that's Mr Robert's younger brother: he's a lawyer, tae, but he's mair high-bendit,' she gabbled on. 'Master James is in the queen dowager's service – whiles at the palace, whiles at the castle – and aye in need of clean linen. Brings me his washing but he's a pernickety one. Says I'm the only one can get his clarty collars clean.' Her bosom puffed out like a doo's.

'The fox keeps his ain hole clean,' Elisabeth murmured.

Cupar, Fife, June 1552

In the market place below Cupar Castle, the prioress struggled to keep a straight face as she watched the players acting out a short scene. A whinging auld jock who'd lost the key to his wife's chastity belt while she was swyving with the Fool, was spouting the most uncouth language. Wait till she saw Lindsay – she'd give him an earful.

After dodging squads of workmen erecting pavilions on the green she found Lindsay instructing the master carpenter in charge of building a scaffold.

'I'll run through it again, for timing is crucial,' he said. 'Once the noose is slung around the villain's neck, you will step on this lever to open the hatch in the platform. The felon will then drop safely on to the ground below. Meanwhile, your journeyman will pull on this rope to hoist up the effigy stuffed with straw. The hangings have to look credible not just comical. By the end of the play, a flock of gallows birds swinging black against the sky should make a fearsome sight.'

'Aye, never fear I'll make sure it's as lifelike as possible, Sir David,' the carpenter replied.

'Or deathlike,' Lindsay muttered as he turned to greet Elisabeth.

She rolled her eyes. 'Davie Lindsay, you're turning into a gruesome ghoul in your dotage! And a filthy auld larbar as well. I've just been watching the banns to advertise your satire.'

Lindsay peered over the rim of his eyeglasses. 'I deliberately wrote a bawdy burlesque to whet the audience's appetite.'

'For a morality play?' Elisabeth said. 'Once the crowd get wind they've been duped, what a reek they'll raise! You'd better beware the mob doesn't put you in the stocks and splatter you with stinking skirlie.'

Lindsay's mouth crinkled. 'So, you think my satire is not entertaining and witty enough to keep them amused?'

Elisabeth harrumphed. 'If pouring scorn and vilification on a well-meaning prioress is a laughing matter then …'

'You've only yourself to blame, Lisbeth, for it was your idea to put on the play.'

'I was clutching at straws, Davie. Folk are becoming restive and are no longer prepared to thole the wanton clergy. Your satire will not only shame those idle fornicators and bring them to heel, it will also show thon righteous Fife lairds we are resolute in stamping out lechery and sculduggery.'

She flashed Lindsay a meaningful look. Those very lairds had conspired to murder Cardinal Beaton in St Andrews and she was never very sure of Lindsay's part in the plot. Better not to know, she thought.

Lindsay chuckled and squeezed her arm. 'My jaggy thistle still can sting. So, if it succeeds, you're to be congratulated?'

Her ferny-green eyes glittered. 'If it doesn't, Davie, you shall bear the brunt of the rabble's discontent. Here comes one of them now.'

A bare-footed lad limped towards them, shouting and waving his arms. 'Sir Davie, come quickly. A fight's broken out. They're knocking skelfs off each other.'

Lindsay rolled his eyes. 'Not another scuffle. The actors from Edinburgh make fun of the local yokels hired for the minor parts. Brawls break out at the slightest slight. I'd better go.'

As Lindsay hirpled away, the lad balanced on one leg to pick out a stone stuck between his toes.

'What's it about this time?' Elisabeth asked.

'Och, there's a loun who's calling my father a liar for saying he was a gallows slave.'

Elisabeth squinted. 'You mean a galley slave?'

'Aye, thon time a wheen of heretics were caught in St Andrews and sent to row for the French …'

Without waiting for him to finish, Elisabeth picked up her skirts and scurried across the field. Lindsay stood in the middle of a circle holding his arms wide to keep two men apart. The lad's father, a local cooper, brandished a menacing fist at his opponent.

'Thon skulking skellum is a damned liar. Says he was never in the galleys but I ken fine he was. His family bide not far from here at Mountquhanie. And I was in St Andrews with Preacher Knox – and so was he.' He turned to Lindsay. 'You were too, Sir David, and I ken you'll back me up.'

All eyes fixed on Lindsay waiting for his answer. He turned and squinted at the accused. 'So you deny you were in the galleys, Master Balfour?'

Shamefaced, James Balfour waggled his head furiously. 'Aye … I mean nay, but my brother was.'

'Hark at him! It was never his brother. I ken fine it was him. Fibbing bastard!' The cooper spat at him. 'How can he deny Preacher Knox who gave us the true word of God? He's a saint whereas you are a Judas.'

Elisabeth grabbed Balfour's arm and held up her rosary. 'Tell the truth. Swear on Christ's blood that you were in the galleys with Knox.'

Balfour flinched at the crucifix. 'I wasn't there I tell you.'

'String him up!' a voice shouted. 'That's the forfeit for traitors who betray their brothers-in-arms!'

'Aye, let's hang him!' the crowd chorused and surged forwards. 'There's a gibbet ready and waiting.'

Lindsay steered Elisabeth away with a firm hand. 'You won't get the truth from him, Lisbeth. Thon lawyer is a proven liar and, like Peter the apostle, not ashamed to deny his master three times. Forbye, I sense bloodlust: this Fife mob is full of reformist sympathisers and raring to throw a noose round the liar's neck. However much I despise Balfour's deceit he doesn't deserve a hanging. Wait for me in the pavilion, Lisbeth, lest they set upon the papist prioress.'

'That I will not,' Elisabeth replied. 'I fain would witness your trial, Davie.'

Lindsay shrugged. 'Ever my jaggy thistle. Then stand well back, Lisbeth.'

He waved his staff to quieten the crowd. 'Tak tent!' he yelled. 'Justice shall prevail and I shall devise the perfect punishment for a liar.' With a theatrical flourish, Lindsay unrolled his script. 'First I charge the accused to take part in the play.'

Balfour scowled. 'I'm no actor, Sir David.'

A smile crinkled Lindsay's lips. 'Ah, now, there I beg to differ. You've trained as a lawyer, have you not? A profession that practises dissimulation if not downright deceit requires the skills of an actor.' Lindsay tapped his quill on the scroll. 'Now, which rôle would be more fitting? Falsehood or Deceit? Hmm, Falsehood, I think.'

Before Balfour could open his mouth to protest, Lindsay addressed the whooping crowd. 'I sentence Falsehood and his blackened soul to be strung up. Does that please you?' When the mob roared their assent, he said, 'Then come and see him hang tomorrow.'

Elisabeth took his arm. 'Well, directed, Davie. You have a gift for calming an angry rabble. But Balfour seems a cunning carl, I pray the queen knows what she's doing. I dread to think she's playing cards with the devil.'

When Elisabeth arrived with Lindsay early next morning, the master carpenter was spread-eagled on the scaffold shouting at a worker crawling underneath.

'Call yourself a journeyman, the only timber you've ever bored is your wooden skull.' He scrambled to his feet. 'My ain lad has left me in the lurch, Sir David. Last seen carousing in the tavern yestreen – which isn't like him. For all I ken he's lying in a ditch, sleeping it off. But this chiel has stepped in at the last minute. Says he's a journeyman and served his time in the boat yards but he seems gey rusty to me.'

'He kens he's also to be an executioner?' Lindsay asked. 'Has he got his hood?'

'Oh aye, we've had a wee run-through. Never fash, Sir David, it'll all come out in the wash.'

Once Elisabeth and Lady Morham had dressed the girls in their costumes, they took their seats on the front bench.

'The stage is set, the players are ready and the spectator stand is full: we only await Her Grace's presence,' Elisabeth said, looking round anxiously. 'The royal party should be here by now.'

At the sound of rumbling hooves Elisabeth heaved a sigh of relief but the sight of the Hamilton brothers leading a troop of men-at-arms, rattled her. Something terrible must be amiss.

Archbishop Hamilton reined in his horse and called out, 'I forbid this blasphemy to go ahead.'

As the guards dismounted, Lindsay emerged from behind the platform. 'On what grounds?'

'By a law passed by parliament in February of this year.' Hamilton beckoned to an acolyte. 'Read,' he ordered.

The acolyte unrolled a scroll and cleared his throat. 'No printer is to presume, attempt or take upon hand to print any books, ballads, songs, blasphemies, rhymes or tragedies either in Latin or English tongue in any time to come, until the same be seen, viewed and examined by some wise and discreet persons.'

'Well read,' Lindsay said to the scribe. 'Good enough to be given a part in my play.'

'This is no play-acting but a serious matter, Lyon Herald,' Hamilton spluttered. 'The performance must cease. Forthwith.'

Lindsay sighed. 'In my defence, may I point out this is neither book nor ballad nor song. It is a play and as such has not been printed. Written out in my fair hand, I admit, but not published in print. Nor is it a tragedy, though some may beg to differ, but a satire. Nor is it written in Latin or English but in the guid Scots tongue.' He turned to Errant Arran. 'I therefore beseech you, my lord regent, as a wise and discreet person to resolve this dispute.'

'He has no power to do so,' the archbishop retorted. 'As primate of Scotland, I am the higher authority and I deem your play blasphemous.'

'How can you tell – if you've neither read nor seen it?'

'By habit and repute. It's well-kent your play mocks the clergy.'

'So hearsay is heresy? What's your opinion, my lord regent?'

As Errant Arran stroked his rimey beard his eyes darted nervously back and forth.

Lindsay leant in closer. 'Tak tent, my lords, you're not only at risk of becoming a laughing stock but being locked in those stocks.' He tilted his head towards the stand. 'The spectators are becoming restless in the heat. If the play is cancelled I fear you may have a riot on your hands.'

While the two brothers withdrew to lock horns, Lindsay muttered, 'Thon pair belie the adage that two halves make a whole. They own not one complete set of wits between them.'

Elisabeth chuckled. 'Never fash, Davie. The queen attended the first performance at Stirling. She will decide in your favour.'

'We shall see,' Lindsay replied. 'Here comes a royal messenger now.'

But the herald did not bring good news. Trouble had broken out in the highlands demanding the queen's presence to deal with it. He ended with the words, 'Her Grace sends her sincere apologies and wishes you all success.'

'I'd say this amounts to royal assent,' Lindsay said. 'Would you not agree, my lords?'

The archbishop grasped his brother's arm and pushed him towards the seats reserved for the royal party. 'Let the play commence, Lyon Herald.'

Towards the end of the play, all the effigies of the various vices except Falsehood had been strung up successfully. As soon as Balfour stepped onto the stage the volume of jeers and catcalls rose: he froze for a few seconds before recovering.

'Lawyers may be liars, but all craftsmen are crafty and all tradesmen cheat their customers,' he declared and wagged an accusing finger. 'Fleshers blow water into lean meat to make it look fat; tailors cut corners, brewers thin their ale with burn water and bakers mix bread with dust and bran. But who has taught you these tricks of the trade? Falsehood. If you hang me, you'll all die of hunger.'

Falsehood's valiant defence to wriggle out of the gallows was futile: he was sentenced to hang. As the executioner threw a noose round his neck, the master carpenter stamped on the lever and nodded to the journeyman to hoist the effigy. Alarmed, Elisabeth rose in her seat, for the rope was not tied to the effigy but to the noose round Balfour's neck. As he was raised into the air, the dangling man tore desperately at the noose. Struggling for breath his tongue stuck out and his face twisted into an ugly grimace. The mob roared with delight at the grotesque sight but Elisabeth was horror-stricken. The journeyman had made a dreadful mistake.

'Stop! Cut him down!' Lindsay shouted.

The master carpenter lunged across the scaffold and clung onto Balfour's legs to pull him down onto the platform, much to the amusement of the tipsy crowd who cheered even louder. In the midst of the melée Elisabeth glimpsed the executioner, now halted in his tracks and staring at Isabelle stuck in the stocks. For a fleeting second their eyes locked and then Isabelle began frantically flapping her angels' wings and yelling, 'Stop him! Stop the murderer!'

VII

Pride and Prejudice

> And there went out another horse that was red:
> and power was given to him that sat thereon
> to take peace from the earth
> Book of Revelation VI: 3, 4

Newcastle, June 1552

Knox wiped the stoor from his eyes. The cavalcade cantering along the sun-baked High Street of Newcastle had shaken up swirling clouds of dust. The townsfolk ran out to gawp at the train of noblemen resplendent in their bright colours of azure and crimson. The glitter of steel bronze and gold may have dazzled the lieges but Knox was not so easily impressed.

'Earls, lords, knights and squires – these are the new, powerful men of England, Jamie. And I jalouse they've come to carve up Tunstall's Durham diocese.'

Leading the horde was a tall, straight-backed figure riding high in the saddle of a magnificent black destrier. Newly appointed as Warden General of the Marches, John Dudley, Duke of Northumberland, had come north to inspect the fortifications along the border. His flamboyant red cloak billowed out like a sail behind him.

'Beware a man in scarlet,' Knox muttered. In the Book of Revelation red signified war and destruction but it also signalled Dudley's lust for wealth power. Made from the crushed bodies of the cochineal insect imported from the New World, cardinal crimson was the most expensive dye. The sight of Dudley in his flamboyant crimson cloak made him see red. As he'd predicted, the duke had got rid of Simple Somerset and was now King Edward's regent in all but name.

'Will Lord Dudley have learnt about your sermon, master?' Jamie asked, uneasy.

'Without a doubt,' Knox replied. 'And from a man with a notoriously short fuse sparks will be flying fast and furious once the flyting starts.'

He did not have long to wait. The very next evening two guards arrived to escort him to the New Castle. On the orders of 'His Highness' they declared. Knox rolled his eyes. His Highness? Is that how Dudley now styled himself? The duke's pride and presumption knew no bounds. *Pride goeth before destruction and a haughty spirit before a fall. A man's pride shall bring him low.*

Being marched through the Black Gate of the New Castle built to keep out the Scots, Knox braced himself. At the very least he would be incarcerated in the barbican; at the very worst, he would share the Protector's fate – the block.

He was shown into an inner chamber where 'His Highness' was seated at a table set for supper. With a snowy white cambric collar ruffling at the neck of a dark red doublet and scarlet silken hose tucked into cordwain boots of softest Spanish leather, the duke looked every inch the powerful warrior. His steely grey hair glinted in the candlelight. Mars the ancient god of fury and ire, Knox thought. Or Lucifer, with horns of pride, more like. The duke glared severely at him.

'Your ingratitude disappoints me, Preacher Knox. When I gave you Tunstall's position I did not expect such treachery: challenging my authority and denouncing me as corrupt is a hanging offence. I should clap you in irons at the very least for your scandalmongering.'

'*Your Highness* will do what he will,' Knox replied. 'I only utter the truth from the pulpit.'

Dudley jabbed a threatening finger at him. 'The truth! What you're spreading is slander, feeding those poisonous, lying tongues that say I brought down Somerset to further my own ambitions.'

'The Lord Protector was a simple man who championed the poor and powerless.'

'You seem to sanctify Somerset, Mr Knox, but when the Protector turned pretender he wrenched the reins of power to ride roughshod over the Privy Council. Stingy Somerset kept his royal nephew as poor as a church mouse while he swaggered about the court bedecked in jewels. He would listen to advice from no one, not even the Lord God on high, finally. His arrogance gained him enemies and led to his downfall.'

Dudley paused for breath, struggling to control his ire. 'Somerset may have acted in good faith but he was muddle-minded with not an iota of administrative skill or sense. He applied wrong remedies to troubles wrongly diagnosed. There's nothing worse – for the road to hell is paved with good intentions badly administered, is that not so, Mr Knox? Somerset was no saint, but guilty of Lucifer's sin – arrogant pride.'

'But he was your friend once and defender of the faith,' Knox bit back.

'And I defended him to the hilt – at first. Even when he made grave mistakes – for I would never attack a fellow warrior. After defeating your countrymen at Pinkie he should have followed through and conquered Scotland. Just think, Mr Knox, if he'd set up Protestant rule, you wouldn't be here but preaching from St Giles's pulpit in Edinburgh.' He gave a short contemptuous snort.

'For two years I tried to gain his co-operation in the Privy Council but your sainted Somerset was too pig-headed to share power. Since his mulish temper wasn't suited to statesmanship. I advised him to leave court and build his mansion but my counsel fell on the ass's deaf ears. Meanwhile, he was plotting not only to murder me but massacre my whole family and my crew. That was the last straw – he had to go. My mistake was leaving it so late. Somerset should have gone earlier.'

Dudley winced and his eyes welled up with tears of remorse, Knox assumed, until he doubled over, hugging his belly. 'Forgive me, but this old warhorse is crippled with aches and pains from battle wounds. These ailments, merely irksome in youth, creep up stealthily in middle age and poleaxe you. When my temper is riled, my belly burns like the fires of hell.' Straightening up, Dudley clicked his fingers for his retainer to serve wine in engraved silver goblets. 'But good wine, I find, cures all ills.'

Despite himself, Knox sipped slowly to savour the delicate smoothness of the fine French claret but when Dudley raised his goblet to toast the memory of Edward Seymour, Knox threw him a questioning look.

'For all his faults Somerset was brave both on the battlefield and on the scaffold at his end,' Dudley explained. 'God forbid it should ever happen, but I would be proud to face the axe with such fortitude.'

Knox winced for that thought haunted him, too. Then it crossed his mind. Was the duke about to pass judgement on him? Was the wine to soften the final blow?

Dudley knocked back his claret and wiped his lips. 'Now, Mr Knox, will you break bread with me?'

Baffled, Knox scowled. Was the duke making a bauchle out of him?

'You see, Mr Knox, I'm not going to throw you into the bottle dungeon. I respect you for being so forthright and honest. You're the one man in England unafraid to speak up for his beliefs and I greatly admire your courage.'

At the click of the duke's fingers, lackeys brought platters piled high with food. 'Forgive me for the poor table, but in the north the choice of dishes is limited.'

To Knox, leg of mutton with gallandine sauce, boiled capon slathered in cream, and lobster fresh from the creel scarcely constituted a poor table. Wielding a gilded, bejewelled dagger the duke cut off a slice of mutton and laid it on a silver salver.

A supper invitation was the last thing Knox had expected: forbye, he'd need a lang-shanket spoon to sup kail with the devil. He shook his head. 'Nay, I thank you but I'm not hungry.'

'Surely you're not fasting?' Dudley raised an eyebrow in mock surprise. 'While I've been doing my best to stamp out all traces of Rome – abolished the mass, demolished monasteries and smashed stained glass windows – you're holding fast to this papist practice.' An ironic smile flickered over his full lips. 'Am I not the good Protestant?'

Knox detected little spirituality in this warrior whose main reason for professing to be a Protestant, he suspected, was to grab valuable Church land.

'Nay, not fasting, but I cannot justify stuffing my belly as full as a bishop's paunch when the common man is starving. I eat to live, not live to eat. Though for many money-grubbing folk, sheep seem more valuable than human souls.'

Dudley glowered at this jibe; enclosing the land for sheep farming was a deeply controversial practice.

'By fencing off smallholdings and common land,' Knox went on, 'landlords have deprived villagers of their rights to grow crops and graze beasts. Famine is raging everywhere and folk have swapped the grain bowl for the begging bowl. Do you wonder why starving yeomanry are rising up in rebellion?'

Keeping his eyes fixed firmly on Knox, Dudley held out his goblet to be refilled.

'I'm a soldier, Mr Knox, not a shepherd of either sheep or men. The defence of my country and keeping peace in the realm are my concerns. Whatever the cause, unrest must be quashed: that was my charge in Norfolk. Robert Kett was a traitor. I offered him a pardon to disband the rebels but he refused. What was I to do? In the great chain of being, the people must learn to keep their place. Would you not agree?'

'Not if 2,000 folk are killed and over 300 souls executed.'

'But I pardoned many more – despite the local gentry's demand for even more blood. For what shall we then do? I asked them. Shall we hold the plough ourselves, play the carters and labour the ground with our own hands? I, too, am on the side of the poor and oppressed, Mr Knox. You hoisted Somerset onto a pedestal as your John the Commonweal but perhaps I truly deserve that title. However well meaning, the good duke failed to ease the miseries of over-taxation and enclosures. His sympathy for the poor may speak well for his heart but it cost them dearer than indifference. He was an ignorant idealist whose love of liberty produced disorder, whereas I seek to alleviate the plight of the poor by more practical means.'

Dudley leant back in his chair and clasped his arms behind his head. 'You see, Mr Knox, I've learnt much from Somerset's downfall. While he ruled with a rod of iron, I mean to delegate power to those more able in their particular sphere. With no head for figures, I've appointed a treasurer to take care of finance and, since theological matters mystify me, I charge you to take care of the country's religious health.'

Flattered at the offer, Knox nevertheless braced himself to be vigilant. What would 'His Highness' demand in exchange for such advancement?

'King Edward is an enthusiastic Protestant but he lacks a strong champion, an apostle,' the silver-tongued devil continued. 'The bishops are either lukewarm like Tunstall, more concerned about the revenues being diverted from their coffers, or too timid in amending the liturgy – like Cranmer. Throughout Harry Coppernose's turbulent reign, the archbishop weathered more storms than the *Mary Rose*, and like that great warship he'd better watch out lest he come to grief.' Dudley's lips twisted into a wry smile. 'The church is in dire need of a whetstone to quicken and sharpen the sluggish Bishop of Canterbury, so says my Secretary of State. Cecil is proving to be that rare beast in this realm – a shrewd treasurer and wise councillor. He recommends your appointment as one of the king's chaplains. When I return to

London, you shall come with me.'

Knox bristled: he didn't take kindly to being ordered about like one of his men. 'Nay, I will not.'

His reply roused the duke's mercurial temper. Dudley jabbed the bejewelled dagger at him and snarled. 'You're very proud, Mr Knox. I expected more humility from a man of God. More gratitude. You may refuse me but you cannot disobey a royal command.'

'I obey a higher command. God has called me to the north where there's still much work to be done. I fain would bide in Newcastle.'

'No doubt, but Bernard Gilpin is a gifted preacher and shall take over your parish. As a royal chaplain you'll be in a strong position not only to advise the boy king but to convert the ditherers and confront the hunker-sliders who're threatening to return to the old ways. You say you do not hear God's call but perhaps the Lord in his wisdom has sent me as one of His angels – Gabriel is it or Michael? To carry you off to the very heart of the court.'

Knox grunted. 'Michael the mighty warrior angel threw Satan out of heaven while the holy messenger Gabriel delivers God's holy word.'

'That's it!' Dudley sprang up and paced the hall. 'We're destined to work together! A divine duo! You as Gabriel shall preach the gospel while I, as the champion Michael shall defend the faith. Words and swords!'

Knox was sorely tempted. To be near the seat of power from where he could bolster the Protestant faith was an offer made in heaven. Was this where God was sending him? Could he in truth turn it down? Only one thing held him back. He cleared his throat.

'I have other ties here that demand my attention.'

Dudley arched a fine eyebrow in query. 'Pray, tell.'

Unwilling to appear weak before the great warrior Knox hesitated but then recalling the auld saw – *who may woo without cost* – he took heart. 'Marjory Bowes has consented to be my wife but her father is against it. The captain considers me – a man of base estate – too lowly in rank for his daughter.'

Dudley smirked. 'So, I've found your Achilles heel, Mr Knox, or rather the Cupid's dart that has wounded your heart. Wealth and rank are not always the best motives for a match, otherwise how would those blessed with aptitude and ambition improve their status? Besides, stagnant blood needs invigorating.'

He placed a hand on Knox's shoulder. 'Agree to my offer and I shall defend your suit for the captain's daughter. I give you my word.'

PART THREE

I

Horoscope

> This changing and great variance
> Of eardly states up and doun
> Is nocht but casualtie and chance,
> As sum men sayis without reason
> *The Abbey Walk*
> Robert Henryson, 15th Century

London, September 1552

'May the Lord bless our bread and wine and drive the sickness from our door. Amen.'

After Knox finished saying grace, Harry Locke thanked him and held out his arms in a gesture of welcome. 'Now I pray you all make good cheer. An ounce of mirth is better than a pound of sorrow.'

'And he that is merry of heart has a continual feast,' Thomas added. 'Our brother makes sure of that.'

Everyone beamed at their host, a generous young man with a paunch, who neither stinted on food nor hospitality. His wife Anna, pregnant with her first child, gazed up at him, her gentle grey eyes brimming with affection.

Knox gave silent thanks for being accepted into this warm, close-knit family who lived cheek by jowl in Cheapside. The Locke brothers – Harry and Thomas – were partners in a merchant company with their brothers-in-law, Anthony Hickman and Richard Hill: with their respective wives, Rose and Elizabeth, they were all good friends who shared meals together.

Though he enjoyed their company, Knox felt too gloomy to join in their mirth. On the eve of his departure he and Marjory had plighted their troth in front of two witnesses – Mrs Bowes and Jamie – but even though their handfasting was considered a binding contract in the northern counties, it might not be in southern England. Nor did they have her father's consent and this troubled Knox.

'You seem far away,' Anna said, rousing him from his reverie. 'Are you missing Marjory, perhaps?' Her voice was low for she knew Knox did not wish to make his betrothal public yet.

A faint blush stained his cheeks. 'Is my heart sewn so plainly on my sleeve? Forgive me, dear Anna, I was thinking how fortunate you all are to live together as one family – so happy and contented. It makes me miss her all the more. Until the duke keeps his promise to support our marriage, I fear her father will do all in his power to keep us apart.'

A look of profound sympathy crossed Anna's face. 'If I were you, I'd confront Lord Dudley and explain your dilemma. Beneath that warrior's armour of steel lies a bleeding heart.'

'I shall do so, as soon as he arrives home.'

Having chosen to sail south on his brother William's boat, rather than ride the long distance with the duke's company, Knox had reached London in good time.

'Did I hear mention of my lord Dudley?' Elizabeth Hill was always on the alert for titbits of gossip. 'I would be wary of Northumberland. He is notoriously short-tempered.'

'And quick to draw the sword when riled. His warlike visage was enough to persuade the Privy Council to elect him as their Lord President,' Thomas added.

'It's not Dudley who worries me but his daughter,' Rose said. 'Lady Mary is fearsomely clever and corresponds with the Italian mathematician Cardano who teaches her the black arts.'

'The Welsh Wizard was also her tutor,' Elisabeth added, her eyes sparkling. When Knox wrinkled his brow in puzzlement she clucked. 'You must have heard of the alchemist, John Dee. Seeking to transform brass into gold he claims to have found a gem with magical properties.'

'That's nothing,' Harry chortled. 'Every day we mercers transform cloth into gold.'

'And fine wine back into water.' Thomas raised his goblet and gave a broad wink.

Rolling her eyes at her brothers and sister, Rose continued, 'I warn you, she's the one who rules the roost in that house – her father is in awe of his sharp-witted daughter – and her recent marriage to Henry Sidney, a childhood friend of King Edward, gives her greater sway at court.'

'Take heed, Master Knox. I for one, have learnt never to underestimate the power of the weaker sex,' Harry said with a meek smile at his wife.

Durham House

Outside Durham House, the magnificent mansion Dudley had requisitioned after Bishop Tunstall's fall from grace, Knox turned to leave. 'His Highness' had not yet returned home. Halfway down the steps a lithe lurcher leapt at him, flailing its paws and baring its teeth. When it started barking Knox narrowed his eyes. 'Haud yer wheesht, ye crankous cur.'

Cowering at the unfamiliar command, the hound slunk away on its belly to lick the hand of a young woman clad in a costly fur-trimmed cloak.

'Your tongue can subdue the wild beast,' she said in clipped tones. 'You must be the Scots preacher who has captured my father's fancy.'

Knox brushed pawmarks from his breeches and bowed. Lady Mary Sidney bore a striking resemblance to her brother with the same golden tinge in her auburn hair. Whereas Guildford's gaze tended to be dreamy and distant, intelligence glittered in her tawny eyes.

'We expect him any day now. An unexpected hitch delayed his departure. Come in, I'm curious to make your acquaintance.'

After leading him along a hall hung with fine paintings and intricately woven tapestries she showed him into the library and asked him to wait.

Bright sunshine streaming through the hundreds of diamond panes window bedazzled Knox. He blinked and rubbed his eyes. A large globe in the centre of the room drew his attention: he couldn't resist giving it a birl. Seeing the old world and the new spinning round in a blur rattled him somehow. Is this how God viewed the earth from the heavens?

He peered at the gleaming bronze instruments lying on a desk: the complicated cylindrical object made up of cogs and wheels must be a sundial. Brass rods held open two lengthy scrolls; one depicting a map of newly discovered lands pleased Knox because it showed Rome was not the centre of the world, but the other covered in indecipherable hieroglyphs was puzzling. Strangest of all was a large book of bronze pages with rotating disks that represented the heavenly constellations and alignment of the planets.

Dust motes danced in the rays of sunshine that lit up the bookshelves running from floor to ceiling. He examined the titles. So many volumes dealing with arcane subjects: alchemy, algebra, astronomy and astrology. The library revealed a whole new world, one in which he floundered.

At St Andrews, his tutor John Mair had introduced his students to this new knowledge. If Amerigo and Vespucci had discovered lands unknown to classical geographers, finding new planets and stars was not beyond the bounds of possibility, Mair had suggested, for the Bible did not give their number. Even so, Knox feared this sophistry veered dangerously close to heresy.

'I see you've been perusing our books. Quite a collection, is it not? Everything under the sun from Aristotle to Zoroaster. But perhaps the Bible is your only source of reading?'

Before Knox could retort, she went on, 'If we only depended on the Bible for knowledge, our civilisation would grind to a halt, Mr Knox. I believe God has created the world as a giant puzzle for humankind to discover its meaning. By which I mean both men and women. Unless you're one of those stick-in-the muds who think that such deep thinking would swamp our pretty little heads.'

'Nay, brought up in a convent, I have learnt to respect female intelligence. I believe women, too, should take an interest in learning.'

'Only the type of learning you sanction, I trow.' Her eyes glinted with mischief as she opened the book of bronze pages. 'Come, I shall open your blinkered eyes to a brave new world.'

'If you mean astrology, then I'll have no truck with it. The study of the heavens verges on blasphemy for it's flying too near the face of God for comfort,' Knox parried. 'Forbye, I believe the Lord God alone has determined our fate and we should look to scripture for guidance in our daily lives.'

Lady Mary arched a delicate eyebrow. 'While you clearly favour the doctrine of predestination, I don't believe our destiny is fixed forever; rather that God created the heavens as a map to guide us, to warn us what may come to pass unless we use our intelligence and free will to change course.'

Again Knox bristled. Her beliefs were downright heretical.

'Why not? We draw on all kinds of signs and signals to enlighten our understanding. Does not a physician use his eyes, ears and nose to diagnose a person's health? In the same way we read the stars. Astrology has a long and noble history. Why, didn't the Magi follow a star to guide them to Bethlehem?'

'Aye, as part of God's eternal plan, not some silly divination pastime.'

Lady Mary gave a derisory snort. 'You've been a seaman, Mr Knox, not by choice perhaps, but you must have observed how a sailor sails the seven seas. Not only does he use marine charts and a compass to navigate but also the sun and stars, otherwise his boat would drift aimlessly, at the mercy of the winds and waves. Life, too, is a voyage and the wise man reads the stars to learn what course he must take to forestall foundering on the rocks. This knowledge helps us to take control of our lives.'

She reached for the bronze book. 'Do you wish to know what the future holds, Mr Knox? Shall I cast your horoscope? Tell me your birth date – and time, if possible – for the more I know the easier I can work out the conjunctions of the planets. Well then? When is it? Or do you fear my magic?' She smirked.

Though her taunting made his hackles rise, Knox's curiosity was piqued. 'The thirtieth day of November,' he muttered through clenched teeth.

After clicking the bronze pages and twirling the globe, Lady Mary jotted down notes and consulted charts crossed with mystical symbols: signs of the zodiac, the constellations, the times of tides. After a few moments she looked up: a puzzled look creased her face. 'November you say. Are you sure?'

'Aye, for the papists celebrate the feast of St Andrews, the patron saint of Scotland, on that day.'

'Then that would mean Sagittarius.' She scrutinised the charts again. 'It's true you display one of its most striking characteristics – a strong spiritual nature, striving for the heavens – and I foresee your stars will conjoin with the Archer at some point. But Sagittarians tend to be flighty and easily distracted whereas you seem stubborn and strong-minded. The zodiac signs also rule different parts of the body.'

As her keen eyes ran over him, a shiver ran through him. The ill-fated gypsy lass who had read his palm had also questioned his birth date.

She tapped her chin with a delicate finger. 'You seem more rooted in the earth than a fiery flame. With your stocky build and broad shoulders, I would have guessed Taurus the bull: stubborn with a volcanic temper when roused. Besides, Taurus is the sign of the orator. A perfect fit I'd have thought.' She creased her brow.

Knox now put to her the question he had come to ask her father. 'Can you tell me what every maiden longs to know? Will I marry the lass of my dreams?'

Lady Mary laughed. 'So, a tender heart lies beneath your gruff exterior.' With a shrug of her shoulders, she continued, 'I'm at a loss, Mr Knox. I can make no sense of your chart.'

On the one hand, Knox was pleased; on the other he felt a twinge of regret. Despite his beliefs, he was no different from most folk – curious to now what lay ahead.

A stramash broke out in the hall: the sound of boots stomping on the tiled floor, a raised voice shouting orders followed by a high-pitched whine made them both jump.

'Papa is here,' Lady Mary cried and rushed out the door.

While waiting, Knox's attention was drawn to a row of books on the lower shelf: books of occult philosophy forbidden by the Vatican. As he hunkered down to have a closer look, Lady Mary led in her father.

'Damn that cursed lad. Damn him to hell. He's no son of mine,' Dudley fumed.

Settling him into a chair, Lady Mary crouched down beside him. 'What happened, papa?'

'That sly minx sweet-talked Guildford into eloping with her.'

'What? The captain's daughter? When you said an "unforeseen hitch" delayed your return that wasn't strictly true, papa. Didn't I warn you about a golden girl who would turn Guildford's head? The stars never lie,' she paused, 'but did they…?'

'Nay, at least I don't think so. I caught the two turtledoves before anything untoward could take place.'

'I sincerely hope so for his sake. A lowly captain's daughter isn't good enough for a duke's son.'

A stab of pity for the star-crossed lovers pierced Knox's heart – poor Amy would be ruined. He leant back on his haunches, unsure what to do next. Distracted by the family drama, Lady Mary had forgotten about him. Should he make his presence known or slink out unseen at the first opportunity?

'He insists their handfasting is binding and not even I can untie the bond,' Dudley said.

'Handfasting? Is that true, papa?'

'Even if it is, the witnesses are not here to tell the tale. As luck would have it, they were both slain by a raiding party of wild Scots reivers. Handfasting indeed! Whoever heard such nonsense.' His cruel laugh chilled Knox's spine.

'Not a word of this to your mother,' Dudley went on. 'If she hears of the giddy fool's *coup de foudre* it will kill her. She still grieves for our beloved angel, Margaret. And if any of my men blab …'

Hearing him punch his fist on the wooden arm of the chair, Knox flinched.

'You can trust me, papa. As far as I'm concerned, this sorry episode never took place. What's to be done with Guildford?'

'Lock him up until the lovesick pup recovers his wits.'

Lady Mary nodded. 'Guildford's sign is Pisces. Like a fish in water, he lives in his own little bubble. A dreamer who loses his heart easily but as quickly forgets. His horoscope forecasts high status and immortal fame – but only if he chooses wisely and doesn't lose his head again.'

'Those Bowes girls seem to possess an irresistible charm over men. Guildford I can understand for he's a callow youth, but Preacher Knox has fallen head over heels for her sister and bids me support the match.'

'And will you, papa?'

Throughout the seemingly interminable, unbearable silence Knox held his breath. But before the answer came, the lurcher nosed into the library and snuffled towards him. He tried to shoo it away but the hound let out a low growl.

'Haud yer wheesht,' he mumbled. 'Haud yer wheesht,' but this time his reproof was powerless to soothe the savage beast.

'You're still here, Mr Knox?' Lady Mary glared down at him, her tawny eyes burning with disconcerting ferocity.

Behind her, Dudley had drawn back his travel-stained cloak to brandish his sword. Anger etched his face and livid veins stood out on his grimy forehead.

'Where the devil did you spring from?'

'In response to your kind offer, my lord, I fain would borrow this volume.' Knox held up the first book he'd put his hand on.

Lady Mary smirked. 'The *Mirabilis Liber*? So you harbour a secret hankering to study divination after all, Mr Knox?'

II

The Black Rubric

no poor child but a manifest Solomon in Princely wisdom
An Expostulation or Complaynt against the Blasphemies of a frantic Papist
John Bale, 16th Century

Windsor Castle, September 1552

Perched on the grand throne under the cloth of state and dwarfed by two black-robed figures, the fifteen-year-old Edward VI of England seemed weighed down by the burden of kingship. 'This whole realm's most precious jewel' as his father had called his longed-for son and heir, had the fabled red-gold Tudor hair but his brilliant blue eyes glittered with an intense zeal that disturbed Knox – like a will o' the wisp that flared brightly but briefly. Fey, he thought, doomed to an early death: the hairs on the nape of his neck prickled.

The king's boyish smile lit up his smooth face. 'My Lord Dudley gives good reports of you, Mr Knox, and I'm greatly looking forward to your sermons.'

As Knox made obeisance, one of the black-robed stalwarts remarked in a loud whisper, 'So this is my Lord Dudley's latest prize.'

'I pray I live up to your expectations, Your Majesty,' Knox replied, 'and hope to be of more use than a silver tassie won at a jousting tournament.'

The young monarch's hand fluttered to his mouth to stifle a giggle. Composing his face into a solemn mask, he introduced the Archbishop of Canterbury and his secretary. Thomas Cranmer extended a limp hand but Richard Cox, the author of the waspish remark, kept his huge paws clasped. His deep-set eyes glowered with suspicion beneath thick black eyebrows that coiled like the demonic horns of Auld Nick.

'We, too, look forward to your preaching with bated breath,' Cox said. 'Your reputation has gone before you, Mr Knox.'

Once in the pulpit, Knox launched into a vigorous attack on Cranmer's *Second Book of Common Prayer*. Commissioned by the king to revise the first Prayer Book, the archbishop had weeded out most of the outward signs of popery: pardons, pilgrimages, and purgatory, but the tap root – the sacrificial nature of the mass – still had a strong hold. The instruction to kneel during the Eucharist was Knox's main bone of contention because it implied the papist belief in transubstantiation. That bread and wine could be consecrated into the body and blood of Jesus Christ was anathema to Knox and worshipping the host by bending the knee was idolatry.

Throughout Knox's sermon, King Edward hunched forward, listening intently to his arguments but Cranmer's aggrieved expression looked as if he'd swallowed a puddock, while Cox's louring looks betrayed a desire to give Knox a good thrashing.

'So, the Scottish apostle whom my Lord Dudley has fetched from Newcastle is already picking holes in our reformation,' Knox overheard him say. 'We cannot allow this runagate Scot to ride roughshod over us.'

After meeting with the Privy Council, the king summoned Knox together with Archbishop Cranmer and his secretary to hear their verdict.

'My dearest desire is to see the purest form of worship in the church of which I am head. As preacher, Mr Knox has delivered the bread of life without any harmful additions or poison to the hungry souls who cry for food. He deems that whatever is not commanded in scripture is unlawful and ungodly. Since Mr Knox has convinced us of the truth of his interpretation we therefore decree sitting to be the correct posture during communion.'

Cox's eyebrows flew up and frolicked across his brow. 'Forgive me, sire, but there is no direct instruction in scripture as to the posture required. If we followed the custom prevalent in biblical times, why, communion would be taken as the Tartars and Turks still eat their meat today – lying upon the ground.'

Cranmer's objection was more practical. 'Your Majesty, the revised Prayer Book is at the printers this very minute. The paper and ink have been ordered: the press is set up and ready to run. It cannot now be altered unless by sanction of the monarch and parliament.'

'Then I command the presses to be stopped so that the mistake can be corrected,' Edward declared. 'The winds of change are blowing the great ship of England into choppy waters and I appoint Mr Knox to pilot it to safe harbour.'

Dismissed from the king's presence, Cox confronted his adversary. 'Your authority may prevail this time, Mr Knox, but the Church of England shall not tolerate arrogant and unruly spirits who like nothing but what is after their own fancy; who never cease to make trouble when things are most quiet and in good order.'

Cranmer also threw down the gauntlet. 'And I shall set my foot by yours to be tried in the flames that your doctrine is not only untrue but seditious for it urges the king's subjects to break the bridle of obedience due to him.'

Knox scoffed. 'Ordeal by fire, you mean? The Archbishop of Canterbury, primate of the English church, proposes to challenge me, not in a court presided over by a judge but by the superstitious practice of *Judicium Dei*. Do you sincerely believe Almighty God will perform a miracle on your behalf and burn my feet? I wager your fingers will get burnt by such a ritual. I know not whether to laugh in your face or shed piteous tears for you.'

III

The Anabaptist

> Let every man say what he will,
> The gracious God mot govern me!
> *How should I Govern me?*
> William Dunbar, 15th–16th Century

Cheapside, London, 2 November 1552

Stepping out of Westminster Chapel after the service, Knox was shrouded in the dense, freezing fog that hung over London like rancid kail-broth. He pulled his scarf high over his nose as a safeguard against the smoke from thousands of coal fires that mingled with the fetid stench from cesspits. Had this miasma infected the royal lungs, he fretted, for King Edward had coughed throughout his sermon. Knox prayed it wasn't the kirkyard croup.

The theme he'd chosen for his 2nd November sermon had seemed fitting for the time of year. Although the papist feasts of All Hallows and All Souls had been abolished, doom and dread still haunted the bleak, dark winter season when folk remembered their dead. Now, after seeing the king's haggard face, Knox regretted his choice: dwelling on death and Judgement Day seemed inauspicious. With a shiver, he tried to shake off the weird feeling that overcame him.

Scarcely able to see more than a few feet in front, Knox groped his way along walls and fences, squinting to seek out familiar landmarks. Spectral forms flitted past in the swirling mist, footsteps tapped on cobbles and street cries muffled by the fog sounded ethereal and unearthly.

Ahead, Knox glimpsed a small shape ducking in and out of view and behind him, a taller figure dissolving into the shadows. Under cover of fog, picky-fingered pike-purses preyed on the unarmed and the unwary but years of defending George Wishart had taught Knox to be on his guard.

A few yards from the Locke's house he stopped and pressed against the wall, hoping to give his stalker the slip. He inched down the alleyway intending to sneak in through the scullery. The Lockes were not at home: Harry and Anna had taken their newly born son to show off to relatives. As Knox reached out to lift the latch, long, skeletal fingers gripped his arm. From the corner of his eye, he glimpsed a figure shrouded in a black cloak, the face concealed by the hood. When the stranger lunged forward wielding an object in his left hand, Knox froze. Not a petty crook, he feared but an assassin. Sent by Richard Cox.

By clashing with the canon over kneeling at communion, Knox had made a bitter enemy. The Privy Council had ordered a special explanation to be inserted into the new Prayer Book explaining that while kneeling was not obligatory, it was allowed: it could be interpreted as a sign of respect to the minister rather than idolatry. Although this sophistry affronted Knox, the Black Rubric had infuriated Cox even more, for it undermined the authority of the Prayer Book. And Cox was not a man to be trounced.

Had he sent one of his henchmen to mete out retribution? Cox would not shed tears over Knox's spilt blood. If he could knock the weapon out of his assailant's hand ... Moving swiftly, he jabbed at his jaw. The crunch of teeth and crack of bone as the man's skull hit the doorknocker made him wince – the weapon, meanwhile, had drifted silently to the ground.

'Do not be alarmed, Mr Knox.' The quaver in the stranger's voice betrayed fear. 'I mean you no harm. This is no weapon – at least not one that will wound flesh. Like you, I am a seeker after truth and I beseech you to spare the time to read this.' He picked up the fallen scroll with a trembling hand.

Disturbed by the commotion, Jamie dashed out, fists at the ready to land the intruder a punch.

'Nay, Jamie, no need for fisticuffs,' Knox said. 'I took our guest for a footpad.'

Intrigued, Knox invited the night visitor up to his room. The fire glowing in the grate cast eerie shadows on the wall. He lit a candle but kept a firm grip of the pewter candlestick: if the man were lying and did mean him harm, he could use it as a weapon.

But the stranger was fiddling with the scroll, untying the ribbons and rolling it out on the desk. His hood had slipped down and in the circle of candlelight his face became more visible. Shoulder length flaxen hair framed an angelic heart-shaped face with high cheekbones, a marked Adam's apple protruded above his collar. With a start, Knox recognised him.

Robert Cooche, a singer in the Chapel Royal choir, sang with the voice of an angel that rang to the rafters and sent his listeners into divine raptures, but he belonged to a furtive, insidious den that cloaked their errors in piety and righteousness and more dangerously – humanist logic. Cooche was an Anabaptist: a libertine, a free thinker whose belief in free will struck at predestination, the very roots of Knox's theology.

After Luther's original rebellion, a whole host of bizarre cults had sprouted: Protestantism was now a many-headed Hydra swarming with schisms all squabbling with one another – not just Lutherans and Calvinists, but Cathars, Manicheans, Melchiorites and Anabaptists all threatened to invade the pure body of the reformed church. In court circles where the cult of Anabaptism was becoming fashionable Cranmer's tactic for tackling this particular legion of heretics – converting them –

was comedic. Firing cannonballs from the pulpit against the venomous traitors and blasphemers was Knox's technique.

Now face-to-face with Cooche, well educated and trained in logic, Knox was forced into hand-to-hand combat with a formidable opponent. He girded his loins for battle.

'What do you wish to show me? If some profane Anabaptist heresy then I refuse to read it.'

A pained expression crossed Cooche's face. 'I chose to be baptised again in Christ, unlike infants christened without their consent – a practice not set down in scripture, I may add. Before you say anything, Mr Knox, hear me out. I've listened attentively to your sermons, now please permit me to put forward my argument.' He smoothed out the scroll of parchment with long graceful fingers. 'The gist being that by removing the need for morality and conscience your doctrine of predestination leads to sin and depravity.'

Hackles raised, Knox craned his neck to read the title: *The Confutation of the Errors of the Careless by Necessity.*

Cooche poked the parchment with his index finger. 'I seek to propose that predestination is the work of the devil, not God. Furthermore, that Satan created the world and the wicked creatures in it.'

'By suggesting good and evil exist equally in the world,' Knox growled, 'you're resurrecting the Manichean heresy which challenges the absolute power of Almighty God. How could any reasonable person believe things contrary to the true word of God as revealed in the Holy Book?'

'I do not intend to trade passages from the Bible with you. For every quotation you thrust at me, I can parry with one that will contradict it. Besides, Christ continually overturned Old Testament teachings: the most famous example being to turn the other cheek rather than demand an eye for an eye. As for being *reasonable* I intend to apply logic to test whether your assertions stand up to scrutiny.'

'Humanist logic has no place in theological debate,' Knox retorted.

'You've just contradicted yourself, Mr Knox. Besides, there are many *reasonable* men who will contest your religious doctrine.'

Before he could respond Jamie came in with a jug of steaming hot punch – a welcome interruption that gave him time to think.

Cooche wrapped his fingers around his cup and blew to cool down the punch. Over the rim of the cup, his cornflower blue eyes twinkled with mischief. 'According to predestination, God has preordained everything that comes to pass on earth – so that no activity, not even a sparrow falling from a twig, takes place without divine ordination. Do you agree?' A lopsided smile skimmed his girlish pink lips.

Reluctantly, Knox inclined his head.

'Thus, at the beginning of creation, God decided who would be saved and who would be damned to the fires of hell.' Cooche narrowed his eyes: the mischievous twinkle hardened to a cruel, glacial stare. 'Does this not seem the most tyrannical and unjust conduct for even the most wicked man in the world? Or even Satan?'

Refusing to rise to the blasphemous bait, Knox mustered his composure. 'Nay, because God already knows beforehand who is going to sin and therefore who merits salvation and who deserves damnation.'

Coocle stroked his beardless chin. 'So even before the fall of man, Almighty God, the fount of all goodness and mercy, created sin and hell?'

'That I utterly deny,' Knox spluttered. 'God did not create sin. Being sinful by nature, man will always choose sin. Man falls by his own fault: his free will would never allow him to reach out to God. Man is so engulfed in sin there is nothing in him that merits or enables salvation. Therefore God must predestine who will be saved.'

'I must admit I'm confused.' Coocle ran long fingers through his flaxen hair. 'If, as you say, man is born in a state of sin then who, apart from God, created sin? Dare I suggest an alternative …'

'God allowed the conditions for sin to exist,' Knox blurted. 'When Lucifer rebelled and Adam and Eve fell from grace they chose sin.'

'Ah, choice would imply free will, would it not?' A note of triumph pealed in the Anabaptist's voice. 'And they chose to disobey God.'

Knox dabbed at his brow slick with sweat and mopped his lips, sticky from the sweet punch. 'Because they were sinful creatures.'

'Who made them sinful? If, as you maintain, everything is predestined, these sinners had no choice but to reject God. Similarly, when Judas betrayed Christ, he did so to fulfil the prophecy. Denied free will, man cannot be held responsible for his actions: should he also be condemned to hell for being innocent?'

'These reprobates were not elected to eternal salvation,' Knox growled. 'As it is written in Romans, Chapter 8, Verse 30: *And those whom he predestined he also called, and those whom he called, he also justified, and those whom he justified he also glorified.*'

'Oh yes, the Doctrine of the Elect: *For many are called but few are chosen* is proof indeed that God is no respecter of persons. Well, then, let us concede man is sinful, that he commits sin but, according to your doctrine, the sins of the elect will be overlooked whereas the damned will go to hell, whether or not they repent.'

Knox winced. He scratched his neck where sweat was snaking down his collar. 'The elect cannot sin. As it is written: *whoever abides in him does not sin.* They are the righteous whereas whoever sins has not known God.'

'This doctrine seems to contradict his original plan. In Genesis, God created human beings in his own image and likeness − both male and female − and

104

blessed them; at what point did he change his mind and condemn some to eternal damnation? Equally, when did he create hell and consign Lucifer and his fallen angels there? These are very important questions. Tell me, how did sin originate in Lucifer's soul? How did Lucifer become Satan? How did he become the serpent in the Garden of Eden? Only God who created Lucifer could create sin. The one follows logically from the other.'

Knox gritted his teeth. He was conscious of digging a deep pit to fall into: he must beware of rolling a stone that would come back on him. 'God did not create sin, but he did create his creatures with the freedom of choice. When Eve chose to eat from the forbidden fruit, her rebellion was not God's fault, but the result of her own free choice.'

Cooche pulled a face. 'We're back to free will again, Mr Knox. It also puzzles me why a loving God would ordain mankind's plummet from grace. Why create anyone with the intent of inflicting misery? Why elect only certain individuals and not all of humanity? That implies God does not love all humankind otherwise he would show mercy and save every soul.'

'God's divine plan is not revealed to us: his will is hidden. You make the love of God common to all men; and that I constantly deny.' Knox fumed. 'Loving kindness is not an essential part of God's nature.'

Cooche gave a snort. 'Are you insinuating God is not love? What do you say to the layman who believes God Our Father so loved mankind that he sent his only begotten Son to save us from sin and grant us everlasting life? How can the layman understand that salvation can be achieved without doing good works? That his sins may be pardoned without repentance? How can he know he's one of the elect or not? Do you, Mr Knox? A blind belief that you are one of the elect – surely that is tantamount to the sin of presumption?'

Knox waggled his head back and forth in frustration. This argument was making his head dirl.

'How do you intend to persuade people to follow your doctrine, attend church and live righteous lives?' the Anabaptist went on. 'The elect have no need of your services while the damned are, well, damned? That's enough to reduce your reformed religion to a complete absurdity. No reasonable man would believe what you preach.'

'It has nothing to do with reason,' Knox raged. 'Faith is all! I teach that sins can be forgiven by faith alone: without the penances demanded by the papist Church, without buying your way out of an imaginary purgatory with indulgences, without praying to a saint's arm bone to save your soul.'

'May I suggest that, just as the pardoners cheated the common folk, you're taking advantage of their blind ignorance? At least with papist dogma there's hope and mercy: A man can be master of his fate. For did not Christ say: *Repent and be saved – everyone who calls on the name of the Lord will be saved.* Christianity is based on Christ's redemption – freeing us from the bondage of sin and despair.'

Knox scowled. 'The Son of God was made man to destroy the works of the devil. *He who sins is of the devil, for the devil has sinned from the beginning.*'

'Aha!' Cooche clapped his hands in jubilation. 'Then you agree with me. The devil co-existed with God: sin and evil go hand-in-hand. I confess I interpret scripture more liberally but surely that's preferable to taking it so literally you find yourself lost in a maze of confusion? There are so many flaws in your argument, Mr Knox. Yet you propose to found a religion on these unsound principles.'

Knox was shaking from head to foot with rage. 'Nay, it is you who're entering a labyrinth from which there is no exit with your rotten heresies and damnable errors. Scripture is not rhetoric but the word of God revealed through the Holy Ghost. There's no cause assigned why the Almighty has chosen some and rejected others. It's not for us to question his hidden will.'

'No cause means no reason and no logic, either. Ironically, your doctrine seems to me rather haphazard. In fact, I fail to see the difference between predestination and destiny or providence. As superstitious folk would say, you cannot flee your fate.'

What's for you will no go by you. You maun dree your weird. Betsy Learmont's auld saws sounded in Knox's ears.

'Yet most reasonable people believe free will – the ability to think for oneself and make choices – sets us apart from the beasts of the field,' Cooche continued, 'otherwise we are as sheep plodding along a rutted path from which there's no straying.'

Struggling to counter the Anabaptist's arguments Knox felt hot and prickly. In contrast, his adversary seemed cool and composed.

'So, to conclude, this is my thesis. Predestination gives the elect no incentive to live a moral life on earth, for they will be saved regardless of how they live. They are the "careless by necessity" in the title of my document: as careless as libertines who live a dissolute life. In fact, I would argue those "careless by necessity" are more injurious to God than atheists and even blasphemers.'

Knox stiffened. 'How dare you cry God's elect libertines! You're not only a blasphemer, but a devil incarnate . . . a vile slave of proud Lucifer.'

Cooche held up an elegant hand. 'Assertions are not arguments and those who use them only grasp a hilt without a sword. Waving your cudgel to bludgeon me into submission will not thrash me; I prefer fencing with a rapier to make my points.'

Fury knotted Knox's tongue. In the cut and thrust of such intense theological debate, he realised he was losing the argument on logical grounds. As the ground shifted beneath him to the point of near contradiction, he was painfully aware of his shortcomings.

First and foremost he was a preacher, not a rhetorician. Forbye, he'd never had time to systematise his theology; his pragmatic aim was to appeal to the common man. Now as God's mouthpiece, his watchman, he must defend the faithful against the Anabaptist threat but Cooche was boxing him into a corner.

'The doctrine of free will is an abomination!' Knox spluttered. 'How can you say God is imperfect! How can you deny God is not the Supreme Being, the fountain from which everything springs? You're none other than a limb of the Antichrist intent on destroying Christianity!'

Cooche's soft lips curled into a sneer. 'Nay, it is you who are a limb of the Antichrist, by spurning our saviour's sacrifice. Continue with this doctrine and I greatly fear you and your Calvinist friends will create a race of monsters – proud beings who believe themselves to above the laws of morality and common decency.'

A red tide of anger swirled within Knox's breast, bubbling up in his gorge and choking his power of speech. No words would come forth.

'Do you like to sing, master Knox?'

Cooche's question took Knox by surprise. He'd last sung as a student in the choir at St Andrews University before his voice broke. 'Aye, but why do you ask?' His voice was hesitant.

'Do you remember the joy of singing with others to reproduce the sound of a heavenly choir? The sheer ecstasy of reaching those high notes? Oh, forgive me – as God's trumpeter you would prefer to play a horn – but no matter. Would you not wish for every one of God's creatures to spend eternity in such bliss?' Cooche asked before answering his own question.

'But no, you choose to believe in the avenging God of the Old Testament, Mr Knox, whereas we Anabaptists elect to follow the teachings of Jesus Christ who offers hope and redemption to the sinner. Which is more Christian in your opinion? Can you even call yourself a Christian? Because nothing you've said to me this night stems from Christ; the Judaic religion would be more fitting for one of your temperament and doctrine.'

'How dare you say I'm no Christian! At least I'm humble enough to admit I cannot know God's hidden will. Whereas you, the proud Anabaptist, are a henchman of Satan who denies the power and the glory of Almighty God. You deserve death as a blasphemous heretic.'

Cooche's lips curled. 'Perhaps we shall meet again on the pyre in a joint burning. Our martyrdom will fuel both our causes. Are you willing to sacrifice your life for your faith and fly straight to your maker?'

'I should go straight to the magistrate to denounce you,' Knox retorted.

Cooche tipped his head. 'As you wish. It is your duty – failure to do so will lead to your arrest as well as mine. Never fear, no one saw me come in. I always take pains to keep my movements secret.'

He brushed a golden lock from his brow. 'I've no wish to cause you any trouble. I intended our discussion this evening to be, if not a meeting of minds, then at least an airing of our views so as to understand each other's doctrines. It's better to know thine enemy before attacking, don't you think?'

Knox shrugged. 'We have indeed discussed weighty matters. I, too, give my word to reveal our meeting to no one. Forbye, once truth prevails, your false doctrine will die a natural death.'

Cooche's fair face darkened as he rolled up his parchment. 'I see there's nothing more to be gained from our conversation. It's clear I shall need to consult with more learned men than you, Mr Knox, to confront the crucial issues I've raised.'

Closing the door behind the Anabaptist, Knox glimpsed a dwarfish figure emerging from the shadows to follow him. Sitting at his desk, he buried his head in his hands: the visit had left his brain feeling as murky as the London fog. He regretted not copying the scroll: he would have liked to analyse the scriptural contradictions that Cooche had raised in order to come to a clearer understanding.

IV

Bishop of Rochester

Be sure you keep some great man always to your Friend
Precepts
William Cecil, 16th Century

Whitehall, November 1552

Knox cast his eyes over the colourful parchments spread across the desk and gave a knowing smile. The various armorials and heraldic rolls depicting shields and coats of arms and blazons betrayed Cecil's task. Anxious to establish a noble pedigree for his recent knighthood, he was in the midst of drawing up a family tree.

When the secretary stood up to greet his guest, Knox raised a hand. 'No need to rise, Sir William. You've risen enough lately. Have you found a fitting crest? With your flair for bending with the wind I'd say you were sprung from the willow rather than the oak.'

Cecil frowned at his boldness but Knox knew it to be true. On Somerset's demise, Cecil had been detained in the Tower of London but had ingratiated himself with Dudley. Skilful footwork, Knox thought – or more likely handiwork – for the thirty-two-year old Cecil was proving to be an able clerk. In the short time Knox had known him the ambitious innkeeper's son had worked his way up from humble scribe to Secretary of State.

Cecil had got to grips with the intricacies of law and finance and, more astutely, grasped that knowledge was power. It was no secret he'd woven an intricate web of spies and informers in every corner of the realm and throughout Christendom. Little wonder Dudley had wasted no time in taking on this invaluable recruit.

But Knox was leery of this shrewish clerk who dressed in clerical black. Cecil was one of those who clung onto the coat sleeves of those on the rise, swiftly letting go on their fall from favour. Even those who lived by the word did not always escape death by the sword.

'If you mean to rap my knuckles for not informing you of the Anabaptist's visit, may I say in my defence I vowed never to reveal our conversation to anyone. The theological matters we discussed are of little interest to a layman such as you. Forbye, I'm no clype but a man of my word.'

'I do not doubt it, Mr Knox. How ironic to take the papist defence – refusal to betray the secrets of confession. No matter. I did hear but am taking it no further. Besides, the chorister belongs to a special breed of men: in former days, they would have lived a monastic life among their own kind. Whatever his beliefs, Cooche is beyond reproach, protected by an invisible ring of friends and admirers in very high places.' He tapped the side of his nose. 'Nay, I've called you here on behalf of my lord Dudley who desires to give you a token of his esteem. Your brother, William, is a merchant seaman, I believe.'

Knox nodded, though wondering what the secretary was leading up to.

'On the duke's recommendation, the Privy Council has agreed to grant him liberty to trade – for a limited period – in a vessel of one hundred tons burden to any part of England. As I'm sure you will agree, such a letter granting safe conduct and sure passport patent will be of enormous benefit to your brother's business.'

After a cursory scan, Knox rolled up the documents. 'That's very generous: I'm sure he'll be grateful.' He gave a curt bow and made to leave.

'Not so hasty, Mr Knox. Though signed, the patent isn't valid until the privy seal has been attached. I shall do so after discussing another matter. Your request to return to Newcastle is most unexpected. Surely the bully Cox hasn't ground you down already?'

'Nay, that's not the reason. I must go where God calls me and I truly believe my mission is to serve my congregations in the north. Forbye, I'm restless without a parish and one sermon a week at the royal chapel does not slake my evangelical thirst.'

Cecil took out a fine lawn handkerchief and wiped his eyeglasses. 'The duke is not well pleased. After all, he brought you south to thwart Cranmer and his cronies.'

'My task here is over. Despite my opposition, the Black Rubric has been inserted – I can do no more. Forbye, the duke has failed to honour his promise to gain Captain Bowes's consent for me to wed his daughter. I must go and do my ain wooing.'

Cecil balanced his Florentine eyeglasses on the bridge of his long nose. 'You cruelly malign my lord Dudley. He has not forgotten about you.' He waved a parchment. 'I have today received this letter in which he writes: *I would to God it might please the king's majesty to appoint Mr Knox to the office of Rochester bishopric.*' He peered over the top of his eyeglasses. 'How does that please *you*, Mr Knox?'

Knox glowered and waggled his head. 'Not at all. Not in the least.'

'I can understand your antipathy but, until parliament changes the law, a bishopric is the only means we have to reward a parson. In addition, the post comes with a generous benefice – enough to support a wife and, in due course, a family.' A smile crinkled his lips. 'Captain Bowes can hardly deny you his fair daughter's hand on the grounds of poverty.'

Sleekit as the snake in the Garden of Eden, Knox thought, tempting him with the apple that was Marjory.

Before he could reply, Cecil went on, 'In response to your objection that you're a preacher not an administrator, Mr Knox, may I assure you the duke and I shall be responsible for the day-to-day running of the bishopric.'

'So you may cream off the taxes and teinds? As you do in the mighty see of Worcester and Gloucester?'

'Bishop Hooper found fit to agree to our conditions in return for being granted custody of so many souls.'

'Your ploy may have worked with Hooper but no matter what gewgaws you dangle in front of me, I refuse. I cannot abandon my flock in the north and I'd work until my finger nibs bled gore rather than take your thirty pieces of silver. You can convey my answer to your master.'

Cecil rubbed his eyes. 'If I were you, Mr Knox, I would think again. You would not wish to lose my lord Dudley's favour. The recent controversy over the Prayer Book leaves you a target for Archbishop Cranmer and Canon Cox. You run the risk of biting the hand that feeds you.'

Knox fell silent. Perhaps he should be grateful to the duke but deep in his heart he believed Dudley to be a devil's limb who should face judgment and retribution for spilling Simple Somerset's blood. Dudley's promises were as false as a spaewife's prophecies. He should gang warily.

'I'm not afeart to bite off my lord Dudley's fingers — nor to cut off my nose to spite my face. I sook up to neither statesman nor churchman. I must be free to preach the true word of God and that I cannot do if my tongue is tied and my wings fettered. As yet I know not what you crafty corbies are scheming but I ken fine that biding here is not part of God's divine plan for me. I am the Lord's instrument, not a pawn in your political game.'

Cecil polished his eyeglasses. 'Would you refuse the king's offer? His young majesty values the spiritual solace you give. He depends on you.'

Knox swithered. An attack of measles the previous April had aggravated the king's consumption and over the last few weeks the flesh had melted off Edward's slight frame. He'd taken to stooping and hunching his shoulders to shield his chest racked by constant coughing. While the courtiers swore love and loyalty to the king, they were counting his days as he coughed the winter out and gambling on their chances once he coughed his last lungful.

'The king is a kindly soul but he's a Daniel in a lion's den of place-seekers and whoremongers who not only keep their strumpets shamelessly in the same house as their wives but offer them to their friends. Thon closet papists are thirsting after the king's death so as to return to their Romish practices.'

'That's why you're needed here. King Edward needs you to push against the backsliders.'

'The king will not live to see another Christmas,' Knox predicted.

'Dangerous words, Mr Knox. You do know that forecasting the monarch's death is a treasonable offence. I could you string up for that.'

Knox clenched his jaw and thrust out his beard, 'Do as you will, for I believe my days with the English church are numbered.'

Cecil shrugged. 'You are – what's the Scots expression – thrawn. Then I warn you, Mr Knox, we shall be keeping a close eye on you in your northern lair. You're not the kind of firebrand that can safely be left burning in the Northumberland bailiewick and at the slightest hint of your kindling a blaze the duke will snuff you out. Meanwhile, I leave you to inform the duke of your decisions.'

'That I shall. Unlike you, I'm not afeart of rousing the duke's fiery temper,' Knox replied. 'Will you then consign my brother's patent letter to the flames?'

Cecil gave a sour smile. 'That is for my lord Dudley to decide.'

V

The Corbie Messenger

> Now therefore take, I pray thee, thy weapons,
> thy quiver and thy bow, and go out to the field
>
> Genesis XXVII: 3

Newcastle, 24 December 1552

Knox blotted the parchment and sat back to read over his Christmas Day sermon. With foresight of trouble to come he'd refused the bishopric of Rochester and returned to Newcastle. The bear pit of the royal court sickened him: it was rotten to the core. His ministry there had failed to amend the dubious morals of noblemen who survived through flattery and bribery and sycophantic courtiers who twitched their noses like curs, sniffing out who was in favour and then licking their backsides.

Lord Dudley was proving to be the worst. We'll see what he has to say about this, Knox thought. For no miscreant would be spared the lash of his tongue in tomorrow's homily. Once he'd delivered his damning sermon, he'd pursue his suit of Marjory and together they'd settle down to live a quiet life in the north.

Jamie shivered as he laid a bundle of branches by the hearth. 'It's colder than a grave-digger's behouchie out there and my moules are fair itching.' He blew on his chill-blained fingers and tucked them under his oxters to warm them. 'But the fairies found me some rowans to burn on Sowans Nicht.'

'I've never heard of that before,' Knox said. 'What's that about?'

'On Christmas Eve we burn rowan twigs to redd out any bad feeling there's been atween folk throughout the year, then boil up a brose – oatmeal steeped in water – and drink the broth to auld lang syne.'

'Thon might warm your cockles and put hairs on your chest but sounds gruelling to me,' Knox chuckled. 'Mayhap I'll give it a by.'

At the sound of the six o'clock curfew drum, Jamie smoored the fire, sprinkling a thin layer of ash on the coals to keep it going overnight. When a blustery wind blew up and rattled the window shutter Jamie's face paled but when this was followed by a series of light, repetitive taps he looked horror-stricken.

'I'll no answer it, master. No on Sowans Nicht when ghouls will be stravaiging about the land.'

'Ghosts and ghouls rarely chap at doors, Jamie, and on Christmas Eve it wouldn't augur well to chase away a weary traveller seeking shelter.'

To be on the safe side, Jamie thrust the iron poker in the fire and took up a position behind his master. Cautiously, Knox opened the door a few inches, enough to see a pair of wild eyes burning above sunken cheeks and a matted beard.

'Master prophet, it's me. Let me in. Afore I'm seen.'

With a quick backward glance into the alley, Robert Stewart sidled in and leant against the door. He looked as if he'd been dragged through several hedges backwards and dunked in stinking ditches. With only a tattered cloak and clarty cloths tied round his feet, his gaunt frame trembled with cold.

While Knox sat him on a settle by the hearth and threw a blanket round his shoulders, Jamie plunged the glowing poker into a jug of ale. With a grateful nod, Stewart wrapped his freezing hands round the beaker.

'What brings you to Newcastle?' Knox asked. 'Have you fulfilled your mission?'

Stewart nodded. 'Aye and nay, but it's a long tale.' He leant forward to whisper. 'One for your lugs only, master prophet.'

Once Knox had sent Jamie off to bed, the archer slurped the ale and wiped his lips. 'It started in London, master prophet, where Sir Henry Balnaves offered me a goodly sum to snoop for him at the French court. But how could I? Tarred as a heretic, I'd be burnt to a cinder. But Sir Henry came up with a plan to ensure me free passage. Under a new name I was hired to escort his adopted son to Paris.'

Knox was perplexed until recalling how Balnaves had taken in the son of Sir John Melville of Raith, a Fife laird beheaded for his part in Cardinal Beaton's murder. It surprised Knox that Marie de Guise would allow a heretic's son to serve as a page at her daughter's court – unless it was a ploy on the part of the guileful dowager. By showing mercy to a son innocent of the sins of the father, perhaps she hoped to win favour among the Fife lairds – or the loyalty of the callow youth.

'I was telt to report to William Kirkcaldy, commander of the queen's French bodyguards,' Stewart continued.

Again the name brought Knox up short. How had one of Beaton's murderers wheedled his way into the Scots Guards? Someone of standing must be backing him.

'I signed up under the name Fletcher but my code name is Corbie.'

Knox snorted. 'Corbie as in corbie messenger – a most fitting *nom de guerre*.'

'Kirkcaldy is Corax and our spymaster is the Raven, but I'm no sure who he is.'

But Knox had an inkling who the black clad bird of prey guarding the Tower of London might be.

'All I ken is that Balnaves was drafting a bond to marry our Queen Mary to the English King Edward,' Stewart went on, 'but there was the tricky wee problem of the dauphin. Even though the shilpit prince is a corpse on legs, he couldn't depend on chance and so he sent me to get rid of him. With scant chance of lodging an arrow in his skull, I settled on poison.

'Then I thought, where's the use in doing away with the prince yet let the queen live? She's the one who'll keep Scotland papist. So as to fell both birdies with one stane I put arsenic in their favourite sweets – frittered pears and marchpane *rillettes* – just a wee droppie at a time. Because both weans were aye whining with the gripe, no one would jalouse they were being poisoned.'

Knox's jaw dropped. 'You tried to murder Queen Mary?'

Stewart nodded. 'Aye, for that was the right thing to do, so God telt me.'

'You heard the voice of God?'

'As clear as I'm hearing you now, master prophet. And I nearly succeeded – until the queen fell sick after gobbling up all the *rilletes* in one go. Thon wee Scots lassie sniffed something was up and alerted Dr Bog, the Scots doctor. When the finger was pointed at the pastry cook, I heaved a sigh for I'd got away with it, but then under torture she blamed me.'

Stewart wiped his brow and took a long quaff of ale. 'Corax put me on a ship to London where Balnaves sheltered me but some Scotsman – Henderson or Henryson – got wind of it and began blabbing. When it reached his ears, Lord Dudley said he'd have to arrest me, but no to fash – he'd free me once all the fuss died down. Then the French began bleating. Demanded that a head roll. Mine. Dudley got the jitters and passed me onto his secretary.

'Thon weasly wee whitrat ferret face Willie Cecil said he'd have to hand me over but, since I kent too much, he was loath to do so. Then, swifter than I could nick an arrow into my bow, a body was handed over to the Frenchies – one of the Cornish rebels Cecil hadn't strung up yet.

'He bundled me off on a boat to Ireland where I lay low for many months waiting for God to guide me. I may have missed the chick and the auld hen but I'll no fail again. For God has given me another mission.'

Stewart's bloodshot eyes blazed with either fever or fervour. Knox hoped it was the former but suspected the latter. This man's presumption knew no bounds. Shifting the blame for his evil schemes onto the Almighty was surely blasphemous. His temples throbbed with the heavy pressure of a louring migraine.

'What are you saying? That you're still planning to murder our queen?'

'Aye, along with her mother and the rest of thon papist crew. Thon whore of Babylon with her Frenchified ways and Romish rites must be hounded out of Scotland. Forbye, Regent Hamilton wants rid of thon galliard, d'Oisel, who's got above himself. I'm the very man to redd out the whaups in the nest. Thon traitor Blasphemous Balfour is now one of the queen's lickspittles. I should have throttled the turncoat's thrapple when I had the chance. But I'll no miss him again. I'll be like thon …' Stewart scratched his lice-ridden head. 'What do they cry him? Jock the Baptist who cleared the way for Christ's coming.'

'Aye, but he got his head chopped off for his pains.'

'That'll never happen to me.' Stewart prodded his chest with his finger. 'I'm too canny to risk my neck. Forbye, if I'm to fulfil his purpose, God will look out for me.'

The archer's gibbering jingled Knox's nerves and jangled his ears. How could his ideas be so warped? 'Murder is wrong,' he insisted. 'Mind the fifth commandment: Thou shalt not kill. Forbye, those who live by the sword perish by the sword.'

'Only the ungodly. Were you no glad to see Beaton's bloated corpse stabbed through like a porcupine and pickled in a vat of brine? The queen mother and her henchmen are murderers. We must avenge the spilt blood of the martyrs.'

Knox pressed his palms against his head to ease his throbbing temples. He yearned to stuff his fingers in his ears to stifle the burbling stream of drivel – and pinch his nose against Stewart's brackish stench as he leant towards him.

'But the evil one is thwarting my attempts, master prophet. Every time I was about to do the deed thon witch with tawny cat's eyes was there, giving me the evil eye. I maun ding her doun afore I can go on. Dressed in the garb of a nun but with a soul as black as the devil's, she kens how to concoct cantrips and conjure up familiars.'

Who was he talking about? This novice nun who'd accompanied the queen mother to France? Knox sat bolt upright. Isabelle! The wee orphan lass he'd rescued! Jamie's sister!

'Afore I do anything else, I maun get back to Haddington. It should be easy. She's only a lass – a quick twist of the neck …' He flexed his fingers. 'Then I'll hurl the witch into the Tyne.'

'Nay!' Knox shrieked. The memory of the gypsy lass drowned in the Tyne made him sick to the stomach. He lowered his voice. 'You cannot murder an innocent lass.'

'She's no harmless, Master Knox. She's Auld Nick's handmaid.'

Knox floundered in the face of such folly. Somehow he had to steer Stewart from his skewed course. How to reason with one who believed himself to be of God's elect? In some twisted way, Stewart had imbibed John Calvin's doctrines.

As if struck by a thunderbolt, Knox gave a jolt. The Lord had answered his plea. With an exaggerated gesture he raised his eyes to heaven and clasped his hands. Stewart gawped at him expectantly. 'The Lord has spoken to me,' Knox said at last.

Stewart's mouth gaped open. 'In truth?'

'Aye, you're to continue the Lord's work, but not in England or Scotland – but Switzerland where the great reformer, John Calvin, is beset by enemies on all sides. The Inquisition, the Liberals, Anabaptists – all threaten the true faith. Dr Calvin is a thinker not a warrior and has need of someone like you – an experienced bodyguard and one of the elect. The Lord has chosen you go to his aid.'

Stewart listened, agape. 'You hear and see things I do not: that's why you're a prophet.' His forehead furrowed. 'But what of the lass?'

'The Lord works in mysterious ways. You must never presume to know his will.

Her fate lies in his hands. In the meantime, you'll sail with Skipper Will to Holland and then make your way to Geneva. I shall write letters of introduction.'

'Never fash, master prophet. Your will is my command.'

Whether through a stroke of luck or divine thunderbolt, Knox gave thanks for sloughing off Robin Stewart who had been sticking to him like a cocklebur.

VI

Treason

> Treason doth never prosper: what's the reason?
> Why, if it prosper, none dare call it treason.
>
> John Harrington, 16th Century

Newcastle, January 1553

'No sign of Skipper Will, Jamie?' Knox asked. As he struggled to secure the window shutters, sleet mingling with salty sea spray stung his face.

'I was down at the harbour this morn, master, but the waves were lashing high over the wall. I nearly got swept off my feet. Not even the boldest mariner would sail in this weather.'

Since St Stephen's Day, the severe winter storms battering the east coast had ceased all shipping and Knox fretted that he'd had no word from Marjory – or else his letters had been intercepted. It would be no surprise after his scathing Christmas Day sermon at St Nicholas's, condemning those in power for their disloyalty to the king. When he caught sight of Brandling, the mayor of Newcastle, wriggling with rage as if he had fleas in his breeks, he knew he'd hit the mark.

After supper, Knox and Jamie had battened down the hatches when loud knocking disturbed them. Knox shuddered – not Robert Stewart again. Jamie answered the door and returned with a parchment wound in a thick woollen cloth. 'A messenger from the Lord Lieutenant of Durham gave me this.'

Reading the scroll, a shiver ran through Knox.

'Is it bad news, master?' Jamie asked.

'Aye, lad. Thon hugger-mugger Brandling has complained to the Privy Council. Lord Westmorland orders me to repair unto him immediately, as I will answer at my peril.' His eyes glazed over. 'I had foreseen one day or other to fall into their hands, for more and more the members of the devil rage against me. I've aye lived in dread of the knock on the door that could spell death with torture, dishonour and ruin. This is it, Jamie.'

'You cannot go anywhere in this weather, master.'

'I must – or risk being put to the horn. Whistle up the Free Fishers, Jamie lad. They will find a way.'

In the dark hours before dawn, Knox penned what might be his last letter to his beloved Marjory. By morning, the storm had abated and a Free Fisher came with the news that Skipper Will had landed.

'What do you think of *Saltire 2*, Johnnie?' Will said, proudly showing off his new boat. 'She's grand, isn't she? My wee coble could never have handled such waters. I've you to thank for this. You must be held in high regard at court. Who could have foreseen it? My brother as chaplain to the king himself and me a royal warrant holder.' He patted the pocket of his jerkin.

'My luck has run out, I wager,' Knox said, 'for this summons may signify my death knell but I fear I'm not yet ripe nor able to glorify Christ by my death.'

As his body trembled with cold and fear, Skipper Will put a hand on his shoulder.

'Never fash, Johnnie. You lead a blessed life. The Lord looks after his ain. Forbye you've got mair lives than a wildcat.'

Knox was unconvinced. He'd never felt so low and vile since the day his feet had been chained in the galleys. 'Whatever the Lord has in store for me, will you please give this to Marjory.' Tears smarted his eyes as he handed Will the letter.

Be sure I will not forget you and your company, so long as mortal man may remember any earthly creature.

London, February 1553

In the courtroom of Guildhall, Knox noticed Thomas Cranmer and Richard Cox on the bench of privy councillors and churchmen, heads together in covert whispering. He'd spent all night preparing answers to the set of articles these two schemers had drawn up. Why was he being so sorely tried? As yet there was no sign of his patron on the bench – only Secretary Cecil.

'My Lord Dudley is not present?' Knox asked.

Cecil scowled. 'The duke thought it prudent to take himself elsewhere. He was not well pleased at your refusal of the bishopric. In fact, he was greatly peeved by your ingratitude and washes his hands of you.'

Knox chewed his lip. Being abandoned by his patron did not augur well.

'Notwithstanding, my Lord Dudley wishes you well,' Cecil went on. 'He has appointed his deputy Warden of the Marches to preside.'

After opening the proceedings, Lord Wharton called on the Archbishop of Canterbury to begin the interrogation. Cranmer struggled to his feet. 'Mr Knox, why did you refuse the benefice of Rochester? Is it because you believe this post to be too akin to papist practice?'

'Many things need reformation in the ministry of England but that was not my reason. I would refuse no office that might promote God's glory and the preaching of Christ's Gospel. My conscience told me I might profit more in some place other than in London.'

When Cranmer then questioned him about kneeling at communion, Knox rolled his eyes. Not that again? Had this not been picked over and over like a scab?

'Let others do as they wish but I refuse to kneel and worship a crumb of bread.'

Cranmer harrumphed. 'I'm sorry to see you have a mind contrary to the common order.'

'If, by that, you mean your common Prayer Book, I'm only sorry the common order should be contrary to Christ's institution. Kneeling is a human invention. We ought to follow Christ's example, which, you must agree, is the most perfect.'

While some of the councillors chortled at his boldness, Cranmer's group huddled in whispered negotiation. After they called for an adjournment, Cecil took Knox aside.

'I have great respect for sticking to your principles, Mr Knox, but this time I beg you to consider some kind of compromise. Otherwise ...' He tilted his head in the direction Cranmer and Cox, clearly at loggerheads with Lord Wharton.

'I shall be sent to the Tower for treason?'

Cecil inclined his head. 'Not only that, I fear you're fanning the flames of your own pyre.'

'I'm sure it would give Cox the greatest pleasure to tie me to the stake and wring my neck with his ain great paws.'

'No doubt. However, I shall do what I can to smooth the ruffled clerical collars.'

When the court reconvened, Cecil begged leave to speak. 'I wish to remind the council that, however inflammatory his views, Preacher Knox not only retains the duke's protection but the king's gracious favour. No man shall be so hardy as to vex him for setting forth the king's most godly proceedings.'

Before Cox could object, Cranmer cringed and clasped his hands. 'Please let it be known to His Majesty that, far from bearing Preacher Knox ill will, I greatly esteem him.'

'In truth, the court highly approves of his sermon,' Lord Wharton echoed. 'The council clear you of all charges of treason, Mr Knox.'

While Cox stamped a petulant foot, Cecil stifled a smug smile. 'Then my lord, perhaps something might be written to Mayor Brandling. To the effect he may have reason to regret his rash complaint and may now wish to withdraw it.'

'Of course. I shall rebuke him at once for his malicious accusation,' Lord Wharton replied. 'No one should offend such an esteemed chaplain as Mr Knox.'

Outside the court, Knox breathed deeply. Heinous were the charges laid against him, and many were the lies that were made but in the end the truth had prevailed – thank the Lord. He could now return to Newcastle with a light heart and, more importantly, put Marjory's mind at rest. As he skipped down the steps, Cecil caught up with him.

'Not so hasty, Mr Knox. The Privy Council have taken Lord Wharton's recommendation to heart. In an effort to bestow honour on you, they're appointing you vicar of All Hallows Church in London. Though a lesser appointment than the bishopric, it's still one of the most lucrative and illustrious positions in the Church of England.'

Knox stared at Cecil in disbelief. Had he heard him aright? Another southern post?

'In your position, I would consider it most carefully, Mr Knox. A refusal this time would most definitely land you in the Tower – and take it from me, it is not the most pleasant of prisons. The only exit for most is to the scaffold on Tower Hill.'

VII

Whitsun Weddings

That women change, and hate where love hath been,
They call them false...

Sonnet vii

Sir Thomas Wyatt, 16th Century

Chapel Royal, Whitehall Palace, May 1553

Knox prowled round the vestry of the Chapel Royal, clenching and unclenching his fists. He would refuse the vicarage of All Hallows. It was not an offer but an order with Cranmer's stamp on it – a ploy to place him under the watchful eye of the bishop of London, Nicholas Ridley.

Well, he could see through it. He loathed the helpless feeling of being in the claws of these ravens circling around the king's deathbed. Was he the only one who could see Edward was dying? Mary Tudor's succession would pitch them all back into the puddle of papistry, or more seriously, onto the pyre. His whole world could unravel.

He squeezed his head in his hands to quieten the vein throbbing in his temples. At times like this, battling with life's unexpected twists and turns, he could not think clearly: he feared his brain was decaying, that he was becoming doitered. More worrying, all this fash and bother drowned out God's voice. He yearned to return to the north to be with Marjory and Mrs Bowes – loved ones who understood his wretchedness.

A niggle in his side signalled the flare-up of the gravel: a kidney stone would soon be scraping its way down his bladder. He hoped it would pass before being called to the pulpit.

'Ah, Mr Knox, you're proving to be quite an attraction,' a high voice trilled. Above his chorister's immaculate white ruff, Robert Cooche's angelic face beamed. 'The chapel is overflowing with folk eager to hear the provocative Scots preacher's latest assault. Your Lenten sermons proved to be quite a draw but I fear you're fighting a losing battle. As I warned you in our discussion, sin and depravity are rife in this world where evil and good exist side by side.'

A piercing pain from passing gravel made Knox gasp. He grasped the back of the chair to steady himself and gulped for air.

'You're in some distress, I see.' Cooche's face crumpled with concern. He unlocked the vestry cupboard and took out a jewel-encrusted chalice and a flagon. After sprinkling some drops from a phial into the wine, he handed the chalice to

Knox. 'Take this remedy to numb all ills and raise the soul to heaven. I swear by it.' Then the chorister intoned in his high treble, '*Asperges me, Domine*, not with hyssop but laudanum.'

Though grateful for the relief it brought, Knox scowled at the reference.

Cooche winked. 'I know what you're thinking, Mr Knox but take it from me. We'll be chanting Latin prayers and singing the mass ere long.' So saying, he broke into *Te Deum Laudamus*, the papist hymn of joy and thanksgiving, before capering out.

He only meant to goad him, Knox thought, before recalling what Cecil had said about Cooche having friends in very high places. Could the Anabaptist also have foresight of trouble to come? He had laid his thumping head against the chair back, praying for the laudanum to take effect, when the vestry door banged open.

'Ah, Mr Knox! How are you?' Guildford Dudley flicked back an unruly lock of auburn hand and grinned. Garbed in a doublet of finest black velvet slashed with platinum satin and silken hose, he looked very gallant. 'You're the first to hear my good news. I am to marry Lady Jane Grey,' he blurted. 'The king has given his consent – and a generous gift of this rich apparel.' He stretched his arms wide.

Dulled by laudanum, Knox struggled to make sense of his words. Lady Jane?

'My mother had desired a more royal match but my smart sister objected. Since Princess Mary is a Catholic and Princess Elizabeth is a bastard, she suggested Lady Jane instead. A match made in heaven everyone says. The fair sex are such clever creatures, don't you think? Much more shrewd than we dull-witted males! Lady Jane is only sixteen but very learned – eye-wateringly so. Young girls nowadays are all so serious, perhaps too serious,' Guildford chuckled.

'And so well read, always talking of weighty subjects and … oh, I know not what.' His hand fluttered in the air. 'Can you guess her first question to me?' Without waiting for an answer, he prattled on. 'Who's my favourite writer? I must admit I blinked at that, Mr Knox, for between you and me, I rarely read. Whereas hers, she informed me, is Plato. In the original Greek. She even corresponds with some Helvetic theologian – in Latin.' He leant in closer. 'Between you and me, she's well named for she's a grey, mousey creature and not at all as pretty as my beautiful Amy.' His eyes took on a wistful look.

'Nor her delightful twin sisters, Mary and Beth. Such charming creatures. They're like little lapdogs who come when you call, obey all commands and most importantly are forever silent! They would make perfect wives. I used to tease them saying I would wed them both in a trice if Amy hadn't already bewitched me.'

The smile faded from Guildford's face. 'I did love Amy – very much. It broke my heart when father told me she'd forsworn me to wed another. He must be Lancelot to steal my Guinevere away from me. Only a perfect knight could have bewitched my Amy into betrayal.' His handsome features twisted into a mask of grief before smoothing out again.

'Mary says it's for the best. According to my horoscope a match with Amy did not bode well. She has done me a favour, setting me free for a more beneficial liaison. With royal blood flowing through her veins, Lady Jane has a claim to the crown. Besides, our fathers are distant cousins and …' he lowered his voice, 'have been scheming to put her on the throne.'

'Guildford! There you are!' Lady Mary had slipped in silently and was glaring at her brother. 'What have you been saying, you giddy Gillyflower?'

'Only that Jane and I are to be married within the month.'

'You were told to keep your mouth shut, you silly ass,' she hissed before turning to Knox with a forced smile. 'What's that quaint Scots phrase of yours, Mr Knox? *Haud yer wheesht.*'

Guildford pouted his pretty lips. 'Preacher Knox can keep a secret. He'll be as quiet as the grave, is that not so?'

Lady Mary narrowed her eyes. 'He'd better be, if he has no wish to end up in one.'

Guildford cupped his hand to whisper in Knox's ear. 'She also read my cards and says I may even be king one day. Just imagine – me – King Guildford of England!'

'I told you to haud yer wheesht, Guildford. Really, this lad cannot stay his tongue. It will be the death of him.'

She grabbed her brother's sleeve to hustle him out of the vestry but Guildford dug his heels in. From inside his velvet doublet, he pulled out a clarty rag. 'Amy gifted me this handkerchief.' His eyes moistened. 'If you see her, will you please give it to her in memory of me?'

By the time he was called to preach, Knox had passed the gravel stone and his migraine had lifted, but the flash of precious metals and jingle of jewellery from courtiers vying to outsparkle each other in glamour and glitter made his blood boil. Gnashing his teeth, he pulled his Geneva gown round about him. Let proud papist prelates parade themselves in gaudy vestments to do their prattling and prating, but Protestant preachers were humble before the Lord, preferring to preach God's word in a plain black robe.

Unable to stand, the frail young king was carried into the chapel on a bier and laid in front of the pulpit. His starry eyes, fever-bright with fervour, gazed up at Knox. When frightful coughing fits wracked his skeletal frame, a physician held a cloth to catch the foul matter the king spewed up. The greenish yellow phlegm flecked with blood alarmed Knox. The young monarch was not long for this life: the end was in sight.

'Oh Absalom, Absalom!' Knox wailed.

In his dirge of a sermon, he lamented how in biblical times, great princes such as David and Hezekiah had been ill served by crafty counsellors and dissembling hypocrites. Questioning why this was so, he raised his voice to a climax. 'Either the evil counsellors had such an abundance of worldly wisdom, foresight and experience to make them indispensable to government or else they kept their malice so well hidden that no one recognised it.'

Why, if even Jesus counted the traitor Judas among his disciples, what hope was there for a young and innocent king to identify deceit?

The comparison between biblical advisers and treacherous Tudor counsellors sent sniggers and snorts rippling throughout the congregation but the dying king's starry eyes sparkled with unshed tears. When a sunbeam streaming through the window illuminated his rosy-gold hair like a halo of supernatural brightness, a profound sadness and deep foreboding for this angelic prince swamped Knox's soul.

Blinded by tears, he stumbled down the pulpit steps. As he wiped his eyes, John Willock, a fellow Scots preacher took his arm and guided him to the vestry. Recently appointed as chaplain to the Duke of Suffolk, Willock begged leave to present his patron's daughter.

Lady Jane Grey had the pallid complexion of a scholar who spent hours studying indoors. Her braided red hair pulled back from a high forehead and her small mouth tweaked into a tiny bow made her look prim but she held her small, slight frame high and her gold flecked eyes did not flinch from his gaze.

'Your outspoken words verify your reputation as being the only man on this island to speak his mind, Mr Knox. I admire your courage and wisdom and now beg leave to ask your advice. I've received a proposal of marriage from Guildford Dudley. Should I accept?'

Taken by surprise, Knox replied, 'My lord Guildford is a comely young man.'

Her bow-shaped lips puckered. 'But he's a featherbrain. How can I wed a man who never reads? Why do I have to marry at all?' She seemed on the brink of tears.

'It's the natural law, my lady. Matrimony is the perfect state for woman created to be man's helpmeet and bear his children. Forbye, since womankind is rash, foolhardy, and easily swayed, she must be guided by man.'

She pouted. 'You disappoint me, Mr Knox, for sentencing me to submit to my lord Guildford – a lad with nary a whit of wit between his two ears and even less wisdom.'

'Your marriage may not be one of minds, I grant you, my lady, but …' he recalled Guildford's words, 'it's a match made in heaven – that will ensure the future of our cause.'

Her high forehead creased and her eyes widened. 'Why so Mr Knox? Is it true you have the gift of prophecy? What do you foresee?'

'Sadly, I see an early death for King Edward. And, of the three women in line for the throne, you are God's chosen one.'

At these predictions – not only ominous but treasonable – Lady Jane's face turned deathly pale. To reassure her, Knox explained, 'God in his inscrutable wisdom has raised you up to defend the reformed faith. England's destiny lies in your hands, but since a woman cannot rule on her own, you need a consort.'

Now she gave him a long, sceptical look. 'You may have the second sight, Mr Knox, but you fail to see what's in front of your eyes. Guildford is no champion but a chump whose blockhead would be unfit to wear the crown.'

As Lady Jane left on John Willock's arm, Secretary Cecil stepped out of the shadows. 'You've not only irked my Lady Jane, but the Privy Council are vexed by your sermon. Your words were not wise, my friend. Thundering out *the threatenings of God against obstinate rebellers* was a bit too near the bone for comfort. By condemning the councillors so publicly, you only encourage Mary Tudor's papist supporters to pursue her claim to the throne. And that will lead to the restoration of Roman Catholicism. Is that what you wish?'

Knox shook his head. 'Nay, by no means.' But the sight of the congregation glittering in their rich finery still rankled. 'Nevertheless, I cannot stay silent and watch the carrion crows circling to tear up his carcase.'

'You've tried our patience, Mr Knox. By overstepping the line between God and government you've angered the Privy Councillors.'

'If I may not speak my mind I resign my chaplaincy. Forbye, I have no stomach for this. I shall refuse All Hallows and return to Newcastle. Preaching the gospel is more precious to me than promotion.'

Cecil's near-sighted eyes narrowed into chinks. 'You seem to think you're free to go where you will, but that is not so. You're a royal chaplain, subject to the king's will. However, I shall support your refusal of All Hallows – on condition that you go forth and spread the word throughout the shires. My lord Dudley fears a revival of support for Princess Mary amongst the common folk who have no inkling she is Catholic.'

'Where do you plan to dispatch me?'

'To Amersham in Buckinghamshire where John Wycliffe began his ministry.'

'And where the Lollards were burnt at the stake.'

'That will not be your fate, Mr Knox. Not if you keep a discreet silence. But mind and keep to your scripture, Mr Knox. Leave statecraft to those whose sphere it is.'

VIII

The King's Will

Holding faith, and a good conscience;
which some having put away
concerning faith have made shipwreck:
I Timothy 1:19

London, June 1553

On his way back to the Lockes in Cheapside, Knox walked along the riverside path trying to calm the turmoil in his brain. Every time he tried to unfankle himself from the fetters of the English church he was yoked up again. Marjory must think he had deserted her. All he desired was to take the highway north to claim her, but now he was being herded along the road to Amersham, far enough from London to cause least bother – yet near enough for Cecil to keep an eye on him. How could he pull himself out of this quagmire, this swamp? The heat of the afternoon intensified his throbbing head.

He stopped in front of Durham House where a crowd had gathered around soldiers hammering stakes into the ground. Their comrades were dragging two prisoners along the sward: blood dripped from the gash where their ears had been cut off. As the soldiers stripped the two wretches to the waist and chained them to the posts, Knox's blood ran cold. When the soldiers flexed their knouts, the jeering crowd fell silent.

Taking it in turns to whip their bare backs, the torturers ripped the skin from their shoulders down to their buttocks. Knox had not only witnessed sailors being scourged in the galleys but his own back bore the scars of countless floggings. The sight of this woman's pale, flaccid skin and the sound of her high-pitched shrieks set his teeth on edge. He flinched at every lash, feeling their pain and stood transfixed as their skin peeled away in blood-soaked strips. Only when the pair fell to the ground unconscious did the brutes cease scourging.

He grabbed hold of a soldier's sleeve. 'What monster has ordered such a spectacle?'

'The Duke of Northumberland. All loudmouths who spread malicious slander are to have their ears cut off – with a flogging for good measure. Dare to call my lord Dudley a monster again and you'll be next in line for a beating.' The soldier snarled at them and flexed his knout.

Knox glanced towards the library window where a hand drew the green velvet curtains tightly shut.

By the time he arrived at the Padlock, his headache had intensified into a full-

127

blown migraine blurring his vision. Describing the brutal scene to the menfolk – it would be too distressing for the ladies – Knox dug his fingers into his palms to ward off pain.

'Why is he torturing the lieges?'

'Malicious tongues have ignited Dudley's tinderbox temper,' Anthony Hickman said. 'They say the great tyrant Northumberland is poisoning the king so as to take the crown for himself and divorcing his wife to marry Princess Elizabeth.'

'It's also rumoured he's been seeking the support of King Henri and plotting to hand the country over to the French,' Thomas Locke added.

Knox rubbed his temples. 'That is hard to believe.'

'This isn't idle tittle-tattle, Mr Knox. Our Worshipful Company of Mercers has a network of spies that Cecil would envy. The French ambassador was seen being smuggled in the back door. Henri would stoop at nothing to gain control of England. His ward, Mary Stewart, has a strong claim to the throne.'

'That can never be,' Knox replied. 'In his will, Harry Coppernose barred the Scots Stewarts from the English throne.'

'Never underestimate the duke's cunning,' Thomas replied. 'Wills can be overruled. Dealing with the French is not such a cock-eyed idea. When Mary becomes queen of France, she'll need a regent in Scotland to govern for her. Her mother won't live forever. In this way he plans to unite the two kingdoms.'

'Practising which religion?' Knox asked.

Hickman shrugged. 'Whichever suits *His Highness's* purpose.'

The next morning, while waiting at the quayside for the skiff to take him upriver, Knox bade farewell to the Lockes.

Anna touched his sleeve. 'We're sorry to see you go, John. We shall miss you.' Her dove grey eyes moistened.

Clasping his hands behind his back, Harry Locke rocked back and forth on his heels. 'Trying times, but right shall prevail. I've heard rumours that those who now fawn over Dudley will soon sell him.'

The sound of loud gunfire coming from ships on the Thames made them all jump.

'Are Canons Cranmer and Cox so glad to see the back of my carcase they're firing a farewell salute?' Knox remarked.

Henry laughed and pointed to a barge flying the royal pennant being rowed down the Thames. 'His Grace is being moved upriver to Greenwich Palace where the cleaner air is judged to be more beneficial for his lungs.'

Like a flock of scavenging seagulls, a flotilla of wherries carrying colourful courtiers glide behind the royal barge. One of them split away and drifted towards the quayside to let a royal herald leap out.

'Good sirs, will you please direct me to the Locke's house in Cheapside.'

Henry cast his wife an anxious glance before answering, 'I am Mercer Locke. May I ask your business?'

'My business is with Mr Knox: I have a message for him.'

His friends looked worried but Knox gave a resigned shrug. What will be will be, he thought. Forbye, what was the alternative? Jump in the river? He stepped forward.

'His Majesty requests your presence at Greenwich,' the herald said. 'You are to come with me at once.'

Their wherry followed the flotilla and as the royal barge approached the Tower of London, more cannons fired. To Knox, the great booms sounded a sombre note of farewell reinforcing his presentiment. This was the monarch's final passage: King Edward VI would never again return to the gloomy rooms of Whitehall.

Greenwich Palace

In the king's antechamber, Dudley gripped Knox's arm. 'What are you doing here?' he growled. 'You should be on your way to Amersham.'

'At His Majesty's request. He wishes to speak with me. Perhaps I may be of some comfort in his dying hours.'

'The king is well enough and whatever sickness he *may* have been suffering from he's now improving. The physicians assure me His Majesty will live to a ripe old age.'

'Of course they will say that – the punishment for predicting the king's demise is death. To save their own skin these quacksalvers are scared to tell the truth.'

'Not only physicians. Girolamo Cardano predicts a lifespan of at least forty years.'

Knox scoffed. 'The much-vaunted Italian magus is a spendthrift who'll say anything for a groat. I don't need to cast a horoscope to foresee our monarch will not see his sixteenth birthday. His fate is clearly inscribed on his wretched face.'

A purple flush crept up Dudley's neck: he drew Knox aside. 'If you don't believe me, Mr Knox, will you believe the truth of your own eyes? Come. See for yourself.'

In the bedchamber the royal grooms were lifting the monarch on to a chair by the window. Henry Sidney balanced the crown cautiously on his friend's head with one hand and raised his powerless arm with the other so that Edward could give the royal wave.

'To scotch rumours of his demise the monarch is presenting himself to his subjects,' Dudley said. 'Now do you see?'

Tears pricked Knox's eyes at the sorry sight. 'What I see, my lord, is a pitiful figure dressed up like a doll in his velvet robes of state and propped up by his puppet masters for the mob to witness. Had Henry Sidney not caught him he would have flopped onto the floor. What a pathetic charade. You must face reality. Our monarch is not going to get well.'

When Knox was next admitted to the chamber, the king was lying in bed with his eyes closed, scarcely breathing. The room was stuffy and humming with bluebottles. The scented smoke from burning herbs could not disguise the odour of decay nor deter the swarm of flies buzzing around.

Knox fought back tears as he gazed upon the king's emaciated body. The shrunken head was covered in a linen cap to hide his balding skull. Poor wee lad, he thought. He craves to curl up into a ball – like a newborn babe yearning to return to his tragic mother's womb. He swatted away a fly landing on his blue-tinged lips.

Nicholas Throckmorton, the king's favourite, who was hovering round the bed, pressed Knox's hand. 'Thank you for coming. I can't think what to do to entertain His Majesty. He has no wish to play board or card games.'

'Perhaps a prayer or two will comfort his soul,' Knox said.

At the sound of his voice, the king's eyelids flickered and opened. He fixed milky eyes on Knox. 'Ah, it's you. I fain would hear my favourite passages from scripture – the Psalms of David.'

While Knox leafed through his Bible, Throckmorton paced up and down twiddling his thumbs and tunelessly humming to himself. Longing to throttle the glaikit courtier, Knox located Psalm XXIII.

The Lord is my shepherd, I shall not want,' he began. Tears blurred his eyes as he recited the lines, *'Yea though I walk through the valley of the shadow of death I will fear no evil for thou art with me; thy rod and thy staff shall comfort me.'*

'Haud yer wheesht,' a sharp voice said. While Knox's head reared up, Throckmorton's jaw dropped.

'Not you, Mr Knox.' Lady Mary shot him a conspiratorial look before whispering, 'That silenced the fool's maddening drone. Is his Majesty awake? We need him to sit up. My father has a document for him to sign.'

'By your leave, my lady, if I may finish reading this psalm,' Knox muttered. 'It greatly comforts His Grace.'

Lady Mary inclined her head. 'Forgive me. Please go on.'

'Surely goodness and mercy shall follow me all the days of my life; and I shall dwell in the house of the Lord for ever.' Knox paused before adding, *'Consider mine enemies for they are many and they hate me with cruel hatred. Let integrity and uprightness preserve me. Amen.'*

'Amen,' the king whispered.

'Amen to that,' Lady Mary said. 'Though I don't recall those last lines in the twenty-third Psalm.'

'Nevertheless, in the circumstances, they are right and fitting would you not agree?'

Her eyes blazed at him. 'Let us look upon his affliction and his pain, shall we?'

As she pulled down the coverlet, her eyes widened at the broad bands of linen crisscrossing the king's puny frame. 'What have these leeches done now?' She crooked a finger at the chief physician. 'Why is the king swaddled like this? You're suffocating his lungs. He can't breathe.'

With jaw clenched the physician retorted, 'His Grace keeps clasping his knees to his chest, but we need to keep his limbs straight.'

Lady Mary lifted up the sheet. 'Look! His arms and legs have swollen up like pork sausages. The bandages are too tight. And his fingers and toes are turning black!' She pointed to a foot peeking out from a bandage and drew away in disgust. 'His flesh is putrid. Can't you smell the stench?'

The physician glared at her. 'We shall set maggots to feed on the decaying flesh.'

'Nay, they will be feasting on him soon enough. Have you carrion crows nothing better to offer? Bloodletting with leeches and cutting his veins have only worsened his condition. There's scarcely a drop of blood left in his veins. You're only plunging him into deeper and deeper pain.'

'We're doing everything in our power, my lady. We physicians have taken the Hippocratic oath.' He gave her a scathing look.

'Above all do no harm,' Lady Mary said crisply. 'Isn't that your vow? Hippocrates would be ashamed of you. You're making our monarch suffer a living hell.'

'I have private business with His Majesty,' a commanding voice broke in. 'Sit him up and then leave.'

Obediently the physicians bowed to his bidding, but Knox remained behind. Lord Dudley glowered at him. 'And you, too, Mr Knox. This is highly confidential.'

As Knox turned to leave, the king stirred. 'Where's my sister, Princess Elizabeth?' he whimpered. 'I long to see her before I die.'

When Lady Mary shot her father a worried glance, he patted the bedcover. 'You will, Your Highness,' he replied. 'Why, she's on her way at this very moment.'

Closing the door, Knox detected deceit in his voice: Lord Dudley was lying.

In the privy chamber, members of the Privy Council were huddled in disparate groups, whispering and glancing furtively over their shoulders at each other. In the sweltering heat of the August day, Sir Robert Bowes, Master of the Rolls and Marjory's uncle, mopped his brow, sweating beneath his state robes of heavy velvet and brocade. When Knox approached him, Bowes pointedly turned away.

'Mr Knox,' a sharp voice said. Archbishop Cranmer rose from the chess game he'd been playing with Bishop Ridley and confronted him. 'You're free to leave. We shall attend the king in his final hours.'

After a brief glance at the chessboard, Knox moved one of the pieces. 'Checkmate. If it pleases Your Grace, I should like to keep watch awhile.' Ignoring Cranmer's louring look, he settled on a window seat and opened his Bible.

Appearing at last, Dudley called on the council members to gather round the writing table where he smoothed out a parchment. 'His Majesty has altered his will and now bids you to sanction it.'

Cranmer scowled. 'In what way has it been altered? The Device for the Succession stipulated that if Edward died without issue, the throne would pass to the heirs male of Lady Frances, Duchess of Suffolk and, failing that, the heirs male of her daughter, Lady Jane Grey.'

'That is correct but with the king's failing health, there is no time for either lady to produce a male heir.' Dudley's tone was tetchy. 'It's the king's wish to go to his grave knowing his sister Mary shall never inherit the crown. Only then shall he rest in peace.'

Cranmer squinted at him. 'I repeat – in what way has it been changed?'

'Read for yourself, archbishop.'

As he scoured the will, Cranmer's face grew livid. 'I see the wording in the provision *the heirs male of Lady Jane Grey* has been altered. The crown will now pass to *Lady Jane and her heirs male.*' He glowered at Dudley. 'Who made the alteration?'

'As Lord President of the Council, I did, with Henry Sidney as witness. He inked the pen and handed it to His Majesty who wrote it in his own hand.' Dudley said, striving to restrain his temper. 'It's not as if it's a great change.'

'Perhaps not, but it benefits Lady Jane. Who happens to be your son's wife. Besides, this Device clearly contravenes the Third Succession Act. I wish to speak to His Majesty. Alone.'

As Cranmer stepped towards the door, Dudley barred his way. 'That would not be wise. I shall advise His Majesty to assemble all his councillors in order to ask them to support his last wishes.'

Edward Montague, the Lord Chief Justice spoke up. 'Archbishop Cranmer is right. These proceedings are patently illegal, my lord.'

'In what way? The sovereign's will overrides any law. And for daring to disobey His Majesty's explicit command you are both traitors,' Dudley warned. 'Furthermore, you and the archbishop are gutless cowards and I'd fight in my shirt with any man in this quarrel.' Dudley pulled at the fastenings on his doublet and put up a threatening fist.

With a languid wave of his hand, Montague withdrew his objection, a signal for the other councillors to line up and sign the king's will.

Dudley slumped onto the window seat beside Knox. 'Lily-livered poltroons every one of them. You understand why I had to do it, don't you, Mr Knox? So as to protect the Protestant succession and ensure England remains a Protestant state, for if the Catholic Mary Tudor grabs the throne, England is lost.'

Though Knox appreciated the ends, the means – and Dudley's motives – were more questionable.

'I guarantee when this is all over you shall have your pick of posts in the English church,' Dudley went on. 'How does the Archbishop of Canterbury suit? I promise to give you a free hand in religious affairs.'

A tempting offer, Knox thought, but could he trust the duke?

Scanning the line of councillors, Dudley frowned. 'Secretary Cecil seems to be absent. His signature is necessary.'

'It isn't like Sir William to miss such a momentous occasion,' Knox said.

Dudley tapped his chin. 'Aye. What does the Raven know that I don't?'

Greenwich, Sunday, 2 July 1553

Just before the start of the Sunday morning service, Dudley hurried into the chapel shooing a forlorn-looking Cecil before him. As Knox moved along the bench to make space for them, Dudley shot him a wink.

'The honourable member of the Privy Council has been languishing in his privy,' he said. 'My daughter's vile concoction – spearmint, liverwort and cinnamon, I believe – has cleared his weak stomach and invigorated his brain. Now that he's thinking more clearly he has chosen pragmatism over cowardice. Is that not so, Sir William?'

Looking jaundiced and jaded, Cecil only glowered in reply and hugged his stomach. Then, during the prayers for the faithful, Cecil's leg started twitching. 'Mr Knox, did I hear aright? Did the archbishop omit to pray for the Princesses Mary and Elizabeth?'

When Knox nodded, Cecil's long face sagged. 'What's he up to?'

Accosting Dudley afterwards, Cecil's voice shook. 'That omission was a grave mistake on the archbishop's part, for it clearly indicates the king's will has been altered. This palace is a sieve, full of holes. The news will be winging its way to them now. We've given the princesses time to prepare.'

Brushing off his secretary's hand, Dudley scoffed. 'You disappoint me, Sir William. If I hadn't come to you with Lady Mary's receipt and forced you to sign the king's will, why, I do believe you'd have been off and running. I never took you for a coward under fire, Sir William.'

When Cecil's yellow face flushed with shame, Dudley put a hand on his shoulder. 'I'm giving you the chance to earn your spurs. Don't let me down this time. Princess

Mary is on her way to London to see her dying brother. We must detain her.'

Cecil shook his head. 'My sources tell me she's now en route to Keninghall, a Howard stronghold in Norfolk. With their support, she could pose a real threat.'

'A mere woman, Mary will never gather enough military to press her claim. I suspect she'll make her way to the port and flee abroad. To Flanders, if she has any sense, and throw herself upon the mercy of her cousin, Emperor Charles. If so, let it be known she'll be given safe passage.'

Cecil gave a high-pitched squeak of alarm. 'My lord, I beg to differ. This is no *mere woman* but a Tudor princess with a strong sense of her birthright. She's been planning her strategy for months. You greatly underestimate her resolve under fire. Possession of power is a matter of the greatest importance. Will you suffer Princess Mary to escape and not secure her person?'

The thought that Catholic Mary Tudor might prevail filled Knox with dread. A Catholic queen on the throne was monstrous. It must be prevented at all costs. Breaching courtly protocol, he spoke up. 'My lord, forgive me if I speak out of turn. However weak his stomach, Cecil has a shrewd head on his shoulders, my lord. If I were you, I would heed his advice.'

Dudley shrugged his shoulders impatiently. 'Then I shall order my son Robert to bring her to London. A small company of horse should suffice. Meanwhile, Mr Knox, you will set off immediately for Amersham to resume your mission: sound the trumpet for Lady Jane Grey and toll the knell for Mary Tudor.'

IX

The Great Shipwreck

> O my good lord, remember how sweet life is,
> and how bitter ye contrary.
> *Last Words*
> John Dudley, Duke of Northumberland,
> 16th Century

Amersham, Buckinghamshire, July 1553

On 6th July, black clouds sweeping up the Thames valley turned the afternoon sky as dark as night. Towards evening, thunder cracked and a powerful storm flashed over southern England. Knox and his congregation were leaving the church in Amersham after evening prayers when forked lightning struck the steeple. Knox looked up in fear and awe before bowing his head.

'The king is dead,' he said quietly. 'Long live Queen Jane.'

'How do you ken?' Jamie asked.

'What the spaewives call the weird feeling has come over me, Jamie. Let's pray the people take the new queen to their hearts.'

Despite his misgivings about a female ruler, Knox had obeyed Dudley's order to garner support for Queen Jane, consoling himself with the thought that the reins of power would pass to her consort, Guildford. While he preached on her behalf, the local landowner, Sir Edward Hastings, raised 4,000 men for Queen Jane.

But nine days later in Amersham market square Hastings proclaimed, 'God save Queen Mary!' and showered down a bonnetful of gold coins to the jubilant crowd.

Knox knew then all was lost.

'What do we do now?' Jamie asked. 'Stay here?'

'Look at the fickle mob, Jamie, scrambling for their thirty pieces of silver. Nay, it's not safe here. We'll go back to London and seek refuge with the Lockes.'

Before leaving Amersham, Knox preached a final sermon.

'O England, how is God's wrath kindled against thee! A woman on the throne is a curse, a freak of nature, my dear brethren, and heaven and earth are in revolt. Hail as red as blood lies upon the grass in London gardens. What dreadful monsters have lately been born in England! A child with one body, two heads, four feet and hands. Cataracts have flooded houses and turned city streets into rivers; trees have been torn up by the roots and whirled through the air. These celestial signs forecast ruin and desolation, division and bloodshed throughout the realm.'

He ended with a warning to Queen Mary. 'O England, if you contract marriage,

135

confederacy or league with such princes as do maintain and advance idolatry then assuredly, you shall be plagued and brought to desolation!'

London, August 1553

'Hark at that clamour, Jamie. Church bells that have lain silent for years now peal night and day.' The glorious carillons that greeted them on the outskirts of London did not resonate in Knox's heart.

After struggling to negotiate their nags through the crowded streets, they were brought to a halt near Bishopsgate. Guards posted along the way were straining to hold back an angry mob eager to tear their victim to shreds.

'Traitor traitor! Death to the traitor! Murderer! Poisoner!'

'Look, it's Lord Dudley,' Jamie said.

By his scarlet robe shall ye know him. The sight of the duke in his mud-bespattered crimson cloak astride his black destrier stunned Knox. For scarlet also signified the gore of martyrs. With velvet cap in hand, Dudley was bowing to the mob in a desperate effort to elicit their compassion, but men spat on him while women and children hurled muck and animal dung. Loutish lads leapt up to rip his cloak off his back. Whether for shame or protection, Dudley kept his face covered with one hand until reaching the Tower. Meanwhile, his retainers were tearing their badges out of their caps out and trampling on them.

And so they all forsook him and fled.

Cheapside, London, 21 August 1553

'Tower Hill is crawling with ghouls waiting to drool over Lord Dudley's hanging.' Anthony Hickman strove to calm the tremble in his voice as he reported back to the faithful few. Knox and Jamie had joined Henry and Anna Locke, their family and other faithful Protestants who'd taken refuge at the Padlock. Every so often Hickman ventured out to bring back snippets of news.

'He's asked for a confessor to repent of his sins. He's been taken to St Peter ad Vincula, the Tower of London chapel, to hear mass and take communion.'

'What?' No words could have shocked and angered Knox more. 'He must have been tortured to partake of the papist sacraments.'

Hickman pulled a doubtful face. 'Perhaps. Because of this, Bishop Gardiner has gone to plead mercy from the queen.'

'That's a papist ruse,' Knox said. 'The bishop is scheming to make Dudley's conversion a triumph for the Catholic cause. Does the duke believe his living penitence will be more useful than his death?'

Though pierced to the core by this betrayal, Knox was not altogether surprised.

It confirmed what he always suspected: Dudley may have been a fearless soldier but he was never a true believer and trifled with religion for his own selfish ends. Having climbed to the highest rung of the ladder, he'd fallen from grace like Lucifer. The cause of his downfall was lack of God.

At supper, Hickman brought the latest news. 'If Dudley hoped to gain a pardon by his conversion, he was greatly misled. Emperor Charles V's ambassador has advised Queen Mary not to spare his life. However, the duke will not suffer the grotesque humiliation of being hanged, drawn and quartered: his head is to be severed from his body by the deadly stroke of the axe.'

'I wonder how he'll face his death?' his wife Rose mused. 'With grace and bravery, or disgrace and cowardice? Will he lose his nerve at the sight of the gallows? Will he be too fuelled with grog to care? Will his dying speech be one of contrition or defiance?'

Hickman grimaced. 'Rose, don't be such a ghoul. You're worse than the ravens in the Tower that feast on the corpses of the slain.'

Undeterred Rose continued, 'How a man faces death tells much about his character, don't you think, Mr Knox?'

Knox fell quiet for these questions also niggled him. If called upon to be a martyr how would he behave? Would he follow the example of those martyrs Wishart and Hamilton who'd met their fate fearlessly and defiantly? Or would he capitulate like Dudley and recant?

'Aye,' he replied at last, 'Rose is right. The execution will be at the usual time – eight of the clock. I shall rise early to get a place near the scaffold.'

Anna nearly dropped the soup tureen. 'You're not going to the beheading are you? Lord Dudley was your patron. If recognised, you risk arrest. You must not go.'

'Once Mr Knox makes up his mind, nothing will stop him, my love,' Henry Locke said. 'Do not fret, I shall go with him and keep him safe.'

Tower Hill, 22 August 1553

'What in Christ's holy name is this? A man's execution or a carnival?' Knox muttered.

They had set out early before dawn but Tower Hill was already bustling with brewers carting beer barrels and vendors and hawkers setting up stalls and booths. Minstrels and songsters strolled through the crowd while jugglers and tumblers entertained the spectators in the balconies and windows overlooking the scaffold.

'Plenty of folk are willing to pay the inflated rent to watch the macabre performance in comfort,' Locke said. He stopped a baker's lad balancing a tray on his head and bought two freshly baked mutton pies. He handed one to Knox. 'To break your fast.'

Knox shook his head – he had no appetite – but it didn't go to waste for Locke wolfed down both.

'And the balladeers broadsheets are selling like hot pies,' Locke said. 'Hark at this one describing Dudley's dastardly deeds. Mary Tudor is now a saint while John Dudley is the great devil. The duke is not only a traitor but a murderer – for poisoning King Edward.'

'It wasn't the duke who poisoned him but the royal physicians with their potions,' Knox snarled. 'They tortured the poor lad to death with their treatments. Stretching him on the rack would have been more merciful.' He snatched the broadsheet from his astonished friend and tore it up, stamping the scraps into the mud.

'See how quickly the mood of the mob can switch: from reverence to ridicule in the twinkling of an eye.'

He scowled at a peddler hawking souvenirs – remnants of Dudley's infamous scarlet cloak. 'Now they're casting lots upon his garment like the Roman centurions at the foot of Christ's cross.'

With the crowd as tightly packed as herring in a barrel, there was no room to sit down. For a better view, some spectators balanced on stools while others paid a silver groat to be hoisted up onto a blacksmith's hefty shoulders. Seized by cramp in his legs, Knox stamped his feet to make the blood flow. The waiting was tortuous.

A roar from the front signalled John Dudley's appearance on the scaffold and then a hush fell over the crowd: the duke was making his final speech. Knox craned forward to catch his words.

'I have always been a Roman Catholic and only feigned to be a reformist for King Edward's sake.'

At first Knox could not believe his ears but why should Dudley's deceit surprise him? That was bad enough, but the Judas's tongue spewed forth more lies.

'And I blame these new preachers for seducing me with their false and erroneous preaching and infecting me with their plague upon the realm.' He raised his voice above jeers from the crowd. 'Beware these seditious preachers and teachers of new doctrine, who pretend to preach God's word, but in very deed they preach their own fancies. They know not today what they would have tomorrow. They open the book, but they cannot shut it again.'

Locke's generous mouth dropped open. 'Is he pointing the finger at you?'

'Now the abyss has opened up beneath him, the miserable man has no faith, no hope and no shame,' Knox muttered.

Towards the end of his speech, Dudley knelt and a deathly hush descended. 'I have one more thing to do. I beseech you all to believe that I die in the Catholic faith.' With that he took his time to recite the Latin prayers – *Miserere*, the *De Profundis*, and the *Paternoster.*

After waiting patiently for him to finish, the executioner begged the condemned man's pardon. Dudley leant forward to stretch himself upon the beam, but rose again to fiddle with the blindfold.

'What's he doing?' an irritated voice shouted.

'Praying and delaying!' another replied.

'Does he think his prayers will save his life and get him a last minute reprieve?'

'Now, he's making the sign of the cross!'

For Knox, this final betrayal was not only a stab in the heart but a knife skewering his bowels, drawing out his entrails. At last John Dudley laid his head upon the block. The axe fell on his neck, severing his fine head and spurting a scarlet fountain onto the block. *Beware the man in red.*

'My lord Dudley has sounded the death knell to our cause,' Knox muttered. 'Our champion has betrayed us.'

'Listen to the baying mob,' Locke burbled in alarm. 'They're turning before our very eyes.' His voice trembled and his florid face had paled to blotchy pink. 'I must get back to Anna and the children.'

As they turned to go, a hand tugged at Knox's gown. 'Follow me,' the dwarf said. 'If you want to save your head.'

Had it been wise to come? Knox thought as he paced up and down outside Cecil's study. Was the Raven at this very moment signing his death warrant? His warning not to meddle in politics was spitting in the wind as far as Knox was concerned. Discreet silence was contrary to his nature. When he was finally admitted, Cecil was busy leafing through sheaves of documents and scribbling on them. With a flourish he put down his pen and blotted the parchment.

'There, that's the last one. The poor lass had no time to sign many royal decrees.'

Knox peered at the document: the secretary had crossed out the signature, Jane the Queen, and written beside it in Latin, *Jana non Regina.* The callous bureaucrat then gathered up the papers and filed them away in a strong box.

He heaved a sigh. 'The first woman to be declared queen of England in her own right has been deposed. It's a great pity, for Lady Jane would have made a virtuous monarch. For her age and sex, she was a brave soul. She stood up to Dudley, you know, and scotched his schemes by refusing to allow Guildford to be king. It wasn't right, she said.' His wistful eyes looked beyond Knox. 'Queen for only nine days. A significant number, for nine is the number of months a woman carries a child: it signals both the end of her labour and the beginning of life. And nine days is the length of time an illness runs its course.'

'As the Scots saying goes: *A wonder lasts but days nine days afore the puppy's een are open,*' Knox remarked.

'In truth, for Lady Jane has accepted her fate gracefully.'

'Is there really no hope for her now?' Knox asked.

Cecil took off his spectacles and rubbed his eyes, red–rimmed from lack of sleep. 'My lord Dudley should have listened to me. I warned him to secure Princess – I mean Queen – Mary but he kept delaying. When he did rush off, not only was it bad timing, it was bad tactics. He should have stayed in London. While his men's feet marched forward, their hearts marched backwards, and his army melted away to Mary's side. Dudley may have been a brilliant soldier but he failed to take into account the people's will.'

Cecil squinted at Knox. 'For you see, the people of England might loathe papacy but they abhor injustice even more. In their eyes, Mary is Henry VIII's legitimate heir and Lady Jane Grey was an imposter. Now we must accept the situation and move on, and that includes supporting the rightful monarch.'

Knox scoffed. 'So you're now serving an ungodly rule.' While faith always came first and policy second for Knox, the reverse was true for these new men who'd swap religion to gain power and further their careers.

'I am the people's servant, Mr Knox, not God's. A modest scribe who has dedicated my pen to the service of the state regardless of whoever holds the reins of power. Since the people have chosen Mary Tudor as their sovereign, I shall offer Her Grace my humble services.'

'Then may I suggest the willow as your emblem, loyal secretary. No matter which way the wind bends, the willow will aye take root again.'

Cecil tilted his head. 'Mayhap, but not only is the wind blowing against you, Mr Knox, you have no patron to lean on. Your preaching license will be revoked —especially after your last sermon at Amersham.'

Balancing the eyeglasses on the bridge of his nose, he glared at Knox. 'Not only did you preach against idolatry – one of your favourite themes – you also railed against a queen on the throne. Is this true?'

Knox knitted his brows. 'All I asked was for God to illuminate the heart of our sovereign lady, Queen Mary, and inflame the hearts of her council with his true fear and love.'

Cecil harrumphed. 'As if Mary, a devout Catholic who has suffered for her faith, would take heed of you and *suffer no papistry to prevail in this realm* as you insisted. But to lambast her cousin, Charles V, the Holy Roman Emperor, as being *no less an enemy unto Christ than Nero ever was* – that's overstepping the mark, Mr Knox.

'Furthermore, if Queen Mary should become espoused to his son, Philip, this will be viewed not only as a direct challenge to the queen but an insult to her prospective father-in-law. Your misplaced words have shocked the Imperial Ambassador presently prowling around the court. Monsieur Renard, a wily fox as his name suggests, has complained you've preached scandalous things to rouse up the people. You understand what I'm saying, Mr Knox.'

'I only say the truth,' Knox retorted.

'I advised discreet silence and instead you bawled from the pulpit. These words may well come back to haunt you, for if the emperor's wrath is roused, who knows what vengeance he may seek.'

'Vengeance is mine sayeth the Lord.'

Cecil's shortsighted eyes narrowed. 'That may well be, but your day of judgement may come sooner than you think. Bishop Gardiner who is in charge of our inquisition has asked me for a list of all traitors.'

X

Aftermath

> The last trumpet is blowing within the realm of England,
> and therefore everyone ought to prepare himself for battle.
>
> John Knox, 16th Century

London, 1 October 1553

The bonfire ablaze at Cheapside Cross to celebrate Queen Mary's coronation kindled no warmth in Knox. Apprentices and barrow boys flung faggots and firewood to fuel the pyre, taking turns to leap over the flames. Foolish lads – they wouldn't be so merry and blithe when the Catholic queen stoked the fires.

Atop St Paul's spire, rigged with yards like a ships mast, a reckless – or drunken – sailor sat astride the weathercock, five hundred feet in the air, waving a bottle.

In the street, women ran back and forth from their houses, their arms laden with all kinds of foodstuffs – roast capons and chickens, pies, tarts – to heap on trestle tables. Their menfolk rolled out barrels of beer and ale and stacked them along the cobbles. But Knox would not be joining the party.

While all England rejoiced, Knox wept.

At the Padlock, Knox considered how to comfort his faithful flock gathered together like the apostles after Christ's crucifixion to lament. This motley crew looked to Knox for guidance but their captain was glum.

'This signifies the great shipwreck of all our hopes and achievements. They will rue it long and bitterly in more places than London. But for the present we must be prepared to stand trial for our faith.'

When the front door rattled, three widowed refugees huddled together like frightened kittens but it was Thomas Locke returning from the Mercers' Hall where he'd dared to go for news.

'Are you the dove bearing the olive branch of hope from Noah's ark – or the corbie messenger?' Knox asked.

'The bishops Cranmer, Latimer and Ridley have been rounded up and imprisoned in the Tower,' Thomas reported. 'If found guilty of treason, they will be condemned to death.' At this the widows squeaked in fear.

'But the people are hostile to the prospect of a Catholic Spanish king who will lead us to war,' Thomas went on.

Knox perked up. 'So there is hope? Once folk have recovered from their drunken jubilation, God's trumpeter shall preach a series of sermons to warn them that the last trumpet is blowing within the realm of England. Everyone should gird himself for battle. For if the trumpet is silenced, it shall never blow again with such force till the second coming of Jesus Christ.'

All nodded enthusiastically except Thomas. 'Not so fast, brother Knox. Further preaching would not be wise. Evangelical orators who hold outdoor meetings and scatter inflammatory placards about the streets are being arrested. But more seriously, parliament has decreed that, as from 21ˢᵗ of December, no form of service other than the mass shall be permitted.'

'Mass!' Knox snarled. 'The mass is not only a papist abomination but a pagan sacrifice! How can they condone idolatry?'

Thomas nodded. 'More dangerously, Queen Mary's decree of universal toleration has been overturned.'

Anna's face crumpled. 'When she forbade her Protestant and Catholic subjects to interrupt each other's services, I had thought the queen to be merciful.'

'The amnesty for heretics expires on 20ᵗʰ of December,' Thomas said. 'You have three options, brother Knox – to lie, fly or die.'

'To lie? You mean recant? That I shall never do. I would rather die first.' Knox raised a clenched fist in the air, but when Anna touched his arm, his face softened.

'In that case, the only option is to fly,' Thomas said quietly.

Knox glanced round at his flock. Though he knew them all to be stalwart supporters, he could detect fear flickering in their eyes. He couldn't put his dear friends in any more danger.

'I must leave England,' he said, sending the three widows into floods of tears.

'What about Marjory?' Anna asked. 'She must be distraught.'

Knox bowed his head. 'Marjory begs to be at my side in coming trouble and I fain would take her with me. But with her father refusing to acknowledge our handfasting, I have no claim on her. So far she's resisting his demand to convert to the Roman Church. She's risking her life for me.'

'She's a brave girl,' Anna said. 'You're fortunate to find such a treasure, John. There must be some way you can free her from his grasp. You must never give up hope.'

'Aye, I promised my wee bird to *Keep Tryst*. You're right. There may be a way.'

He took out the letter he'd received that morning from Mrs Bowes. 'She urges me to petition the captain's brother and remind Sir Robert of the favour I did him in the past.'

'That sounds promising, John. What was the favour?'

'After I put in a good word for him to Lord Dudley, he recommended him to the Privy Council and then appointed him Master of the Rolls.'

Thomas rubbed his chin. 'But where does he stand now? Sir Robert may have supported Dudley and Lady Jane Grey but I hear he's now professed undying loyalty to Queen Mary. Like so many turncoats, he's hoping she'll pardon him, but nothing is certain in these uncertain times. I wager he lives in fear of the knock at the door.'

'He may owe me a favour but his imprisonment after the battle of Haddon Rig may have turned him against the Scots,' Knox replied. 'He may not look kindly on my suit.' Weariness crushed him.

Anna tugged his sleeve. 'Surely it's worth a try, John.' An impish smile twitched her lips and her dove grey eyes twinkled. 'Besides, faint heart never won fair lady.'

As Knox passed through the archway into Rolls Court, he glanced backwards into Chancery Lane to check if he was being followed. Reassured, he knocked on the grand door of Rolls House.

'Did anyone see you come here?' Sir Robert's voice was edgy and his lined face tense. 'Bishop Gardiner has spies posted everywhere. If you've come on behalf of Henry Grey, then I have no wish to hear.'

Knox shook his head. He, too, had heard rumours that Grey was conspiring to restore his daughter, Jane, on the throne but even knowing about the plot was tantamount to treason. 'I've no wish to put you in danger, Sir Robert, only to crave your kindness. I fain would wed your niece, Marjory, and I come to beg your support and ask you to petition your brother for his consent.'

Sir Robert put up a defensive hand. 'Staunch your bleeding heart, Mr Knox, for I will not be persuaded. Where's the use? If parliament repeals all clerical marriages, married priests will either have to put away their wives or resign.'

Knox struggled to douse his fury. 'I'm no longer a Catholic priest, nor ever will be again. May I remind my lord of the favour shown to you in the past?'

A crimson flush crept up Sir Robert's neck. 'I'm no longer Master of the Rolls. I've seen fit to relinquish that post. The tide has turned and the time has come to turn with it, but you seem hell-bent on offending the new order. Do you deny censuring the queen's marriage and insulting Emperor Charles from the pulpit? What were you thinking of? With these words you've signed your own death warrant. You're a marked man. How could I possibly consent to my niece being yoked to a renegade such as you? Begone, Mr Knox, and never darken my door again.'

Infuriated by his ingratitude and pierced by his spiteful words, Knox consoled himself with the thought that one day Sir Robert would suffer divine punishment for his cruel disdain. In the meantime, he was prepared to risk life and limb in pursuit of his beloved Marjory.

XI

Skeletons in the Closet

I know how to content myself in others lust;
Of little stuff unto myself to weave a web of trust;
And how to hide my harms with soft dissembling chere,
When in my face the painted thoughts would outwardly appear.
Description of the Fickle Affections, Pangs, and Slights of Love
Henry Howard, Earl of Surrey, 16th Century

Norham Castle, December 1553

Locked up in the turret of Norham Castle, Marjory shivered, struggling to keep warm. Hoar frost sparkled on the iron bedstead and a sheet of ice lay on the chamber pot. Everything was cold to the touch. There was no fireplace only a brazier to take the chill off the air and the only light came through a narrow arrow slit. The December days were short and Marjory dreaded when darkness fell.

She tugged the bristly blanket more tightly and hobbled over to the arrow slit where a shower of sleety rain blasted her face. High in the night sky the old moon lay in the young moon's arms, casting an eerie glow over the landscape sparkling with frost. A bad omen, Molly believed, and though Marjory always spurned such superstitions, it deepened her disquiet. Goose pimples prickled her skin and her teeth chattered. She strove to vanquish the gloom threatening to engulf her. She must *endure fort* and pray that Knox would *keep tryst* and come for her.

But what if he didn't? Fear numbed her. What if her father were to marry her off? Like he did with Amy. Her failed elopement with Guildford had marked her as soiled goods but butcher Robson had been willing to take her on. He'd also struck a bargain with Robson. In lieu of a dowry he'd promised the twins to his two strapping sons. How could he be so cruel? Two halves of a scallop shell, MaryBeth should not be prised apart.

The sound of the key grinding in the lock lifted her spirits: the warden was coming to light the brazier. The thick studded oak door creaked open but he stood back to let someone in. Her father. Before, she would have thrown herself upon him, eager to feel his lips sprinkling her cheek with kisses, his strong arms hugging her close. But now she hugged her arms tightly to her chest.

'Have you come to set me free?' she asked, her voice as bitter cold as the air in the chamber.

The captain smiled and held out his arms. 'You know I'd do that in a trice, my Sweet Marjoram. All you need do is renounce your Scots preacher and come back to the true faith. I cannot stand by and let you be arrested as heretic.'

She chewed her bottom lip to bolster her resolve. 'I cannot reject everything I hold most dear. I'm no apostate.'

The captain's face darkened. 'How can you be sure your angel of light is not a false prophet? Times have changed, Marjory, and so must we. Your preacher has been put to the horn: he's now an outlaw, a renegade. If he flees abroad, you'll never see him again. Forget your fusty old Scotch heretic. I shall find you someone more fitting – a young, strong-limbed, handsome lad.'

'I don't wish anyone else, father. Now we are betrothed, Master Knox is my lawful spouse. We made our solemn oath before witnesses.'

He scoffed. 'Since clerical marriages have been forbidden, do you wish to be a priest's whore? Nor is so-called handfasting recognised in law. To break this mock betrothal all you need do is admit that you did so under duress, against your will.' His voice softened. 'Your mother pressed you into this so-called contract, didn't she?'

'I pledged my troth willingly: I will not forsake him.'

His face twisted into an ugly sneer. 'I cannot stand by and watch you fall into their trap. The Scots preacher doesn't love you. He's infatuated with your mother and she with him. He's bewitched her with his foxy tongue and weasel words.'

Marjory gawped at him in distress. 'You're lying. You're only saying this to drive a wedge between us.'

'Would that I were. Do you never wonder how they spend their time together? Well, I'll tell you.' He drew a crumpled letter from the pocket of his jerkin. 'Listen: *Since the first day it pleased God to bring you and me in familiarity, I have always delighted in your company and when labours would permit, you know I have not spared hours to talk and commune with you.*'

Indignation inflamed Marjory's cheeks. 'You stole Master Knox's letters to mama?'

'I didn't steal them. Coming across the pair of them closeted together in a cupboard, your uncle, Henry Wickcliffe, became so concerned that he copied them. Besides, a husband has every right to read his wife's correspondence – especially if he suspects she's being unfaithful. My men laugh behind my back and mock me for being a cuckold. The captain of Norham can't keep order in his own house, they jeer. Gossip is rife, and no wonder. Listen to this.

'*Call to your mind what I did standing at the cupboard in Alnwick. In very deed I thought that no creature had been tempted as I was. And when I heard from your mouth the very same words that trouble me, I did wonder, and from my heart lament your sair trouble ...*'

Marjory stared at him in disbelief. *It could not be true. He's making it up.*

'So you see, your holier than-thou preacher is a filthy fornicator, an adulterer who has tempted your mother to break her sacred marriage vows. Knox may have turned my wife's head but he shall not have my daughter!' Lowering his voice, he pleaded, 'Give him up and come and live with me, Sweet Marjoram. Isn't that what you always wanted? Obey your papa who loves you most in the world.'

He opened his arms wide but she stood firm, biting her lower lip to fight back tears stinging her eyes.

'I can never live with you, papa. You accuse mama and Master Knox of adultery, yet why do you look at the speck of sawdust in your brother's eye and pay no attention to the plank in your own eye?' She drew in a breath before continuing, 'I know all about the harlot you keep here in this very castle. And your bastard son – Little Dicken.'

His face darkened to a dark purple hue. For a few seconds, a silence as taut as an archer's bowstring hung in the air between them. The blow came swiftly, unexpectedly, as he smacked the side of her face with the flat palm of his hand. Her eyes stung and her cheek smarted, but Marjory did not flinch. She fixed blazing eyes on him before slowly and deliberately turning her head to offer him the other cheek.

XII

The Wicked Carcase

The blind love that I did bear to this my wicked carcase,
was the chief cause that I was not
fervent and faithful enough in that behalf
A Faithful Admonition
John Knox, 16th Century

North of England, December 1553

The louring black clouds deepening the early December gloom threatened snow. Weak to his very core, Knox plodded on, head down, following in Jamie's footsteps along a rutted track. Skipper Will had been right – the lad had a homing instinct. Drop him off anywhere and Jamie could find his way back.

When he could no longer see in front of his nose or hear sounds carried on the wind, Jamie sniffed the air. As a sailor can smell dry land, he could smell habitation – smoke from a homestead, stench from a town or miasma from a city – but they'd need to find shelter for the night soon.

Large fluffy flakes swiftly covered the landscape in a snowy shroud. Knox chewed his frostbitten lips to stem the agonising pain from gravel stones. His aching body yearned to curl up in a soft bed of snow, but that would surely become his grave: no one could survive these freezing conditions. In his pack were letters for Marjory and Mrs Bowes written at his lowest ebb. Life seemed to vanish like smoke before the blast of the wind. Would he see his beloved Marjory before bidding his last good night on this earth?

Scarcely able to lift one heavy foot after the other and blinded by the whirling blizzard, he stumbled into Jamie who'd come to an abrupt halt.

'We'll need to make a snow hole, or we'll no see the morn's morn.' He hollowed out a cave where thick snow had drifted against a dyke for Knox to burrow into. 'I've a hunch we're near Newcastle but you're too weak to make it, master. Wait here till I come back for you.'

Knox didn't argue – he scarcely had strength to nod his head. In this weather they'd be lucky to reach Berwick this side of Christmas. Knox had left London with a plague of fleas in his ear from Sir Robert and less than ten groats in his pouch but all along the way, faithful followers had given them food and shelter. In return, a grateful Knox had preached – at great risk to their necks.

It was surprisingly warm in the snow hole and drowsiness soon overcame him. He'd dozed off when Jamie shook him awake. His nose had sniffed out a byre on the edge of Newcastle. Better to wait there than enter the city.

Once again they were on the move, but as Knox blundered behind Jamie, his feet grew heavy as if hampered by shackles. His brain slowed down and became sluggish. He couldn't remember where they were going and why. As his legs crumpled beneath him, Jamie grabbed hold of his arm and led him into a shed.

'This is Robson's place. He keeps pigs and kye here. Stay here, master, until I get a message to Skipper Will. The brotherhood will help us.'

Knox crawled about the earthen floor looking for clean, dry straw that was not soaked in piss and keech. Though the snuffling kye gave off warmth, he dared not snuggle up close for fear of being crushed to death. When the byre door scraped open, he murmured, 'Over here, Jamie.'

'It's not Jamie,' a woman's voice answered.

Knox's heart leapt: it was Mrs Bowes. He struggled to sit up.

'It's me, Amy. My husband has gone with his sons to the castle where papa is organising a search party for you.'

Knox sank back onto the hay. Amy the butcher's wife was growing stout like her mother.

'Uncle Robert has told him you've come north to start an uprising. Is this true?' Her voice trilled with fear.

'I can barely put one step in front of the other never mind lead a rebellion,' Knox slurred. His tongue felt thick in his mouth. 'All I crave now is the strength to reach Berwick where Marjory is waiting. Then we shall leave you all in peace.' His head flopped onto his chest.

Amy gave him a shake. 'Papa won't let you. He's locked Marjory up in Norham Castle.'

His beloved Marjory a prisoner? With effort, Knox raised his head.

'For her own good, papa says. Mama's religious frenzy is harming Marjory and he doesn't wish her to become a martyr.'

'And your mother?'

'Mama is as stubborn as ever. Uncle Robert is leaning heavily on papa to make her convert but she'd rather die than live under papist rule. Because no one would force an invalid to go to mass, she's taken to her bed.'

'Ah, Sir Robert,' Knox murmured. The ill-starred interview with Bowes still stung. He was not a good orator in his own cause, he thought ruefully. 'May I shelter here until I recover my strength …'

'You can't stay here. You're putting our whole family in danger,' she said and placed a protective hand on her belly. Her thickening waist, Knox realised, signified she was with child.

'Many in the north have gone over to the queen's side – including my husband.

Since Robson supplies the fort at Norham, he's no wish to cross papa.'

'So, my dear sister, will you turn me in?' Knox's lips were numb with cold. 'Then I shall bide here and await my fate for this wretched carcase is in no state to crawl far less flee.'

'What else can I do?' Amy snapped. 'You reformist traitors have brought enough grief to my family.' Her eyes glistened with unshed tears. 'You can stay here tonight but you must be gone by morning. If not, I shall tell papa – I cannot risk harbouring a heretic.' Amy tucked her kid-gloved hands into fur-lined sleeves and left the barn.

Knox bedded down in the straw. Is this how his life would end? Not aflame atop a pyre as he aye feared but freezing in a manger on Christ's nativity? His body shook with violent shivering and then stopped. His toes had gone numb – not an unpleasant feeling – but his hands seemed to be on fire. When he wrenched off his sheepskin gloves, his fingers looked puffy and thick, like thumbs. The skin on the back of his hands was turning blue and the ridged veins stood out like contours on a map. He studied his palms. Was his future written there? He traced a line down to his wrist. He could feel no heartthrob. Had he come to the end of his journey – of his life?

He drifted into a fitful sleep, disturbed by vivid visions and dreams. Ice seeped into his veins and his bones began trembling like the wheels of a cart trundling along a cobbled street, towards the Lawnmarket where witches and heretics were burnt in Edinburgh. Flames began leaping up his legs – he was atop a bonfire – his worst nightmare. He couldn't breathe – he must undo the cords binding him, the noose strangling him. He gasped for breath. In the hellish heat, he tore off his rags, exposing his skin to the flames. His blood bubbled and his eyes seared in their sockets. In his agony he called out, 'My God, my God! Why hast thou forsaken me?'

He awoke with a jolt and stared into the darkness. He had a great drouth on him and his tongue stuck to the roof of his mouth. The wind blew the byre door open and two silvery figures bearing lighted tapers floated towards him. At the hour of his death the Lord had sent guardian angels to accompany him. They leant over him, wafting their warm, sweet breath into his nostrils.

One of the angels held a flagon to his cracked lips and he drank thirstily – the small beer tasted like the sweetest wine. The other unwrapped a cloth and fed him morsels of bread and crumbly cheese that tasted like manna from heaven. Throughout this celestial feast Latin phrases from the Catholic mass crept unbidden into his mind.

Domine, non sum dignus
Sanctus, sanctus, sanctus
Agnus Dei … qui tollis peccata mundi … miserere nobis.
Dona nobis … pacem

While the bread and wine sent the blood coursing through his veins again, a stinging, tingling sensation in his bladder signalled a stone was on its way. He urgently needed to pass water. The angels averted their heads as he knelt among the straw and groaned with pain. With tears of relief in his eyes he sank back into his manger. 'Thank you, dear angels. You are indeed heaven sent.'

Shivering in flimsy cotton nightgowns and sucking furiously on their thumbs the heavenly messengers uttered peculiar high-pitched squeaking sounds like piglets. Knox blinked. In his delirium he hadn't recognised the twins, Mary and Beth. Two sets of identical eyes gazed mournfully at him and two sets of rosy lips mouthed a single word, 'Guildford?'

Informed that Guildford and Lady Jane Grey were imprisoned in the Tower, their fair heads drooped like wilted roses, their pink faces stained with teardrops.

'Will they die?' Mary or Beth asked.

'I don't know,' Knox replied, 'but if they do they shall be martyrs.'

'Will Guildford go to heaven?'

Unsure what to answer, Knox simply nodded. He didn't know how the Lord would judge their souls but if anyone deserved paradise those two innocents certainly did.

'If we're good, shall we go to heaven, too?'

Again the question took Knox off guard. What weird, fey creatures, he thought, with their wan, drooping faces and fascination with the afterlife. Again he simply nodded.

'Then we may yet meet Guildford in paradise.' They waggled their heads and beamed at each other, seemingly satisfied with his answer.

'Oh, I nearly forgot.' He drew the embroidered handkerchief, now crumpled and grubby, from his bundle. 'Guildford asked me to give this to Amy but since I might not see her again, will you please pass it on.'

MaryBeth pounced on the handkerchief and gabbled excitedly in their incomprehensible language before running off. Knox heaved a sigh. He should have also asked them to deliver his letters to Marjory and Mrs Bowes.

In the early hours, Amy shook him awake. 'Papa has got hold of Jamie.' Her voice was jittery. 'He's thrown him into the dungeon at Newcastle. If he finds out you've been here and I didn't tell him, he'll be furious.'

'Never fash, I'll go but afore I do ...' Knox was scrabbling for the letters when the byre door opened.

Amy gave a start. 'He's here! I've found him,' she shouted before squeezing past the figure looming in the doorway and darting out of the byre.

Knox's heart jolted. So Amy was his Judas. She'd delivered him up. So be it. He tried to get up but his legs gave way beneath him. As he fell face down in the hay, a low voice said, 'Sinclair, is that you?'

Hearing his slogan, Knox struggled to sit up.

'The fraternity sent me. You're to come with me.' The man wrapped a heavy worsted cloak round Knox's shoulders and wound a scarf round his face before bundling him into the back of a cart full of sheep fleeces.

'Where are we going? Berwick?'

'Nay, Chester. I've to deliver fleeces to the port there,' the carter replied.

'Chester? On the west coast? That's miles away – on the border with Wales.' Knox's spirits plummeted – he had no strength for such a journey.

'That's my orders. Since they'll be looking for you at all the ports, north and east, Skipper Will says it's safer to leave from the west. A merchant called Goodman is to arrange your passage along with his son who's also fleeing.'

'What about Jamie?'

'Have no fear. We'll look after the lad. The fraternity have given their word.'

PART FOUR

I

Cautious or Cowardly

> O Lord, how lang for ever will thou forget,
> And hide thy face from me? Or yet how lang
> Shall I rehearse thy counsel in my heart?
>
> Psalm XIII: 1

Dieppe, France, Late January 1554

Dieppe. Knox's hope that he'd seen the last of the French port had been in vain for here he was again, chased out of England by a woman. Though he would not be condemned for fleeing Mary Tudor's persecution, Knox felt ashamed for abandoning those whom he loved most dearly in the world to their fate. How Marjory must despise him for leaving her in the lurch. Would she ever forgive this faint-hearted and feeble soldier?

Bitter resentment simmered in his breast. 'Those abominable idolaters may triumph for the moment but the hour approaches when God's vengeance shall strike not only their souls but even their vile carcases shall be plagued.'

Christopher Goodman laid a hand on his sleeve and glanced around the tavern: *Auberge au Port* was bursting with refugees arriving every day from England.

'Calm yourself, brother. You never know who may be listening.'

Knox nodded – but grudgingly. His sanguine temper was too easily riled, his blood fired up too quickly whereas his new companion was of phlegmatic humour. With his stocky, thickset build and permanent scowl on his rugged face, Goodman looked more like a boxer than a former Professor of Divinity at Oxford, but he kept his composure. He was right. They must watch out for the prying eyes and flapping lugs of crooked clypes who would betray them to the Catholic authorities.

'Here, a cheering draught should quench your ire,' a voice boomed. 'May I join you?' asked their couthie host, John Wedderburn. When he beckoned to a serving lass for a pitcher of steaming mulled ale to be planked on their table, they budged up the bench to make room for his generous frame. 'Did I hear you making moan, Mr Knox?'

Goodman's sideways glance said, *I told you so.*

'Not without reason,' Wedderburn went on. 'Your ringing sentiments struck a chord in me. Your words, full of fervent passion, are worthy of Sir David Lindsay himself.' He placed a hand on his heart and recited:

'And I have power great princes to doun thring
That lives contrair the Majesty Divine

Against the truth which plainly does malign
Repent they nocht I put them to ruin.'

'High praise indeed but I cannot be spoken of in the same breath as the makar,' Knox replied. 'I'm proud to have performed the rôle of Divine Correction in his *Satire*, though some said I wasn't acting – merely being myself.'

Wedderburn's eyes boggled in admiration. 'I envy you, Mr Knox. What a great honour. No one could match Sir David for scurrilous satire, especially not my brothers hounded out of Scotland – not for heresy, I tease them, but wanwordy writing.' He rolled out a parchment. 'I, too, like to scribble. I'm putting together a collection entitled *The Good and Godly Ballads*. Would you do me the honour of listening to these verses?'

Knox swirled his ale round the mug and nodded. He could hardly refuse his big-hearted host. Wedderburn's family were wealthy Dundee wool merchants, whose business he managed in France. A staunch Protestant, he was kind enough to share his good fortune, paying for the board and lodgings of struggling refugees in Dieppe.

The makar manqué cleared his throat to read:
'Banished is faith now everywhere
By the shaven sort, I you declare.
Alas therefore my heart is sair,
And blyth I cannot be.

But the wallop of a fist hitting the board cut short his recitation.

'Never fash, the shaven sort shall be chastised,' Knox muttered, eyes starting out of his head. 'Their cities shall be burnt, their land shall be laid waste, their enemies shall dwell in their strongholds and their wives and their daughters shall be defiled, their children shall fall on the edge of the sword; they shall find no mercy because they have refused the God of all mercy.'

When Wedderburn wriggled uneasily at this surge of curses, Goodman whispered in Knox's ear. 'It behoves you ill to vent your anger on our generous patron.'

Knox dipped his head. 'Forgive me. The spiced ale has inflamed my doited brain. I meant no insult.'

Wedderburn rolled up his parchment. 'None taken. I'm sending these ballads to be printed in Strasbourg where Gutenberg perfected his printing press. As soon as they're published, I shall give you both a copy. For the present I shall leave you two gentlemen in peace. I have poetry to scrieve.' With a bow and a flourish of his pen, he left.

Waiting until he was out of earshot, Knox murmured, 'He's wasting his time. What good are words now? Princes, nobles and clergy refuse to take heed and call us prating knaves.'

Wedderburn's verses had touched a raw nerve. Why had the Lord allowed the wicked to triumph? Railing at God and boiling with rage at the papist usurpers did little to allay the guilt niggling his conscience. Nor did hurling tirades drown out the taunting voice: *Feardie-gowk! Feardie-gowk!*

'We should not have fled England,' Knox muttered.

'At a time of persecution, we could do no other. *If they persecute you in one city,* Christ said, *flee to another.* But all is not lost. There may be hope.' Goodman refilled their cups and glanced around to check for eavesdroppers. 'Thomas Wyatt and Henry Grey are whipping up revolt amongst opponents of Mary Tudor's marriage to a Spanish Roman Catholic. With all the might of the Holy Roman Emperor and the Vatican behind him, tolerance will not be one of the new King of England's virtues. Let's pray for the success of their revolt. For be in no doubt – once Philip becomes king, the Spanish Inquisition will set England alight with their funereal pyres.'

Knox shuddered. He'd already fled the flames once, leaving Wishart to face the pyre alone. He'd gone into hiding – unlike Adam Wallace who'd continued to preach the gospel until Archbishop Hamilton finally caught up with him. Knox was racked with guilt and fear. While he'd bolted, Wallace, a simple man of no great learning, laid down his life for his beliefs. Would he be brave enough to go to the stake for his faith?

As panic rippled through him, his breathing grew shallow: his heart hammered so strongly he feared it would burst. *Feardie-gowk! Feardie-gowk!* He drew back from the fire blazing in the hearth and mopped his brow. If only he had some laudanum to calm him. 'I cannot salve my conscience. We were cowards for abandoning our friends in England.'

'What good would it do if you were to go up in flames?' Goodman asked. 'For a form of religion you dispute? Did you not say the English church is taking a direction that offends you?'

'Aye, the English reformation has been a mingle-mangle. Sparked off by the worst intentions – a strutting monarch's lust and greed. I've done my best to scour out the popish dregs but my efforts are aye thwarted.'

'Time and patience are the strongest weapons in this battle,' Goodman said.

'I've not much left of either, I fear.'

'Nay, my friend, time you have aplenty. And though patience may be bitter its fruit is sweet, so the Greek philosopher Aristotle tells us. Besides, God has called you to be a preacher not a martyr.'

'Aye, you're well named. You're a good man and a deep thinker. But as a scholar you have no parish, no pastoral care of a flock who depend on you. You're free to leave whereas I ...' Knox faltered. 'I should return to my flock and lend my support. As a bitter tasting medicine restores health, these troubles will pass. I promise to join the battle before the conflict ends – even if it were at the very hour of my death.'

'Don't be too hasty. For the time being, let's wait to hear from England.'

When Skipper Will brought the long-awaited news, it was not good. 'Wyatt's rebellion has failed and Mary Tudor is now betrothed to Philip.' He drank deeply from a tankard of beer and wiped away the bubbles of froth clinging to his busy seaman's beard with the back of his hand.

'Wyatt's already been strung up and gralloched and Henry Grey is in the Tower, awaiting the block. His wife, Frances, has been licking the new queen's feet and pleading for mercy but Bishop Gardiner has closed his lugs to any pardon for the young pair and demanded the death sentence: burning for Lady Jane and gutting for Guildford. At least Bloody Mary showed some mercy, for the lambs were both beheaded. The streets of London are now running with the gore of more than ninety rebels.'

Knox touched his brow to make the sign of the cross but his hand swiftly fell again, as if scalded. Cross with himself, he rubbed his forehead in a sign of irritation instead.

'Such innocents! By just laws and faithful witnesses they can never be proved to have offended by themselves.'

'No quarter is to be shown to traitors who proclaimed for Queen Jane,' Will continued. 'Bishop Gardiner is calling for these *rotten members* to be lopped off afore they stir up rebellion. Since he's declared Protestantism to be treason, folk are creeping back to papistry, like dogs slinking back to their boak. Edward's death on the anniversary of Sir Thomas More's execution was a sign of divine anger, he claims, and God has placed the Virgin Mary on the throne for their redemption.

Knox groaned. 'Even worse. England is plummeting into darkness and superstition. I fear the great shipwreck of God's true religion is breaking up even more.'

'However disappointing this may be, we're in no position to blame the weakhearted,' Goodman said. 'Hiding away in the comparative safety of Dieppe, it's easy for us to urge our followers to stay firm. If the penalty for refusing to attend mass is to be burnt alive, we cannot blame folk for recanting in their droves.'

'I'm a bad shepherd who's abandoned his flock,' Knox blurted. 'A good shepherd would defend his sheep, whatever the cost, even if it meant defying lawful authority. And at present, lawful authority lies in the hands of women whom God created inferior to men in every way. It's neither right nor fitting that Mary Tudor in England and Marie de Guise in Scotland should hold the reins. It is a monstrous perversion of nature.'

Wedderburn held up a hand. 'What I am about to say may shock you, gentlemen, but there may be a solution. You've heard of the Magdeburg Confession?'

They had not. 'That doesn't surprise me. Such a heretical document could set the continent on fire. When Charles V tried to smash Protestantism in the cities of his Holy Roman Empire, only the citizens of Magdeburg stood against his imperial army. Nine pastors drew up a doctrine to justify their stance. They claimed divine law is not only superior to human law but unlimited obedience to the state is the devil's invention.'

Seeing the shock on their faces, Wedderburn puffed out his broad chest. 'I'm not simply a scriever of baleful ballads: I also translate subversive pamphlets from Latin. This Confession has fallen into my hands only recently. From memory – since I daren't let untrustworthy eyes have sight of it – the gist of their argument is this: when the state makes laws commanding us to do what God forbids, or makes laws forbidding us to do what God commands, we should obey God rather than the state. Furthermore, they base their arguments on scripture, history, law, and reason.'

Knox grasped Wedderburn's hand: this was the divine message he'd been praying for.

After swearing to keep it secret, Knox shut himself in the garret to study the secret Confession. At daybreak a few days later, a hubbub in the courtyard outside disturbed him. Knox raised his head from the table and rubbed his eyes, bleary from a sleepless night. Hearing a knock at the door he swiftly scooped the fiery document into a drawer and locked it.

'I've come to bid farewell.' Wrapped in a travelling cloak Goodman held out his hand.

'You're leaving? Are you in danger?'

'Not imminently. Fearing the French authorities will not abide this pocket of dissent for long, a band of pilgrims is setting out for Strasbourg. They've asked me to go with them as their pastor. Will you come with us?'

Knox considered for a moment before shaking his head. 'Nay, the Lord has shown me a different path.' Though where it would lead was still uncertain.

After bidding Godspeed to Goodman, Knox walked briskly down to the harbour to blow away the cobwebs from a sleepless night. If only God would give him a clear indication of what to do next. He sat on the sea wall, lost in a dwam, paying little heed to the boat docking at the quayside until a bluff voice roused him.

'Brother, are you well? See what the tide has washed up.'

Knox blinked and sprang up. Skipper Will was standing before him with an arm round Jamie's shoulder.

'Jamie! You're safe! I thought you were locked up in Berwick Castle?' Knox wanted to hug the lad.

A broad grin stretched across Jamie's face. 'They couldn't keep me in the jougs o'er lang.'

'Crossing a greasy palm with silver made sure our young sailor was set free,' Skipper Will winked. 'Our Free Fishers have as many tentacles as thon fabled sea monster, the Kraken, reaching into every neuk and cranny.'

Knox said a silent prayer. 'The Lord has sent you in my time of need, Jamie. Come, leave your fishing net and follow me. We have an overland journey to make.'

II

The Timid Scholar

God send every priest a wife
And every nun a man
That they might leave that holy life
As first the kirk began
The Gude and Godlie Ballads
The Wedderburn Brothers, 16th Century

Geneva, February 1554

Undeterred by rain, mud and glaur of roads flooded from thawing winter snow, Knox and Jamie at last drew up outside the white walls of the City of God.

Jamie squinted at the initials JC gates emblazoned on the gates. 'Do they stand for Jesus Christ?'

'Nay, lad. For John Calvin, the great scholar and author of *The Institutes of the Christian Religion*,' Knox replied. 'Only he will be qualified to answer my questions.'

They made their way to the address Wedderburn had given them. Walter Milne, a former Roman Catholic priest who'd fled Scotland after Wishart's execution, now lived in Geneva with his wife, a former nun.

'I'm pleased to meet another of Baal's shaven sort who's had the wisdom to grow whiskers,' Knox said.

Well-stricken with age, Milne ran gnarled fingers through a grizzled beard and chuckled. 'At heavy cost, for I'm become a shaveling with this monk's tonsure.' He took off his bonnet and patted his bald pate framed by a circlet of wispy hair.

His wife Marta, a pared stick of a woman, warmly welcomed them, at the same time apologising for the humble accommodation in a low-ceilinged loft.

Knox laid his bundle on the iron bedstead. 'After bedding down in barns and byres for weeks, a pillow to lay our heads on is luxury for worn-out travellers. But before I can rest, I must have paper pen and ink.'

In a fit of feverish activity, he translated his burning questions into French, Calvin's native language. Only when his petition had been sealed and sent off, did Knox feel able to join his hosts for supper. While Marta ladled out thick cabbage soup into trenchers of dark rye bread, her husband filled their wooden goblets with honey-coloured ale.

'You must be thankful for finding shelter here in God's own city, far from the boorach in both Scotland and England,' Knox said.

Milne gave his wife a sidelong glance. 'Aye, we're fortunate indeed.' Keeping her eyes cast down, Marta rose from the table. 'But though I give daily thanks to the Lord for bringing me here, my love for my homeland has never left me. I've a hankering to end my days among my ain folk.'

'I'd gang warily, if I were you,' Knox warned.

Milne shook his grey head. 'From what I hear, Mary of Guise tholes evangelicals. Forbye, what risk is there from an auld man like me who's seen seventy-eight winters? Nearly four score already. I wish to see my eightieth in Scotland.'

'Kept in check by thon nobles who've converted to our cause, the queen dowager seems loath to light pyres – for the time being,' Knox said. 'But the Catholic primate, Archbishop Hamilton, craves to cremate more martyrs.'

Sweeping aside Knox's forewarnings, Milne rambled on. 'I've a mind for these auld decrepit banes to be buried amongst my ain kith and kin.'

When Marta brought in a pot of pork stew to refill the trencher bowls, Knox asked, 'What about you, Marta? Are you willing to leave your homeland?'

She placed a hand on her husband's shoulder, a grim expression on her gaunt face.

'Has Walter told you the real reason for his return?'

'Wheesht, Marta. I've no wish to entangle Mr Knox in my mission.'

Paying him no heed, Marta went on, 'Walter has been translating pamphlets and tracts into Scots for Dr Calvin's brother to publish. He means to take them back to Scotland to spread God's word.'

'A noble mission indeed,' Knox replied.

'But one that's fraught with danger. Walter may wish to bury his bones in his own kirkyard but I fear this risky venture will hasten his death.'

Milne cackled. 'If I'm tied to the stake, these knotted auld banes will crackle and burn like dry twigs and quickly turn to ashes.'

Marta sighed. 'No matter what I say, he's made up his mind. Since we've taken sacred vows to remain together until death do us part, then so be it.'

Milne gazed at his wife with rheumy eyes and gave her a gummy smile. Taking her hand, he pressed his withered lips against it.

Their evident love and affection touched Knox but a pang of envy also pierced his heart. Would he and Marjory ever be so blessed?

'Then I can help you,' he said. 'My brother, Skipper William, will arrange safe passage for you both. Never fash, the *Saltire* will get you home safely.'

When days passed and no reply came from Dr Calvin, Knox chafed at the bit. On Sunday, he accompanied the Milnes to hear him preach in the cathedral church of St Pierre. Thrilled to hear the true word of God ringing round the rafters of the plain white space, Knox was eager to speak with his hero but the cordon of guards blocked his way.

'The Servetus affair has made Dr Calvin many enemies,' Milne said. 'He was great friends with Michael Servetus, the Spanish theologue and physician, and they corresponded for many years – until Servetus questioned his views in a long volume of ravings. The blasphemer even declared Christ was not the Son of God, merely a prophet! He also poured scorn on the doctrines of the Trinity and predestination. Though justifiably furious, Calvin ignored him.

'When Servetus threatened to come to Geneva, Calvin advised against it, for he couldn't assure him safe conduct. Fired up by satanic pride, the Lucifer came anyway to challenge our leader. What could he do? Calvin had no option but to denounce the heretic. Nevertheless, he couldn't bear seeing his old friend burnt alive and suggested beheading instead. But when the council insisted on the original sentence, Servetus was set ablaze atop a pyre of his own blasphemous books. By doing what was right, Dr Calvin raised the wrath of the faithless libertines.'

Hearing of Servetus's fate, Knox fingered his throat to loosen the icy grip of fear on his thrapple. Was Calvin's silence a sign of his displeasure?

Combating his apprehension, Knox plucked up courage to call on Dr Calvin the next morning.

As Milne had described, the entrance of No 11, Rue des Chanoines, with its two large oak carved doors was both impressive and intimidating. The city government had enticed Calvin to Geneva with this grand mansion, formerly the property of a cathedral canon and large enough to house his family, Milne explained.

Knox was about to knock on the smaller door at the side belonging to the printing workshop, when a nose pressed up against one of the windowpanes. Seconds later a woman with a bairn clamped to her breast and two more tugging at her skirts opened the door.

Embarrassed, Knox averted his eyes. 'Forgive me. I must have mistaken the address.'

'What's amiss? Have you never seen a mother nursing her babe before? You're one of Dr Calvin's disciples, no doubt.' She sneered. 'Monks without monasteries.'

A man wearing an ink-stained printer's apron put a hand on her shoulder. 'No need to be rude to our guests, my love. You must be Mr Knox. My brother has been expecting you. I am Antoine Calvin – and this is my wife, Annette, with three of our children.'

Shrugging off his hand, Annette shot him a scornful look and gathered up her brood. As she set off down the long hallway, Antoine's gaze lingered on his wife's swaying hips. When curious faces poked out of half open doors, he chuckled and said, 'As well as my wife and offspring this leaky ship gives bunk and board to an assorted crew – relatives, friends and devout disciples. Relationships here are complicated, Mr Knox.'

Stopping at one of the doors, Antoine rapped loudly. When there was no reply, he put an eye to the keyhole. A young woman came down the stairs and glared at him.

'Dr Calvin is resting. You mustn't disturb him.' Her voice had a keen edge.

Antoine rolled his eyes. 'Please meet our good sister, Catherine. My brother's keeper and vestal virgin.'

Plainly dressed in a grey worsted gown, her hair tucked under a white linen coif, Catherine stood straight-backed and stern. Her frown deepened the groove etched between neat eyebrows. 'Someone needs to keep a hand on the tiller of this leaky ship. Someone needs to look after the master in the midst of all this chaos.' Her voice rose to a shrill, peevish wail. 'It's impossible for my good brother to get any peace and quiet in this swarming household.'

'Then I shall come back another day, at a more suitable time,' Knox replied.

Catherine cocked a curious eyebrow. 'You're the Scotsman who's been writing to him? Come, I'd like a word, if I may.'

Her chamber was as bare as a nun's cell – a pair of stools, a narrow bed with a dark grey coverlet and a small bedside rug. An enormous leather-bound Bible lay on a desk piled with papers.

Catherine offered him one of the stools. 'Madame Annette may be the senior housekeeper but as Dr Calvin's ward, I'm responsible for his welfare. Otherwise his needs would go unheeded in this messy ménage. Not that he'd notice. Dr Calvin preaches every weekday morning and twice on Sunday – with no time off at all. As you know, he's written countless theological works. Commentaries on the Bible, a catechism, the Genevan Psalter.' She pointed to a row of neatly stacked books on a shelf above her desk.

'Yet he still finds time every day for pastoral visits. All this unceasing labour has taken its toll on his health and too much fasting has left him greatly afflicted by a plague of ailments.' She counted them on her fingers. 'Arthritis, cramps, gout, gravel, haemorrhoids, infections, itchy skin.'

'I can sympathise with his suffering,' Knox said. 'I, too, have not had my troubles to seek and suffer great discomfort.'

'Not just discomfort, Mr Knox, but agony.' Catherine's thin lips compressed into a tight line. 'As if he didn't have enough to bear, migraines constantly torment him. Little wonder his temper is frayed at times. More seriously, in this city of sin, he's fighting a moral battle as great as that between Gabriel and Lucifer.'

Knox was astounded. 'The city of God is a city of sin? How can that be?'

'Oh yes. The so-called Children of Geneva oppose his attempts to impose discipline. Their leader Ami Perrin urges them to stir up hatred against religious refugees who've sought asylum here. They decry us as outsiders, trespassers who're imposing our rule of law on all the citizens of Geneva. These Perrinists grumble our commandments are too strict when in fact their morals are too lax. They justify living their lives as they please without church discipline, by saying they're only following Christ's teaching.'

As she took a deep breath, her expression oozed loathing. 'Not only is Perrin a libertine but a hedonist. A proud peacock who struts about elaborately dressed in the finest of clothes, a gluttonous roué who stuffs his belly until bursting with the best of food.'

'I heartily agree,' Knox replied. 'To remedy folk's morals their souls must first be cleansed.'

'But they're reprobates, Mr Knox, whose souls will never be purged. They are the damned.' She could not veil the venom in her voice. 'Like cockroaches they infect even the cleanest household – scuttling and crawling everywhere, dragging in filth and dirt on their hairy feet.' She shuddered with revulsion. 'The City of God is being tossed about like Noah's ark in the waters of the deluge and Dr Calvin fears the wicked will throw him overboard. Not only sinners, but heretics in the guise of scholars are threatening our status quo.'

'If Dr Calvin fears a repeat of the Servetus affair then please reassure him I've no intention rocking your ship of state.'

Her eyes narrowed in suspicion. 'Our experience with Servetus has warned us to be on our guard. We assumed he was one of the elect until Satan seized his soul. We rejoiced at overpowering the devil until you came along.'

Knox was dumbfounded. How could she compare him to Auld Nick, the father of lies when he, God's messenger had come to sound the trumpet of truth?

'You see, your question about deposing a tyrannical ruler has greatly alarmed us for it would give these Perrinists a pretext to rebel. They've already set their dogs on Dr Calvin and spat on him calling him a tyrant and pope of Geneva, the Protestant Rome. Dr Calvin is no despot like Herod, but Moses leading his people out of the desert to the Promised Land. He's striving to convert Geneva into the first Kingdom of God on earth, a city for the elect.'

Catherine fixed fierce eyes on Knox. 'Then, like the serpent in the Garden of Eden you come along to … to… ' She threw up her hands in frustration. 'To upset the apple cart.'

'I assure you, I'm no devil in disguise,' Knox began but Catherine had already flung open the door onto the landing where Madame Annette was yelling down the stairwell.

'Pierre! Pierre! Where is that idle dwarf?'

'This is the sort of thing I'm up against, Mr Knox. Even in this house there lurks a nest of vipers.' She led him back downstairs and rapped three times on Calvin's door. This time a grumpy voice answered, 'What is it now?'

She ushered Knox into the book-lined study. 'He's been complaining of a headache this morning,' she murmured before changing her tone. 'That's no way to greet Mr Knox who's journeyed over 500 miles to see you, dear brother.'

Seated in a high-backed chair of black oak, his elbows leaning on its thick arms, Calvin seemed more shrunken, less daunting than the doommonger in the pulpit. With a grouchy harrumph, he pulled his scholar's black velvet bonnet down over his ears and continued reading his book.

'He dislikes being interrupted while in deep thought,' Catherine said. 'Wait until he addresses you first. I shall bring him a physick.'

Knox studied his hero close-up. With a grey-streaked pointed beard and pallid complexion, John Calvin looked much older than his forty-four years. Thin faced, with high-cheekbones and a long nose, the renowned reformer had the gaunt look of an ascetic.

Suddenly he snapped the book shut and screwed up deep-set eyes to peer at his visitor. 'So, you're the Scots firebrand I've heard so much about.'

Without returning Knox's smile, Calvin gestured for him to sit down. When he drew a document from the untidy pile heaped on his desk, Knox recognised his list of questions, now heavily annotated in the margins.

Calvin took his time reading out the questions one by one punctuated by pauses in between.

'Does divine right entitle a woman to rule or govern and, if so, can she transfer her rights to husband?

'Is it obligatory to obey laws that enforce idolatry?

'If the nobility oppose a monarch can the people support them in certain circumstances?'

Calvin tapered his beard to a point. 'These are indeed burning questions, Mr Knox. Although I respect your zeal, if the answers you seek were to be applied they could encourage other nations, other communities to follow suit. The implications are terrifying. Too inflammatory in fact, for such questions will not only lead *you* to the pyre but may ignite rebellion, chaos and anarchy. They must be extinguished at once.'

Knox stiffened. 'With all respect, Dr Calvin, may I remind you that there are precedents, such as when the Protestant pastors rose up against Charles V in Magdeburg. I've no desire to foment rebellion here in Geneva. My questions arise from the situation in England and Scotland.'

Calvin's gaunt face twisted into a grimace. 'I am but a timid scholar who believes true and lawful monarchs ought to be obeyed. Although I don't approve of female rulers, it may be argued they could and should hand over rights to their husbands if that was in accordance with the law of land.'

When Knox sucked in a breath at this, Calvin frowned. 'I see my answers do not satisfy you, Mr Knox, in which case I shall be like any good physician and pass you on for a second opinion. Like you, Pierre Viret in Lausanne is a popular pastor. Preaching sermons that win over the most unyielding hearts has earned him the sobriquet the Smile of the Reformation.'

Before Knox could protest, Calvin passed a frail hand across his scholar's forehead.

'That's quite enough for one day, Mr Knox,' Catherine clucked as she brought in the tisane. Shooing him out the door she murmured, 'Your reckless behaviour makes Dr Calvin nervous. In these troubled times he prefers to tread softly, like the angels, whereas you're playing with hellfire.'

III

An Answer Given to a Certain Scotsman

> It is better to trust in the Lord,
> than to put confidence in Princes
> Psalm CXVIII: 9

Lausanne, April 1554

'Nothing is too much trouble for a fellow preacher in need, especially one who's travelled from afar to see me.' Bursting at the seams with bonhomie, Pierre Viret gave Knox a hearty slap on the back. 'Buffeted by the storms of life, we must all row together in the barque of the Lord.' His arms mimed pulling at oars. 'As you did so bravely in the galleys.'

His jovial greeting raised Knox's hopes of gaining his support. Such a convivial man would surely tackle any hurdle with enthusiasm.

Once the dinner platters had been cleared away, Viret refilled their wine goblets and leant his elbows on the table. Forming a bridge with his hands, the Smile of the Reformation beamed benignly at Knox. 'Now, tell me your woes so that I may draw you out of deep waters.'

As Knox repeated his questions, the benevolent smile gradually slipped away from Viret's face. He twiddled his thumbs and sucked in a breath. 'I'm a preacher not a theologian, Mr Knox. I'm not learned enough to rule on serious matters of doctrine. I would advise you to consult the Oracle.' A shadow of a smile flickered briefly before fading again. 'Dr Bullinger is far more knowledgeable than I am. I'm sure he'll set you on the right course.'

Striving to curb his temper, Knox rose. 'In which case, I shall trouble you no longer. We shall set off at once.'

Outside, Jamie was peering at the cloudy sky through his sunstone. 'Did you get your answers, master?' he asked.

'Nay, but my questions took the wind out of his sails. We're off to Zurich and on foot, for I doubt we've enough money for a mule. Just as well our shanks are sturdy, for they'll be our nags for the journey.'

'Which direction, master?'

'North. Never mind your lodestone, Jamie. Just point thon trusty neb of yours in the direction of Zurich.'

The late spring weather was kind and they made good progress through the Swiss valley, on foot most of the time and if God smiled on them, begging lifts on carts. Bumping about on the back of a wagon, Knox filled his lungs with the crisp clean air blowing down from the jaggy snow-covered Alpine peaks and admired the lush green meadows of the foothills, so different from the wild, unruly Scottish braes covered in unforgiving bracken, gorse and heather. Beyond the smartly painted wooden houses by the lakeside, grazing cows dotted the rich pastures.

'Everything's so dinkie and douce here! Look at thon kye! Fat well-fed beasts, no like oor scruntit runts!' Jamie said.

Not only the cattle were plump. Knox chortled as Jamie, his eyes rounded like scallops at the flaxen-haired, cherry-cheeked milkmaids, *mademoiselles* and *frauleins*.

'Helvetia is indeed blessed by God,' Knox said, 'but not without a struggle. Many were martyred in the fight to fling off their Roman fetters, including the great reformer, Dr Zwingli. But his legacy lives on in Dr Bullinger whose thundering sermons have led folk to think that Zwingli is not dead but resurrected like the phoenix. Let's hope his heir will support my cause.'

Zurich

Outside Das Grossmünster, the minster whose twin towers loomed over Zurich, Knox glanced up at the inscription above the main door: *Come to me, all who labor and are heavy laden, and I will give you rest.* The quotation from Matthew XI: 28 lit a lantern of hope in Knox's darkness as he went in search of Dr Bullinger.

This former monk married to a former nun clearly revelled in family life, indulging the boisterous children who ran hither and thon playing hide-and-seek around his legs.

'Matrimony is the perfect state,' he said. 'I recommend it for every man. It promotes the mutual love of husband and wife thus protecting them from sexual sin and temptation. And of course it enables procreation. Children are our future. We must take care to nurture their souls and mould their natures.'

'As you did for Lady Jane Grey,' Knox replied. 'Your stout instruction fostered her faith and emboldened the young lass to become a true martyr.'

Bullinger's eyes moistened. 'She was an example to us all. For one so young her courage was admirable. Anxious to appear modest and prudent while walking to her death, she asked me what adornment was becoming in a young woman professing godliness.'

'But was her sacrifice in vain? Papistry has returned to England. For her sake, if nothing else, I implore you to endorse my proposals.'

As he read them through, Bullinger's brows knitted into a frown. 'Do I understand correctly? Is it your aim to incite rebellion amongst the English?'

Knox thrust out his chin. 'Aye, it is. To repel the ungodly violence of those authorities who enforce idolatry and condemn the true religion.'

Bullinger drummed his fingers on the desk. 'It's hazardous for godly persons to set themselves in opposition to political regulations. Due obedience must be given to magistrates, rulers and princes without tumult, grudge or sedition.'

Knox bristled. 'God's prophet, Jeremiah, did not shy away from treason. If the people rise up and depose the Jezebel, God will not be offended. But if Mary Tudor's authority is maintained, England will be made a desert and the spawn of a Spaniard will usurp the English throne.'

Bullinger rose to pad up and down his study, tweaking his beard and scratching his chin. 'Though there may be some cases when resistance is acceptable, anarchy must be averted. For who would then take control?'

'A common weal of the people,' Knox replied. 'For where is it written that kings have a divine right to rule?'

'To suggest sovereignty lies with the people rather than an aristocracy is, dare I say, Mr Knox, revolutionary. Who decides whether a ruler is evil? For wicked men may feign godly motives. I agree we should not obey the king or magistrate when their commands are contrary to divine law but the current times are too full of danger. Our situation here is precarious. Though Zurich is a City State, it remains under the Holy Roman Emperor's jurisdiction. Besides, without sufficient knowledge, it would be foolish to recommend anything specific.'

Knox's heart sank. 'So you're saying that, in order to respond to my questions, you would need to know the answer?'

Bullinger held out his hands. 'What I'm advising is patience and endurance while we await the Lord's deliverance. We must not be too hasty in case we do mischief to …' He fluttered his fingers in the air, 'many worthy persons. Prayer will give us the wisdom to know when the time is right.'

'Surely death is preferable to allowing idolatry to thrive?'

Bullinger waggled his head. 'Not if we, the elect, abstain from all superstition and idolatry. Besides, I have eleven children and numerous grandchildren. I must think of their future.'

Knox sucked in a breath. 'If we don't annihilate the legions of Satan now, our children will have no future. When Christ called upon his apostles to put down their nets and follow him did they falter? Did your mentor and martyr Zwingli hesitate to go into battle? He gave his life so you could practise your faith freely. You may lie in your cosy marital bed free from the fear of persecution but my people are suffering.'

'I'm sorry you feel so strongly, Mr Knox, but for the present, I advise caution. I shall let Dr Calvin know my thoughts and await his response.'

Wending his way to Das Grossmünster to meet Jamie, Knox seethed with anger. In stark contrast to the martyr Zwingli, Bullinger and his like were all cowards, still steeped in the papist indoctrination of their seminary education.

'I see why it's cried the gross monster,' Jamie pointed to the grotesques carved on the great doors. 'Thon are monstrous.'

Knox chuckled. 'You always ken how to cheer me up, Jamie lad.'

Dieppe, April 1554

At *L'Auberge au Port,* Knox threw his bundle on the bed in the garret room. 'God's own country has let me down,' he moaned. 'I'll have no more dealings with hen-heartit Helvetians: nor shall they silence this lone voice.'

'Never fash, brother,' Wedderburn said. 'You're guaranteed a safe haven here in Dieppe for as long as you wish.'

'What's the latest news from England?'

Wedderburn handed him a wad of letters. 'You may read for yourself.'

Greedily, Knox tore open Marjory's letter first. The good news was that her father had freed her from the turret and sent her to live with Amy, far from her mother's malign influence. The bad news concerned MaryBeth whose bloated bodies had been washed up at the mouth of the River Tweed.

'Saddest of all, in death the poor wee mites were still clinging to each other and strangest of all, their hands were tied together – with the handkerchief I embroidered for Amy. It's a mystery how they came by it. Amy is convinced they were so grief-stricken by Guildford's death that they took their own lives. If so, I worry that their souls will be forever damned. But if they are of the elect, will they be angels in heaven?'

The news greatly distressed Knox. Had the twins not come to his rescue that winter night, he surely would have perished: but had he not encouraged their desire to be united with Guildford in paradise they might still be alive. Were their souls damned as Marjory fretted? Though suicide was a mortal sin in the Roman Church he could think of no passage in scripture that condemned it. On the contrary, he could cite cases – such as Samson's sacrifice – where it was justifiable, even pardonable. If only he could explain all this to Marjory himself.

Mrs Bowes's question was simpler but no less easy to answer – when was Knox coming to save them from persecution?

At supper he poured out his woes to Wedderburn. 'I'm no a moudiewort, a blind mole content to grovel in deepest darkness. I must return to England as soon as possible to join my troubled brethren greatly afflicted in these dolorous and dangerous days. I've heard that the flocks I so carefully tended are now enlisting in Satan's leagues and converting in droves. If I could enlist the support of some assured men, I would jeopardise my own life to show what must be done.'

Wedderburn's jovial jowls slackened. 'That's either very brave or very reckless. As soon as you set foot on English soil you'll be seized.'

Knox tugged at his beard. 'Then I can only write to encourage them, to give advice.'

'How many letters can you send in a day? Forbye, they may fall into the wrong hands. A more rigorous campaign is required. Not a few stray arrows – but a cannonade, a bombardment. Come, I have something to show you.'

Down in the laigh, Wedderburn grappled with the key of a rusty iron lock. He heaved open the oak door leading into a barrel-vaulted cellar dimly lit with slit windows high up at street level. A huge object hidden beneath a counterpane poked above the casks and barrels.

'Since it's now too dangerous to send documents to Strasbourg, I bought this ingenious engine.' Wedderburn whipped off the cover and patted the printing press proudly. 'It will produce more copies an hour than you can ever hope to scrieve in your lifetime. It is at your disposal, Mr Knox.'

He opened a kist full of blocks of moveable type. 'Printing is quite a skill. All the words have to be reversed. The letters are placed back to front, which is fiddly at first, but I'm getting my eye in. I maun be chary of Titivilllus, the printer's devil, though.'

Knox chortled. 'So the patron demon of scribes that sprinkles manuscripts with mistakes has wheedled its wicked way into printing.'

Wedderburn nodded and grinned. 'Aye, the devil is my excuse.' With black ink staining his hands and face, he looked very much a wicked imp. 'I've found my true vocation at last.' He grinned with delight. 'Not poet – but printer and publisher.'

Eager to make use of the press, Knox hastened to his garret to scribble a stout reprimand to the faithful in England.

In the cellar, Wedderburn read over the *Admonition*. 'Not keeping your powder dry, I see,' he chortled. 'Decrying the cruel council as bloodthirsty wolves who would devour Christ's small flock. Demanding the blood of thon blind buzzards, the bishops – wily Winchester, butcherly Bonner and your *bête noire*, dreaming Durham, Cuthbert Tunstall. Gardiner fair gets the edge of your tongue: son of Satan, brother of Cain and fellow to Judas the traitor, no less.' His beefy shoulders shook with laughter.

'Not forgetting the treasurer – William Paulet,' Knox retorted. 'He who once called Mary an incestuous bastard who'd never reign in England is now a minister in her council, crouching and licking her feet. A legion of fiends – tyrants, turncoats and hypocrites all.

'As for Queen Mary! The most evil women in the Bible pale beside bloodstained Mary. Jezebel never erected half so many gallows in Israel as malicious Mary has done in London. The howdie should have strangled her at birth like a deformed bairn. That way, the fruits of her cruelty could have been forestalled. Under an English name, she bears a Spanish heart. Witness her marriage to Philip of Spain.'

Wedderburn tapped an inky finger on his chin. 'Strong words, Mr Knox.'

'But are they strong enough to rouse the sleepwalkers from their stupor?'

Emptied of bile, Knox lay in his iron bedstead in great pain. Foul juices heaved in his stomach and hammers clamoured inside his head.

Jamie tiptoed in with a jug of wine. 'Are you able for a visitor?'

Before Knox could answer a black clad figure approached his bed.

'Sir William! You are here!' Knox raised himself up. 'Have you read my epistles? Have you news? Will the people rise up? Is there hope?'

Cecil scowled. 'Nay, I'm on my way to meet with Cardinal Pole, the papal legate, to discuss matters of extreme importance concerning Her Majesty.'

Knox's eyes narrowed to arrow slits. 'So the whore of Babylon has entrusted you to talk with the Antichrist! You, too, are a Judas! A corbie messenger!'

Cecil held up a hand. 'Sticks and stones, Mr Knox. I'm but a humble servant whose only loyalty is to the people of England. I've come to warn you that your epistles have not only aroused the anger of the Catholic bishops but struck fear and alarm into the hearts of those Protestants brave enough to remain in England. Pouring vitriol has only succeeded in fuelling the flames of their pyres. Until now I've fostered respect – reluctant at times – for your integrity but now I fear for your wits.'

'My wits? Do you dare to tell me I am mad?' Knox howled.

Cecil took out a parchment and balanced his eyeglasses on his nose.

Let them all drink the blood of God's saints till they are drunk and their bellies burst yet they shall never prevail! For a kingdom born out of tyranny and blood can neither be stable nor permanent. With one blast they shall be consumed so that their palaces shall be a heap of stones! With such severe curses, what else am I to think?'

'What I say is God's honest truth,' Knox retorted. 'The fear and reverence of the Lord's holy name is quite banished from their hearts. Never fash – death shall devour them in haste. Let the earth swallow them up and let them go quick to hell.'

Cecil let out a long sigh. He rolled up the epistle and tucked it under his cloak. 'Such a tirade overshoots the limits of tolerance even for me. The die is cast, Mr Knox. You've crossed the Rubicon and burned your boats. Dieppe is no longer a safe haven for you – it's too close to England. I would advise you to return to Geneva forthwith.'

With a swish of his black cloak, Cecil swept to the door where he stopped and turned. 'Your epistle has made your return to England impossible. At least while Mary Tudor reigns.'

IV

Pilgrimage to Loretto

> Gif him the habit of ane freir,
> The wyfis will trow, withoutin weir,
> He be ane verie Saint!
> *Ane Satire of the Three Estates*
> Sir David Lindsay, 16th Century

Edinburgh, April 1554

'Praise be the Scottish crown has been safely placed on the queen regent's head. Is that not a matter for rejoicing, Davie?'

Elisabeth was in a merry mood as they rode home after Marie de Guise's coronation at the Edinburgh Tolbooth but Lindsay only grunted in reply. Ignoring his ill humour, she prattled on, 'Did you see Errant Arran's crabbit face when he shambled forward to resign the regency? I feared he might change his mind at the last minute. Or that Matthew Lennox would spring up and snatch the crown, but now that Marie de Guise is Queen Regent of Scotland the commonweal will be in safe hands, *Dei Gratia,*' Elisabeth said and drew out the pearl rosary tied to her girdle. When she made the sign of the cross and kissed the silver crucifix, Lindsay winced.

'Alas we have no king,' he muttered before quoting from his poem,

'Ladies no way I can commend

Presumptuously which doth pretend

To use the office of ane king

Or Realms take in governing.'

'What? How can you say that women should not govern, Davie? Am I too feckless to run the abbey? And what of the much-vaunted Henry of England? Harry was no great skipper. He used religion as a tiller to steer the ship of state in his misguided direction leaving a huge tide of destruction in its wake —families split up, wives wrenched from husbands, heads hacked from bodies, and not least, monks and nuns defrocked and thrown out of monasteries.'

When Lindsay looked sheepish, Elisabeth berated him. 'Would you prefer twa-fangelt Arran, thon Lord of Misrule, with as much sense as a slug? Nowhere on earth could you find a fairer and more forbearing monarch than Marie de Guise. She struggles to sort out the miserable state left by your feeble Stewart kings and the havoc wreaked by fushionless regents. Forbye, she had to seize the regency to foil a conspiracy concocted by Hamilton and Mary Tudor to install Matthew Stewart not only as regent but king of Scots.'

'However venerable, Queen Marie is the puppet of Henri and her de Guise brothers who desire to make us a colony for France to plunder,' Lindsay replied.

'No worse than our own lords looting the treasury. Errant Arran for one has bled the country dry, running up a debt of over £30,000. Why, there isn't a bawbee left in the coffers. That's how well a man runs the country's finances.' She sneered.

'Châtelherault is a thieving rogue who readily took the queen's bribe. In swapping the regency, she had to promise not only revenues but grants of property and titles and goodness knows what else to the Hamilton clan. Our queen mother will raise our infant Scotland to be a grown-up nation – and not a bleating lamb depending on an auld yowe for suckle. In what way is she unfit to rule?'

As she paused for breath, Lindsay leapt in. 'The queen is too much swayed by Cardano's magic wand. He's a magician and a gambler who uses his mathematical skills to win – and lose – large sums of money.'

'Girolamo Cardano is no necromancer but a physician who cured Archbishop Hamilton of his malady,' Elisabeth replied. 'He suffered so badly from shortness of breath he was struck dumb and couldn't speak for ten years.'

Lindsay snorted. 'That was no curse but a blessing. For who'd want to hear Hamilton's long-winded sermons? How did Cardano heal him? By dooking him in a tub of holy water or tapping him on the brow with the bone of a dead saint?'

Elisabeth cocked her head. 'He drew up some kind of astrological chart to show the stars in the heavens at his birth.'

'Sounds like joukerie-pawkery to me. What did this sleekit tod find?'

'That his sickness was caused by Saturn being in the fore at the moment of his birth and once the moon loomed nearer the planet, he'd be cured.' Her face creased with concentration. 'At least I think that's how it worked.'

Lindsay's mouth crinkled into a mischievous smile. 'An auld spaewife could come up with a better cantrip than that, Lisbeth. Dares to call himself a man of science. Why, he's no physician but a gleb-gabbit quacksalver.'

'Whatever you may think of him, Cardano worked a miracle on Hamilton.'

'More's the pity,' Lindsay murmured. 'How much did this so-called cure cost him?'

'Two thousand gold crowns – and the offer of a place at court.'

'What? And where did Hamilton get such a sum? From his brother the erstwhile regent? No wonder our poor land is bankrupt. Or perhaps he raided the diocesan coffers? Even more scandalous – robbing the tithes hardworking folk have struggled to pay.' Lindsay gurgled and spat into the grass verge to clear his throat.

Spotting the specks of blood amongst the spittle, Elisabeth became concerned.

'Don't you see, Davie? If Cardano can cure the archbishop, he can help you. Your wheezy chest is a kistful of whistles. There'll be no bloodletting, no cutting, no foul medicine – just reading a horoscope chart. He's still in Edinburgh. Please, Davie, will you see him?'

He wiped his lips. 'Nay, Lisbeth. I'll have no truck with starry-eyed charlatans. Cardano's no better than the hypocrite hermit of Loretto. Speaking of which …'

He tilted his head at the horde streaming across the auld Roman Bridge over the River Esk at Musselburgh and glowered. 'Pilgrims on their way to the shrine at Loretto,' he sneered before reciting:

'Young men and women singing on their feet
Under the form of feigned sanctitude
For to adore an image in Loretto.
Many came with their fellows for to meet
Committing their foul fornication.'

Elisabeth's face crumpled. 'Davie, why do you think the worst of poor folk hoping for a miracle to relieve their misery?'

'Sad but true,' Lindsay replied. 'There may be some who visit the shrine to gain salvation and remedy from earthly harm but for most a pilgrimage is an excuse for whoring. And not only unmarried lads and lasses are tempted.

'For I have known many good women pass from home
Which have been trapped with such lusts rage
Have returned both with great sin and shame.'

'No wonder Sister Agnes gets all kittled up. She has you doomed for a heretic. If she could hear you now.'

'For condemning the worship of false gods and the selling of false promises? Since the clergy have corrupted Christ's ideals for their own selfish ends, it's they who are in need of reform, Lisbeth. Too many are attracted to the spiritual estate for worldly gain. Where are the true vocations? Where are the virtues of poverty, devotion and chastity?'

Suspicion glinted in her green eyes. 'Are those forced into the nunnery blameworthy for failing to meet your saintly standards, Davie?'

Lindsay looked shamefaced. 'Will you ever forgive me for disrobing the prioress to show her red kirtle under her habit, Lisbeth? It was too dramatic an opportunity to miss.'

Here eyes sparkled with mischief. 'Forgiveness is too merciful for you, Davie. Let that lampoon forever prey on your conscience.'

As Lady Morham cantered towards them, her face radiated excitement. 'I've heard that touching the Virgin's statue heals the sick. Cripples have flung away their crutches and the blind can see.'

When Lindsay opened his mouth to object, Elisabeth gave him a light tap with her riding crop.

'Folk have even come from the north of England to give thanks that a Catholic sits on their throne once more,' Lady Morham went on. 'With Harry Coppernose dinging doun all the holy places there's nowhere for them to pay homage. Jean and I would fain visit the shrine. May Isabelle come, too?'

Elisabeth nodded. 'Why not? My novice should learn about such places.'

'New shrines are springing up everywhere like mushrooms,' Lindsay muttered. 'The Marian cult is gaining strength because a Catholic monarch named Mary sits on the English throne, but it's no more than superstition. Fostering this cult of Mary, Virgin and Mother is blatant blasphemy.'

'Surely not,' Elisabeth replied. 'In scripture, God rewards Mary the mother of his son by taking her bodily into heaven after death. That surely proves her spiritual worthiness.'

'Mary as Mother of God: Mary as Virgin. Is that not a contradiction?'

'She signifies all aspects of womanhood,' Elisabeth retorted. 'Forbye, in this wretched world where we have to endure war, plague and death, folk look to a mother for understanding and sympathy. What's so shocking about that? A mother is a port in the storm of life, where a child can aye be assured of safety and protection.' She looked thoughtful. 'Now that Mary Tudor is on the throne, John will not be welcome in England. I fain would give him shelter here. Have you any news, Davie?'

'John is not only unwelcome – he's in grave danger,' Lindsay replied. 'The saintly Mary Tudor will suffer no heretics. All I ken is he's on his way to Geneva.'

Distress clouded her face. 'To the lair of thon devil incarnate, Calvin.' She gnawed her lip before brightening up again. 'All the more reason to beseech Our Lady to deliver John from the beast's claws. Will you come with us, Davie?'

Lindsay spluttered. 'To kiss the clagged tail of the hermit? Over my dead body, Lisbeth. Such a sacrilege would fling me to kingdom come. Thon so-called hermit is a wolf in wedder's clothing who pulls the wool over folk's eyes. There are none so blind as those who will not see.'

Elisabeth was peeved. 'I wager you didn't scance at your beloved monarchs whenever they set out on pilgrimages. Why, didn't James V trudge barefoot to Loretto afore wedding Princess Madeleine? And afore fateful Flodden, his father rode non-stop to St Duthac's shrine at Tain?'

As Lindsay's anger waned he looked woebegone. 'My jaggy thistle still kens how to sting. What good did it do either of them? One slain in battle and the other driven to death by despair. Thomas Doughty is a pox-ridden, lecherous knave who should be libbed like a gelding. He claims to have a papal dispensation to breach his vow of celibacy.'

Elisabeth's eyebrows shot up in surprise.

'Bizarre as it may seem,' Lindsay continued, 'he alleged that abstaining from hauchmagandie caused his genital organs to swell up so much he couldn't piss and for the sake of his health he was urged to lie with a maiden. Thon hypocrite insults the Blessed Mary by defiling her reputation as mystic rose, virgin most pure. If you take Isabelle and Jean within a mile of him, I warn you, your virgins will not return intact.'

'They shall indeed,' Elisabeth retorted. 'You have my word on it, Davie Lindsay.' She dismounted and handed him the reins. 'Look after our nags, while we have a daunder. Who kens? Lady Morham is a creaking gate, aye smitten with some ailment or other. The laugh will be on the other side of your face if she's cured.'

Weaving a way through the pilgrims' camp, a shambles of makeshift shelters and tents, Elisabeth and Lady Morham swerved to avoid the higgledy-piggledy stalls and booths where pardoners thrust crude copies of the miraculous statue and other geegaws in their faces.

'Let's seek out the shrine,' Lady Morham said. 'I imagine it'll be made of alabaster gilded with gold leaf and studded with precious stones.'

Overhearing them, a hirpling old hag with a withered leg snorted. 'Huh. The sleekit English knaves set fire to the chapel and hermitage during the Pinkie rout. Over yonder is the hermit's tent. The one flying Our Lady's colours.' She pointed a gnarled finger at a blue and white striped pennant. 'And thon's the hermit.'

A figure in a hempen tunic and leather sandals crawled out of the pavilion and mounted a wooden platform.

'With thon lank straggly locks, he looks more like a wild man than a holy man,' Elisabeth said. 'Let's hear what he has to say.'

'Tak tent, tak tent, good folks,' he began and waved a pewter flask. 'I, Thomas Doughty, may only be a humble friar but on Mount Sinai, the Angel Gabriel appeared to me with a message: to find the statue of Our Lady of Loretto. Who, you may speir, is the Lady of Loretto? You're all acquent with the crusaders, the brave Christian knights who took up the cross to wrench the Holy Land from the Moslem invaders?'

'Aye,' the spectators chorused.

'Thon Saracens, rampaged through Jerusalem and Bethlehem defiling many sacred sites in the name of their God, Allah. These heathens were hellbent on burning the holy house in Nazareth where the Angel Gabriel told Mary she was to bear the Son of God. But then angels appeared and carried it across the sea for safety to the village of Loreto in Italy.

'Since then, many have gone on pilgrimage to thon faraway land and God has rewarded them for their faith with countless miraculous healings. But it's not an easy passage for you folk living in this far-flung corner of Europe. That's why Gabriel came to me in a dream. Go to the Holy Land, he said, and take the statue of the Virgin Mary carved by St Luke himself back to Scotland. Gabriel has guided me here to this sacred spring whose water will cure all ills. That's why this shrine is dedicated to Our Lady of Loretto.' He held up the pewter flask. 'Now, who shall be the first to benefit from Our Lady's miraculous powers?'

He scoured the rows of spectators with a snakelike gaze, trawling for victims before alighting on someone in the front. 'Come with me pilgrims.' When he jumped down from the dais, a line of spellbound pilgrims followed him to his tent.

Elisabeth shivered. 'Thon hermit makes my flesh creep. Let's away from here.' Turning to go, she felt a tug at her sleeve. A beggar, his unseeing eyes showing white, held out a phial. 'Here's for your charity, mother. Water from St Mary's holy well in Nazareth.'

'Poor wee laddie, blindness is a terrible affliction,' Elisabeth said and rummaged through her pocket for a coin. From the edge of her vision, she caught a flicker in his eyes but as she turned her head, he darted off, ducking and diving his way through the throng.

As they passed a spaewife's tent, a gypsy in a multi-coloured costume held out her hand. 'Cross my palm with silver, kind ladies, and I'll tell your fortune.'

Lady Morham's eyes lit up but Elisabeth shook her head. 'I'm a nun, mind. I cannot be seen dealing with the devil.'

Setting off for a daunder, Elisabeth caught sight of Lindsay dozing on a saddle blanket. After sneaking up on him she crouched down and sprinkled him with the holy water.

He stirred and shook his head. 'Is that the rain on?' Spotting the phial in her hand he laughed. 'It'll take more than being drookit in blessed water to restore my health – or my faith in the Catholic Church.'

The effort of kneeling on all fours made Elisabeth groan. 'Auld age doesn't come itself. I should steep these ancient bones in holy water,' she moaned as she swung her legs round.

'Davie, who are the Saracens the hermit was havering on about? He said they destroyed many Christian shrines in God's holy name. Are they reformers like thon wife-slayer, Harry of England, who razed our religious houses to the ground?'

Lindsay shook his head. 'Moslems or Moors or Saracens are the followers of Mohammed who claims to be a prophet of God, or Allah as they cry him. Islam is their faith and the Q'ran is their holy book.'

Elisabeth creased her brow. 'If Christianity is the one, true faith why does God allow other faiths? Isn't the Bible the true word of God? And if the Lord sent his son, Jesus Christ, to be crucified on the cross to save us why, then, did he also give his word to Mohammed?'

Lindsay chuckled. 'I always said you were a wee heathen, my jaggy thistle, with your lack of religious instruction. Well may you ask. But we can never know the mind of God who moves in mysterious ways. The path of man's search for truth takes many twists and turns. But this midden isn't one of them.' He waved a hand at the camp. 'Overtimes I think our religious observance is regressing. Look at them with their tongues hanging out – like pagans worshipping the golden calf.'

Elisabeth shaded her eyes. 'Here's Jean. Let's hear what miracle Doughty worked on her.'

Jean Hepburn flopped onto the blanket, red-faced and breathless.

'Thon horny auld hermit invited me into his tent to show me his magic wand,' she blurted. '*Do you want to witness a miracle, my young maiden?* he asked. *Lay your virginal fingers on this and it shall spring into life.* Then he pulled up his louse-ridden habit and tried to make me fouter with his wizened auld whistle. What does he take me for? Yeuch. It's enough to make me puke. Thon holy hermit is a filthy auld fornicator.'

V

Troubles at Frankfurt

> Then began the Tragedy, and our consultation ended.
> Who was most blame-worthy, God shall judge!
>
> *History of the Reformation*
> John Knox, 16th Century

Geneva, November 1554

The squiggles and hieroglyphs jiggling and wriggling across the page like tiny black imps made Knox's eyes cross. The key to the truth lay in deciphering the original languages of the scriptures but how could he possibly make head or tail of the Hebrew alphabet? It was all tapsalteerie and reading a scroll back to front made his head birl. No wonder scholars made so many contradictory interpretations. He scratched his scalp with his quill. Mastering the language of God was going to be more difficult than he thought.

In Geneva he planned to live the calm life of a scholar without fear of arrest or persecution and undertake his own translation of the Bible. In the tiny room tucked under the eaves of Calvin's gabled house, Knox had everything he needed: table and stool, paper and pen, and books from Calvin's library. All he needed to complete his contentment was a parish so that he could send for his beloved Marjory but what did Dr Calvin have in mind for his future?

As he wondered how to broach the subject, Catherine summoned him to the great scholar's study where he found Calvin gazing out of the window. Knox waited a few moments before coughing politely.

Calvin turned and dabbed damp eyes. 'This garden gives me great pleasure – so full of fond memories of my beloved wife. Idelette was my faithful helpmate and best companion of my life, ever ready to share all my trials, not only banishment and poverty but even death itself. When she was taken from me, my grief was very heavy. Matrimony is indeed God's gift to man, Mr Knox.'

With Calvin in a reflective mood, perhaps now was the time to grasp the nettle. Knox cleared his throat. 'I share your feelings, Dr Calvin, and I bid you look kindly on my request for a parish so that I may invite my betrothed to Geneva.'

Calvin fixed him with cold eyes. 'All in good time, brother. In the meantime, I've received a request for your ministry.'

Knox's heart soared – being given a parish would fulfil his greatest wish – but when Calvin read out the letter it sank again. The parish was not in Geneva. It wasn't even in Switzerland. Twenty-one members of the English Protestant congregation led by William Whittingham were inviting him to serve as their pastor in Frankfurt, Germany.

'Your fame has spread, Mr Knox. You must consider it a great honour.'

Knox did not and Calvin's words were little consolation. His worn-out carcase yearned to stay still, in one place, with his mind set on higher things.

'Frankfurt has attracted many French Huguenots as well as fugitives fleeing Mary Tudor's persecution in England,' Calvin explained.

So many differing factions signified trouble, Knox suspected. 'Is there no one else to take on this mission? Forbye, I don't speak German.'

'Don't let that trouble you. Your congregation will speak either English or French and you're fluent in both. Besides, Brother Whittingham one of my most able disciples has a facility for languages. He will interpret for you. I had a mind to keep him here in Geneva but, because he also speaks German, he's of more use in Frankfurt. However, he's not yet an ordained pastor.'

Knox tried another tack. 'I fain would finish my new translation of the Bible.'

'There are scholars aplenty to take that on, Mr Knox, but you're a man of action. I've heard good reports of how you calmed the breast of the savage beast in Berwick. No stranger to controversy, you're the one best fitted to create order out of chaos. Frankfurt needs you.'

But Knox did not need Frankfurt. The prospect filled him with despondency. Could he thole a long tramp to northern Germany? 'November is not the most favourable month to travel. Many of the Alpine paths will be impassable, knee-deep in snow ...' he trailed off.

'You're a well-seasoned traveller, Mr Knox. The Lord will guide you.'

Knox took a deep breath before blurting, 'I do not see God's hand in this mission, Dr Calvin, and I'm unwilling to go where God has not called me.'

Taken aback, Calvin shot him a cold, contemptuous look. 'God doesn't always speak to us directly, Mr Knox, as I have learnt. On my way to Strasbourg, a local uprising forced me to make a detour through Geneva. I planned to stay for only one night until William Farel pleaded with me to stay and help him. But Geneva was a whirlpool of revolt and I was a young and timid scholar who desired nothing more than peace and tranquillity to study.

'When I resisted, Dr Farel reminded me of Jonah's fate in attempting to flee the Lord: he was cast into the sea and swallowed by a giant fish. When he then laid a curse on me, striking terror into my very soul, I felt the hand of God stretching down from heaven to hold me here. And thus I yielded to God's will.' Calvin narrowed his eyes. 'I shall not lay a curse on you, Mr Knox, for I know you will not refuse this beleaguered congregation. Their plea is the voice of the Lord calling you.'

That may be so, but deep down a voice told Knox this was not God's will but

Calvin's. How could he defy the patron on whose goodwill he depended?

'Once your mission there is accomplished, Mr Knox, I give you my word a parish shall be your reward.'

Given this promise, Knox could hardly refuse and resigned himself to packing up his bags yet again.

On the morning of his departure, Catherine drew Knox aside. 'You'll be meeting some of Dr Calvin's associates and … one of his pupils.' Blushing deeply she dropped her glance. It was unlike Catherine to appear so bashful. 'Master Whittingham … is a most worthy and dependable … brother.'

She fumbled in the pocket of her skirt and drew out a letter. 'May I ask you to give him this?'

Knox gave a wry smile. 'With a joyful heart, for it gives another purpose to my journey: winging my way to Frankfurt to play Cupid.'

Frankfurt-am-Main

Tucked away in the poorest corner of Frankfurt, the lofty four-storeyed house with a steeply pitched roof and gable end built into the city wall loomed lonely and forbidding. Above the door, a macabre skull ringed by writhing serpents was carved on the lintel.

'Thon place gives me the creeps, master. It looks haunted,' Jamie said, echoing Knox's presentiments.

When the door slowly opened on squeaky hinges and a tall figure shrouded in a black gown emerged, they both gave a jolt.

'Welcome to Das Pesthaus, Pastor Knox. I am William Whittingham.'

'The pest hoose?' Jamie muttered. 'Even worse. What kind of beasties crawl about here? We'll need to burn a wheen of fleabane to get rid of them.'

'You're right. This was the plague house,' Whittingham replied, 'but do not fret. There's been no Black Death here for over two hundred years. Nevertheless, fleabane may be useful in purging the plague of two-legged pests that currently infest our abode.' He tossed back a lock of flaxen hair and winked at Jamie.

Knox warmed to him at once. Little wonder that Catherine was attracted to the handsome young pastor, he thought as he delivered her letter. 'From Dr Calvin's good sister.'

'Ah, you mean Catherine. Thank you.' Whittingham gave a bashful smile and tucked the *billet doux* into a pocket.

Over the next few days, Knox witnessed with dismay the discord amongst his congregation. Though largely illiterate, his Berwick flock had been eager to take instruction, whereas here university trained theologians and scholars wrangled incessantly. Living cheek by jowl in Das Pesthaus caused their petty squabbles to flare up into huge rows.

'Sadly, education doesn't always lead to enlightenment and harmony,' Knox grumbled over a frugal meal of bratwurst and rye bread in the refectory. 'They would quarrel over how many angels can jig on a pinhead.'

'This is a veritable Tower of Babel,' Whittingham replied. 'Whereas the Genevan church is united under Dr Calvin, the Frankfurt faithful are deeply divided. Until we English arrived, the German Lutherans and French Calvinists lived in harmony. I've done my best to reconcile the warring schisms but I'm not experienced enough as a pastor to keep the folk in order. That's why I sent out a call to all the exiled parsons inviting them here – but they all declined.'

'No wonder,' Knox retorted. 'So I'm the pastor of last resort?'

Looking sheepish, Whittingham shook his head. 'Nay, not at all, brother. You are Dr Calvin's chosen one, sent to calm the waters. This is our dilemma.' He ran his fingers through his floppy hair and sighed. 'When the French Calvinists allowed us to worship in their Church of the White Ladies – provided we follow their liturgy – I devised a form of service that satisfied both their condition and my flock. However, the recent influx of refugees insist on using the English Book of Common Prayer.'

Knox groaned. 'So Cranmer's Prayer Book is rearing its evil head again. Thon's a travesty. Fretting over the colours of chasubles – they're worse than maidens preparing for a party. It's a waste of God's good time.'

Whittingham's shoulders sagged. 'They're loathe to leave their liturgy behind. But now Magistrate Von Glauberg has threatened to withdraw permission if we persist in using the English Prayer Book.' He cast Knox a pitiful, pleading look. 'I see no end of this contention unless one party relents.'

Though he sympathised, Knox could not yield on truth. 'I'm sorry, brother, but it cannot be me. Unlike you, I'm not a natural diplomat. It sticks in my craw to give in. I bent the knee once before when I agreed to the Black Rubric but I will not do so again. I knew then it was wrong and I've been proved right for it has caused nothing but strife. Let the devil get a foot in the door and he'll make himself at home.'

Seeing his colleague's downcast face, Knox tugged at his beard. 'Here's what I propose. I shall continue to preach but I refuse to administer the sacrament. Let someone else dole out their blessed wafers while they kneel and stick out their tongues like frogs catching flies. If they object, then I shall resign.'

Knox secretly hoped they would, for he loathed his Frankfurt ministry and had sent repeated requests to Dr Calvin to liberate him from his post. So far they had gone unheeded. Lest his correspondence fall into the wrong hands, he'd signed with his *nom-de-guerre*, John Sinclair. Perhaps Calvin did not recognise his signature?

At the next meeting, when the vote was taken on Knox's proposal, the majority of hands shot up to object. As he addressed the congregation, he strove to mask the smirk on his face. 'In the spirit of reconciliation I've done everything I can to compromise.' He held out his arms in a gesture of compliance, 'But you have rebuffed me. I now beg to be released from my ministry here.'

Knox sat down beside Whittingham to await their decision. 'That should take the wind out of their sails. I'll no be shedding any tears leaving here. Frankfurt is the bleakest place on God's earth. I yearn to be back in God's own city.'

Whittingham gave a heart-rending smile. 'If truth be told, so do I. I greatly miss Catherine. We met in Geneva when I was a student of Dr Calvin. I'd hoped to ask for her hand.' He gave a short laugh. 'I often wonder if he's sent me here to prove I am worthy of his ward.'

'Indeed you are, brother, and I would support your suit. Catherine seems,' Knox hesitated before choosing his words, 'a devoted and diligent handmaid.'

Whittingham nodded his thanks. 'Aye, beneath that prickly coat lies a soft heart. She has a sad history. Everyone knows her as Catherine Calvin but her own name is Jacquemin. Her parents – wealthy French Huguenots – followed Dr Calvin to Geneva but tragically fell victim to the plague of 1540. The widow Stordeur took in the orphan and when she married Dr Calvin, he adopted Catherine as his ward to protect her inheritance. She may appear austere but Catherine is her stepfather's guardian angel.'

'No need to explain,' Knox replied. 'Blessed is he who can find a virtuous woman. For her price *is* far above rubies. Thanks to the Lord I, too, have found such a one.'

'Will she be joining you in Frankfurt?' Whittingham asked.

Knox slowly shook his head. 'Alas nay. As yet my beloved Marjory is not my spouse and it sorely grieves me that she still languishes in England.'

Whittingham placed a hand on his shoulder. 'That must distress you, brother, I shall pray for her safe deliverance.'

As the congregation deliberated over his resignation in heated whispers, Knox began to fidget. 'Why are they taking so long?' he grumbled. 'I thought they'd be thrilled to see the back of this thrawn Scotsman.'

At last their spokesman disentangled himself to give their verdict. While they agreed to continue using Pastor Whittingham's order of service for the present, in no wise could they consent to Pastor Knox's resignation.

At his wits' end, Knox felt like tearing his hair out. 'Is there no way out of this mire?' he appealed to Whittingham. 'In answering Dr Calvin's call, I quashed the niggling doubt this was not God's plan. Now my suspicion has been proved right. I'm serving no useful purpose in Frankfurt. Forbye, my presence here is only fostering schism when it should be a focus for unity. It's better for all concerned that I depart forthwith.'

'Nay!' Whittingham yelped in alarm before dropping his voice. 'You cannot leave us in our hour of need. What will Dr Calvin say? You cannot go against his wishes. You cannot resign without his blessing. He takes a dim view of those disciples who act without his approval.'

'Then I shall ask him if I may now stand down with a good conscience. I've patched up the leaky vessel as best I can to steer a course through choppy channels. Now's the time for the skipper to hand back the tiller.'

Though no answer came from Geneva, the spring thaw sent fresh contingents of English exiles from Strasbourg and Zurich – led by Pastors Grindal and Lever, both staunch Cranmer supporters. With a sinking heart, Knox and Whittingham watched them herd their flock through the door of Das Pesthaus.

'Why so gloomy, brothers?' A bulky figure elbowed his way between them and landed two large paws on their shoulders. 'I've heard all about your trials and tribulations, brothers, but never fear, I'm on your side and eager for the fray.'

While Christopher Goodman's pugilistic face broke into a broad grin, Knox was on the verge of tears at meeting his friend again. Wiping his eyes, he heard a female voice in his ear, 'I fain would have a word with you, Mr Knox.'

Her words were tinged with a distinct Scottish burr: Knox whirled round to face a buxom matron of middle years.

'I'm Elizabeth Macheson, wife to Miles Coverdale.' She tilted her head towards a scrawny wee man with a scrunched up face and bulbous nose resting on an iron bound oak kist.

'The renowned translator of the Great Bible?' Knox asked in admiration and surprise.

'Aye, it is,' the buxom matron, answered for him. 'But the journey has greatly wearied him. We've stravaiged the length and breadth of the continent hoping to find a quiet haven. When thon Jezebel, Mary Tudor, took the throne, we sailed to my sister in Copenhagen where her husband is professor of theology.'

Knox's eyes widened. 'You mean John Macalpine?'

'Aye, the very one. Though they cry him Maccabeus. When he heard you were in Frankfurt, he advised us to come here. He sends his good wishes. 'Meanwhile, we would be glad of a cot to lay our weary heads.'

'Never fash, my lad Jamie will find you a room at our inn.'

At supper Knox expected the usual cold collation but was astonished to be served a bowl of steaming stew and warm white rolls. Meanwhile, Jamie dashed around the refectory plonking flagons of spiced wine on the trestles, under the watchful eye of Mrs Coverdale.

'I pray you have no objection to my wife lending a hand in the kitchen,' Coverdale said.

'None at all,' Knox replied savouring the smell of roasting meat in his nostrils. 'Praise be to the gentle sex. Mistress Coverdale kens the way to a man's heart. Until now we've lived like monks in a monastery. Starved of womenfolk, we eat in a refectory, sleep in dormitories and worship in a Cistercian cloister. All that is lacking are habits, cowls and tonsures. Some men flee the company of women, but others wilt without the gentle sex to succour and comfort us.' Knox's tone was wistful.

'Women have their uses, as long as they know their place,' Goodman grunted and wiped his bowl clean with a hunk of bread. 'Though I wager she's the master in their house,' he muttered and gestured with a downturned thumb.

Mrs Coverdale carried over a pot to dole out second helpings. 'We're here to help in any way we can, brother. My gude brother tells me those who favour Cranmer's liturgy are thwarting your attempt to practice a purer form of worship.'

Knox sipped the spiced wine and licked his lips. 'Aye, and we seem to have reached a stalemate.'

'Then a higher authority is needed to arbitrate,' Mrs Coverdale said. 'Why not ask Dr Calvin to be the final judge?'

How did such simple solution not occur to him, Knox thought. 'Why not indeed? I shall set out our case forthwith.'

Knox's summary of the Prayer Book greatly amused Goodman who kept breaking out into raucous laughter. 'This is particularly wry, brother,' he chuckled. *'We must rid our church of all the apish pageantry of papistry and popelings* ...Your poetic turn of phrase can hardly fail to rouse Dr Calvin into action against the apostates.'

'By deliberately drawing attention to the mumbo-jumbo and hocus-pocus of papist practices therein I hope to show him the serpent we're wrestling,' Knox replied.

Calvin's response came quickly – by return – causing Knox to wonder if he had received his resignation but was deliberately ignoring it until he'd fulfilled his mission. For only then would he be rewarded a parish – and Marjory.

The next Sunday, Knox read out Calvin's reply in which he gently upbraided his Frankfurt brethren for being so attached to popish dregs before ordering a committee, including Knox, Whittingham and Goodman, to draw up a completely new service. Striving to lower the note of triumph in his voice, Knox ended with Calvin's exhortation: 'Be reasonable and yield to their instruction.'

By the time Knox came down from the pulpit, the sheep belonging to pastors Grindal and Lever were bleating their objections.

'Look at them,' Goodman grunted. 'What a despicable spectacle. Beating their breasts over the loss of their papist pigswill.'

'There will be weeping and gnashing of teeth ere long,' Knox retorted.

Somehow the herd reached a compromise. Lever informed the threesome that Whittingham's service would be followed until a vote was taken at Easter.

'Then we shall win,' Knox said. 'They will not dare to gainsay Dr Calvin's will.'

On Maundy Thursday, Goodman entered the refectory with a grim look on his bulldog face. As he leant across the board for a hunk of bread, his jaw clenched more tightly.

'Just as we were steering our ramshackle ship towards a safe berth, a cannonball has been fired across our bows.' He crumbled the bread between his fingers. 'Another flock has arrived from Strasbourg.' Knox and Whittingham let out low anguished, groans, but there was more.

'This time, their shepherd is none other than Canon Richard Cox.'

'Never fash,' Knox said in a bid to overcome their frustration. 'Knox will be more than a match for Cox.'

VI

Failure in Frankfurt

> I fear not the tyranny of man,
> neither yet what the devil can invent against me.
>
> John Knox, 16th Century

Frankfurt, March 1555

Every time the studded oak door of the White Ladies opened, a cold wind whirled round the porch where the trinity of Knox, Goodman and Whittingham took shelter. The Coverdales and other supporters stopped to greet them but many scuttled past, heads bowed, ignoring them. After filing up the nave, the folk parted ways: the Knoxians to the left and the Coxians to the right.

'I'd hoped the vote at Easter – the season of renewal and hope – would heal the rift,' Whittingham said. 'Now that Canon Cox has arrived from Strasbourg with his followers, I fear it will be opened up again.'

Goodman, however, was more cynical. 'This is no coincidence but a scheme for the Coxians to outnumber the Knoxians and undermine our authority.'

'It looks as if they will,' Whittingham murmured. 'Mary Tudor's recent cull of bishops has deeply distressed our flocks. Hooper, Ridley and Latimer all went heroically to the stake.'

'Yet Cranmer, the source of all our troubles, has recanted.' Knox was full of contempt for his rival.

'I dare say prison has broken his spirit,' Whittingham said. 'Nevertheless their sacrifice troubles our people. How can they cast aside the work of these martyrs? Besides, many hope to return one day to a Protestant England where Cranmer's Prayer Book will be the cornerstone of their faith.'

'That may be so,' Knox replied, 'but here in Frankfurt today, our church is riven with the schism it has caused.'

When a gaunt-faced mother in a shabby cloak struggled to open the door for her fatherless bairns, Knox, whose heart never failed to be touched by the plight of widows and orphans, hastened to her aid. Anna de Tzerclas, widow of Bishop John Hooper, would surely side with him but catching sight of Knox, she lifted her chin high and threw a withering look that stopped him in his tracks.

She raised her voice to marshal her brood to troop past the trinity. 'Keep to the right of the nave, children, and stay together. No straying from the righteous path,' she added.

'Thanks to secretary Cecil circulating your inflammatory *Admonition to the faithful*, many blame you, Brother Knox, for stoking the fires of Bloody Mary's crusade,' Whittingham murmured. 'Widow Hooper believes you've added oil to the flames of her husband's funeral pyre.'

This noble lady of Burgundy was no *Stabat Mater dolorosa*, Knox reflected. The silent accusation etched on her face pierced him to the very core: *You* may be still alive, but my husband did not flinch from the flames. As a chill ran through him, Knox stamped his feet and thwacked his arms against his ribs to warm up.

'She spurns us as cowards for fleeing England, yet she doesn't seem to hold Cox in contempt,' he said.

'She cannot see through the canon's pious mask,' Whittingham replied. 'Cox is not only a coward but a barefaced bully. As headmaster of Eton, he was notorious for his cruel floggings. Then, as Chancellor of Oxford, he purged the university of all vestiges of popery – burning books and manuscripts, destroying ornaments and cancelling endowments. Because of his ruthless crusade, we nicknamed him the Cancellor. I bid you beware, brother. Cox takes no prisoners and his *modus operandi* hinges heavily on badgering, bullying and blackmail. His favoured tactic in an argument is to talk over his opponents in a loud booming voice until they fall silent and cave in to his browbeating.' His shoulders slumped. 'If he uses his bullying tactics here, the Coxians will outvote us. Our cause is lost, I fear.'

'Do not lose heart, brother,' Knox said. 'I was loath to come here but now I believe the Lord has sent me to confront Cox and stamp out this papist abomination once and for all. Cox is one of the Hydra's many heads, the beast I maun slaughter. Never fash. Cox and his retinue are not yet members of our congregation and so cannot vote.'

A blast of wind as the church door opened cut short their conversation.

'Here comes Cox now with his henchmen,' Goodman muttered. 'By all appearances, they're out to make trouble.'

The corpulent canon wobbled to a halt in front of his opponents. His bulbous eyes bulged out of their sockets and he rubbed at an unsightly swelling on his neck. Gluttony had bloated his belly and pride had swollen the goitre, Knox reflected.

The canon's eyebrows sprouted like demonic horns. 'I await your sermon with bated breath, Mr Knox. You never fail to inflame passions – and tempers.'

From the pulpit, Knox surveyed his divided congregation. To his right, his loyal supporters clustered round Whittingham – the minority – to his left, the serried ranks of Coxians sat behind their leader flanked by his menacing henchmen – the majority.

Never mind, Knox was confident right would win over might: his reasoning would carry the vote. Before he began, one of Cox's henchmen, a shilpit, whippet-faced man with sleekit eyes and a pointed beard, produced a flask for the canon to sip from – a heaven-sent signal.

'Shall we drink of the popish dregs?' Knox began. 'Shall we continue to use this liturgy which demands dressing up in copes of many colours? A vain display for which a bishop gave his life. Did the martyr Hooper die in vain?'

Widow Hooper lowered her eyes at this reminder: her husband's defiant refusal to wear ceremonial vestments had led him to the stake.

'While others give their lives for the true faith, the English church is sinking into the depths of depravity. Among its leaders sloth, greed and pride are rampant – the very same vices that cursed the Roman Church. Letting the church slide into the old, idolatrous ways is sloth. Receiving generous revenues from multiple ecclesiastical offices is utter greed.'

Having aimed this shot at Cox, a holder of several benefices, Knox was gratified to see the canon's florid face deepen to a purple hue and the veins stand out on his brow.

'With these ill-gotten gains, they buy the support of mealy-mou'ed henchmen whose lickspittle feeds their puffed-up pride! And all of these vices incur God's wrath!'

Paying no heed to the shuffling in the front row – the Coxians squirming in their seats, no doubt – Knox flicked through Whittingham's prayer book to locate the first prayer. He was about to start reading when someone scrambled into the pulpit and dug him sharply in the ribs. Before he could catch his breath, strong arms dragged him down the stairs and out the side door.

Meanwhile, from the pulpit, the whippet began reciting loudly and emphatically from Cranmer's liturgy.

Seething with rage, Knox confronted the presiding pastor but Lever only threw up his hands and tilted his head towards the Coxians bleating the responses like sheep. Knox stormed outside to wait for the whippet.

'How dare you interrupt my service.'

'How dare you slander the reverend canon,' the whippet hissed, splattering Knox's face with his spittle.

'However reverend your canon may be he does not merit being revered. What have I said that is slanderous? Do you deny benefiting from his largesse?'

The whippet waggled his finger. 'You'll pay for this, Mr Knox.'

Stepping between them, Whittingham turned to the whippet. 'May I remind you that you are a guest in our church and should behave as such.'

'For the present,' Lever broke in. 'Until such time as the new arrivals are granted full membership of our congregation.'

Goodman glowered at him. 'Over my rotting corpse. You're not only a Trojan horse, dumped in our midst to destroy us from within, Brother Lever, but a Judas.'

Knox put up a hand. 'Enough carfuffle. Fisherrow fishwives bickering over creels of herring are more civil. Let's discuss this at a later date, when tempers have cooled.'

At the Wednesday meeting, when Whittingham's faithful few threw out Lever's proposal to admit them, Cox and his colleagues walked out.

'That's the end of that,' Goodman declared. 'Good riddance.'

Knox shook his head. 'If they agree to accept our liturgy and repent of past idolatry, then we must accept them as members.'

While Whittingham was speechless, Goodman was incredulous. 'You're championing their admittance? Surely we cannot allow that.'

Knox was unflustered. 'Because, brothers, it is not only right, it is their right. Otherwise they'll crow that fear has caused us to turn down their request.'

'But the Coxians will then be the majority,' Goodman growled. 'They'll ride roughshod over us.'

Knox put a hand on his sleeve. 'Never forget the Lord is on our side. And a man with God is always in the majority.'

On Knox's recommendation, the congregation voted to admit the Coxians. Business over, the trinity rose to leave when Lever detained them. Canon Cox wished to propose another motion. When the whippet seconded it, Whittingham sprang to his feet. 'This is preposterous! You cannot do this!'

'We can and shall,' Lever replied.

A show of hands indicated the majority were in favour of the motion: to expel Mr Knox as minister of their congregation.

A cruel sneer smeared the canon's lardy face. 'We've had enough of your meddling, Mr Knox,' Cox jeered. 'The majority has spoken.'

As he packed up his books and papers to leave, Knox felt a great weight lift from his shoulders. He was thoroughly scunnered with Frankfurt where he'd come against his will but the irony that his foe Cox and not Dr Calvin had finally answered his prayer amused him.

'We're saddened to see you go, Master Knox,' Mrs Coverdale said as she handed him a parcel of food for his journey. 'But who can blame you, for the devil has claimed Frankfurt for his own.' She shivered. 'And the malevolent spirits who possess this Pesthaus have stifled the Lord's voice. Be assured that wherever you go, Miles and I shall follow.'

'Thank you, dear sister, and I shall be glad to see you both in Geneva.'

'Brother John, you may not have to leave.' The cry came from Whittingham wheezing with excitement as he ran up the stairs. 'I've warned Magistrate von Glauberg about serious trouble if these newcomers dismiss the rightful preacher and he's agreed to arbitrate. Come quickly! He's about to address the congregation.'

In the pulpit of the White Ladies, Von Glauberg began by admonishing the audience like a schoolmaster scolding a class of wayward pupils. Had he not opened the door of the White Ladies on condition they used the Calvinist service? He now threatened to close it again if they did not. No further argument would be tolerated.

'Let's see what Cox makes of this,' Knox murmured.

'Let's pray he walks out and takes his henchmen with him,' Whittingham replied.

When Cox stood up to give a grovelling apology to the magistrates, the trinity could hardly believe their ears. And when he made a solemn promise to obey their diktats, Goodman ground his jaw. 'I don't like all this bowing and scraping. It sets my teeth on edge.'

Whittingham, however, looked hopeful. 'Does this mean you'll stay with us, Brother John?'

Knox shrugged. 'Let's see what Sunday brings.'

In Das Pesthaus refectory, Cox and his crew hogged the benches by the large fireplace, consigning the Knoxians to the outer reaches, the coldest corner of the draughty hall. To spite the tyrannical canon and despite his protestations, Mrs Coverdale ensured that the Knoxians were served first at table.

'Keep your lugs pinned back, Jamie,' Knox murmured as the lad went back and forth serving supper, 'and find out what they're conniving.'

It wasn't long before Jamie reported back. 'He's telling his cronies to go along with the magistrates' order – for now. Says it'll no affect their prayer book once they're back in England. But he's plotting something else with whippet face that I couldn't catch.'

Whether it was this news or the tingling in his bladder that signalled a gravel stone, Knox felt queasy in the pit of his stomach. Unable to face food, he bade goodnight to his colleagues. When he came out of the privy, a Cox's sentinels barred his way.

From behind them, the whippet elbowed his way through. 'I'd like to speak with you in private, Mr Knox.' His words were polite but his expression hostile.

'Another time, I'm off to bed. It's been a tiring day.' When Knox tried to push past him, two guards grabbed his arms and marched him along the corridor. 'Unhand me at once. Shackling only steeks my tongue. Forbye, I never give in to threats. Especially from persons unknown to me.'

After introducing himself as Edward Isaac, the whippet gave a nod to the brutes to release their captive. Reluctantly Knox let him in to his room but slammed the door in the guards' faces.

'In your latest missive to Dr Calvin you pour scorn on our Prayer Book,' Isaac said.

'That was a private letter. You must have purloined it.'

'However it fell into my hands is neither here nor there. You mock our order of service as being a garbled version of the Latin liturgy. You've done this out of sheer spite to promote your own form of worship. You're well known as a man who speaks his mind, Mr Knox, but I'm here to warn you: continue to speak out against Dr Cox and you'll be cast into the deepest dungeon at the very least. That I can guarantee.' His look was filled with menace. 'However, moderating your opposition will be to your advantage.'

Knox's weariness lifted: his hackles rose. 'As I said, I never yield to threats — veiled or otherwise. You have no grounds to arrest me.'

'Not yet, Mr Knox.'

'What do you mean?' Knox lunged forward and shoved his face into Isaac's.

'Stay your hand, Mr Knox,' he said, edging backwards to the door. 'One whistle from me and the guards will burst down that door.'

'No need for that.' Knox lifted the latch. 'I'll let you out like the bleating lamb you are.'

24 March 1555

On the Saturday before Knox's final sermon, delivering a missive with the seal of Frankfurt legislature, Whittingham could hardly contain his excitement. 'This will be from Van Glauberg, ratifying our agreement to use the White Ladies.'

Knox tore it open. 'Nay, it appears to be a diktat from the Frankfurt council forbidding me to preach. So, Knox has met his match in Cox,' he said in a voice weighed with weariness. 'I'd foreseen my fight to be against that synagogue of Satan, the Roman Catholic Church, but it seems the horde of darkness is gathering strength in the English church. Cox has denounced me.'

Whittingham slapped his cheeks. 'Forgive me, brother, this is all my fault.'

Shamefaced, he confessed. At the council's request, he'd translated Knox's pamphlet, *A Faithful Admonition to England,* into Latin for them to read and thought no more of it – until receiving a summons to appear before them.

'I was at pains to tell them how learned, wise, grave and godly you were. Of your excellent qualities they were in no doubt, but some passages seriously concerned them. In fact,' he hesitated, 'they might even be construed as treasonable. Cox has been stirring up trouble. Reminding the council that you condemned Emperor Charles as being, *no less an enemy to Christ than Nero was,* he has accused you of high treason. With the imperial army encamped nearby at Augsburg, the magistrates are scared. However sympathetic they may be to your plight, they've no wish to be charged with harbouring a traitor.'

'Never fash, brother, the answer is quite simple,' Knox replied to comfort him. 'I shall leave Frankfurt forthwith.'

'Nay! For that means Cox has won. How can that be? Surely God intended his visible army, the elect, to strike at the horde and win?' Whittingham ran his fingers through his flaxen hair in frustration.

Knox had no answer for he, too, felt forlorn. He believed God had rolled out a path for him to follow, one ending in the pulverisation of papistry, but if so, why had he failed in Frankfurt? Why had God forsaken him? Had he blundered in his dealings with Cox and his Satanic cohort?

'The English church is so stuffed with reprobates that truth is stifled. Forbye, I see the writing on the wall. Before the year is out, Frankfurt will have bishops and the surplices and rosaries will follow. If this is to be the face of the English church, there is no place in it for me.'

VII

The Godfather of Geneva

> But fornication, and all uncleanness, or covetousness,
> let it not be once named among you, as becometh saints
>
> Ephesians V: 3–5

Geneva, April 1555

'I'm glad to out of thon pest house, master. It gied me the jitters,' Jamie said as they left Frankfurt behind. Seeing Knox hauch and spit thick phlegm into the mud, Jamie wrinkled his brow. 'I hope you haven't caught the pest, master.'

Knox shrugged. 'Who kens? Frankfurt has stuck in my craw: I pray it hasn't leached into my lungs.' He croaked a laugh. 'Lungs fit for a preacher. That's what Betsy Learmont used to say about me. Now I can scarcely raise a whisper.'

By the time they arrived in Geneva, Knox was so worn out that Jamie had to haul him out of the saddle and drag him upstairs to his garret.

'I'm footsore, saddle sore and heart sore,' Knox mumbled to the distress of Catherine who'd heard from Whittingham how Frankfurt had unjustly treated the Scots preacher.

'Rest assured you shall be shown the warmest of Christian charity here,' she said. 'I shall make sure of that.'

Madame Annette was not so bountiful, however, as Knox overheard her complaining to one of the maids outside his room. 'I'm not blessed with supernatural powers. She needn't expect me to run after another invalid. My hands are full tending to my own brood as well as all those wretched refugees who come knocking on our door, begging for help and handouts. And I have to manage Antoine's business when he's away.'

Knox lurched towards the door. 'Madame Annette, please don't bother about me,' he croaked. 'Jamie will look after me. And he'll be glad to lend you a hand, too.'

Annette halted halfway down the stairs. 'He'll do nicely. At least one of the scroungers will earn their keep.'

After a few days of bed rest, Knox craved fresh air and exercise. Downstairs in the kitchen Jamie, stripped to the waist, was turning the iron handle of a spit spiked with a suckling pig over the open fire. Knox chuckled. 'She wasted no time in putting you on the spit, Jamie lad.'

'I'm melting in the heat and my arms are dropping off but I daren't rest lest the fat catch fire.'

'You're doing a fine job,' Judith reassured him.

Jamie's face reddened even more – and no wonder. Calvin's eighteen-year-old stepdaughter was a comely lass. As she stirred chopped neeps into a cauldron steaming on the stove, a pink glow suffused her cheeks and tendrils of damp golden hair clung to her brow. The way her deep blue eyes cast a knowing look at Jamie raised Knox's concern for his innocent lad.

'And I'm happy to have a healthy young body to share my load.' Pierre dumped a truckle of logs by the hearth and straightened his humped back as best he could. 'Though Master Antoine employs me, Madame Annette has me at her beck and call, chopping wood, running errands. But I'll have to keep an eye on those two,' Pierre sniggered. 'I wager Judith will have young Jamie stripped naked e'er long. She knows more than she shows.'

Madame Annette rushed in and wagged a finger at him. 'That's enough of your bawdy talk. Now fetch some more logs. The fire needs stoked.'

'I'll wager.' Mischief glinted in Pierre's black eyes. Pulling a face he looked like a wicked goblin. Perhaps it was true what they said about hunchbacks – that they possessed the glamour, the gift of bewitching women, Knox thought.

'Pay him no heed,' Madame Annette said, 'his mind is full of filth. Jamie, if that pig's roasted, fetch some butter from the market.' She watched as Jamie put his sark back on and then turned to Judith. 'As for you, stop your brazen flirting and start supper.'

Judith rolled down her sleeves. 'I'll take no orders from you.'

Annette lifted her hand but, catching sight of Knox's horrified face, let it drop. 'You are your mother's daughter. *Putain.*'

'If anyone's a trollop …' Judith picked up her basket and left. Despite the defiant sway in her gait, she was snivelling.

Knox made his way to the garden bench at the foot of the garden where Judith was looking out towards the lake.

At the sound of his footsteps, she swivelled round. Welling tears intensified the blue of her eyes. 'My mother loved this view,' she said, wiping her nose on her sleeve.

Knox shaded his eyes to gaze at the shimmering waters of Lake Geneva. A rainbow – the sign of hope – hung over the azure water before dissolving into mist. 'It is indeed wondrous.'

'And this garden was maman's pride and joy,' Judith said before dropping to her knees beside a mass of tiny blue flowers. 'I planted these in her memory. *Vergissmeinnicht*! Forget me not! They're a sign of faithfulness and enduring love.'

'And the very shade of your eyes,' Knox replied, unsure how to console her.

Judith blushed and buried her nose in the flowers. 'Whenever I feel miserable, I come here to be near her: this is the only place where I feel at home.' Her voice dropped to a bitter whisper. 'Maman would still be alive today if the witch Annette hadn't bullied her into an early grave. She never forgave her for marrying Dr Calvin and ousting her as mistress of the house. When every child born to my mother died, cruel-hearted Annette declared God was punishing her for her past sins.'

Astonished, Knox asked, 'What sins could she be guilty of?'

Judith sniffed. 'She was an Anabaptist. Does that shock you?'

Though taken aback, Knox reserved judgement until hearing the whole story.

Judith sat back on her heels and squinted at him. 'Because of their beliefs, my parents weren't legally wed but chose to plight their troth solely in the sight of God. For that Annette calls her a whore. They had to flee Belgium for fear of persecution but Dr Calvin converted them from heresy.'

'In that case, their errors would be forgiven,' Knox replied. 'And since your mother married Dr Calvin he would make sure her sins were absolved.'

Judith heaved a rueful sigh. '*Maman* was a saint. She raised Catherine and me as sisters until her death. But all that changed when Annette became mistress once again. Because she's a wealthy heiress Catherine is treated like a daughter, while I'm banished to skivvy in the kitchen.' Her voice oozed with resentment. 'My stepfather may wield power throughout Geneva but he has no money. Without a dowry, no decent man will have me, though Annette torments me by saying it's because I'm a trollop's daughter.'

Judith picked a stalk from the basket to chew on. 'She's the one to talk. I know all about her and Pierre.' Her hand flew to her mouth. 'But I'd better hold my tongue or I'll be scourged for blasphemy.'

When Knox raised a quizzical eyebrow, she confided. 'You can't trust anyone in this city. Everyone is snooping on everyone else – even children are urged to spy on their parents.'

Knox shook his head. 'I'm no clype. And never fash, a bonnie lass like you will soon find love.'

She let out a sigh. 'I have done – only to lose it again. Life is unfair, Mr Knox. Why do we love those who don't love us back? And what of those who don't deserve love?'

Sensing she was about to confide in him Knox leant forward, but when the garden gate creaked open she leapt up.

'Yuck, Jamie! Where have you been? Swimming in a sewer? You're stinking.' Judith screwed up her face and pinched her nose for Jamie's clothes were slathered in all kinds of muck: soggy cabbage leaves, stinking vegetable skins and bloody animal guts. While she went to fetch hot water, Knox gave the lad an enquiring look.

'A gang of louts set on me, master,' Jamie explained. 'I tried to gie them the slip by nipping into a lane behind the market but two lads blocked my way.'

'Petty pickpockets or street fighters looking for a brawl,' Knox said.

'Nay, that's what I thought but their clothes were too fancy. They were right wee fops with gleaming white linen frothing out of their collars and cuffs. But I wasn't feart. I learnt how to defend himself at sea.' Jamie put up his fists to demonstrate.

'Two lads wrenched my arms behind my back while the others circled round us. They asked if I was the servant of the Scotsman, a colleague of the tyrant Calvin. They don't like foreign invaders telling them what to do – especially a Frenchman who's set up his own personal Vatican city with himself as pope. They threatened to put the *grésillons* on me. Do you ken what they are, master?'

As Judith brought out a pewter ewer she sucked in a breath. 'Iron grills that torturers screw round your hands and wrists until you pass out with pain.'

'What we cry pennywinkis in Scotland,' Knox said.

'Aye, the lads twisted my wrists and I had to scrunch my teeth to keep from crying out,' Jamie said as he stripped off his sark. 'Then they tried to put me on an *estrapade*, or something.'

'That's where they truss you up like a pig on a spit and raise you into the air before dropping you just short of the ground, leaving your feet to dangle,' Judith explained, her eyes drawn towards Jamie splashing water over his naked torso.

'I kicked one of them in the groin and threw the others off. But before I could flee, they all leapt on top of me and squashed my face against the cobbles. I thought I'd had it, but luckily the city guard came chasing after them and they scarpered.'

Offering him a cloth to dry himself, Judith's hand lingered on Jamie's arm. 'Your attackers are libertines, the Children of Geneva. They resent my stepfather for ruling the city with a rod of iron.' She lowered her voice. 'And who can blame them for he forbids any kind of amusement. Gambling I can understand – for it's a madness that leads to poverty – but how can singing and dancing be the devil's inventions? What's so wrong with serving sweets at wedding banquets? Is he afraid bonbons will rot our souls as well as our teeth? Wrongdoers are severely tortured for the mildest offence.'

'Strong measures are needed to bring folk to heel,' Knox replied, 'until they follow the righteous path.'

Judith snorted. 'We're not dogs to be trained but human beings with souls and hearts. Why, folk are banished or even put to death for loving each other. He's made Geneva a prison. If only my mother were still alive: she could temper his fanaticism but when God took her from him he became bitter and twisted. What does that say about divine mercy? Sometimes I yearn to run away and never come back.'

Knox caught the wistful glance she gave Jamie. He'd have to keep an eye on his lad lest he be tempted to say or do something he might regret.

VIII

The Riot of May

Doctrine is not an affair of the tongue but of the life
Institutes of the Christian Religion
John Calvin, 16th Century

Geneva, May 1555

'Calvin! Come here!'

Startled to hear the respected doctor's name being called out so rudely in the street, Knox stumbled down the steps of the Auditory. He was even more surprised on seeing a dog cocking its leg against a wall before running back to its master. Clearly not everyone revered the bishop of Geneva.

The ringing of the town crier's bell drew Knox into the main square. Curious, he craned his neck over the bystanders to see a bedraggled man clad in a hair shirt and carrying a torch being jostled along by the city guards. Dragging his bare feet, the penitent sang in a rasping, plaintive voice. Every time he stumbled or stopped singing, one of the guards lashed him with a whip. His piercing cries rent the air and chilled the blood. When the town crier read out the accusation, the onlookers fell silent.

The guard flexed the cleesh. 'Stand well back. I need space for a good crack at the knout.'

Knowing what was about to happen, Knox could not bear to watch. He turned away, flinching at every lash of the whip. Only when a howl of disgust arose from the crowd did he dare to look at the penitent who had fallen to the ground – unconscious or dead. The guards bellowed at the mob to disperse while they scooped him off the ground. The squad of scaffies on standby scurried in with brushes and buckets of water to clean up the mess. No blood must be left to stain the cobbles of God's own city, Knox thought ruefully.

In the kitchen of Rue des Chanoines, Jamie was pummelling a mound of dough with his powerful fists, closely supervised by Judith. Every so often she tore off a blob of the springy dough and stretched it out before shaping it into a roll.

'I saw a poor devil being flayed in the market place today,' Knox said. 'What was his crime, do you ken?'

Judith shoved the rolls around on a tray before setting it on a shelf above a simmering cauldron. She drew a forearm across her sweating brow. 'Speaking evil and vile words against our lord and master.'

'Who? God? Is that no blasphemy?' Jamie blurted.

'Blasphemy indeed!' Judith scoffed. 'Not against God but an even higher authority! The wretch was scourged for daring to criticise Dr Calvin at a banquet. No doubt strong drink had loosened his tongue. They say the high priest hasn't closed down the taverns yet, but after that he soon will.' Her searing look of contempt scalded Knox. 'There is great unrest amongst the Children of Geneva. I fear this unjustly cruel punishment may spark a riot.'

'Calvin! Calvin! Calvin!'

The cry jolted Knox awake. It must be someone looking for his dog, he thought, and turned over, pulling the blankets over his head to muffle the cries. When the shouts grew stronger and louder he became alarmed. This was not a master bringing his dog to heel but a howling pack of ravening wolves. As he pulled back the shutter, a stone came flying through the window, followed by another.

In the street below, a group of drunken louts were flinging stones up at the windows and smashing bottles against the walls. They were jeering and calling for the tyrant Calvin to be hauled out and strung up.

Knox roused Jamie and rushed down to the kitchen where the rest of the household were gathering. Looking pale and frail in his nightgown and cap, Calvin was remonstrating with Antoine while Annette tried to comfort the wailing weans.

Wrapped in a cloak to cover her nightdress, Catherine paced the kitchen. 'Where are the servants?' she asked.

'They've all fled – terrified for their lives,' squeaked Pierre cowering under the table. 'The libertines are taking over the city. This will be the end of the Calvinist reign and the beginning of Perrinist rule.'

Jamie grabbed a broom and made for the door. 'We cannae just sit here and let them run roughshod over us.'

Calvin put up a hand. 'No, that's not the way. We must wait for the consistory guards.'

Passive resistance may have been Calvin's stance but it was not Jamie's. The lad was itching to knock heads together.

'Listen to Dr Calvin, Jamie,' Knox said. 'What can we do against the rascal multitude? Never fash, the Lord will protect us.'

Unconvinced, Jamie glanced round the kitchen. 'Where's Judith?'

Pierre scrambled out from under the table. 'She's not under here with me.'

No one had seen her.

'The reprobates may have taken her hostage,' Antoine said. 'To demand a hefty ransom for her return.'

'What if those godless heathens ravish her?' Catherine cried and pulled the cloak more tightly round her shuddering shoulders.

Annette hugged a sleeping babe closer to her chest and scoffed. 'You think Judith has been taken against her will, but I wouldn't be surprised if she's joined the libertines. After all, her parents were Anabaptists. It's in her blood.'

Calvin shot her a look of black hatred. 'I will not have my beloved wife's memory besmirched – especially not by you. Besides, your friendship with the Perrinists has dishonoured us enough already.'

Annette tossed her head and snorted. 'So much for your Christian forgiveness.'

Exasperated by their speculations, Jamie made for the door. 'I'm away to look for her.'

Before Knox could stop him, he'd gone.

Throughout the long night, Knox and the others huddled in the basement kitchen, listening to the clash of street fighting. He prayed his reckless lad would come to no harm. In the early hours, the door was kicked in and a huge wolfhound baring its fangs bounded into the kitchen.

'Never fash!' a voice rang out. 'We've smashed Satan's spawn!'

Grey-faced and red-eyed from lack of sleep, Knox stared at the city guard waving a bloodstained sword above his head in triumph.

'It's me, master prophet.'

Knox winced. Robert Stewart. Of course. At his suggestion Stewart was now serving the consistory to defend the City of God.

'I'm bringing back your brave laddie – though I've a mind to keep him for he's a bonnie fighter.' He stood back to let the guard carrying Jamie lay him on a bench. 'He's a bit battered and bruised but no bones broken. We've rounded up the ringleaders,' Stewart went on. 'Thon clumsy crew of mutineers had no chance against a canny mercenary, like me and my trusty horde. We'll soon skelp the skin off thon scunnerous skellums.'

IX

Timor Mortis

> I see that makaris amang the lave
> Playis here their padyanis, syne gois to grave;
> Sparit is nocht their facultie:
> *Timor Mortis conturbat me*
> William Dunbar, 16th Century

St Mary's Abbey, Spring 1555

'Listen to thon wind, wailing like a soul long forgotten in purgatory.' Elisabeth crossed to the window to fasten the shutters. '*Remember me* it seems to be crying.'

'That's if you believe the myth that souls languish there awaiting the magic words to be sprung free,' Lindsay replied. 'Another false belief with no basis in scripture.'

Her brow knitted, creasing the smudge where the priest had signed a charcoal cross for Ash Wednesday. When Lindsay leant forward to rub away the stain, she drew back.

'It's a *memento mori*, to remind us we are dust and shall return to dust. But afterwards, like the phoenix rising from the ashes, our soul will live on.'

'I pray that it is so, Lisbeth, for there will be nothing left of these creaking bones to rise.'

'This may signal the start of the doleful season of Lent, but don't be such a ghoul, Davie. You're aye talking of death. You're no ready for your shroud yet. Forbye, with dark clouds hiding the sun since Christmas, we're all gloomy.'

Lindsay pulled his fur-lined cloak more tightly round his hunched shoulders. 'I'm just an auld larbar with a wheen of frailties spreading like rust over iron. Forbye, I'm nearly seventy-years-old. The allotted span for this auld birkie will soon be up. You pass through life, squandering time and effort, treading water and then all of a sudden, like a fall of snow in the night, old age is upon us. With it comes the ever-growing fear of death – all consuming, gnawing at one's vitals – and then the abyss. *But the day of the Lord will come as a thief in the night,*' he murmured. 'Just as well we do not know what troubles lie ahead nor the cruel death we maun endure when we least expect it. When my time comes, Lisbeth, swear to me there will be no corbie clerics swooping down on my corpse to pray for my soul.'

Irritated by his dark mood, Elisabeth replied, 'All this talk of the Last Days, the End of Time, the Great Judgement is a madness, Davie. It's birling your brain. You must rest.'

'No peace for the wicked, Lisbeth.' His mouth crinkled at the corners then drooped again. 'My auld wounds have come back to torment me. This dreich dampness is seeping into my bones and making my leg throb at the spot where it broke all those years ago,' he said and rubbed his calf.

When he began shivering, Elisabeth stoked the fire high with logs and settled beside him. His forlorn expression as he stared into the flames made her uneasy. His melancholy seemed to be deepening by the day.

'This *tedium vitae* is choking my thrapple,' he said before muttering,

'All men begin for to die
The day of their nativity.'

Elisabeth pulled a face. 'Have you nothing more cheerful to lift this pall of gloom on Ash Wednesday?'

'Not only my personal plight troubles me, Lisbeth, but the present state of our realm. The queen regent may be a prudent leader but she's up against thon witless gowks, the Hamilton brothers who have scant regard for any principles – human or divine – and will do everything in their power to hinder her. All I can do is rail against stupidity and injustice with my pen – and ink – which has run out.'

With a sheepish expression on his face, he held up the empty inkpot. 'I daren't ask Sister Agnes for her special blend for I ken she begrudges me. There's one person who will be glad to see me laid in my grave.'

'How can you say such a thing! Sister Agnes is one of the kindest, most caring souls.'

'But she resents my attacks on the Church. I don't seek to undermine her faith – I only mean to show up corruption and hypocrisy in order to fortify Christ's kirk. She wants no more ink spilt in that cause.'

'Never fash. I'll ask Isabelle to make some.'

'Thank you, my dearest love. The Franciscans' ink is pish-poor: they water it down with vinegar.'

Helpless to stop Lindsay writing, Elisabeth could only ply him with receipts to clear his chest and ease his breathing. She kept a careful watch for blood-flecked sputum, a sign that his cough had crept into his lungs causing consumption.

Late one evening, she found him slumped over an open book. Cautiously removing the pen from his inky fingers, she noticed he'd been underlining verses in his last poem. *Ane Dialog betwix Experience and ane Courteour* seemed to be a collection of advice to a young monarch:

'My son, now mark well in the memory
Of this false world the troubles transitory,
Whose dreadful day draws near ane end.
And every day, my son, *Memento Mori*;
And watt not when nor where that thou shall wend.'

Had he been thinking of John? If so, she vowed to pass on this precious copy to him one day. What could be a more fitting *memento mori*?

Alarmed to see Lindsay growing weaker by the day and coughing up more blood, Elisabeth moved him into her bedchamber to nurse him. She slept on the truckle bed so as to be near at hand and comfort him whenever dark thoughts assailed him. Hearing him cry out in his sleep one night, she clambered onto the bed beside him.

'Davie, was it the same dream? Of the shipwreck?'

'No dream but a nightmare,' he gasped. 'I'm leaning over the side of a boat, staring down into the dark silt of the sea bottom where shapeless creatures like enormous reptiles lurk. When one of the monsters stirs from the murk and heaves its great bulk higher and higher, I'm scared that in another minute its huge snout will overturn the boat. I screw up my eyes to see what this thing is but the waters dim again and the beast sinks into the mud to lie still – except for a slight flicking of its scaly tail.' As he wheezed for breath, he turned deathly pale and his startled eyes stood out on stalks.

'And on the destined day, it will capsize the boat. For that monster is death, Lisbeth. I thought I'd face it with more courage but the nightmare makes my whole carcase tremble with terror.'

Fear gripped Elisabeth with its icy fingers. The deep dread of losing her love overwhelmed her. All she could do was hug him close to fend off the terror. 'You must not let despair defeat you, Davie.'

'Oh my jaggy thistle, my dearest thistledown!' His frail voice cracked with emotion. 'What a squandering of time and effort life is. I've spent my life trying to reform the Church but to what end? My greatest wish was that John would pick up the torch but he's overleapt the bounds to go his own misguided way. I foresee bad times coming, Lisbeth. Where did I go wrong?' Seized by a fit of coughing, he cradled his painful ribs. 'Do you blame me for tearing a son away from his mother?'

Wiping away tears, Elisabeth shook her head. 'As Betsy used to say, John maun dree his own weird. As long as his fate doesn't lead to the pyre, what more can we hope for?'

'I shall never see John again.'

The regret in his frail voice brought a lump to her throat. 'Aye, you will. We both will and when we do we'll tell him the truth and give him this.' From her shift, she drew out the ring she always kept close to her heart; the ring with which they had plighted their troth many years before. As she peered at the engraving, Elisabeth's heart cramped, for the skull and crossbones signified yet another *memento mori*.

'If I'm gone afore then,' Lindsay murmured, 'promise me you'll tell him.'

'Aye, I will Davie. Cross my heart.'

She slipped off the bed and dug out a bottle buried at the bottom of her oaken kist. The seal on the bottle of holy water from Loretto depicted St Mary and her infant son in a galley. Mary, Star of the Sea, was the patroness not only of mariners but for souls racked with self-doubt and in need of spiritual succour at approaching death. She drew in a breath. Was Davie's life ebbing away? Please God, no.

She broke the seal and poured the water into a goblet of wine. With a furtive glance towards Lindsay, she recited the *Ave Maria*. He would be furious if he knew – but what harm could it do?

Holy Mary, Mother of God,
Pray for us sinners now and at the hour of our death. Amen.

She raised his head and put the goblet to his lips. He took a few sips and then sank back against the pillows. After quaffing the remainder, Elisabeth lay down beside him and cradled him in her arms.

'Davie, do you mind our first kiss and how I cracked your nose?'

'*Nemo me impune lacessit.* Who dares meddle with you, my jaggy thistle?' His laugh turned into a choking fit. 'Dearest Lisbeth,' he gasped, 'love of my life, my thistledown – forgive me for all the times I failed to keep tryst.'

'Nothing to forgive, Davie, my auld larbar. You're here now.'

He smiled and closed his eyes. She pressed her body against his and rocked him gently to sleep. After a while she dozed off, but woke with a jolt in the wee hours. Davie's breathing had become shallower; short gasps followed by a troubling gurgling sound.

She nudged him gently. 'Davie.' When he didn't respond, she gabbled on nonsensically, saying whatever came into her head. Memories, experiences they shared. For hearing was the last sense to leave the body.

But what about touch? She put her arms round him and held him close, feeling his last gasps against her cheek. If only she could breathe life into his lungs as she'd done with thon bairn all those years ago. She counted the seconds between each breath – the gaps becoming longer each time. Each one could be his last. Hearing a burble in his lungs, she let out a plaintive whimper, 'Don't leave me, Davie. Love of my life, please don't go.'

She burrowed her face in his neck, moistening his beard with her tears. She half-expected him to open his eyes and make some quip about dampening his spirits. She dearly wished to see thon quirky smile crinkling his lips, the mischievous twinkle in his grey-blue eyes for one more time. She rubbed his cooling hand to warm it up. He took another breath – more a long-drawn out sigh – followed by an unnerving ruckle. Please no – not the death rattle. She waited. Did he just breathe again? Aye? Nay? Maybe? She couldn't tell. Curbing her own breath, she placed a palm to his mouth and waited. Not a puff. Nothing. She laid her head on his chest.

Not a whisper of a heartbeat.

A look of unspeakable peace passed over his careworn face. The crow's feet round his eyes relaxed: the years melted away. Davie had slipped his moorings and was drifting away on the morning tide.

'Rest in peace, my love, my ain one, my only one,' Lisbeth murmured. Hot, salty tears seared her cheeks as she kissed him for the last time on his cooling lips.

PART FIVE

I

The First Supper

> For I here tell Divine Correction
> Is new landed, thankit be Christ Our Lord:
> I wait He will be our protection.'
> *Ane Satire of the Three Estates*
> Sir David Lindsay, 16th Century

Geneva, Summer 1555

Thrilled to see a letter from Marjory amongst his latest delivery of correspondence, Knox pounced on it, eager to know how his wee bird was faring. Her sister had given birth to twins, she wrote, the reincarnation of the ill-fated Mary and Beth, so their mother believed. But this happy event had created a dilemma for Marjory.

Amy asked me to be their godmother at the Catholic baptism and couldn't understand why I refused. It's more than just a naming ceremony, I told her. As godmother, I would be responsible for their religious upbringing and that I cannot do for a religion I reject. Dear John, did I do right?'

Reading of her bravery in keeping faith brought a lump to Knox's throat but her next words stuck in his craw. Amy was pestering Marjory to wed whichever of her stepsons pleased her best.

But neither of these two brawny butcher's boys pleases me. Amy sweeps aside my objection that I'm already betrothed to you and claims that mama forced me against my will. Unless you come for me soon, I may be forced into matrimony.

A letter from Mrs Bowes contained another *cri de coeur* for she, too, was at the end of her tether. Her husband was pressing her to convert to what he falsely called the true faith or else be flung onto Mary Tudor's pyres.

While he brooded over their plight, Knox opened the next letter – a *cri au secours* from the Scots lords begging him to return to Scotland. Now that the Queen Regent was showing tolerance towards reformers, it was safe to do so, they claimed.

How could he refuse to quench the fervent thirst of his Scottish brethren, night and day sobbing and groaning for the bread of life? More importantly, how could he close his ears to pleas from his damsel in distress? Thoughts of their suffering plagued Knox's conscience. How could he live in comfort and safety while she and her mother were being persecuted?

'I detect the hand of God in their appeals. We must leave the sanctuary of Geneva and go to the rescue of all my beleaguered brethren,' he explained to Jamie.

'Including Mistress Marjory,' Jamie replied looking rather peeved, hands stuffed into his pockets as he kicked the leg of a chair.

His mood worried Knox– it was not like the lad to be so gloomy – but ever since the revolt led by 'the comic Caesar' as Calvin mockingly called Perrin, he'd been miserable.

'If we pass through Berne, mayhap I could look for Judith,' Jamie muttered.

So that was it. He was hankering after Judith who'd gone missing the night of the May riots. While most of the ringleaders had been caught and condemned to death, it was rumoured Ami Perrin and others had fled to Berne.

'What will you do if you find her?' Knox shook his head. 'Nay lad, if she's gone with the libertines then she's joined the legion of the damned. A libertine life is not a life of liberty.'

Greatly alarmed by the riot, Calvin had vowed to tighten the screws on hardened sinners and reprobates. His stepdaughter would not be exempt, Knox predicted.

'But if I save her, master, she'll become one of us and then I can wed her. Surely if a sinner confesses she'll be saved? Didn't Christ show mercy to Mary Magdalene?'

Knox sighed. How could he explain to Jamie there was no salvation for reprobates who were already damned? 'I would forget about Judith, Jamie. Forbye, she's in God's hands.'

Dieppe

After another journey of over six hundred miles, they arrived once again in Dieppe. Before Skipper Will opened his mouth, Knox knew from the dour expression on his usually cheery face he had bad news – but he did not anticipate his next words.

'Sir David Lindsay has passed away?' Knox tugged at his beard, unable to believe his ears. Once back in Scotland, he was hoping to seek his mentor's wise counsel. The skilled director, who'd urged him to preach his first sermon at St Andrews, would advise him how best to trumpet the cause. With a pang of sorrow, he recalled the time in Berwick when Lindsay had warned him against being too bombastic.

All it took for Joshua to bring the walls of Jericho tumbling down was a trumpet.

Knox sucked in a deep breath. 'Lindsay was not only a true champion of our cause he was like a father to me. He gave me the courage to follow this path infested with thorns and thistles. His death leaves a great emptiness in my life and a huge hole in my heart.'

'Aye, we were all greatly saddened by Sir Davie's passing, but your godmother, Prioress Elisabeth, is grief-stricken. She was very fond of him and cared for him in his last days at the abbey.'

Strange, Knox thought until remembering how the sisters had nursed Lindsay in his guise as Friar Lazarus after breaking his leg. Falling into a dwam, Knox heard his godmother's voice reciting lines from Thomas the Rhymer:

'O see not ye yon narrow road,
So thick beset wi thorns and briers?
That is the path of righteousness.'

And then her image drifted into his mind, as she was at their first meeting: a divine vision: Queen of Heaven, Queen of Fairyland, swathed in the scent of lavender. Presenting her with a feather, he'd felt her soft touch on his hand. The tiny hairs on the back of his neck prickled and tears nipped his eyes at the memory. He gave himself a shake. That was in the past.

'If you have time, mayhap you could visit her,' Will continued. 'Forbye, she may have a minding for you. Something to remember Sir Davie by.'

Knox shook his head violently. 'Never, Will. I can never go back to the abbey.'

Scotland, Summer 1555

Knox was hoping to pick up Marjory and Mrs Bowes on the way but when the *Saltire* sailed past Berwick and up the east coast, beyond the Firth of Forth, he became worried.

'It's too dangerous to land you anywhere near Berwick or Edinburgh – or even St Andrews,' Skipper Will said. 'Never fash, I'll fetch them when you're settled. In the meantime, you'll be met at Montrose by the laird of Dun Castle in Angus. John Erskine is one of the richest landowners on the east coast: his silver paid for this voyage. You're lucky to have such a wealthy patron but you'd better be mindful, for he slew a priest in Montrose belfry. An accident he claimed, but if so why did he pay the blood-price to the priest's father afore fleeing abroad?'

Knox chuckled. 'You seem to ken a lot about him, brother.'

There was a pawkie gleam in Will's eye as he winked. 'I'm a Free Fisher. I make it my business to ken everything about everybody.'

On meeting John Erskine, it struck Knox that his host had neither the face nor indeed the temperament of a murderer. In fact, the lithesome, sweet-natured man reminded him of George Wishart who, as it turned out had not only been Erskine's neighbour at Forfar, but close friend at King's College, Aberdeen.

'Then we both left to study abroad,' Erskine went on. 'George by choice and me by necessity.'

'I heard about that ... incident,' Knox said.

'Accident,' Erskine retorted. 'I'm no killer but you ken how clishmaclaver corrupts truth. I'll tell you how it came about one day.'

'I jalouse you'd be more likely to behave like Wishart and save a priest's life rather than take it.' Knox said, remembering his master's act of mercy.

Erskine nodded. 'In my view, killing is never justified. That's why my dear friend's barbaric execution inflamed me so much. Had my family's wealth and influence not saved me, I would have shared his fate: now I help those who walk in his shoes. I've vowed to do everything in my power to support the true faith.

'I heard you preach in Berwick, Mr Knox, and your sermons moved me deeply. No one – not even Calvin – preaches with as much passion and commitment as you do. You're the true successor to Wishart and we're truly grateful you've returned.'

The following day, Erskine took Knox to the village of Fordoun to show him something of great interest. At Pittarrow House, John Wishart, George's uncle, an auld man bent with age, led them to the Great Hall, the walls of which were painted with large scenes.

'Wishart's frescoes,' Knox mumbled in a breaking voice. 'He mentioned them in passing – in his usual modest way. I'd no idea they were so skilful.'

'They're as good as any by thon artist Holbein. Indeed, art was George's first love,' Erskine said. 'He gave up his studies to travel to Germany to study under Holbein.'

That was news to Knox. He turned his attention to a vividly coloured fresco depicting a grand procession of cardinals: Behind them the pope, dressed in full papal robes and crowned with a tiara, was mounted on a mule.

'Is this the much vaunted Basilica of St Peter's in Rome we paid for?' Knox asked.

As he squinted at the lines scribbled in Latin below, Erskine translated. 'Thy merit, not thy craft; thy worth, not thy ambition, raised thee to this pitch of eminence. The Papal Curia, as we well know, gives freely to the poor, nor grudges its gifts.'

Knox looked doubtful. 'The Wishart I knew would never have praised the Antichrist.'

'It's a *pasquil*, a lampoon,' Erskine said. 'Such humorous verses were popular amongst students at continental universities. To appreciate the full satirical significance, it should be read backwards. Thus: *The Papal Curia, as we well know, grudges its gifts, nor bestows on the poor freely. To this pitch of eminence thy ambition raised thee, not thy worth; thy craft, not thy merit.*'

Knox gave a hearty laugh. 'That's more like my master.'

'Aye, George had a wicked wit but come and see this. I ken fine your opinion of false idols but this is a most precious image.' He pointed to a small portrait hanging in a corner of the hall.

Knox staggered backwards, stunned by the faithful rendering of Wishart's familiar features: the long beard, the melancholy eyes and on his head, the well-kent black velvet French bonnet.

'Some say the master Holbein painted this but I believe it was Wishart himself,'

Erskine said. 'It's so true to life and captures his spirit.'

Knox wiped away a tear. 'Wishart had many talents. What a tragic loss to our cause.'

Edinburgh, 1555

Keen to introduce Knox to the leading reformist supporters – all good men and true – Erskine organised a supper party at his house in the Canongate. Knox was surprised to see John Willock, former chaplain to Lady Jane Grey, who had fled to Emden in the Protestant duchy of Friesland. Or so he thought.

'Where I practised medicine to earn a crust,' Willock explained with a chuckle. His skills had brought him to the attention of Duchess Anne who appointed him as a diplomat to negotiate trade agreements with Scotland.

'So, here in Edinburgh, I'm taking the opportunity to catch up with the evangelists. But I never dreamt one of them would be you, brother. The Lord in his mercy has sent you to rally our troops.'

'Amen to that,' Erskine said and steered his honoured guest into the oak panelled supper room.

When Knox tilted his head towards a solemn looking young man seated at the far end of the table, Erskine lowered his voice.

'Thon is Lord James Stewart, ill-begotten son of James V and Lady Margaret Erskine, his favourite mistress and my cousin. Mind you, his mother claims that since she was handfasted to King James her son should be legitimised. James is a surly lad, but who can blame him? Being cried *Jacques, Bâtard d'Ecosse* when he thinks he should be King of Scots.'

A lanky lad with the long face of the Stewarts, Lord James had the dour demeanour of a preacher. He didn't say much but listened attentively and watched, his dark eyes shifting beneath hooded eyelids. This grave young man may have inherited his father's melancholy but not his wild gaiety, Knox thought.

In contrast, the silver-tongued William Maitland relished the art of oratory. The eldest son of the poet, Sir Richard Maitland of Lethington, he was clearly a man of good learning. A lively debater, he asked probing questions and tested Knox with his rapier sharp wit and reasoning. But everything in his manner warned Knox to be leery of this worldly-wise gentleman who picked up his food with delicate tapered fingertips and constantly dabbed at his moustache with a fine linen handkerchief.

After a supper of cock a'leekie and salted mutton, Knox preached a short introductory sermon outlining his plan to return to the gospel in all its naked simplicity, as it was first delivered to plain unlettered men.

'We must add nothing to it and take nothing from it. We must cut off the last rags of superstition and break away from Roman ritual with its popes, purgatory, penances pilgrimages and all sic-like baggage! And the first step is to break the thousand-year-old habit of the mass. It is a dead rite.'

Dipping a comfit to sweeten his wersh wine, Maitland looked up. 'Here in Scotland, where Roman Catholicism is still the religion of state and crown, what harm can it do to attend mass as well as follow the reformed doctrine? Did not St Paul attend the Jewish temple and pretend to pay his vow?'

Knox's eyes glinted with suspicion at the unacceptable hypocrisy and apostasy of this challenge. Maitland's question suggested someone more interested in furthering his own career than the reformist cause. A man to watch, Knox decided.

'Paying a vow is one thing, for God has sometimes commanded it, but attending mass is idolatry. Forbye, I greatly doubt whether Paul's participation pleased the Holy Ghost because soon afterwards a mob put him in fear of his life.'

Satisfied with Knox's riposte, the others murmured their assent. Not to be outdone, however, Maitland rebounded with a sardonic quip. 'Arguing with Mr Knox is like a foretaste of Judgement Day. I see very well that all our shifts will serve nothing before God, seeing they stand us in so small stead before man.'

Shooting a disapproving glance at Maitland, Erskine raised his goblet. 'This very night we have laid the keystone of the reformed religion in Scotland. Let's drink to our first supper and crave God's blessing it will not be our last.'

II

Black Friars

Why will ye, merchantis of renoun,
Let Edinburgh, your nobill toun,
For lack of reformation
The common profitt tyine and fame?
To the Merchants of Edinburgh
William Dunbar, 15th–16th Century

Edinburgh, Spring 1556

Throughout the winter, Knox travelled the length and breadth of Kyle and Ayrshire, preaching freely in privy kirks and administering the Lord's Supper. In God's own country, where the brethren still held true to the faith of their fathers, the Lollards, he felt as if he'd truly come home. Returning in triumph to Edinburgh, he wondered how its citizens would welcome him.

'The bruit of your pilgrimage has gone before you, brother,' Erskine said, as he showed Knox round the Black Turnpike, a large stone-built mansion set behind St Giles. 'The Edinburgh folk will flock to hear you preach, that's why I've rented the Bishop of Dunkeld's residence for you. My humble abode cannot accommodate their number. Needless to say, I haven't apprised His Excellency of his tenant's identity.'

Knox chuckled. From the latticed window of the Black Turnpike, he could see the lantern steeple crowning the collegiate church. 'This will do very well, brother. Until I storm the pulpit of St Giles, the trumpet will blow the old sound from here.'

It would also do very well as a home for his bride. Knox felt a pang of guilt for staying away so long in the west but his pastoral mission took precedence over personal happiness. Now safely back in Edinburgh, he would send for Marjory.

Alexander Cunningham, Earl of Glencairn, came puffing up the turnpike stair to warn him that William Maitland wished to speak with him. 'I've never trusted thon Wily Willie. His mind is a mirk mirror. Shall I give him short shrift?' He thrust out his double chin defiantly.

Glencairn, who'd followed Knox from Ayrshire, was proving to be one of his most devoted recruits. He had the stocky build and burly shoulders of a seasoned warrior but was no mindless bodyguard, all brawn and no brain. In his youth he'd been banished for writing scurrilous attacks on the Roman Church, including a satire slating the hermit of Loretto. Unlike lords such as the Machiavellian statesman, Michael Wylie, Glencairn acted out of religious belief and not personal gratification: because of that Knox was inclined to listen to him. On the other hand, since Maitland

217

always had his lug to the ground, he was curious to hear what he had to say.

'I thought you should know Archbishop Hamilton is after your blood,' Maitland said in his haughty tone. 'At his brother's mansion in Kirk o'Field, I happened to overhear him sound a battle cry. *Something has to be done about thon knave Knox. The French queen regent's laissez-faire policy will be the death of us.* Those were his very words.'

'No one has forbidden me to preach,' Knox replied.

'While Her Grace may wink at your private sermons to those of higher rank, Hamilton objects to your preaching to the common folk. He fears you're stirring up rebellion by spreading heresy in these privy kirks.'

Denied access to church premises, folk worshipped in their own homes where Knox urged them to include servants and tenants in their daily Bible readings.

Knox guffawed. 'Heresy! For preaching the true word of God to all! Faith is above class. This from a concupiscent cleric who keeps a concubine in his Kirk o'Field! The prating priest can only prattle in Latin: he cannot recite one word of scripture.'

Maitland twitched his nose at him. 'Since the queen regent refuses to outlaw you, the archbishop means to apply canon law and charge you with heresy. Stand trial and you'll be condemned to burn at the stake: the verdict is already predetermined. He's cocksure this threat will scare you off and send you back to Geneva like a scalded cur.'

'Let him try,' Erskine replied. 'Has the archbishop not seen the crowds clamouring to hear Preacher Knox? A grossly unfair trial might swing it even more in his favour and may even may be a signal for the folk to riot.'

'Hamilton has also taken legal advice from one of the queen's most trusted advisers.'

'Who might that be?' Erskine asked.

Maitland shrugged. 'I've already said more than enough.'

Watching him leave, Glencairn screwed up his eyes. 'Thon birkie may strut around like a cock o' the walk but he whirls around like a weathercock atop a steeple. He's no to be trusted.'

'Glib in the tongue is aye glaikit at the heart, as the auld saying goes,' William Keith remarked preening his grey moustache. More cautious than headstrong Glencairn, Keith the Earl Marischal was another recent convert to the reformed faith.

'Aye, there's truth in these auld saw,' Knox replied. For Maitland reminded him of another William – Cecil in England – always on the lookout and ready to change tack depending on the wind's direction. Like Cecil he, too, was near-sighted – but as another auld saying went, the man with the shortest sight had the longest vision. Knox wrinkled his brow. 'One of the queen's most trusted advisers, so Maitland said.

Do you ken who?'

Glencairn grunted. 'Henri Cleutin, I'll wager. The Frenchie fop has more than the queen's lug, I jalouse.'

'Och, away with you,' Marischal said. 'D'Oisel is one of us − a warrior, tried and tested on the battlefield, and respected by our Scots lords. He follows the rules of combat − French ones, mayhap − but ones we all stick to, nevertheless. Not ones made up willy-nilly by the likes of thon popinjays who've never tasted blood.'

Erskine laughed. 'Aye, he's right. At least you ken where you are with the lords − the deepest purse ensures their loyalty.'

Glencairn put up a warning fist. 'I'm black affronted at that.'

By way of apology, Erskine bowed. 'Not in your case, my lord. Forbye, these glib young men with their continental learning crave not gold but power. They've all read the Italian Machiavelli's doctrines on statecraft and studied astrology, cosmology…'

'And alchemy, I trow.' Knox glowered. 'All works of Auld Nick. They'd be better off reading the Good Book. Everything they need to ken about the world is there.'

'That may be so,' Erksine replied, 'but you have the worldly-wise Maitland to thank for the queen regent's tolerance of our faith. He rides so high in her esteem that she wished to promote him to secretary of state.'

'If he's in the queen's favour, why did he warn me?' Knox asked.

'To spite Châtelherault who objected to his appointment,' Erskine replied, 'claiming he's too young to be given such an eminent position. A man like Michael Wylie does not forget a slight. Forbye, his keen nose has sniffed out the mood in the causeway and tells him you're winning folk over to your side. Maitland plays a double game.'

Champing at the bit, Glencairn broke in, 'So what about this summons, Mr Knox? How do we tackle it? Flight or fight?'

'Fight, of course. I've had to fend off accusations of heresy many times − even from Grey Friars. An encounter in Black Friars holds no fear for me.'

Glencairn raised a triumphant fist. 'Then you have our support, Mr Knox. You shall not be black affronted in Black Friars.'

Edinburgh, 15 May 1556

Early on the morning of the trial, a great host of men on horseback gathered outside the Black Turnpike. At their head, Glencairn in helmet and full armour waved an unsheathed sword. 'I've raised a corps from amongst our most powerful lords, Mr Knox.'

'These men are armed to the hilt,' Knox hissed. 'There must be no civil disturbance, no shedding of innocent blood. Those who'll suffer are the common folk. I wish no other armour but the power of God's words and the liberty of my tongue.'

'Never fash, Mr Knox,' Glencairn replied, 'a wappenschaw is how the Scots lords have aye dealt with a false accusation.'

Curious crowds spilled into the High Street and heads poked out of tenement windows to cheer on the cavalcade as it wound its way towards Black Friars Wynd. Outside the church, Maitland the diplomat dismounted to confer with the archbishop's counsellors. Glencairn's men remained mounted swords drawn.

'Who's thon?' Knox asked. There was something familiar about the other negotiator.

'That's the queen regent's lawyer, James Balfour.'

'Blasphemous Balfour?' Knox queried. 'Then I shall have words with him.' As he swung his leg to dismount, Glencairn put a hand on his bridle.

'Steek your gab, Mr Knox. Let Maitland deal with this. As you're aye saying, words not swords.'

Knox gripped the reins to control his rising anger. How he wanted to box Balfour's ears. The man with whom he'd shared a bench in the galleys, the man who'd saved his life, was a cowardly traitor. 'Let's get on with the trial,' he muttered. 'Why the delay?'

Stamping on the cobbles and snorting their steamy breath into the air, the horses, too, were impatient. At last Maitland came over. 'The summons has been withdrawn. It seems Master Balfour has detected an error in its execution.'

Knox scoffed. 'So no trial? And no execution for me?'

'For my part, I strongly advised against proceeding with the prosecution, for it would not be prudent to make a martyr out of you, Mr Knox.'

Knox thanked Maitland, though not without some reluctance. As one who thrived on confrontation, he'd been looking forward to trouncing Archbishop Hamilton.

As they trotted back up the High Street, Erskine drew up his horse beside him. 'That was canny of Glencairn to fall back on the auld practice of compurgation.'

Though trained in ecclesiastical law, Knox was not acquent with the term.

'If the accused swears an oath of innocence, his name can be cleared by witnesses vouching for his character,' Erskine explained. 'Your followers have come out in force as compurgators to defend of your good name and show the magistrates the strength of our support.'

Knox chuckled. 'Intimidate them by a show of arms, you mean?'

'Overawe, I should say. Ofttimes it's the kindest way.'

When news of the clash swiftly whirled round the city, folk streamed into the High Street, waving and cheering and thronging the closes and wynds. Greatly encouraged, Knox stopped to give an impromptu sermon to the enthusiastic crowd, much to Erskine's approval.

'I believe this is the start of our reformation, Mr Knox,' he said afterwards.

Outside the Black Turnpike, the lad hunkered on the doorstep leapt to his feet. 'Dean Barron's wife is cowping her creel. Will you come, Preacher Knox?'

Elizabeth Adamson, the Dean of Guild's wife, was one of Knox's regular correspondents: he could not refuse her dying wish.

At her home, a black-frocked priest had already arrived and was setting out the contents of an ebony kist on a tray. As a former priest, Knox recognised the paraphernalia used in the papist sacrament of Extreme Unction – the blessed wafers, chrism oil and holy water. Another corbie harangued the dean who was blocking the door to his wife's bedroom.

'Your wife has lost her wits. In her death throes, she knows not what's she's doing. She cannot be denied the last rites,' the priest said.

'And I cannot deny her last wish. She refuses all your papist rituals and wishes Preacher Knox to pray with her. His correspondence has sustained my wife's faith.'

The dean drew Knox aside. 'Getting wind her life was ebbing, these ravens flew to her bedside but Elizabeth summoned the strength to curse them.' His lips quivered with emotion.

Knox glowered at the two clerics. 'Did you hear that, sergeants of Satan? The dean's wife has given you short shrift – now shrive yourselves. Before she's even cauld in her grave you twa corbies are here to snatch the mort cloth. Well, you can wait till kingdom come, for no death duties will be paid into the Roman church's coffers.'

Having shooed away the priests, Knox prayed with Mrs Barron until her last breath. Though in deep grief, the dean thanked Knox. 'Your presence here at the hour of her death is a sign of God's grace.'

When Knox returned to the Black Turnpike, Glencairn and Marischal were locked in heated debate. Inflamed by success and French cognac purloined from the bishop's cellar, the warriors were discussing the next step in the campaign.

Glencairn raised his goblet. 'Now we have the upper hand, Mr Knox, we maun grasp the thistle but with a gloved hand. We're thinking if the dean's wife could cast off the papist faith so readily why not a queen?'

The Earl Marischal burped and wiped his lips with the back of his hand. 'Aye, we maun invite the queen regent to join our congregation. If your preaching can sway a pagan like me, why not Queen Marie? Once she hears the true word of God she, too, shall see the light.'

Knox rolled his eyes. 'Ask the papist queen to convert, you mean? That's the drink blabbing, I trow. Or are you playing hunt-the-gowk? I've been traduced as a heretic and accused as a false teacher and seducer of the people. If all these rumours were true, I would be unworthy to live on this earth. I doubt the queen will lend me a lug.'

'All thon clishmaclaver and scurrilous reports have deafened *her* lugs to God's truth and your innocence,' Glencairn said.

Meanwhile, Erskine was nodding sagely. 'Don't be too hasty, brother, there may be some sense in their wild suggestion. Marie de Guise tholes our cause and may even have had a hand in gaining your stay of execution. Young Maitland has hinted as much – and he's no gowk. He's high in the queen regent's favour.'

Knox mulled this over. What if converting the Catholic queen regent was his God given mission? The reason he'd been called back to Scotland? 'I doubt she'll attend my sermons or give me an audience.'

'Then you maun scrieve your case in a letter – and I'll bell the cat,' Glencairn said.

III

Till Death us Depart

Where thou goest I shall go
Ruth 1:16

Edinburgh, June 1556

Knox paced the quayside at Leith, trying to quell his excitement. Marjory was on her way at last. As the *Saltire* drew near, the first person he saw was Mrs Bowes waving furiously. He was also heartened to see Pastor Milne and his wife clinging to the side rail. But where was Marjory. Had something gone wrong?

'I never thought I'd live to see this moment,' Mrs Bowes cried and threw herself into his arms. 'Oh, my dear son, if you knew the agony I've endured. I feared you'd forgotten about us.'

Gently prising her arms from round his neck, Knox asked, 'Your husband didn't thwart you?'

Mrs Bowes harrumphed. 'The captain will be quite relieved to be rid of his troublesome spouse. I shall be a burden and an embarrassment to him no more. And no longer will papist priests pester him to bring his wayward wife to heel. Let him say that incompatibility of religion has caused our separation. I don't care if I never see his face again either in this life or in the next.'

As Knox looked about for Marjory, Pastor Milne's bony hands gripped his arm. Tears trickled from the corners of his rheumy eyes. 'Thanks to you, I'm going hame at last, Brother John, hame to my ain folk. My banes to be buried next to theirs in the Aberdeenshire soil.'

'Before that sorry day, we have work to do.' Marta waved a bundle of leaflets. 'Here are some tracts we've translated into Scots.'

'Aye,' Milne said, 'we shall play our wee part in spreading the gospel.'

'The Lord bless you both,' Knox replied. 'You're very brave to make such a move at your time of life.'

'Like you, Brother John, we go where and when God calls us, regardless of time and place,' Milne mumbled. 'We're fortunate to have each other and we wish to say how pleased we are that you, too, are blessed with a kind-hearted companion to share your life,' he rambled on. 'May the Lord bless you both with the happiness that he has gifted my beloved Marta and me all these long years and may he give you the strength and courage to overcome any difficulties in your passage through this vale of tears.'

With tears glistening in his rheumy eyes, Milne pressed Knox's hand. 'For these are uncertain times, brother. Just as well we're blind to what lies ahead.'

When Marta gently drew her husband away, Knox caught sight of Marjory standing alone with her head bowed. His heart lurched. Why did she look so sad? Was she seasick? Did she regret coming here? He ran forward and clasped her to his breast.

'My wee bird, I thank the Lord for your safe arrival,' he whispered his voice husky with longing.

'This won't do,' Mrs Bowes said as they sat down to supper. 'Who do these burgesses' wives think they are? They sweep in here in their wealthy weeds to worship at the feet of the master, and expect wine and sweetmeats to be served.'

Exhausted after a long day, Knox's spirits sank. He'd risen at cockcrow to read the Bible before setting off to preach in the privy kirks. Now in the early evening a large following of Edinburgh ladies had gathered at the Black Turnpike to consult him.

'They treat me like a housekeeper and Marjory like a skivvy,' Mrs Bowes whined.

Knox glanced across at Marjory's miserable face: she had not cheered up since arriving.

'What I cannot abide is how they dangle their daughters as bait before you. Something must be done. Why, if you don't make an honest woman of my daughter you may have to make do with the mother.' Mrs Bowes simpered and threw him a coy glance.

Without warning, Marjory sprang up, tears brimming in her eyes, and left the table.

'There, see how unhappy she is,' Mrs Bowes said. 'When are you going to name the day?'

'I'm waiting to hear from Pastor Willock. I've asked him to make our marital arrangements,' Knox retorted and rose to follow Marjory. He caught up with her in the lobby and steered her into his study.

'You don't seem happy, my wee bird. What troubles you?' Kneeling beside her, he clasped her hands. 'Have you changed your mind? Do you no longer wish to be my wife? Is that it? My dearest one, please tell me.'

Marjory cast down tear-filled eyes. 'I don't know what to think. My mind has been in turmoil ever since...' she faltered. 'Ever since father told me something awful, something cruel to vex me.'

'Then please tell me, so that I may put your mind at rest.'

She blushed and looked away. 'He accused you and mama of...' she broke off to lick her dry lips, 'of fornication and adultery.'

Anger coloured Knox's face. 'What calumny! What slander! These are gross lies borne out of wounded pride.'

'But he had proof.' Marjory's voice was a low, sad whisper. 'When Uncle Henry saw you embracing mama in Alnwick, he copied your letters to show papa.' She gulped deeply. 'You wrote: *In very deed I thought that no creature had been tempted as I was.*'

Furious, Knox tried to tamp down his temper. 'My dearest bird, we were discussing religious matters, not indulging in carnal affairs. Your father is twisting my words to wreak revenge. Being spurned by his wife and daughter sticks in his craw.'

Marjory sniffled. 'Seeing how she warmly she embraced you at Leith and how she pours out her heart to you has sparked my niggling doubts.'

'That's your mother's way, my wee bird. She cannot help baring her soul: she's tortured by the fear her papist past may hamper her path to eternal bliss.' He lifted her chin to gaze into her eyes. 'But you are a pure soul, untainted by popish trumpery, bereft of the anguish that afflicts your mother. As my rock, my lodestone you have a special place in my heart. How could you think I would ever betray you? We made a vow to keep tryst, mind?'

Marjory chewed her lower lip. 'Aye, we did. I'm sorry I doubted you.'

Knox drew her close. 'And I promise never to let anyone come between us.'

True to his word, Knox summoned Pastor Willock who cringed with apology. 'Forgive me, brother, for the delay in your nuptials, but I'm awaiting Dr Bullinger's response.'

From the corner of his eye, Knox glimpsed Mrs Bowes's arms folded firmly across her bosom – a clear sign her dander was up.

'And what has a Helvetian scholar got to do with their marriage, pray?' she demanded.

'Protocol, my dear lady. Since Marjory is a minor, a marriage contracted without the knowledge or consent of parents may not be legitimate. Therefore I wanted to know if once wed, they may continue to live piously and lawfully in holy matrimony.'

Mrs Bowes harrumphed. 'Nonsense. I'm her mother: I've given my blessing. What more is required?'

When Willock dipped his head sheepishly, Mrs Bowes drew herself up to confront him. 'Are you trying to say only a father's consent will do? That his word carries more weight than that of a mother who bore her child for nine months and then laboured to give birth? Is that it? That a woman is no more than a womb for a man to plant his seed?'

Willock waggled his head from side to side. 'Nay, I only mean to ensure the marriage is sound, that no objections can be raised and no calumny be rained down on Brother Knox.'

'Since my husband has disowned me and disinherited Marjory, his approval will not be required. Does that ease your conscience? If so, can we please get on with the marriage.'

Willock wavered. 'There is another concern.'

Mrs Bowes opened her arms wide and raised her eyes heavenwards. 'The Lord give me patience. Are you trying to thwart this union?'

'Nay, in Scotland we have not yet established a Protestant marriage ceremony. In England, I used Cranmer's rite but knowing Brother Knox's aversion to the Prayer Book, I hesitate to suggest it.'

'Before we decide, let's take a look,' Knox said.

Resting his bowed head on his hand, he listened to Willock reading the *Form of Solemnisation of Matrimony* from the English Prayer Book. A reverent silence filled the room before Knox looked up and dabbed his eyes.

'Though there is much I lament in Cranmer's accursed liturgy, he must have been divinely inspired when he composed this rite. His words are indeed right and fitting. I will be honoured to plight my troth with these vows. And you, dear Marjory?'

She bowed her head. 'I will.'

'Where shall the banns be read out?' Mrs Bowes asked. 'We have no parish church.'

'This chamber shall be our chapel,' Knox replied. 'For as Christ Our Saviour said, *where two or three are gathered together in my name, there am I in the midst of them.*'

'Amen to that,' Mrs Bowes said. 'As for the ring – you may have mine.' She yanked her gold wedding band from her finger. 'I have no more need of it.'

On the Monday after the third Sunday, Pastor Willock addressed the small gathering of wedding guests. 'Dearly beloved friends, we are gathered together here in the sight of God …'

Standing by Marjory's side, Knox felt his heart drumming against his chest. He stole a glance at his bride. Her pale face looked anxious and solemn. When Willock joined their hands and asked them to make their vows, Knox gave hers an encouraging squeeze. Yet when the time came for him to repeat the marital pledge, God's trumpeter wavered as he stumbled over the words.

'I take thee, Marjory, to my wedded wife, to have and to hold from this day forward, for better, for worse, for richer, for poorer, in sickness, and in health, to love and to cherish, til death us depart: according to God's holy ordinance: And thereto I plight thee my troth.'

When it came to the bride's turn, Marjory held her head high and quietly but confidently repeated similar vows – with the added promise to obey and serve her husband.

With shaking fingers Knox slipped the ring onto her finger and heaved a relieved sigh when Willock uttered the immortal lines: 'Those whom God hath joined together: let no man put asunder.'

'Amen to that,' Knox whispered and kissed his bride.

As they drew apart, Marjory begged leave to say a few words. Fixing her hazel eyes on her husband, she spoke in a clear, determined voice: 'Whither thou goest, I will go and where thou lodgest, I will lodge. Thy people shall be my people, and thy God, my God. Where thou diest, I will die, and there I will be buried.'

Swelling with pride and admiration for his wee bird, Knox thought his heart would burst.

Mrs Bowes sniffed back tears and blew loudly into her handkerchief. 'Well chosen verses, my dear daughter. The words of Biblical Ruth to her mother-in-law, Naomi, echo my own feelings.' She elbowed her way between the newly-weds and clasped her son-in-law to her bosom. 'Now we three shall never be put asunder.'

The shutters were closed and a fire burned in the grate to take the chill of the marital bedroom. While Marjory undressed behind a screen, Knox stood like a stookie, unsure how to approach his bride so as not to scare her. When she slipped between the linen sheets and beckoned to him, he was unwilling to take off his shift. She mocked his coyness.

'Why so shy, John?'

'I'm ashamed my wicked auld carcase, scarred from floggings in the galleys, might repel you.'

She gave a knowing smile. 'You forget how I washed you when you were ill. If not disgusted then, why should I be now? Come here, John.' Emboldened by the nuptial toasts, she took his face in her hands and kissed him.

'Your lips taste of wine,' he whispered.

'Not too wersh, I hope?'

The laughter that followed this reminder of their first encounter relaxed them enough to put the final seal on their marriage and become one flesh.

Afterwards, Knox brushed her hair from her forehead. 'My beloved wife,' he whispered, 'you have made me whole. Before this blessed day I was only half a man. My life is now complete.'

Marjory stood at the latticed window and watched the workmen scampering like mice over wooden scaffolding. Up and down the High Street, masons and hammermen, carpenters and thatchers, were repairing the damaged tenements and filling in the gaps.

It was unlike her to be idle, but Marjory couldn't settle to her sewing: she was still getting used to her new state. How strange to be the wife of John Knox, she thought. That such a powerful man could sink to his knees before her and express gratitude.

It saddened her that, after only a few days together as man and wife, Knox had set off again in response to Glencairn's appeal to preach in Kyle, the receptacle of God's people, the Lollards. He couldn't refuse the earl. The fervency of his followers there had far exceeded all others he'd seen. Marjory had begged to go with him, but that would be too perilous. Better to stay in the relative safety of Edinburgh.

Her mother joined her at the window. 'I detest this stinking city. Auld Reekie is well-named. The reek of burning coal stings my eyes and the stench of herring nips my nostrils.'

She pointed to a steaming midden heap, where skinners and fleshers hurled animal skins, blood. 'Look at the filth they fling into the street – vegetable peelings, shells, fish bones, cattle dung – even night soil from chamber pots. Why, the gutters are stinking sewers. Just look at my shoes!' She glanced down at her feet and turned over first one shoe then the other to study the soles. 'I'll have to buy a new pair. The mud – or worse,' she shuddered. 'Slurry sticks to them and rots the leather.'

'Wear clogs, mama, or pattens. They'll keep your feet out of the muck.'

'And give those haughty Edinburgh hussies the pleasure of sneering at me? Nay, Marjory, no lowly wooden soles for me. The cordwainer is making me a pair of high-heeled shoes. They're the height of fashion – Mary Tudor wears them to make her look taller. That will teach them to squint down their snooty noses at me. Now that you're the wife of the most important man in this city, you'll have to step out and put your best foot afore you. But not shod in clogs.'

When Marjory rolled her eyes, Mrs Bowes clucked. 'Fashion aside, there are more serious matters we need to discuss, my dear daughter.' She spun Marjory round and studied her face. 'Well?'

'Aye, mama, I am quite well.'

'I'm not enquiring after your health, my dear. I'm only concerned to know …' Mrs Bowes faltered.

Marjory's eyes rounded innocently. 'To know what, dearest mama?'

'To know if …' she broke off. 'To know if you are well … and truly a wife. That you're no longer *virgo intacta*,' she added in a rush.

'Mama!' Marjory's eyes widened even more. 'How dare you ask such a thing!' She wriggled free and picked up the woollen hose she'd been darning.

Mrs Bowes pulled up a stool beside her. 'I ask only out of concern that, if there's anything amiss, I may be of help. Being so young you're in need of a mother's advice and experience.' She leant in closer. 'Men have different needs from women. Oftimes they have strange requests or odd practices or particular difficulties. Whereas youths are too hasty, older men find the carnal side of matrimony harder … I mean to say…' she sputtered to a halt.

Exasperated, Marjory jabbed the needle in and out of the stocking as her mother angled for information. Let her flounder, she wouldn't fish her out of the mire.

Trawling for any titillating snippets, Mrs Bowes grabbed hold of Marjory's wrist. 'Is that a welt? I hope he's not too rough with you. He's not rowing in the galleys now. Men often mistake marital relations for martial ones − tussling and wrestling and grappling.'

Marjory drew her hand away. 'Mama, that's quite enough,' she snapped. 'Did you not always say whatever passes between a man and wife in the bedchamber should stay there? So please don't keep asking.'

When Mrs Bowes heaved a frustrated sigh, Marjory threw down her sewing.

'Mama, you may be privy to John's mind …' She hesitated for his Christian name sounded strange on her lips, 'but as his wife, I have his body − and that I will not share with you. Besides, Amy has given me all the advice I need. And she should know.'

IV

A Pasquil

Superfluous and foolish it shall appear to man that I,
a man of base estate and condition
Letter to the Queen Regent
John Knox, 16th Century

Holyrood Palace, June 1556

The sound of raucous laughter coming from the queen's presence chamber disturbed Elisabeth waiting outside. A thickset man with a balding pate came out and glared at her. His deep-set eyes scrunched into an angry skulk as he pushed rudely past her. 'Papist strumpet,' he mumbled.

What was thon uncouth lout, Glencairn, doing here? Elisabeth wondered.

In the royal privy chamber, members of the queen's council were hooting like schoolboys at some prank. Propped up on her throne with cushions, with eyes half-closed, Marie de Guise seemed unaware of the rowdy gathering. When her lady-in-waiting announced her arrival a weak smile wickered over her colourless lips.

'*Merci, ma chère amie,*' she murmured in a feeble voice. Extreme fatigue etched the queen's refined face and sinister dark circles shadowed her eyes. With a glance at her feet resting on a footstool, Elisabeth noticed her ankles were puffy. The queen sighed frequently, and her breathing was short and shallow – all signs of heart strain.

Fearing that the queen's sluggish heart was causing the dropsy, she drew out a phial from the pouch tied at her waist. After cautiously adding a few drops to a beaker, she handed it to the queen. 'By your leave, madame, this should ease your breathlessness.'

The queen took a sip of the bitter liquid, choked and spluttered. '*Sacre bleu*, that's strong.' She gave a wry smile. 'Are you trying to poison me, dear prioress?'

'Not at all, madame. The tincture of foxglove will open up your lichts – your lungs – and quicken the blood.'

Despite being dubbed dead woman's thimbles or dead man's bells, the foxglove had curative qualities. Elisabeth had learnt from her old nurse, Betsy Learmont, how to steep the dried powdered leaves in *aqua vita,* but the doses had to be administered with great vigilance – too low and it was ineffective, too high risked death. As long as she kept careful note of the measure and time of each dose, it should help ease the queen's swollen ankles.

'And this wine will sweeten the blow.'

The queen drank deeply and sat back. 'You're a dear and trusted friend, Elisabeth.

It's a pity there are so few I can depend on.'

'Aye, you can never depend on that fickle bunch. But your men seem merry today, madame. What has sparked their mirth?'

A rosy glow now bathed the queen's cheeks Elisabeth was pleased to note.

'Lord Glencairn has delivered a missive from Mr Knox, but my eyes are too bleary today. I've asked my lord archbishop to read it but for some reason it seems to amuse them all greatly.'

Elisabeth glanced over at the Archbishop of Glasgow, James Beaton. The nephew of the murdered cardinal had used this connection to wheedle his way into the queen's favour in order to oust his archepiscopal rival, Hamilton. 'I pray, share your hilarity with us.'

Beaton bowed. 'In brief, Preacher Knox urges Her Grace to reform religion and give greater freedom to the Protestants in Scotland. Even more drastically, he desires her to convert to the true faith and join his congregation.'

At this, the lords broke out braying like a herd of jackasses.

'The gowk should be strung up for his conceit,' James Balfour snarled.

There goes the kettle calling the pot black, Elisabeth thought. She must keep an eye on this weasel who'd sneaked into the royal sanctum.

'Or else his wits have been doited,' Beaton retorted. 'For the only true faith is that professed by the one, holy, catholic and apostolic Church of Rome. Why would Her Grace reject truth for falsehood? This former priest is asking our queen to become a heretic – for the good of her soul!'

'He must be joking. This surely must be an April Fool!' Balfour guffawed.

'Too late in the year for that, but the pastor may have written a *pasquil*,' Maitland said. 'It means a type of lampoon in Italian, a satirical scrieving.'

When this produced even greater peals of laughter, the queen waved a dismissive hand.

'I shall read it later. Meanwhile, leave us, my lords. I wish to speak with Dame Elisabeth in private.' Once the whinnying pack had shambled out, the queen sank back into the cushions. 'These men drain me. There's enough strife in the land without their constant squabbling.' She heaved a sigh. 'Trouble has flared up in the marches again.'

Elisabeth could commiserate. The borders were a running sore, an open wound that never healed. Despite the queen's efforts at holding justice ayres to enforce bonds of assurance between warring chiefs, tempers had flared up again and the Debatable Land remained in dispute.

'I've a mind to appoint my Lord Bothwell as Lieutenant General of the Marches to lead a campaign against the rebellious thieves and traitors.'

Elisabeth drew in a breath. 'You mean to entrust Patrick Hepburn with such an important task? Setting a thief to catch a thief is a risky strategy, madame.'

The queen regent nodded. 'To demonstrate his loyalty, he planned an insurrection with Percy of Northumberland against Mary Tudor.'

'His loyalty?' Elisabeth scoffed. 'You mean his luckless bid to regain your favour, madame. That plot failed as all his ventures do.'

She hardly needed reminding. When the servant he'd sent to negotiate with Percy on his behalf was caught, Patrick laid the blame on the queen regent, thus forcing her to calm Mary Tudor's ruffled feathers.

'Patrick is heart-lazy and can scarcely organise a game of hunt-the-gowk never mind an intrigue. His plans are aye apt to go agley,' Elisabeth continued. 'I'd think twice before entrusting him with the wardenship of the wild borderlands.'

Queen Marie sighed heavily. 'What you say is true, dear prioress, but his willingness to make amends for past failures has persuaded me he will not let me down this time. Making the poacher gamekeeper may turn his fortunes around.'

'Never mind his sheer lack of smeddum, Patrick's lungs are weak and choked with the quinsy. I have more faith in his son. Master James is made of sterner stuff than his humfie-backit father. He's expected home from France any day now.'

After draining the wine, Queen Marie rubbed her eyes and yawned, clear signs she was about to nod off. She pointed to the letter on the table. 'Please read it, dear prioress, and tell me what all the fuss is about.'

Leaving the queen to snooze, Elisabeth took a seat in the anteroom and perched her *occiale* on her nose. Old age, she grudgingly admitted, had weakened her eyesight but these Italian eyeglasses riveted onto a bone frame – a gift from Lindsay – made reading easier. Thank you, Davie, she whispered. This habit she'd acquired of talking to Lindsay was consoling: it filled the aching void of grief.

Describing himself as a 'man of base estate and condition', Knox started off politely enough – humbling himself to the very dust as a wretched worm to beseech the honourable princess to show loving kindness to the elect. Courteous to the point of cringing, Elisabeth thought, and quite out of character. His request for the queen to convert was also couched in tactful terms. Love compelled him to warn her of the sycophants and flatterers who blinded her to the truth. Because of this, Her Grace might lack the freedom and power for a public reformation but he hoped she might at least grant religious tolerance.

So far his petition was worthy of anything Lindsay the courtier might have written, so what had caused the lords' mirth? Reading on, Elisabeth sucked in a breath. Knox's tone veered from the fawning of a lickspittle courtier, to the doom-mongering of an Old Testament prophet. The Roman Catholic religion was corrupt and if the queen regent continued to drink from this poisoned cup, death and damnation would ensue. Fail to heed this heart-felt cry and she would feel the heavy hand of God. But if she hazarded all for the glory of God, her terrors would vanish. *Lay the book of God before your eyes and let it judge*, he demanded.

Elisabeth sat in a daze. Such bluffness, nay rudeness, was not the way to the heart, mind and soul of any woman, never mind a Catholic queen. The letter lying in her lap gave an insight into how far down the path of perdition her son had gone: he truly believes he's Divine Correction, God's messenger. Was there any way back? If the queen took his challenge seriously, she would surely arrest him. The best thing would be to burn the obnoxious letter. She was on the point of tearing it up when someone leaned over her shoulder.

'What's your opinion, Dame Prioress? A burning offence?' Maitland's lips curled into a smug, knowing smirk.

Elisabeth distrusted Sir William – dishonest and disloyal with a sleekit tongue like the rest of the Maitlands who were aye challenging the abbey's rights to lands that bordered Lethington estate. She felt sure this corbie messenger was waiting for her to die so as to get his talons on Hepburn property.

'Aye, indeed, Sir William, that's the answer. This offensive letter is full of blaw and bluster. Burn it.'

'Or laugh at it as a lampoon – as the lords suggest.'

Elisabeth itched to swipe the smirk from his face. That would be no way to respond to Knox. Ridicule would only rile his anger and offend his pride. He'd never forgive the queen if he heard mockery had been her reply. On the other hand … 'Aye, of course, Knox must be joking – and I should ken. I'm his godmother. John has a wicked sense of humour.' Like his father, she thought. 'Pray, tell him Her Grace acknowledges receipt of his letter and will respond in due course.'

'I shall do what I can to see he receives your honest response – if he hasn't fled the country by now.'

'What do you mean?'

Wily William gave a polished smile and bowed. 'The archbishop is growing impatient with his evangelising fervour and as soon as Knox returns from his progress in the west, he means to lay hands on him. If he escapes his clutches again, Hamilton shall hold his young wife to ransom.'

V

Visitation

O see not ye yon narrow road,
So thick beset wi thorns and briers?
That is the path of righteousness.
The Ballad of Thomas the Rhymer
Traditional

Edinburgh, July 1556

Elisabeth glanced up and down the lane as she rapped urgently on the back door of the Black Turnpike. 'I hope no one saw us come here, Isabelle. With prying eyes and wagging lugs everywhere, we cannot be too careful.'

'Even if they did, they wouldn't ken us in this garb.'

To avoid being recognised the prioress had dressed in her finely tailored riding outfit while Isabelle wore a plain frock and a shawl to cover her head.

'All the better to veil our movements,' Elisabeth said as the door opened.

Jamie gawped at them goggle-eyed and slack-jawed. 'Dame Elisabeth! Is that you? And can this be my wee sister Isabelle?' He hurtled forward and swept her off her feet.

'Aye, Jamie, it's me. I've grown a few inches but you've bred a braw set of muscles. You're squeezing the breath out of me.'

Jamie laughed and put his sister down. 'The master's no at hame.'

'I ken, Jamie, but we're no here to speak with him. Isabelle, you go with Jamie while I speak with the mistress of the house.'

'What's going on?' The doughty-looking middle-aged matron ambling down the hall confronted Elisabeth. Her podgy face wore an unwelcoming glower. Surely this was not the woman Knox had married?

The matron folded her arms. 'I'm Master Knox's mother-in-law. May I ask your business?'

Elisabeth's hackles rose. 'I am John's godmother.'

'Master Knox has never spoken of a godmother.'

'An oversight on his part, I'm sure. I'm Lady Elisabeth Hepburn, aunt of his liege lord, the Earl of Bothwell. Now, be so kind as to tell Mistress Knox I am here.'

The corners of Mrs Bowes's mouth twitched. 'Doubtless you're used to giving commands in your castle, but that doesn't give you the right to issue orders in my son-in-law's house.'

The two matriarchs stood glowering at each other, neither willing to back down until Marjory appeared. 'Mama, what's going on? Jamie tells me we have a visitor.'

'She claims to be John's godmother and wishes to speak with you.'

'Alone if you don't mind,' Elisabeth said, her tone crisp.

'Of course, my lady, you are most welcome.'

While Marjory showed her guest into the parlour, Mrs Bowes hurled a black look.

'You must forgive my mother's rudeness,' Marjory said. 'Life has been very difficult for her recently, so many changes, so many people to deal with. She becomes impatient with Master…' she faltered, 'my husband's faithful flock who pester their pastor at all hours of the day and night.'

'I understand. Your mother only desires to separate the sheep from the goats.'

When Marjory stifled a giggle, Elisabeth felt a stab of pity. Why, she's just a lass, not much older than Isabelle. She'll have a hard furrow to plough, yoked to the rebel preacher.

Marjory's face clouded over. 'I never knew John had a godmother. He never speaks of his former life. I only know his brother. Skipper Will is our lifeline.'

'And mine too,' Elisabeth said. 'We'll be calling on his help again very soon because of a threat on both your lives. Archbishop Hamilton has petitioned the Vatican to raise charges of heresy against Protestant evangelicals. If he wins, they can hope for nothing but persecution and certain death.' She hesitated. 'John's name is top of his list.'

Marjory's hand flew to her mouth. 'How can I warn him? He's gone to the west.'

'Never fash, I shall make sure he receives word, but for now I'm concerned about you. To ensure he gets his claws on John, the archbishop means to hold you as hostage.'

Whatever double games Maitland was playing, Elisabeth was grateful for this precious nugget of information.

Marjory wrung her hands and chewed her lips. 'What should we do? Where shall we go?'

'Listen carefully. Jamie will take you to Finlayston, the Earl of Glencairn's house on the River Clyde. From Dumbarton, Skipper Will's boat will ferry you all to Dieppe. Isabelle is helping Jamie pack provisions at this very moment. You must leave at once.'

'But how shall we get to Finlayston?' Her voice trailed off. 'We've no money.'

Elisabeth held up a pouch of jingling coins. 'This will aid your passage.'

When Marjory looked uncertain, Elisabeth explained. 'This is John's pension from his service as notary at St Mary's Kirk in Haddington.'

Marjory shook her head. 'I don't think he'll accept that. A papist church supporting an evangelical preacher? It doesn't ring true.'

'What about you, Marjory? It cannot be easy making ends meet, living on the broch from other folk's tables. Forbye, with God's grace you'll bring bairns into the world. The pension will give you a regular income.'

When Marjory gnawed her lip, Elisabeth patted her hand. 'The Knox motto, *Moveo et proficior*, means move on and prosper. This will give you the wherewithal to do that. And *Keep Tryst* is the Hepburn's. Never fash – only three folk need ken about the pension – you and I and Skipper Will who'll bring it to you wherever you are.' She glanced at Marjory's rough-hewn clogs peeping out from under her hem. 'This way you can keep yourself decently shod.'

Marjory glanced round furtively before tucking the pouch in her pocket.

Elisabeth nodded her approval. 'For what use is a godmother if she cannot lend a helping hand when necessary. John may wish to disown both Rome and me – that is his choice, but he can never sever the strong bonds that tie us. Nor can he douse the love of those who care for him.'

She considered her words carefully before continuing, 'I gave John his first breath. At his birth, I blew into his struggling lungs to save his life. As his godmother, I witnessed his baptism and when he and Will were orphaned, I raised them. John fancied me to be the Queen of Elfland who brought Thomas the Rhymer three gifts – poetry, prophecy and truth – a tongue that would never lie.'

Marjory looked pensive, 'Pastor, prophet and poet – that describes John very well.' Though her words saddened Elisabeth to the core, she was glad John was blessed with a sympathetic helpmate to share his life. Marjory may be young, but she was wise beyond her years. Being forced to forego Lindsay had blighted Elisabeth's life. How could she begrudge John love and marriage?

'Before I forget, I have one more gift.' She handed her a paper poke. 'I believe John suffers from the gravel. This powdered saxifrage should help ease his suffering.'

VI

Farewell to Edinburgh

> My galley chargèd with forgetfulness,
> Through sharp seas in winter nights doth pass,
> Tween rock and rock, and eke mine enemy alas.
>
> *Sonnet V*
> Thomas Wyatt, 16th Century

Mid Calder, July 1556

After an exhausting but fruitful mission to Ayrshire to garner support, Knox broke his journey at Calder House, the home of James Sandilands. He would leave early at first light, to ride the fifteen miles to Edinburgh, and by nightfall he would be embracing his bride in the comfort of their marital bed. The thought sent a frisson of desire through him. He'd been loath to leave Marjory so soon after their wedding but needs must. As he tried to divert his thoughts back to prayer, a soft tap at the door disturbed him.

'There's a man outside wishes to speak to you,' a stable lad whispered.

Knox pulled a cloak over his nightshirt and made his way down to the stables. The gloaming of the summer evening cast eerie shadows and he nearly jumped out of his skin when a tall figure emerged from the darkness.

'Forgive me for the subterfuge, Mr Knox, but I bring important information.'

Knox gasped. 'So it's you, Wily Willie. Why are you here? Did the queen regent send you? What does she say? Will she recant? Has the Lord illuminated her soul with the light of truth? If so, our trauchle will be over.'

The fifteen-mile ride from Edinburgh had dishevelled the well-groomed Maitland. He mopped the sweat from his face with a linen handkerchief and shook the dust from his velvet bonnet. 'I'm sorry to say Her Grace has declined your invitation to convert to the true faith. In fact, she was greatly amused by your *pasquil*.'

'My *pasquil*?' Knox growled.

'Aye, it's a lampoon, a satire.'

Knox grimaced at Maitland's snooty condescension. 'I ken fine what it is.'

'Her Grace handed your letter to Archbishop Beaton and said...' Maitland cleared his throat to mimic a high-pitched voice. 'Please you, my lord, to read a *pasquil*.'

'She said that?' Knox clenched and unclenched his fists. 'So she was making a bauchle out of me? Then I fear she's far too deeply mired in the puddle of papistry ever to be prised out.'

'I jalouse Her Grace will not be shifted in *her* stance before God,' Maitland replied with his characteristic sardonic smile.

Glowering at this reminder of their first argument, Knox wagged a finger at Maitland. 'It was you who led me to believe she might convert, my lord.'

Maitland beat his breast. '*Mea culpa. Mea maxima culpa.* I confess I was mistaken but it was with the best of intentions. Who knew if the Lord might have moved her to hear his word?'

Knox raised a clenched fist. 'So who has been making a fool out of me? The queen or you, Michael Wylie?'

Maitland inclined his head. 'Had you given me sight of the letter before sending it, Mr Knox, I would have advised against such a diatribe. In my humble view, your request was couched in terms too bluff for a queen accustomed to the refined language of diplomacy. More sophistication would have aided your cause, perhaps.'

'Sophistication? You mean sophistry – for that is the art at which you excel, my lord. Never trust the silver-tongued for they are deceitful.' Maitland was cut from the same cloth as Lord Dudley, Knox suspected, a man for whom courtly ambition was more important than faith.

'Then I can do no more for the queen regent.' Knox snarled. 'I've done what I can to bring this wanton widow mistress to salvation but she is a reprobate. A murderess who poisoned her husband to cavort with the bloodthirsty Cardinal Beaton and who now dallies with the French fop d'Oisel. They're all damned to hell.'

He glared at Maitland. 'And you, Michael Wylie, whose side are you on?'

Pinning on his mask of mystery, Maitland examined his fingernails intently. 'Things are never as black and white as you'd like them to be, Mr Knox. As you know, I support the reformist cause – which is why I've risked coming here tonight – but the time is not yet ripe for root and branch reformation. Until then, I intend to keep my cards close to my chest. At present the reformers can hope for nothing but persecution,' he paused. 'Archbishop Hamilton has already put you to the horn. I would advise you to leave the country forthwith.'

VII

Burnt Offering

> It is better to marry than to burn
> I Corinthians, VII: 9

Edinburgh, July 1556

In the queen regent's mansion on Castlehill, Elisabeth peered through the long window towards the port of Leith. The *Saltire* would have left by now on its way to Dumbarton to collect John and his family. Not a moment too soon, for if Knox did not leave Scotland within twelve hours, Archbishop Hamilton would roast his carcase.

The sudden thought that she'd never see her son again and fulfil her promise to Lindsay stabbed Elisabeth's heart. Would it matter if he never knew who his parents were? Soon he would be safe in Geneva where he could preach to his heart's content to folk who shared his beliefs. There would be little to disturb his peace there, except ... the wicked thought made her chortle.

'Why so canty, Dame Prioress?' Isabelle asked. She draped the riding cloak round the prioress's shoulders for the journey back to St Mary's.

'I was thinking Marjory seems a gentle, loving creature – she may be the one to tamp down John's frantic fanaticism – but as for his mother-in-law! I wouldn't wish such a harridan on my worst enemy. Let us pray the old adage is proved wrong in their case,' she paused. 'Like mother, like daughter.'

They both dissolved into giggles before Elisabeth became serious. 'Forbye, it's for the best, and Queen Marie will rest easier in her bed knowing the heretic Knox is no longer at large in Scotland.'

As they left Nairne's Close, the sound of raised voices and hundreds of feet clattering along the cobbled causeway made them draw back in. The High Street was crowded with folk surging up from the Grassmarket and flowing down the Lawnmarket.

Bewildered, Elisabeth caught hold of a fishwife's arm. 'What's going on?'

'There's to be a burning!' the fishwife cried. 'They're torching the heretic Knox at the Mercat Cross!'

Elisabeth's skin prickled with apprehension. Had Hamilton and Beaton already caught John before he left Scotland? Knowing that a public trial would cause an uprising, had they found him guilty in private? And were they burning him before the queen regent returned from the borders? When the queen's away, the cats will play – was that their cowardly game? For Marie de Guise would never sanction his execution.

As fear flooded her veins, her heart pumped harder against her breast. For years Elisabeth had lived with the horror that one dreadful day, her son would perish in the flames. To keep steady, she gripped Isabelle's arm as they followed the mob moving towards the Mercat Cross. Already street vendors and hawkers were taking advantage of the festive mood. Luckenbooths around St Giles were doing a roaring trade peddling their wares. Balladeers were making up songs on the hoof setting new words to well-kent tunes. Elisabeth kept her eyes on the unicorn atop the lofty shaft to guide them. The Mercat Cross, where folk gathered to hear public proclamations, was also a place of execution.

When the west portals of St Giles opened, Hamilton's episcopal guards trooped out and formed a cordon to protect the procession of clergy. A choir chanting a dirge led acolytes carrying a huge cross. Bringing up the rear, the clergy, attired in lavishly embroidered robes that flaunted the wealth of the Roman Catholic Church, processed to a wooden dais.

'Dame Prioress!' James Beaton called out. 'Come and join us to watch the devil go up in flames.'

Before she could object, the sisters were being hauled up onto the dais. Scrutinising the crowd, Elisabeth could see no sign of Knox's followers. Where were the reformist lords and other members of his faithful flock? Had they like Peter and the apostles abandoned their saviour in his hour of need?

The kindling stacked in front of the Mercat Cross didn't seem enough to roast a rat, never mind a man. Did they ken what they were doing? The executions of Patrick Hamilton and George Wishart had, by all reports, been badly botched. At least with poor Janet Douglas, falsely burnt as a witch, Elisabeth had smuggled in some belladonna to ease Jinty's death throes. If she'd know aforehand, she could have done something for John.

The jeers rose higher as the cart carrying the doomed man trundled into the square. The whooshing of blood in her ears mingled with the clamour of the crowd. That it should end this way – that John, her son, should be sacrificed at the stake, with her being there to witness his horrific death – was a cruel quirk of fate. Darkness threatened to engulf her in this living nightmare.

Isabelle clasped her hand tightly. 'We must pray for his soul. If he recants at the last second he'll be forgiven. God's mercy is great.'

'Let us pray that it is so.' Elisabeth gathered her wits and scolded herself. She mustn't give in to self-pity. She must be brave. She mustn't swoon. Nay, when the time came she would cry out, *John! I'm here*, so he'd know she was with him at the very end to share his agony. For, whatever their religious differences, the bond of blood between mother and son could never be broken. *Keep Tryst! Endure Fort!*

The cruel laughter from the mocking crowds rang in her ears, growing louder and louder as a figure clothed in black was heaved out of the cart and tossed onto the steps of the Mercat Cross. Elisabeth screwed up her eyes: panic blurred her weak vision even more. John looked so frail so small – more like a puppet with floppy arms and legs. Had they tortured him and broken his limbs?

In his pompous voice, Archbishop Hamilton read out the sentence. 'There shall be no last rites and no confession or absolution, for the Lord shall consign the heretic's blackened soul at once to the fires of hell.'

When the executioner tossed the figure onto the pyre with a pitchfork, the crowd whooped with laughter. Elisabeth slumped on the bench: her cry died on her lips and her mouth fell open. The figure had caught fire in a trice; the black cloak was already blazing like a torch. Flames shrivelled the hair and scorched the skin, the face, the eyes. The pungent smoke stung her eyes and nostrils. Elisabeth covered her face with her hands and squeezed her eyelids. She couldn't bear to watch.

Isabelle tugged at her sleeve. 'Dame Elisabeth, you must look.'

Slowly she opened her eyes. The acolytes were poking at a bundle of blackened straw smouldering on the scaffold.

'It was only an effigy stuffed with hay,' Isabelle murmured.

James Beaton grinned at them. 'Did our *pasquil* amuse you, Dame Prioress? A pity it wasn't Knox in the flesh. However, since our prey has already flown the coop, we've burned him *in absentia*. Never fash, this is only a rehearsal. We'll catch him up one day and incinerate the heretic.'

241

VIII

The Prodigal Son

Liberalitie and Loyalty, baith are lost,
And Cowardice with lordis is laureate
And Knichtlie Courage turnit in brag and boast.
The Dreme
Sir David Lindsay, 16th Century

Seton Chapel, 8 September 1556

'What do you think of my feeble attempt to withstand the heathen horde?' Abbess Joanna asked.

Elisabeth waggled her head in admiration. 'You've done grand work restoring the chapel to its former glory, dear sister.'

For Seton Chapel had been a victim of Harry Tudor's rough wooing, destroyed when his troops had rampaged their way to Edinburgh, burning everything in their path. His English brigands stole the bells and organ before setting it alight. Apart from the spire, most of the repairs have been done.

'It was my wish to erect a fitting memorial to my beloved George who sacrificed his life for king and country.' Joanna stopped in front of a granite tomb adorned by an effigy of George III, 5th Lord Seton. 'Here's his final resting place – may he rest in peace – and my own one day soon.'

'Not so soon, dearest sister,' Elisabeth said. 'You have years ahead of you.'

'Lisbeth, I'm nearly seventy-years-old, mind, an old crone who's not long for this earth.' She made the sign of the cross and kissed the jewel-encrusted crucifix dangling on her girdle. 'Forbye, I long to be united with him, wherever his soul may languish. In heaven, I pray. Dedicating the chapel to St Mary and the Holy Rood will have gained a plenary indulgence to release his soul from purgatory. I also have a requiem mass sung for him every day.'

'Aye, best to be on the safe side,' replied Elisabeth who was doing the same for Lindsay's soul. In view of his vehement denial of such a state, she could imagine what he'd have to say about that. If not purgatory, where would his soul be now? she mused. Heaven or hell? Grief squeezed her heart – wherever he was, she sorely missed her beloved Davie here on earth – but unlike Joanna, she was not yet ready to join her beloved yet. She still had work to do.

After the requiem mass for the fallen at Flodden, Elisabeth took her time hirpling back to the castle. She was still haunted by memories of that fateful day. The sky was overcast and light drizzle glistened on the grass and leaves. The weather was not as wet as it had been that sodden September of 1513 but still damp enough to chill the bones. She drew her cowl loosely over her wimple.

In the murky light, her failing eyes glimpsed something moving towards her. She squinted and, as the figure drew near, her skin prickled. For, looming out of the shadows was the shade of her brother Adam, exactly as she'd last seen him forty-three-years ago on Flodden eve, a sturdy warrior of twenty-one years, clean-shaven and bristle haired. A chill ran through her from head to toe. To see such an apparition was a bad omen because it heralded the death of close kin.

'I've come with news,' the ghost murmured.

Elisabeth let out a breath. It wasn't her brother but her great-nephew, James, the very image of his grandfather Adam.

After five years in France, nineteen-year-old James Hepburn had matured, if not into a fine gentleman, then a force to be reckoned with. His rugged looks and brusque manners could never turn James into a Frenchified fop. Broad shouldered and dark-haired, with the swaggering gait and slightly bowed legs of a born horseman, James exuded the confidence and self-assurance his father Patrick lacked. His greenish-brown eyes, peaty like a Moorfoot burn, fixed on her as he awaited her response.

Elisabeth gave herself a shake. 'We'll catch our death standing in this drizzle. Come with me.'

In the turret chamber at Seton Castle, Hepburn prowled up and down like a caged beast: his dark brows knitted into an angry glower. 'My father is mortally wounded in Dumfries and is hours away from death.'

So James's appearance was a portent, Elisabeth thought. Poor Patrick 'It grieves me greatly to hear that. The queen had high hopes of his success in daunting the borders.'

James snorted. 'Despite having a wheen of troops at his command, my father's military strategy has been disastrous – with at least eighteen dead and forty or so taken prisoner.'

Fury flashed in his eyes. 'Reiving, raiding and riding with the enemy has given the Hepburns a bad name. Not only was he a fushionless, shiftless soldier he was a feckless father. In France, I begged for funds but he never even answered my letters – for he'd squandered everything. Like a pauper I had to beg, borrow and pawn to keep body and soul together. At least I didn't stoop so low as to steal.'

'When invited to Queen Mary's birthday celebrations, I feigned illness. How could I present myself to the queen in breeks so threadbare you could see my arse? As the heir to the first earldom in the land, I should command respect, but mention his name and folk jeer or spit at me, crying me a traitor's son. He's betrayed our family motto: *Keep Tryst*. I'm ashamed to call him kin, far less father.'

Elisabeth gave a heartfelt sigh. 'He'd hoped to earn not only a goodly reward to pay off his debts but, more importantly, his son's esteem.'

James ground his teeth. 'That's the last thing he'll do, for he's one of the captives. There's no honour in being taken prisoner. It would have been better if he'd been slain. May he die in excruciating agony.'

Elisabeth sucked in a breath. 'Will you and Jean go to make your peace with him in his last hours?'

'Jean will not. Not after he sold her to Blinksalot.'

Elisabeth looked puzzled. 'Blinksalot.'

'That's what she cries Robert Lauder of the Bass whose skellie-eyes make him blink a lot. Forbye, he's bandy-shanked and hen toed. But his father is a rich landowner who seeks advancement and agreed to take Jean with no dowry. A match with a high-ranking earl's daughter is worth its weight in gold to him, but thon howe-backit haddie is hardly a catch for our Jean.'

James clenched his fists. 'The cringing coward shall die the death he deserves – alone and friendless. Then I'll call off Jean's marriage.'

Though pierced by his cruelty, Elisabeth could understand his scorn. Throughout his life, the Fair Earl had vexed and frustrated her but now, at the hour of his death, she pitied her nephew. Left fatherless by Flodden, the eighteen-month-old infant had been abandoned by his mother, Nancy Stewart, who had lowped the dyke, not once but three more times. Packed off to Spynie to be brought up by the iniquitous Bishop of Moray, Patrick had no one to instil in him a code of allegiance and loyalty. Cut adrift, he'd followed his own twisted path, leading him away from his wife and children, kin and country, to prison and exile.

'Then I shall go,' Elisabeth said. 'I may be of comfort to him in his last hours.'

'Where's the use? By the time you arrive, he'll be cold in his grave. As the fourth Earl of Bothwell, I shall inherit land and title but no money. My father leaves only debts. I intend to offer my services to my queen in France and her regent in Scotland. How can I present myself in these ragged duds?' He rubbed his shabby velvet doublet and pointed to his patched leather boots.

Elisabeth narrowed her eyes. 'Will you take the queen's part, James?'

The flash of angry pride in his green eyes made her flinch but she stood her ground. Would he be as fickle as his father, switching sides according to the highest bidder or would he keep tryst?

'I am of the queen's side, of course.'

'So you have not been lured by the reformist lords?'

He shook his head violently. 'Never, thon so-called nobles are untrustworthy. Forbye, my father's behaviour reinforced my resolve to serve crown and country.'

'Then you will support the Roman Catholic Church.'

James glowered and whistled through his teeth. 'Forgive me for saying the truth, Dame Prioress, but I care not a tinker's curse about religion. The wantoness I witnessed at my uncle's abbey at Spynie made me despise the corrupt Catholic Church. I'm my ain man and would fain follow my conscience. My lodestone shall always be the Hepburn motto: *Keep Tryst*. Keep faith. *My* faith.'

His honesty commanded Elisabeth's respect. 'Never fash, James. If you swear allegiance to our young queen, then I shall lend you however much you need.'

Once he had gone, Elisabeth brought to mind the words of her aunt, Prioress Janet: *It's a sorry trait in the Hepburn men aye to be dintit with the king's quines.* Was this Hepburn also destined to be a queen's champion?

PART SIX

I

The Most Perfect School of Christ

> Geneva is the most perfect school of Christ
> that ever was on the earth since the days of the apostles.
> *Letter to Anna Locke*
> John Knox, 16th Century

Geneva, December 1556

On the steps of the Auditory, lightly dusted by the first snow of winter, Knox stopped to breathe in the crisp mountain air.

'Let other men feign miracles, but Geneva seems to me the wonderful miracle of the world. We three are truly blessed to be brought together in his sacred city.'

'After the horrors of Frankfurt, this is an earthly paradise,' William Whittingham agreed. 'I thank the Lord for delivering me out of that lions' den into this sanctuary.'

'And into the arms of your dear Catherine,' Knox added with a knowing smile. 'I, too, am grateful for my beloved Marjory's release.'

Scotland may have thrown him out but his faithful flock had begged him to return to Geneva. An escaped felon no longer, Knox was fulfilling the purpose God had decreed for him: preaching three sermons a week in the Auditory, and preparing a new prayer book with his friends.

More importantly, he shared his life with the ideal wife. Dr Calvin approved his choice: Marjory was a rare find possessing all the qualities he demanded in a spouse – gentle, chaste, modest, economical, patient and interested in his health.

But his young bride's health troubled Knox. Recently he'd heard her retching in the early mornings but she never complained. He hoped his wee bird wasn't suffering some serious ailment in silence. He couldn't bear to lose the love of his life.

Knox nudged Whittingham's arm. 'Let's not overlook Brother Christopher. He should not be denied the joy a good woman brings. We must seek the perfect partner for him.'

Goodman scowled. 'I prefer books: women baffle me. Quirky, unpredictable creatures – even the most complicated texts are easier to decipher than a woman's mercurial mind. I would be better suited to a monastery, shut away from womenfolk.'

Knox laughed. 'Never fash, brother. The monastic life is unhealthy. God has created a mate for every man. In an unguarded moment, Cupid's dart will strike your hardened heart.'

'I doubt it,' Goodman replied. 'I'm too ugly to attract the fair sex. Not even one of those fearsome females who swarm round the foot of your pulpit, like bees buzzing round a honeypot, greedy to suck the nectar of truth from your lips, Brother Knox.'

When a high-pitched wail interrupted their laughter, they turned to see a large, heavily built woman blundering towards them. Her multi-coloured cloak flapped in the wind behind her like the tail of a peacock.

'Preacher Knox!' she screeched. 'Wait for me.'

'Oh no, Madame Amour has broken free again,' Goodman mumbled. 'What bizarre belief has the banshee dredged up today?'

'Better not let her husband hear you calling her that. Pierre Ameaux is a member of the small council but his wife is a poor demented soul,' Whittingham said. 'On St John's Eve she claimed to be possessed by Salome and danced naked in front of Dr Calvin's house until he set the guards on her.'

'With your arrival, she has sniffed fresh blood, Brother John,' Goodman growled. 'Better watch out – the harpy is frantic to sink her grubby talons into you.'

The woman brushed back the grey, streaked hair that flowed freely around her shoulders and fixed wild, burning eyes on Knox. 'Beloved brother in God! Your words fill me with such fervour that the Holy Spirit has pierced my breast and filled my heart with love. I long to share this divine passion with you. For the children of God must love one another. United in body, we shall be transported in spirit.'

She stretched her arms wide. 'So, dearest brothers, let us all live together and lie together as one flesh. The children of God can never sin. To the pure all things are pure.'

Goodman wrinkled his nose in disgust. 'This from a woman who stinks to high heaven! Distorting scripture to excuse her lust.'

'Hearing the gospel preached freely and in words they can understand moves women in mysterious ways,' Knox said. 'God's grace stirs not only their souls but rouses passion in the blood and inflames madness in the brain.'

Goodman let out a horrified gasp. 'So it has! Christ's blood, stop her. She's about to bare her breasts.'

As she fumbled with the lacing of her low cut bodice, they stood transfixed until an angry shout roused them.

'Benoite! Stop that at once.' Ameaux halted in front of his wife and struck a blow that raised a livid welt on her cheek. He grabbed her arm and shook her hard. 'Do you want the city guards to lock you up again?'

'I am the Woman clothed with the Sun.' Her wild eyes rolled about their sockets. 'Everything is permitted.'

'Please accept my sincere apologies, brothers. The council has instructed me to deal with her lovingly but I'm sorely tried by her wantonness.'

'I'm not wanton,' she squealed. 'You twist my words and deeds. My love for my fellow Christians is pure.'

'But not chaste. Did you hear that? Does that not amount to adultery? Her scandalous behaviour is driving me to divorce.'

Knox glared at him. 'Adultery is a very serious accusation which carries a very severe penalty.'

'If she violates the sixth commandment, she must be punished accordingly,' Ameaux said and dragged his wife away.

Concerned by the anxious look in Marjory's eyes, Knox put a comforting arm round her shoulders, prepared to share her worry. But when she explained the reason, he could scarcely speak for the lump in his throat.

'Truly this day my cup runneth over with joy.' Tears filled his eyes as he squeezed her tightly. 'Your joyful news has completed my happiness, my wee bird. I am to be a father. I am indeed blessed.'

Perched on his knee, Marjory nuzzled his face into his beard. 'But I'm scared, John.' Her soft voice reverberated in her throat like a wee cushie doo. 'Childbirth frightens me. So many things can go wrong. A bairn may be stillborn and many women die of the fever...' her voice faded.

Knox felt a pang of guilt. While this auld birkie brimmed with pride and happiness at fathering a child, his young wife was eaten up with fear. He drew her towards him and rubbed her belly where his seed was growing.

'Never fash, my wee dove. Put your faith in God. The Lord looks after his ain. All will be well.'

'I feel so queasy. Food sickens me. Mama says it's natural and will pass within a few months. And I feel exhausted all the time. Worst of all, my mind won't settle. My brain feels like bran mash. I can't concentrate. I worry about making grievous mistakes copying out your work.'

'Then you must rest until you feel better. And never fash your bonnie wee brain about my work. I'll ask your mother to help.' He gave a short laugh. 'The way she tosses out theological conundrums to test my mettle and picks holes in scripture, I wager she knows her scripture better than I do.'

Mrs Bowes's habit of shuffling through his correspondence before giving it to him riled Knox.

'Another missive from one of the dear sisters of Edinburgh,' she muttered in disapproval. 'What does she want?'

'I'll read it later, dear mother,' he said snatching the letter from her.

'Open it now, John, I may be able to help with the reply.'

Knox rolled his eyes. His mother-in-law was proving to be less biddable than his wife, acting above and beyond her secretarial duties. She took the liberty of opening his letters, commenting on the contents and recommending responses. Stand up to her now and she would nag him until he gave in.

'It seems Mrs McGill, Janet Adamson to her ain name, can no longer thole her husband's infidelity and wishes to leave him. What should she do?'

'Poor woman,' Mrs Bowes said with unexpected sympathy. 'I know exactly how she feels. Tell her to leave the lecher – as I did.'

'In your case, dear mother, religious incompatibility caused your separation. Until then you put up with your husband's indiscretions, a most bitter cross to bear, I agree. But if God has willed her husband – who should be her comfort – to become her foe then she must carry her woe with patience. For the limbs must stay with the head. That's the advice I shall give her.'

So saying, he took a fresh quill from his pot and cleaned the nib ready to write.

Mrs Bowes smacked her hand down on the paper. 'What! You don't think infidelity a good reason for a wife to leave her husband? You're advising this woeful gentlewoman, misused and mistreated by a selfish husband, to harness her tongue and tolerate his philandering?' She squeezed her lips into a sphincter of censure. 'I would have thought you'd better admonish the errant husband.'

'James McGill and his father are Lords of Session. Her brother is a burgess. They're generous supporters of our cause, contributing greatly...' Knox's words withered on his lips as he felt the full force of her critical glare.

'Financial patronage should not exempt them from retribution. I thought we'd swept away such papish practices. It's as wicked as taking money for pardons.'

'Nay, idolatry is a more grievous sin than adultery.'

'What if a woman strays? Would you give the same advice to her husband? Remain silent and endure the humiliation of being a cuckold? Or would you drown the wayward wife?'

Thoroughly vexed, Knox slammed down his quill, splashing his letter with inkblots.

'What if the adultery is taking place right under your nose?' She thrust her face into his and hissed. 'What if the debauchery blackens the name of your esteemed master? What would your advice be then?' Her exasperated tone became eerily menacing.

Taken aback, Knox asked, 'What has Dr Calvin got to do with this?'

'So, you're ignorant of the debauchery going on under his own roof?' A note of triumph resounded in her voice. 'The consistory has arrested Madame Annette on the charge of...' After pausing for effect she announced. 'Adultery.'

Knox could not believe his ears. 'There must be some mistake. Some malicious blabbermouth seeks to skaith her name, no doubt.'

Mrs Bowes clicked her tongue. 'There is no doubt. Because of her sin, his brother Antoine has filed for divorce.'

'Divorce Madame Annette? The mother of his bairns? That cannot be.'

II

Les Liaisons Dangereuses

> He that is without sin among you,
> let him first cast a stone at her.
> John VIII: 7

Geneva, January 1557

In Rue des Chanoines, a phalanx of guards lined the way from Calvin's door to a waiting cart. From inside the house, Knox heard a woman shrieking and then the door was flung open. The guards bundled a figure wrapped in a blanket into the cart before rattling off along the cobbles at a breakneck speed. Antoine was about to close the door when he caught sight of Knox. After a quick glance up and down the street, he waved him inside.

In his study, Calvin pulled his black velvet bonnet down over his ears and grimaced with pain. 'All is not well in our holy city, Mr Knox. Thorns and thistles have crept into our Garden of Eden and a cankerous worm nibbles at the core of our golden apple. My brother's wife has broken the sixth commandment.'

'We'd hoped to deal with this matter in private,' Antoine said, 'so no blemish would blacken my brother's name.'

'Indeed,' Knox replied, 'for such a scandal will be as manna to the libertines.'

'Unfortunately it may all become public. The consistory have insisted on proof of infidelity to secure my divorce – and since our word is not enough they have passed the case on to the small council for trial.'

'There would be no need for a trial if Annette confessed,' Calvin said. 'Nevertheless, I'm confident the verdict shall go our way.'

Though reluctant to question the great scholar's judgement, Knox pressed him. 'Pray tell me, why do you insist on divorce?'

Calvin's dour face glowered with an expression as severe and uncompromising as his high-backed oak chair. 'Because Annette is a temptress, a reprobate in thrall to the serpent lurking in the undergrowth. Tertullian and the ancient scholars were correct – woman is truly the portal of evil. Through Eve, sin came into the world and brought about man's fall. History is full of examples of how women have debauched virtuous men.'

'Is it not then the duty of fathers and husbands to guide the weaker sex lest they stray into foolishness and sin?' Knox asked. 'Forbye, is man ever justified to put asunder sacred marriage vows?'

Calvin scowled. 'As it is written in Deuteronomy, when a man discovers his wife's fornication, he can divorce her and send her from his house.'

'Did not Christ forgive the woman taken in adultery?' Knox parried.

'On condition that she go and sin no more,' Calvin retorted, 'but Annette did not. Whenever my brother was absent, she invited strange men into the marital home and made free with her favours. She refuses to repent of her sins. While a worthy wife is her husband's joy and crown, a shameful spouse saps his strength,' he added bitterly.

'To avoid washing your dirty laundry in public, perhaps a plea of insanity would be preferable,' Knox attempted. 'For her own safety, Madame Ameaux has been confined to bedlam.'

Calvin's features warped. 'No longer. The consistory considers being shackled in chains as too harsh a punishment and has commuted the sentence. No such mercy must be shown to Annette. She shall face the full force of the law.'

'What is her punishment if found guilty?' Knox feared to ask.

'According to both civil and divine law, adultery deserves the death penalty,' a stern voice broke in. 'Decapitation for men and death by drowning for women.'

Knox gave an involuntary shiver. Drowning – like a witch or the gypsy lass he'd seen tossed into the waters of the Tyne. Nevertheless, if this was the penalty for discipline to be upheld, then so be it.

When a tall lanky man with a long craig and craggy cheekbones came in and heaved a box full of leather bound tomes onto his desk, Calvin sat up.

'What's the verdict? Has the Jezebel been found guilty?' he asked, his face brightening with hope.

With the mien of a doomster about to pronounce the dreaded sentence, the lawyer and prosecutor Germain Colladon shook his head. 'Unfortunately, the evidence was not compelling enough to secure a prosecution. The council had no option but to pronounce the defendant,' he paused to lick his thin lips, 'Not guilty.'

Calvin's long chin slackened. 'That cannot be. You assured me the trial would be a matter of procedure. We had more than the two witnesses required by law.'

'Under cross-examination, their testimony did not stand up to scrutiny. The evidence of four witnesses who claimed to have seen Madame Calvin and Pierre Daguet sneak into "secret and suspect places" to engage in carnal activities – was dismissed as unreliable.'

Ignoring Calvin's angry cry, Colladon continued. 'For one thing, if they could not see into the windowless back room of the shop, how could they know what was happening there? For another, all the accusations came from servants who bore a grudge against Madame Annette. When they had begged to be taken back after running away on the night of the May riots, she dismissed them.'

'Surely the crooked dwarf's flight strongly suggests a guilty conscience,' Calvin said with a snarl.

'Unfortunately, Pierre Daguet left Geneva and is now in Lausanne, far beyond our jurisdiction. Nevertheless, in his written statement he denied fleeing, claiming his employer, Antoine Calvin, had sent him there on business. He also denied any wrongdoing with Madame Calvin and accused others of besmirching his name.'

'Appeal the verdict,' Calvin growled, 'and make sure of a conviction this time.'

Colladon's head wobbled on its long craig. 'To do so, Dr Calvin, there are only two options: eyewitness evidence – highly unlikely since adultery is a crime committed in secret – or a confession. So far Madame Annette has resisted all inducements ... all ... tools of persuasion to plead guilty.'

A cold shiver spiralled down Knox's spine. 'You mean she's been tortured?'

'In obstinate cases, coercive measures are recommended,' Colladon replied. '*Gresillons* – or iron grills – have been attached to her hands and wrists, but so far have failed to squeeze out a confession.'

No stranger to corporal punishment, Knox was staggered by the woman's ability to withstand extreme pain but Calvin was nonplussed.

'Since Satan has numbed her senses, the witch will feel nothing.' He scrunched his teeth. 'Perhaps more persuasion is needed.'

Colladon jerked his head. 'The council are not convinced. They believe there are too many uncertainties in her story to merit more strenuous torture.'

Frustration distorted Calvin's face. 'She's not only an adulteress but a traitoress. After betraying my brother, she enticed him back to sire her children. Besides, it's not the first time the sly Perrinist in our midst has sinned, is it brother?'

Colladon fixed his legal eyes on Antoine. 'Please continue. The more evidence we have to support your charge the better.'

Antoine took a deep breath. 'Eight years ago, Annette was accused of adultery with Jean Chautemps, a business associate of mine, but the examiners found no sure evidence. Instead, she pled to a lesser charge of immodest behaviour. The guilty parties were released with a reprimand and ordered to stop seeing each other. Husband and wife were to be reconciled. Annette had to fall on her knees and publicly beg forgiveness from both my brother and me. I took her back on condition that if she sinned again, I would abandon her.'

Calvin thumped his fist on the desk. 'And she has persisted. Which only goes to prove that Annette is an irredeemable reprobate, one of the damned.'

Colladon tapped his long chin with his quill. 'If we can demonstrate her conduct with Daguet was not a single unfortunate slip that may happen to a woman surprised by fragility, but involved repeated episodes over a period of time, then we can plead capital adultery. In short, a pattern of adulterous behaviour. To make sure the charges stick this time, we can insist Madame Calvin be tried on both counts.'

A ghost of a smile flickered across Calvin's crabbit face. 'Then do it – and if eyewitness evidence is also necessary, that too may be found.'

The Court Room of the Consistory

Annette's appearance when the jailer brought her in horrified Knox. Her shackled feet and bare legs streaked with blood and glaur – or worse – dragged along the floor. Her filthy shift was ragged and torn and her matted hair straggled across her face, black and blue with bruising. As the jailer shoved her onto a stool, he caught Knox's eye and winked. Robin Stewart. Knox looked away. Was he also her torturer?

When Colladon read out the charge of the 1548 trial, Annette raised her head. Bitter scorn twisted her battered face.

'Now read out the verdict,' she said. Though a thick tongue slurred her words, a note of defiance lingered in her voice. 'I may have pled guilty to immodest behaviour but not adultery. Besides, all the evidence was hearsay. Malicious muck-raking from spiteful, spineless servants.'

'Until now,' Colladon said. 'We have an eye witness.'

'Who? Almighty God?' She grinned, showing a row of broken teeth.

'The woman has no shame,' Calvin hissed. 'The devil has a stronger grip on her than I thought. She must be Satan's bride to withstand another round of torture. Never fear, our reliable witness will crush her.'

When he called on Judith Stordeur to take the oath, Knox was stunned. Had she not run away with the libertines to Berne?

Calvin nudged him. 'I have you to thank, Mr Knox, for sending me this most righteous soldier in Christ,' he said, tipping his bonnet towards Stewart. 'Your compatriot not only hunted down my stepdaughter but he's bridled her bold spirit and rescued her from ruin.'

Judith seemed cowed, no longer brazen but mimsy-mou'ed and meek, no longer buxom but skinny and shilpit. She tucked in a few loose locks that had escaped from the linen cap covering her flaxen hair.

'So they've harnessed the trollop's daughter.' Annette sneered and when Colladon read out the charge of adultery carnal with Jean Chautemps, she howled with demonic laughter.

Judith lowered her eyes and twiddled her thumbs. 'Monsieur Chautemps often visited the shop when Antoine was out of town. Then one day, I heard Madame Annette say her husband wouldn't be at home and asked him to come for supper. Which surprised me.'

'Why did it surprise you?'

'It's unseemly for a wife to invite a man into her home without her husband's permission. Only a woman of ill repute would dare do such a thing. When he came, Madame Annette flirted and acted the coquette with him. After that, he gave her gifts. I saw an expensive ring with a sapphire stone on her finger.'

'How can you be sure these gifts were not from her husband?'

'Monsieur Antoine would never squander money on trinkets that pander to female vanity and lead to sin. Sometimes Madame Annette would miss the afternoon church service, complaining of a headache. Once, when I came back she was still in bed: she'd been lying with him, I supposed.'

'You supposed but cannot be sure. Perhaps Chautemps had been at the service.'

Judith jiggled her head. 'Nay, he wasn't.'

Colladon stroked his chin. 'Amongst all the congregation at a crowded service, you noticed that Chautemps was absent?'

'Aye, she noticed,' Annette screeched, 'because she was besotted with Jean and jealous because he had eyes only for me. She's making up all these lies to spite me. Go on, tell them the truth, you liar! Calvin's daughter, the lovesick pup with cow's eyes. Annette taunted. 'And not only for Jean. Admit it, Judith, you're in love with your stepbrother Antoine, too!'

A crimson flush crept up Judith's neck.

'Steek your gab, woman, or I'll steek it for you,' Stewart threatened in Scots and yanked her chains. Annette's head jerked and her neck made a sickening creak.

'Madame Calvin, in the original trial, evidence was given that Jean Chautemps entered your bedroom,' Colladon said.

'I did not deny it. And neither did Jean. He came into my bedroom but denied having carnal relations. Read out his statement.'

Colladon flicked through his papers. '*If she had been as foolish as I, who knows what would have happened.*' He paused. 'However, if, as you assert, he was in love with you, he may have said that to preserve your honour.'

Judith pointed a finger and squealed. 'But you did! You did lie with Jean on the couch in the print room. I saw you – through the keyhole and when you came out your faces were red with passion and guilt.'

Annette squinted at her. 'What keyhole? That door is latched. There is no keyhole, you lying sneaky.' She flicked back a greasy lock of lank hair and fixed burning eyes on Dr Calvin. 'I'm not blind, nor am I a fool. I can see what's happening here. My fingers have been mashed to a pulp with *gresillons*, my teeth knocked out, my head held under water until I almost drowned and yet I've refused to say what you want me to say. Nevertheless, I will now confess.'

Calvin sat back. A sanctimonious smile slid across his stern face as he whispered, 'Whatever confession she concocts, the verdict will go in our favour. Nothing less than capital adultery.'

Annette glared at him. 'Only if you hear me out: I will have my day in court.' She jabbed a smashed finger at Colladon. 'Assure me I will suffer no interruptions – from any party – including Dr Calvin – and bring me some water!'

Annette took a sip and rinsed her mouth before spraying out blood and bits of broken tooth, narrowly missing her persecutor. 'I confess I was in love with Jean Chautemps and he with me. What was so sinful about that? Yet love has become a crime in this city of suspicion and distrust. We grew up together, played together, and thought we would marry and live together. But my father, Nicholas le Fert, was in thrall to Dr Calvin and his so-called Christian ideals and gave me in marriage to his brother, Antoine. Nay, he sold me.'

Knox and the councillors drew in a collective breath.

'To gain favour with the great reformer, my wealthy father provided a dowry of 150 ecus and a stock of valuable furniture. If – nay, when – I am found guilty, as I surely will be, the Calvin brothers will keep what is rightfully mine. Calvin is a tyrant who thirsts for power. The pope of Geneva would rather we all lived like monks, wearing hair shirts and eating gruel. Like the pope in Rome, he'll brook no opposition.

'Remember the fate of Jacques Gruet – tortured for three years before his head was cut off. Just for hanging a placard on Calvin's pulpit. Mocking the scriptures may be a sacrilege but Almighty Calvin deems it blasphemy to ridicule his sermons and lampoon the dogma he spouts. To cough during his long-winded tirades is a sin.

'Living is not only a crime but dying, too. Folk were forbidden to drink from a miraculous spring that heals the plague for that's akin to idolatry, he says. And those stricken with the pest were burned alive for spreading the disease. That's the kind of holy man Calvin is. But to enforce his will, he needs laws and for that he needs to bribe the lawmakers. Once he gets his greedy paws on my dowry, my money will find its way into your pockets as a reward.'

When the councillors voiced their objections, Colladon raised a hand. He'd given his word.

Annette bared blackened stumps of teeth at them before continuing. 'The lust for power and avarice not only drives the Calvin brothers but jealousy and spite. Antoine envied Jean for being handsome, rich and of higher rank. I never loved Antoine but he lusted after me, desired me. As a dutiful and obedient wife, I never refused him and bore his children. I may not have loved him but his stepsister did.'

As she slurped in a deep breath, blood-specked saliva burbled from the corners of her mouth. 'In return for testifying against me, Judith's reward will be marriage – to Antoine. There, I've had my say. Now, do with me as you will.'

Her legs buckled but before she could crumple to the floor, Stewart caught her and hauled her up onto the bench. Her head fell forward onto her chest.

The trial left Knox in turmoil. Was Annette a Jezebel possessed by Satan with supernatural strength to withstand torture? Or was she telling the truth – that Dr Calvin was so hell bent on acquiring her money that he was prepared to throw her like Jezebel to the dogs. If so, the possibility that the great theologian succumbed to such common human frailties as cowardice, avarice and lust for power disturbed him. But then who was he to judge? Only the Lord could fathom the depths of the human soul.

As he lay with his arms round Marjory's swelling belly, he sought solace in her yielding softness.

'Madame Annette must be very courageous to withstand such torture. I would have confessed at the first screw of the pennywinkis.' She shuddered.

Knox drew her in closer. 'You never know until you're tested. But you'll never be accused of such sins, my wee bird. You're one of God's children and I'm truly blessed to have such a virtuous soul as you for my wife. You are my compass, my lodestone on the narrow path of righteousness. I ken you'll never fail me.'

Marjory shifted her weight to get comfortable. 'Geneva frightens me, John. The maidservants tell me it's everyone's duty – even children – to clype on each other. What's more, his guards have the power to burst into people's houses and quiz servants about what goes on. Wet nurses are forbidden to sleep in the same bed as the children they're breastfeeding. Every day folk are interrogated, arrested and punished. The folk all live in fear. Where is the Christian charity in this City of God, John? Didn't Jesus command us to love our enemies?'

'If we assume to surpass in sweetness and humanity Christ who is the fountain of piety and compassion, woe be unto us.' Knox replied, repeating Calvin's answer to a lady with the selfsame question. Though whether it satisfied Marjory was doubtful, for she let out a long-suffering sigh.

'I wouldn't presume to surpass Christ's compassion, John, just a teardrop of human pity to salve a troubled soul would be enough.'

'Oftimes extreme measures are necessary to tackle Satan's evil power,' Knox replied. 'However harsh he may appear, Dr Calvin is God's chosen vessel, and discipline is our defence against the devil.'

Marjory fell silent before asking, 'What if the wrong person is punished? The other day I saw a young lass with a child at her breast and a sign round her neck. Do you know what it said?' she bit her lip. 'Fornicator. Yet she looked so scared. It seems she was a maid whose master had had his wicked way with her and then flung her into the street to be spat on. Surely that's not just.'

'Never fash, my wee bird. The Lord will punish the evil master in hellfire,' Knox replied. Yet it bothered him that the trials and tribulations of everyday life deafened the voice that spoke so clearly to him in the pulpit.

Marjory curled her warm body against his. 'Dr Calvin's regime is so unforgiving. Promise me you'll never be so hardhearted, John.'

It came as no surprise to Knox when Colladon informed the court next morning that Annette was not fit to attend.

'Since Madame Calvin cannot provide adequate explanations of her previous actions with Jean Chautemps, the council has decided to grant a joint judgment. To Antoine Calvin, we grant a divorce from his wife, Madame Anne le Fert. She's to be exiled from Geneva and, on pain of whipping, shall leave the city within twenty-four hours. Her husband shall have custody of their children and control of her dowry.'

When Colladon declared an end to the trial, Calvin beckoned him over. 'I expected no less a verdict than capital adultery.'

The lawyer dipped his long neck. 'The council are uncomfortable with the death penalty that would ensue from such a verdict.'

'How can we maintain law and order if we fear to mete out severe punishments?' Calvin bellowed. 'It's not enough to exile the sinner from her family, I shall excommunicate the reprobate.'

Colladon coughed behind his hand. 'As you will, but they also fear it may aggravate your reputation as a tyrant and incite riots.'

'I'm no tyrant! I'm only trying to implement God's law. Doctrine is not an affair of the tongue but of life. You see what I'm up against, Mr Knox?' he thundered.

To a certain extent Knox did. On the other hand, there was some truth in the old saying: it's better to be half-hangit than ill-married.

III

Anna Locke

And then not daring with presuming eye
Once to behold the angry heavens face,
From troubled sprite I send confused cry,
To crave the crumbs of all sufficing grace.
Meditation upon a Penitent Sinner
Anna Locke, 16th Century

Geneva, Spring 1557

Knox read the latest letter from Anna Locke with increasing unease and foreboding. Mary Tudor had turned up the heat, fuelling her crusade with countless sacrificial lambs. With no bishops left to burn they were rounding up ordinary folk to tie to the stake: brewers and butchers, blacksmiths and cobblers, masters and apprentices, maids and mistresses, widows and children.

Goodman would be inconsolable to hear that his friend Bartlett Green had become a victim. Despite being tortured, the young martyr had kept faith and, according to Anna, had gone to his death joyfully. Would he be so brave? The thought was always skulking in the darkest corners of Knox's mind, like a deathwatch beetle ticking away at his conscience.

The net was tightening around them, Anna wrote. Already Henry's brother, Thomas, and Anthony Hickman had been arrested for smuggling Protestant literature and ferrying exiles to Antwerp on their merchant ships. Incarcerated in separate cells in the Fleet prison, they expected the death sentence any day. Anna and Rose Hickman were beside themselves with worry.

Knox had just finished penning his reply when he heard Mrs Bowes's step on the squeaky stairs. At the click of the sneck, he hastily blotted the letter and hunched forward. He should steek the door against her for she stomped in without knocking, demanding his immediate attention and disrupting his flow of thought.

Mrs Bowes picked up the heavy tome he'd placed at the door to warn him of an impending invasion and thumped it onto his desk.

'That book keeps falling,' she complained. Like a keen-eyed kestrel stalking her prey, she cast a glance over his desk and spotted the letter beneath his elbows. 'Who are you writing to?'

None of your concern, he fain would reply. Why did she make him feel like a naughty schoolboy? Swift on her toes for someone so stout, Mrs Bowes had nipped round the desk to read over his shoulder. He pressed the letter close to his chest.

How dare she! She drove him to distraction at times. She would try the patience of a saint.

'To my friends in London, mother. Because their lives are in danger, I'm inviting them to Geneva.'

Mrs Bowes folded her arms, her lips puckered as tightly as a laced purse. 'Is that wise? Our house is full – we have no room. Your wife is about to give birth.'

'Even the innkeeper at Christ's nativity found room in a lowly stable.'

'I already have my hands full tending to Marjory and soon there will be a baby to care for. Who else might follow? You're opening the floodgates to a whole pack of outcasts.'

'Her brothers-in-law are already in prison and may be put to death. Would you leave their wives to be driven like lambs to the slaughter? Would you have their children murdered like the Holy Innocents? Would you be more wicked than Herod?'

Her perversity of spirit drove his wrath to fever pitch.

'How can we sit in safety in Geneva while they suffer so? We must pluck them from Satan's bloody claws. Where is your Christian charity, dear mother? When I sought refuge in London the Lockes never shooed me away from their door. Their generosity knows no bounds: despite the risks, they regularly send me sums of money. I'm forever in their debt.'

Her woeful expression made Knox regret his outburst. 'Forgive me, dear mother, but their plight grieves me. I entreat you – be not poor in spirit. Be mindful of Christ's words: *Blessed are the merciful for they shall obtain mercy.*'

Knox heaved a sigh. 'Perhaps I'm being thoughtless and asking too much of you – in which case I shall lessen your burden. When Mrs Locke arrives, I shall ask her to act as my secretary.' Mrs Bowes's face crumpled and she wrung her hands. 'So I'm no longer good enough to be your helpmate, dear son?' Her voice dropped to a wheedling whine.

'Nay, that's not what I meant at all.' Why did she distort his good intentions? He rose and put an arm round her shoulder. 'We must do everything possible to make our guests feel at home. I know I can count on you, dear mother, to look after them.' He pressed the wax seal on the letter and handed it to her. 'Now, may I trust you to pass this on to Jamie to deliver?'

Get thee behind me Satan, Mrs Bowes muttered, but the temptation to read Knox's reply to Mrs Locke was too strong. With shaking hands she broke the seal of the letter and read the first few lines. Now her whole body trembled.

Dear sister,

If I could express the thirst and languor I have for your presence, I shall appear to pass measure. I weep and rejoice in remembrance of you; but that would vanish by the comfort of your presence which, I assure you, is so dear to me that if the charge of this little flock here did not impede me, my presence should anticipate my letter.

The green-handled dagger of jealousy ripped through Mrs Bowes, tearing at her entrails as she read on. *Sometimes I sobbed fearing what should become of you.* The words seared her heart. She'd assumed she was the preacher's only confidante, that she alone shared his most intimate thoughts, but here was proof Knox was offering solace and comfort to another woman. Who was this damsel in distress who had stolen Knox's heart? She must be vigilant.

May 1557

Every day Mrs Bowes kept watch by the window, awaiting the English exiles with increasing trepidation. On the day of their arrival, she stifled her antipathy and greeted them with as much civility as she could muster. It struck a chill in her heart to see that, despite being travel-stained and travel-weary, Anna Locke was a comely creature, with a heart-shaped face peeping out from under her hood and golden curls escaping from her snood. Her blue-grey eyes radiated warmth. Nevertheless, as Mrs Bowes knew, a pretty face did not turn Knox's head: he was attracted to the inner beauty of a soul seeking truth. Was Anna Locke such a one?

'It's so generous of you to share your home with us: it cannot be easy to welcome strangers,' Anna said.

Mrs Bowes pinned on a smile. 'We must do what we can to rescue the weak and the needy and deliver them from the hands of the wicked.'

'My husband is also grateful. Sadly, he cannot leave his business but I've brought our two children. Harry, give our hostess your gift,' she coaxed.

After Mrs Bowes had thanked the solemn-faced five-year-old for his poem, Mrs Locke introduced her daughter fast asleep in her maid's arms. 'The long journey has wearied her, but she'll be as right as rain after few days' rest,' she murmured and gently brushed aside a curl on Annie's forehead.

Knox gave all his guests a cordial welcome but Mrs Bowes watched closely as he greeted Mrs Locke. His face beamed with joy – his cheeks glowed and his blue eyes sparkled – much to her distress. Then, when he kissed Anna full on the lips, lingering longer than necessary, the green bile of jealousy surged in Mrs Bowes's throat. She must be on her guard that this siren did not topple her in Knox's affections.

The refugees had scarcely settled in when young Annie fell ill with a high fever. When a rash flared up round her neck and down her arms, Mrs Bowes vented her concern to Knox. 'You must ask them to leave forthwith.'

'They cannot return to England. Forbye, Annie will soon shake it off.'

'What if Marjory catches it? She's carrying your child.'

'Then tell her to stay in our room until the crisis has passed.'

'On your head be it,' Mrs Bowes mumbled.

The next morning, she interrupted Knox's breakfast to tell him that, as he'd predicted, the crisis had passed. Annie had shaken off the infection.

'Thanks be to God,' Knox replied. 'I'm pleased to hear.'

Mrs Bowes crossed her arms. 'Along with her life.'

'What? You mean to say young Annie has died? This is dreadful news!' Knox pushed back his stool and leapt up, sending papers and quills clattering to the floor. 'Anna will be bereft! I must go and console her,' he cried.

But seeing him hurtle to her rival's side was no consolation to Mrs Bowes.

Marjory dabbed her clammy brow with a handkerchief and ran a hand over her swelling belly. The nausea of earlier months had passed, thank goodness, but stomach cramps bothered her. Was that lurch in her womb? With the baby due any day now, she was on edge: a twinge in her lower back made her shift in her seat.

She glanced across at the table where Anna Locke was engrossed in her writing. Marjory envied her calmness. How could she be so resigned to her daughter's death? Losing a beloved child at such a young age – her grief must be great. How could she bear it?

When Marjory's sewing slipped onto the floor, Anna flung down her pen and rushed to her side. She placed a hand on her damp brow. 'Are you well?'

'I'm fine. Just stiff from sitting too long.' Tears welled in her eyes. 'But I'm so scared Anna. What if I lose the child? I could not be as forbearing as you.'

'I find great comfort in my work, translating and composing the Psalms. Whenever grief threatens to crush me, I try to keep in mind the words of our Saviour. *Come unto me, all ye that labour and are heavy laden, and I will give you rest.* We must put our trust in the Lord who shares our burdens. Do not lose heart, dear Marjory, you're not alone – my sisters-in-law and I are here to help.'

Marjory's pale face lit up. 'Thank you, dear Anna. That gives me heart.'

'And when I bore my children,' she paused, 'this manual was most useful.'

Marjory squinted at the book Anna held out but the title printed in thick black Gothic script made no sense to her.

'Roughly translated it means, *A Very Cheerful Booklet of Encouragement Concerning the Conception and Birth of Man,*' Anna explained. 'Dr Jacob Rueff is an eminent Zurich surgeon with vast experience of delivering countless babes into the world. He decries so-called physicians who think nothing of laying out a corrupt corpse one minute and delivering a babe the next without changing their clothes or washing their hands.' Anna shuddered at the thought.

'They don't seem to realise that miasma from the pest and the pox not only taints the breath and hair but clothing. Similarly, the custom of confining the expectant mother to a dark airless room may harm not only her health but her child's.'

'It never did me or mine any harm,' Mrs Bowes butted in. She stood at the door, arms folded, and glowered. 'There's a carpenter outside with some kind of contraption he says you ordered. Is that true, Mrs Locke?'

'The birthing chair is ready? Thank you for letting me know, dear sister.' She turned to Marjory. 'Dr Rueff recommends sitting on this chair to ease your delivery for lying flat thwarts nature's course.'

Mrs Bowes's face darkened. 'Dr Who? There will be no surgeons at my daughter's confinement. I won't allow it.'

'I quite agree, dear sister,' Anna replied. 'Dr Rueff condemns those so-called surgeons who are no more than butchers or barbers.'

Marjory rose and took her mother's hands. 'No need to fret, mama. I'm blessed to have so many experienced mothers to aid my delivery.'

Knox watched with nervous apprehension as Marjory laid his newborn son in his arms. He'd never held a babe so recently delivered of the womb before.

'Do not vex, you won't drop him.' Marjory loosened the shawl swaddled round the bairn. 'And don't be shocked that he looks like an old man. His skin is still wrinkled and bruised from the birth but Anna assures me it will quickly clear up.'

For Knox, his son was a miracle of creation. He gazed in wonder at the squashed red face with crusted eyelids and tufts of hair. He ran his pinkie round the little whorl-shaped ears and tapped the wee button nose. The bairn's eyelids flickered and opened: his hazy eyes drifted in their sockets before fixing on his father for a brief second. And when the wee mite clutched his pinkie in his tiny fist, Knox thought his heart would burst with love and pride and joy.

'Look, Marjory, he's holding my hand! Welcome to the world, wee man!' Tears streamed down his face into his beard.

'Nathaniel will be a fitting name. In Hebrew it means gift of God. We must give thanks to the Lord for his safe delivery and to you, dear wife, for bearing this rare and wonderful gift.' As he raised his head, his beard tickled Nathaniel's nose. When the bairn scrunched up his face and girned, Knox panicked. 'Wheesht, wee man. Wheesht,' he murmured rocking him back and forth.

Marjory untied the lace of her nightgown. 'He's hungry for his milk, John. Here, give him to me.' She took the bairn and latched him onto her breast.

As he watched his wife feeding his child, a wave of love surged through Knox followed by a groundswell of panic — for this fragile new life brought the added responsibilities of fatherhood. Would he be up to the task? The bairn's cries must have alerted Mrs Bowes who came rushing in only to scold the nursing mother. 'This won't do, Marjory. Only common women have infants sucking at the breast.' Addressing Knox she said, 'She should have a wet nurse.'

'I told you I don't need one, mama. Anna says a mother's milk is best for a babe.'

'And her son Harry is a vigorous young lad,' Knox added.

'But her daughter failed to thrive,' Mrs Bowes retorted.

Marjory gave a yelp. 'Mama how can you be so cruel! Anna's daughter died of a fever!'

Knox, too, scowled at her jibe: her sharp-edged tongue would clip a clout. 'That was most unkind and unworthy of you, mother. If Marjory wishes to nurse our son then so be it. She kens what's best for our bairn.'

'So, everyone spurns the advice of a mother who has borne fifteen children. You, too, think me a dried-up old crone.' Mrs Bowes pouted and stormed out in a fit of pique.

Knox let out an exasperated sigh. 'The Lord hasn't seen fit to bless me with the wisdom of Solomon, Marjory, nor has he made me all things to all women that I might keep the peace amongst them.'

Summer, 1557

A few weeks later, the arrival of two Edinburgh burgesses, Barron and Syme, disturbed Knox's domestic happiness. Reading the letter signed by James Stewart, the Earl of Glencairn and Erskine of Dun, begging him to return to Scotland, raised mixed emotions in Knox. On the one hand he was flattered, on the other he was flattened at the prospect of abandoning his family.

Mrs Bowes's stance was clear-cut, however. 'You cannot think of going back to that land of ruffians when you're making a comfortable life here for all of us. Your wife has just given birth to your first son. You have time to study. You have Calvin's respect. You're the pastor of a trouble-free flock who hang on your every word. Return to Scotland and they'll hang you on the end of a rope and then burn you alive.'

Knox flinched. Most of what she said was true. 'They assure me my life would not be at risk, dear mother. The queen regent may have mocked my attempt to convert her but at least she's not cremating martyrs. And if my people call how can I refuse to be their minister?'

'The Scots Lords have let you down before with their dithering. Besides, what will Dr Calvin have to say? He may not give his permission.'

That would solve his dilemma for, deep down, Knox harboured grave doubts about the lords' motives.

IV

Delay in Dieppe

I am the voice of one crying out in the wilderness
John I: 23

Dieppe, October 1557

In the gloomy cellar lit with rush lights, John Wedderburn rubbed his inky hands on his leather apron and pulled out an upturned cask for Knox to perch on.

'Why have you risked life and limb to travel across this war-torn continent?' he asked. 'Dieppe is awash with French troops and no longer a safe haven for Huguenots. To please her Spanish prince of darkness, Mary Tudor has declared war on France: Spanish and English invasion fleets are moored all along the coast.'

'Why indeed? I've never stopped asking that question since leaving Geneva.'

Knox leaned his chin on his hand. Contrary to his expectation, Calvin had given his blessing. Unless he wished to be unmerciful to his country and rebellious unto God he should heed this call from the faithful eager for his ministry.

Knox had delayed his departure for it grieved him sorely to leave behind his wife and son who had brought such joy into his life. While Mrs Bowes had been irate – and rightly so – Marjory had been more forbearing and practical – packing his bags and slipping pokes of powdered remedies into his pocket. He must do what he believed to be right. But Knox had been led astray so many times by the Scots lords, he no longer knew what to believe.

Despite his misgivings, he had set out on the road with his trusty lodesman Jamie, who could make the journey blindfolded.

'Not the best timing,' Wedderburn said. 'Forbye, Marie de Guise's brother is in charge of the French army and if the duke catches you here, he'll hand you over to his brother the cardinal. The Grand Inquisitor is waging his own war on heresy. If they find my printing press I, too, face having my tongue shredded.' Unease oozed through his pores and his stout frame wobbled with worry.

'Then I must leave for Scotland as soon as possible,' Knox replied. 'Is Skipper Will able to get through?'

'All the Channel ports are either blocked or closed and Calais is under siege, but the doughty Free Fishers always find a way.' He opened up the kist and drew out a leather pouch. 'Your brother smuggled in these letters but I dared not send them on lest the messenger be seized and slain.'

Detecting Maitland's seal on one of them, Knox hastily ripped it open. Skimming the letter, he let out the long low howl of a tortured hound. 'The fickle Scots lords have changed their minds again. They urge me to wait in Dieppe while new consultations take place. What can they mean?'

Wedderburn heaved a sigh. 'The French marriage. Our lords are being lured with the promise of French gold if they support our queen's union with the dauphin.'

The second letter supported the first. 'Even the most frack and fervent lack the boldness and constancy needed for such an enterprise,' Knox read. 'The time for return is not yet ripe.'

Wedderburn looked on helplessly as Knox buried his head in his hands. When he looked up his face was grey with despair.

'Does it not enter their flichtersome heads what I've had to thole in answering their call? It's been no dauner doun the brae to abandon my ministry in Geneva, leave my home and family, and travel six hundred miles across a country at risk of arrest for heresy at any time. Why am I being tested? On each journey I've had to face a trial – the pride of politicians, the disloyalty of lords, the cowardice of scholars, the greed of clerics for power. Am I not God's messenger? Why is he keeping his schemes secret from me? At times I fear the Lord is playing hide-and-seek with me.'

'Though it may feel as if God is playing dice with you, you must not lose hope. Despair is the most grievous sin.'

'I know. But if the Lord will not give me a reason – at least give me a key to solve his puzzle.'

December 1557

By the middle of December, Knox had received no word from the Scots lords. The advent of Christmas only deepened his melancholy: in Geneva his family would be celebrating – not Christ's nativity – but the season of goodwill without him.

'Stuck here in this eternity of waiting, I know not whether I've been pitched into limbo or purgatory,' Knox moaned.

Wedderburn nodded his shaggy head in sympathy as he warmed his inky paws at the fire. 'Would giving a sermon on Christmas morn fill you with good cheer? Word of your presence here has spread amongst the French Huguenots. A noble lady, wife of Captain Ribault, bids you give a sermon in her home. Will you come?'

The prospect of preaching to the primitive kirk of beleaguered souls jolted Knox out of his slough of despond. On Christmas morning, amongst the gathering of Madame Ribault's family and friends, he noticed a drably clad woman swathed in a woollen shawl, cowering at the back of the room. A servant, he assumed, until Wedderburn took his arm.

'This poor mother has walked miles in the depths of winter to hear you preach, brother. She fain would have you baptise her bairn but dare not ask.'

The power of a mother's love never failed to kindle Knox's heart and as she drew back the swaddling, hot tears pricked his eyes. Her baby son's scrunched up face reminded him of Nathaniel. Fatherhood had brought unexpected delight and he'd looked forward to witnessing his son's first steps and teaching him his first words. Now he was missing all his significant milestones – all for the sake of false promises.

January 1558

When the turn of the year brought neither response from Scotland nor respite in the weather, Knox struggled to ward off self-pity and despondency. Sitting by the fire in the tavern, listening to the storm lashing Dieppe, he fretted that bad weather and the blockade in the Channel had delayed shipping. When a strong gust battered the tavern door, he whirled round in alarm, but was relieved to see Wedderburn.

'I've just been down to the harbour,' he said, taking off his sopping wet cloak and spreading it over the settle to dry. 'One of my boats has made it through.' He drew out a bundle of letters tucked under his oxter. 'But it's not good news, I'm afraid. John Rough, the Ayrshire preacher, has been burnt at the stake in Smithfield.'

Knox's blood ran cold – yet another of the glorious company to add to the tally. 'I believed he was safe. Did he not flee to Friesland with his wife and children? To set up in trade knitting woollens, I mind.'

'Aye, that he did,' Wedderburn said, 'but while in London, Brother Rough witnessed the burning of a Protestant preacher. When the martyr's bereft flock recognised him, they pleaded with him to take their pastor's place. Then he, too, was caught.'

The news shook Knox to the core. At St Andrews, he'd stepped into Rough's shoes – was this a sign he'd step into them once more? What should he do? Where should he go? The waiting game was fraying his nerves.

'Here are good tidings to cheer you,' Wedderburn said, interrupting his thoughts. 'My brother Robert writes from Dundee to say the Scottish lords have signed a covenant. They swear to defend Christ's Evangel and congregation from the rage of Satan and remove all abomination and idolatry. Isn't that a matter for rejoicing?'

Knox thumped the table with his fist. 'Is it? Who's behind this? What drives them? These swithering, dithering lords cannot begin a reformation without me. Who will lead them?'

Wedderburn scanned his brother's letter. 'After losing the regency, Châtelherault has taken up the Protestant cause.'

'Twa-fangelt Arran? Thon hunker-slider is only professing God's truth to further his own personal gain and worldly ambitions. How could the Lord raise such a leader from the dunghill? He's up to something. John Dudley was cut from the same cloth – he, too, tailored religion for his own political ends. I must return as soon as possible to aid thon true Protestant lords. Erskine and Glencairn haven't withdrawn their official invitation. Perhaps their reply has gone astray and they are, at this very minute, waiting for me to arrive.'

'Nay, brother, bide here a wee. At the back end of the year, the weather is too treacherous for sailing.'

'No more treacherous than the villainous Scots lords,' Knox muttered. 'The longer I delay, the further thon wayward lords will stray from the right path and support for reform ebb away.'

February 1558

The more his mood darkened, the more his health deteriorated. Knox sorely missed Marjory's attentive ministrations. With an uncanny knack of sensing his symptoms before he did, his wife would be by his side with feverfew to calm a looming migraine or powdered saxifrage to ease the gravel. In her place, Wedderburn liberally dosed him with the best tonic for all ills that he swore by – the finest French cognac.

On a drizzly February morning, Wedderburn roused Knox from fitful slumber.

'Hair of the dog, brother.' He handed him a beaker of hot spiced wine. 'Forbye, it's a dreich day. This will warm you to the cockles.'

As he opened the shutters, Wedderburn's shoulders stiffened. Sensing his unease, Knox staggered from his bed to join him. Down below in the street, folk were scurrying about like frenzied ants.

'Is today *un jour de fête*?' Knox asked. 'Are they celebrating an unhallowed saint's feast day?'

'Nay, not during Lent. A flotilla of galleys docked overnight.' Wedderburn hesitated before adding, 'Ferrying commissioners from Scotland.'

The crowds lined the street to watch outriders on plumed horses, blowing bugles and flying pennants to herald the arrival of the grand procession.

'The French king has offered the lords offered lavish inducements as a reward for supporting Queen Mary's marriage to the dauphin. Now they're on their way to Paris to negotiate the terms,' Wedderburn said ruefully.

Knox shook his aching head: despair deepened his hangover. 'This match will sound the death knell for religious reformation in Scotland. Our flighty lairds will aye follow the gold to feather their own nests. The riches of the corrupt French court will blind them to the true faith and the French will swarm over Scotland like midges. The Duke de Guise will take over the reins of power from his sister and the cardinal will carry on his persecution of Protestants. Thon crafty Salome, Marie de

Guise, is handing Scotland to France on a platter.'

Wedderburn gaped at him in astonishment. '*In vino veritas*, brother. The claret has cleared your mind, I see. Nevertheless, the good Lord did his best to thwart their treachery. A storm cast off a ship transporting their horses while another with costly furniture was shipwrecked off the French coast. No earls or bishops perished, however.'

'More's the pity,' Knox muttered and scrutinised the horsemen cantering past. In pride of place, at the head of the cavalcade, rode James Beaton, the fiend who'd mocked his appeal as a pasquil. No surprise there, but then Knox gave a jolt. Nay, that could not be. In the midst of the procession rode Lord James Stewart and Erskine of Dun, staunch followers and signatories to the covenant. If they had switched allegiance, what hope was there? Knox swigged back the wine to quell the disgust rising in his queasy stomach.

'So once again Satan has reared his ugly snout to taigle me. I fear the moment for reformation has passed.'

Disgruntled, he was about to turn away from the window when men-at-arms led by William Kirkcaldy, caught his eye. Bringing up the rear rode a familiar figure – was it Robert Stewart? Why was thon would-be assassin on his way to Paris?

V

The Last Martyr

I will not recant the truth. I am corn not chaff;
I will not be blown away with the wind or burst by the flail.
I will survive both.

Last Words
Walter Milne, 16th Century

Holyrood Palace, Edinburgh, April 1558

Once all the toasts to the health of the royal couple had been drunk and the trestles cleared away, the minstrels struck up to signal the start of the dancing.

'Time to leave the merry company to their revels,' Elisabeth said.

'Our modest celebrations must pale in comparison to the grand nuptials in Paris but I've done my best to commemorate my daughter's marriage,' Marie de Guise said. 'I greatly regret not being there to see her wed.'

'Let us pray the hitching went without a hitch and Queen Mary will now be a blushing bride.'

'You always lift my low spirits, dear Elisabeth.' But the queen's fleeting smile swiftly faded. 'Now their union has been consecrated, let us also pray for its consummation.'

Elisabeth crossed her fingers behind her back. 'Given time, madame. They are young enough.'

A shadow crossed the queen's wan, puffy face. 'Now that Mary's destiny is in France, she will never return to Scotland. My health is not good and I worry who will take over the regency when I'm gone.'

'You have years left yet, madame,' Elisabeth insisted, though secretly fearful her days were numbered. The queen's heart was causing her concern: her swollen ankles and laboured breathing indicated dropsy. 'But for now you must rest.'

Helped by her ladies, the queen hirpled upstairs to the royal bedchamber where she sank into a chair with a gasp. 'Even so, I must make plans for my succession. What do you think, my dear prioress? Who could replace me as regent?'

Elisabeth considered the various candidates. Despite being James V's merry-begotten son, James Stewart had the support of his pushy mother, Margaret Erskine, and her powerful family as well as the Lords of the Congregation. If bastardry barred him from the throne, becoming regent was the next best thing.

He had a strong rival in James Hamilton, now Earl of Arran after his father's promotion to the dukedom of Châtelherault. As if inheriting folly from his father were not scourge enough the madness infecting his mother's family tainted his blood. With delusions of marrying Queen Mary, Arran was rumoured to be on the verge of lunacy. Worried he might do something reckless – attack the groom or even the bride at the royal wedding – King Henri had ordered the duke to keep his mad son locked up at Châtelherault, his estate in France.

'Not a great choice between the two Jamies, madame. Peerie-heidit Arran's head is birling with bees: there's no telling which way he'll jump. And high-heidit Stewart will scheme to put the crown on his ain head,' Elisabeth replied.

The queen regent chuckled. 'Sad but true. However, there is a third James: your nephew is making his mark. Even Mary Tudor has heard of James Hepburn's exploits. After his surprise dawn attack on Northumberland's men, she plans to send more troops to the border garrisons. But he professes the Protestant faith, I believe.'

'Bothwell is a border reiver who abides by their rules of conduct, madame. Having pledged his trust, even to an enemy, a reiver will keep his promise. James is an eagle to his father's magpie, the devil's bird.'

'I know. That's why I've a mind to appoint him Lieutenant of the Border in place of my Lord Huntly.'

'A wise move, madame. Huntly is heavy with age and even heavier of figure. Too auld and too stout and a highlander, forbye. The lowlanders have scant respect for thon bag of guts as wheezy as a set of bagpipes.'

'Surely you do not share their opinion of the most powerful Catholic noble in the realm, dear prioress?' the queen said striving to keep a stern countenance.

When Elisabeth arched an eyebrow in reply, they both burst into laughter. Their mirth was cut short by the arrival of Maitland whose solemn face heralded bad news.

Wielding a scroll he said, 'I bring a petition from a group of reformers complaining about the recent execution in St Andrews.'

A look of alarm passed over the queen's grey face. 'I know of no execution.'

Uncharacteristically ill at ease, Maitland fidgeted with the petition. 'The archbishop arrested a reformist recently returned from Geneva. He was tried on two counts: heresy and, being an ordained priest, illegal marriage.'

Elisabeth's heart skipped a beat: her hand flew to her mouth. 'They have captured John Knox and sent him to the stake?'

Maitland shook his head. 'Nay. Walter Milne, a former priest, and his wife were caught spreading the gospel. He was burnt on the very site where Patrick Hamilton and George Wishart met their fate.'

Elisabeth let out a long slow breath and mumbled, '*Deo Gratias.*'

The queen's face blanched and her knuckles turned white as she gripped the arms of the chair. 'By sending Milne to the stake, Hamilton has created another martyr. I was not consulted about this.'

'In this ecclesiastical matter, your permission was not required, madame. He did so on the advice of his advocate. As James Balfour reminded him he's responsible only to Rome.'

The queen's ashen pallor worried Elisabeth but also made her angry – any joy at her daughter's marriage had been swiftly dispelled. 'Has Hamilton forgotten the fate of David Beaton for setting Wishart ablaze?' she fumed. 'The cardinal was brutally stabbed and his bloody corpse hung out of the castle window.'

Maitland inclined his head. 'It was not his best decision, I must admit, Dame Prioress, for the memory of Wishart's burning is still raw in St Andrews. The townspeople did everything in their power to delay Milne's execution, refusing to provide fuel for the fire and ropes to tie the martyr to the stake. Only when Hamilton threatened to pull down their houses to stoke the pyre did they acquiesce – grudgingly.'

'Hamilton and Balfour had better look out or their ain carcases will be tossed to the curs,' Elisabeth murmured.

'In truth, for Milne's execution has horrified the populace. Folk were sickened to see the frail preacher with his long frosty beard and wrinkled face hirpling to the stake and muttered how wicked it was to burn such a decrepit old man.'

Elisabeth shuddered. 'No wonder. Most folk don't live to such a ripe old age. Setting aflame an old beard – whatever his beliefs – is shameful if not downright cowardly.'

'Yet Milne faced his fate with courage,' Maitland said not without a tinge of admiration. 'Before committing his soul to God's keeping, he warned that a hundred better would arise out of his ashes.'

'Why has the archbishop done this?' the queen moaned. 'He knows I've always advised tolerance towards Protestant believers. I've no desire to incite a religious war.'

'Indeed, Your Grace, but the archbishop wishes to demonstrate that, while you may show leniency, the Church of Rome will not tolerate heretics.'

A look of anguish crossed her face. 'The people will think I had a hand in it, that it was done with my authority.'

'That may indeed be one of his aims – to cast a slur on you,' Maitland replied.

'And portray you as the Scottish Bloody Mary,' Elisabeth added.

Maitland nodded. 'I fear as much. Folk mumble that faggot, fire and sword is all they will now get from the Queen Regent. Forbye, incensed that his main quarry – John Knox – keeps slipping out of his grasp, Hamilton has burned Milne in his stead.'

Setting aside her own disquiet, Elisabeth comforted the queen. 'Never fash, madame. Hamilton has only brought shame on himself by this.'

'I jalouse the Hamilton brothers will do everything in their power to topple you as regent,' Maitland said. 'While the archbishop is on a crusade against those Protestant Lords who have formed what they cry a Band of the Congregation, his brother is toadying up to them. The Hamiltons are playing a double game.'

Elisabeth harrumphed – pot calling the kettle black for Maitland, too, was a canny player, shifty and nifty on his toes. 'So, nothing new from twa-fangelt Arran? Who else has joined this merry band?'

'The earls of Argyll, Glencairn and Morton, Lord Campbell of Lorne, and Erskine of Dun have signed a covenant pledging to establish the reformed religion in Scotland. They also begrudge the presence of Frenchmen on the council who, they say, are plotting to make Scotland a French colony.'

'There are only two Frenchmen amidst the many officers I retained from Châtelherault's administration,' the queen retorted. 'I've tried my best to act without fear or favour.' She pressed a hand against her heart. 'I'm being squeezed between the Catholic clergy on one side and the Protestant lords on the other.'

Maitland dipped his head. 'What's more, they're seeking to bring back Preacher Knox.' This made Elisabeth's ears prick up. 'If so, the archbishop fears they will triumph, for Knox's eloquent tongue has the power to win over men's souls. In need of a strong theologue to withstand him, Hamilton has requested a papal nuncio from Rome.'

'About time too,' Elisabeth said. 'Her Grace has been petitioning support from the Vatican for years to stamp out corruption – to no avail.'

'There's no one more papist than the episcopal procurator in Rome,' Maitland said. 'Dr John Row is a skilled advocate with degrees in civil and canon law. But for his fragile health he would rise higher in the Vatican.'

'He may be the very champion to replace our late lamented Cardinal Beaton,' the queen regent said.

'However, until Dr Row arrives, Hamilton seeks to fortify folk's faith with a miracle at the Loretto shrine.'

Elisabeth gave Maitland a sceptical scowl. 'How can that be? Since when has the archbishop been blessed with divine powers?'

'By whatever powers vested in him, Hamilton has promised a verifiable miracle to open people's eyes to the truth of the Roman Catholic Church.'

VI

The Trumpet Sounds …

How abominable before God,
is the Empire or Rule of a wicked woman,
yea, of a traiteresse and bastard.
*The First Blast of the Trumpet against
the Monstrous Regiment of Women*
John Knox, 16th Century

Geneva, Late Spring 1558

'Da, da,' the toddler cried and waddled few unsteady steps towards his father.

Knox caught hold of Nathaniel and swung him high into the air. 'Look how much he's grown!' he cried as the bairn shrieked with delight.

Seeing Marjory's face beam with maternal love and pride, his welcome was complete.

Returning to Geneva with his tail between his legs, Knox had laboured to make sense of his failures, his futile wanderings. His strength drained to the very dregs, he thought he could never recover but now, holding Nathaniel in the crook of one arm and hugging Marjory with the other, vim and verve surged through him.

'I feared I'd not only be a stranger to Nathaniel but that you, too, my wee bird wouldn't recognise this auld carcase. I feel as ancient as Methuselah.'

'As long as you live to such a ripe old age then we shall be blessed,' Marjory replied and kissed his lips dry and dusty from the road.

Their laughter at Nathaniel tugging his straggly beard brought Mrs Bowes waddling down the hallway. 'So the weary, wayworn wanderer returns?' she clucked and stretched out her arms.

Knox braced himself for her crushing clinch – instead she snatched Nathaniel from him. 'We'll hear all about it later. Come with me, my wee man. Your grandma has something sweet for you.'

When Knox's eyes widened in wonder, Marjory tweaked his cheek playfully. 'You have a rival. Mama dotes on Nathaniel. Our son has replaced you in her affections.'

Thankful to be with Marjory after such a long absence, Knox took her onto his knee and nuzzled her neck. 'It's good to be home. I never want to leave again.'

They sat locked in a tight embrace until Marjory broke away. 'I've no wish to sour your happiness, John, but I have some sorrowful news. The old man I met on the boat.' She hesitated. 'He's been sent to the pyre.'

Knox slowly raised his head. 'Walter Milne is burned?' He stared ahead with unseeing eyes: his face turned as grey as the cinders of a spent fire. 'Then I have his blood on my hands. I warned him not to return but when he insisted, I arranged his passage – to his death.'

Marjory stroked his cheek. 'Nay, you're not to blame, John. You could not have stopped him. His dearest wish was to die on his native soil.'

Knox shuddered. 'But not like that – his bones charred to ashes.'

All night lurid dreams of martyrs burning at the stake disturbed his longed-for rest. Blistered and blackened by fingers of flame, familiar features dissolved into masks of horror screaming out for vengeance. Terrified, he woke up lathered in sweat but Marjory's warm, rhythmical breathing soon soothed him back to sleep.

'The nightmare has begun,' Knox informed his colleagues the next morning. 'Mary of Guise has given her daughter a fine wedding gift. A burnt offering – the sacrifice of Pastor Milne.'

Whittingham pulled a grim face. 'She's following Mary Tudor's example. Something must be done to stop this carnage.'

'Aye, but what?' Knox scowled. 'Don't think I haven't tried. I've crisscrossed the continent seeking an answer but all the great thinkers and scholars – Calvin, Bullinger, Viret – shrank in fear. Like John the Baptist, I've been a lone voice crying in the wilderness.'

Goodman stretched his squat neck, tense from too much studying. 'Do not vex, brothers, the end is nigh. Sitting on our hands and turning a blind eye has only led to suffering and slaughter. Now is the time for action.' He rummaged through a pile of documents and handed a pamphlet to Knox. 'In your absence, we've been discussing this treatise.'

Knox peered at the title: *A Short Treatise of Politic Power, and of the True Obedience which Subjects owe to Kings.*

'It was published anonymously but I have it on good authority it was composed by John Ponet, former bishop of Winchester, now exiled in Strasbourg.' Goodman picked up his scribbled notes.

'Here's the gist of his argument. Given that the power of the monarch rests on a contract with his people, their obedience is conditional: they will obey him as long as he rules justly. Should he break this contract by depriving his subjects of their goods or murdering them, the people have the right to rebel and replace him with a leader more to their taste. In extreme circumstances they have a right to assassinate an evil ruler.'

Knox furrowed his brow. 'Even an anointed one?'

'That's a spurious mantle,' Whittingham replied. 'For who anoints absolute rulers? Not God, as they falsely assert, but man. Like all of mankind, a ruler is subject to the ultimate power, divine power. Why, a king may no more commit idolatry than a private man.'

'Furthermore,' Goodman went on, 'England has broken the covenant God made with the Israelites. As it is written in Deuteronomy, the ruler must be a native-born male of the true religion. Mary Tudor is unlawful on two counts – not only is she a woman but an evil ruler who has handed our country over to foreign idolaters. She is God's punishment on the English for disobeying his law to shun female rule. Thus the cause of all the present misery in England is the monstrous regime of a murderous woman, and it's the duty of the magistrates or, failing them, the people, to depose her.'

'And not only in England. Scotland, too, writhes beneath the female yoke,' Knox added. 'Female authority is a tainted fountain and no wholesome water can spring from a polluted well.'

Goodman jabbed his stubby forefinger. 'Being feeble and frail by nature, lacking judgement and morality, women are unfit to govern. The only remedy is to take up arms against the pestilent papist queens.'

Knox let out a long, low whistle. Was the solution to the question festering for years like a boil in his brain now within his grasp?

'I've been working on my own call to arms,' Goodman said, '*How Superior Powers Ought To Be Obeyed By Their Subjects: And Wherein They May Lawfully By God's Word Be Disobeyed And Resisted.* I would welcome your opinion, brothers.'

Knox was unsure. 'What will Dr Calvin say? He believes that because God's peculiar providence has permitted the rule of women it should be left alone. Who are we to question divine motives? If he would not support my petition before, why do you think he will uphold yours now?'

'Dr Calvin may have another reason for maintaining the *status quo*,' Whittingham said. 'There still remain many clandestine Perrinists in Geneva who resent his iron rule and who will be swift to denounce *him* as a tyrant. Your call to arms may open the floodgates again in Geneva.'

'I think not,' Goodman said. 'Dr Calvin is not blind. Surely he must see how these women have caused civil chaos and wickedness in our countries. If we present a carefully worded, coherently argued treatise for his opinion, surely he will give it his blessing. Our leaders may turn deaf ears but they cannot stop us from publishing our ideas. Let the people read and decide what must be done. If you fear reprisals, Brother William, we shall publish anonymously.'

Knox's head waggled vigorously. 'Aye, we must destroy the many-headed Hydra, the root of all our misery. I shall add my voice to the cause. I, too, shall sound the trumpet against the monstrous regime of women.'

When the book scraped along the floor, Knox gave a guilty start. Mrs Bowes was pushing her way in, dragging Harry Locke behind her.

'I don't know what plots you're hatching in here, but you'll have to knock some obedience into this very naughty boy.' Sweeping aside their scrolls, she dumped the lad on the desk and snatched a scrap of paper from his grubby mitt. Sniffing back tears, wretched Harry stuck his thumb in his mouth and watched with tearful eyes as she spread his drawing on the desk.

Next to a sketch of woman's scowling face were scribbled the words: *It is better to dwell in the corner of a roof than with a scolding wife in a big house.*

'Not a bad translation of Proverbs 21:9. The lad deserves praise,' Goodman said and winked at Harry.

Mrs Bowes glared at him. 'You may think it a laughing matter but *even a small child is known by his actions, whether his conduct may be pure and right.* Proverbs 20:11,' she barked back. 'If his mother refuses to thrash goodness into this precocious child, someone needs to take him in hand. I shall leave him in your care.'

While Whittingham comforted Harry, Goodman muttered under his breath, 'So the cock may crow but the hen rules the roost.'

Furious at his mother-in-law's intrusion and mortified by her affrontery, Knox stood rooted to the spot, staring at her retreating back. How dare she humiliate him in front of his colleagues. A woman untamed was a monster, worming her way into a man's affection only to sap his strength and grind him down. The subtle daughter of Eve bewitching men with her wiles and leading them down the path of perfidy was more treacherous than a legion of demons.

He banged his fist on the desk, sending a flurry of papers onto the floor and startling young Harry. 'Let's publish and be damned.'

VII

... A Wrong Note

Wondrous sound the trumpet flingeth;
Through earth's sepulchres it ringeth;
All before the throne it bringeth.

Dies Irae
Attributed to Thomas of Celano, 13th Century

Geneva, 24 June 1558

With much to celebrate, Knox gathered his friends together on Midsummer Eve for supper. 'Not to mark the feast of St John the Baptist or Walpurgisnacht – there shall be no head on a platter at our supper table nor dancing naked round a bonfire at midnight,' he said with a twinkle in his eye, 'but to give thanks that Brother Goodman and I have become free citizens of Geneva.'

'That is indeed good news, and well deserved, ' Mrs Bowes piped up. 'But I too have joyful tidings.' A gloating smile spread across her face as she clasped a hand to her heart. 'I am to be a grandmother again. My beloved daughter is once more with child.'

In the midst of congratulations, Knox was not the only one to fire her a furious look. Tight-lipped and unsmiling, Anna Locke patted Marjory's hand. As pale as a wraith and wilting in the summer heat, she wiped her perspiring brow and dropped her gaze.

In the privacy of their bedchamber, Knox vented his anger. 'It wasn't her place: as the father I should have been the bearer of such news.'

Marjory was contrite. 'I didn't tell mama, John. She must have guessed. I haven't been feeling well recently.'

'Why did she do it?'

'Mama likes to be the centre of attention – perhaps she feels neglected.'

'Once the bairn is born, the doting grandma will be kept busy,' Knox replied. Too busy to poke her nose into everyone's business, he hoped.

At his Sunday sermon, Knox's attention was distracted by the stranger seated beside Dr Calvin on the front bench. Tall and spare with a long doleful face and pointed beard, the man never took his eyes off the preacher.

After the service, Whittingham seemed agitated. 'Dr Calvin wishes you to meet Theodore Beza,' he said. 'His former pupil is now a distinguished professor at Lausanne University and reputed to have a powerful intellect.'

Knox replied. 'And a sense of humour forbye, for I believe he has written satires.'

'Aye, in his misspent youth, perhaps,' Whittingham muttered. 'More recently, he defended the burning of the heretic Servetus. The matter must be very important for Professor Theodore Beza to travel from Lausanne. Beware your head doesn't roll, brother.'

In his study, Calvin briefly introduced his guests before returning to the document he'd been reading. Knox held out a hand to Beza, but his hostile glare offered no reciprocal welcome.

'So, you are the famous – or should I say – infamous Scots preacher? The author of this pamphlet, I believe?' He brandished a booklet in the air: *The First Blast of the Trumpet against the Monstrous Regiment of Women.*

Knox was instantly on his guard. 'I am.'

'What about this one?' Beza picked up Goodman's pamphlet: *How Superior Powers ought to be obeyed of their subjects.*

Knox shook his head. 'Nay, that is not mine.'

Beza narrowed his deep-set eyes. 'So, if you now admit to being the author why did you publish the *First Blast* anonymously? Because you are ashamed, perhaps, or because you knew the response it would provoke?'

Knox tugged at his beard. It hadn't taken long to be identified as its author, but in no way was he ashamed. 'Someone had to raise a voice against the English Jezebel.'

'But not one so strident that grates on the ears. I came here to find out how Dr Calvin could allow such a pernicious document to see the light of day. but he tells me he knew nothing of its existence. Being written in English, which Dr Calvin does not read, and printed without a licence, how could he? You must have known he would not sanction it. This displays not only tactlessness but also cowardice on your part. In translating it into French, I trust I've lost none of its original vigour.' Beza jerked his head towards Calvin who kept on reading with his head down.

'Unless I'm mistaken and have misinterpreted your words, Mr Knox,' he went on, 'you're not only urging rebellion but the deposition and even execution of an ungodly monarch. How can you think Dr Calvin would approve of regicide? You vilify Mary Tudor for being a butcher, but you're no less barbaric in your call for all idolaters and unbelievers to be put to death. Why, you sound like a Saracen bellowing for the heads of infidels, not a Christian preacher.'

Professor Beza clasped his hands behind his back and paced up and down.

'If people followed the principles you lay down, no magistrate, no councillor would be able to ride quietly through the streets among such desperate beasts and no master would be safe, even in his own bedchamber. We believed the devil had been cast out from the City of God with the Perrinists but he is here worming his way into our very midst.'

Beza halted and peered at him suspiciously. 'Who are you working for, Mr Knox? Who's paying to publish all this illicit literature?' He picked up a pile of pamphlets and booklets and slapped them back down on the desk. 'The Gutenberg press was a divine invention not a devilish tool to spread lies and incite rebellion.'

Knox bristled at his monstrous accusations but remained undaunted. Professor Beza might be Calvin's revered disciple but he knew nothing about the struggle of the faithful to worship under duress, nor how Satan schemed to slink into the very seams that joined the elect together and wear away thin the fabric of their faith.

'With all due respect, brother, while you and your Swiss scholars rest snug, smug and unseeing in your ivory towers, martyrs are being torched daily at the stake.'

'With your powerful *Blast* igniting the flames.' Beza's thin lips stretched into a tight line. 'Your trumpet has reverberated throughout Christendom, Mr Knox.' He shuffled through a sheaf of papers. 'These are some of the letters I've received from those whose ears are booming with it.'

'I didn't expect my ideas to be warmly received by papists and idolaters.'

'These did not come from the Vatican but from our own community in Switzerland, as well as a number of English exiles whom you've outraged.'

'If you mean Richard Cox and his cronies, I care naught for their opinions. Cox is fixed on perverting the reformist cause for his own selfish ambitions.'

Beza selected one of the letters. 'Not only Cox but Fox attacks Knox.'

Knox paled. He'd believed John Fox to be one of his most staunch supporters.

'Even he is alarmed by your *Blast*, though he attempts to excuse your outpourings as the work of someone in a foul humour or suffering ill health.' He smoothed out the parchment. 'Tears of impotent rage caused by Mary Tudor's cruelty may have blinded your judgement, he claims.'

'My rude vehemence may appear to proceed from choler rather than reason but I was never one to flatter or use soft words, Dr Beza.'

'Your lack of diplomacy and tact is never in doubt, Mr Knox. Perhaps you should have considered the consequences of your affirmations before committing them to paper.' Beza's lips pressed even more tightly. 'You're driven by the belief that you, and only you, hold the key to God's truth. Yet, as you yourself write, Satan has used guile and craft to corrupt God's most holy decrees by infecting men's minds with dreams, inventions, and fantasies. Did it ever occur to you that Satan might be deceiving you?'

'I am always and ever God's instrument,' Knox retorted. 'To me it's enough to say black is not white and man's tyranny and foolishness is not God's perfect ordinance.'

Above his snow-white lace collar, Beza's dour face darkened. 'We must await Dr Calvin's opinion to decide what steps need to be taken.'

Calvin remained absorbed in the document. From time to time he rubbed his temples – a sure sign of an impending migraine – or mounting irritation. Calvin had a short fuse and Knox had anticipated the *Blast* would incur his wrath. He'd steeled himself for a disagreeable interview with the great scholar, not a confrontation with Professor Beza bearing such absurd objections.

At last Calvin finished reading. He took off his eyeglasses and leant his chin on his hand. His face was tense and drawn.

'Mr Knox, you write: *To promote a woman to bear rule above any realm, nation or city is repugnant to nature: contumely to God and the subversion of all good order, equity and justice. For who can deny but it is repugnant to nature that the blind shall be appointed to lead and conduct such as do see?'*

'That is so,' Knox replied. 'The government of women is a deviation from the original and proper order of nature, to be ranked no less than slavery, among the punishments consequent upon the fall of man.'

Calvin and Beza exchanged long-suffering glances.

'Though you claim to have produced this treatise out of zeal not malice, nevertheless it is misguided on many counts,' Beza said. 'In fact your tirade reads like one lengthy outpouring against all women – with more than a hint of henpecked defiance. It screams with the raw rage of an Old Testament prophet.'

Knox jutted his beard in challenge. 'What I write is the truth. Every example I quote is from scripture. My argument is based firmly on Salic Law.'

'Which is much disputed,' Beza replied. 'As for scripture, the Bible contains many contradictions, as you well know. *An eye for an eye: Lie with your daughters.* These injunctions were made to the Chosen People, the Israelites, but since then Christ has shown us the way, the truth and the light in the New Testament. Did he not say? *Render unto Caesar the things that are Caesar's?'*

'The devil has so blinded the senses of many they do not know what belongs to God and what to Caesar,' Knox retorted. 'Because the spirit of God has said: "Honour the king whatever he commands, be it right or wrong", they assume it must be obeyed. But heavy shall be the judgment on those dare to be so bold as to affirm that God has commanded any creature to be obeyed against himself.'

An awkward silence hung in the air before Calvin responded in a quiet but firm voice. 'You're not in the pulpit now, Mr Knox. Much as I admire your zeal, I must insist, however abhorrent, it will not do to meddle with anointed kings. Tyrants must be obeyed in the same way as good rulers, because, as St Paul asserts, God ordains the powers that be, and we resist them at our peril. The need to preserve the peace is of prime importance and I always urge obedience to rulers, however imprudent they may be.'

'Even if that ruler commits idolatry and embraces a religion God has not approved?' Knox snapped. 'Those who do so give no true obedience; they are not only apostates to God but traitors to their princes, whom they confirm by flattery.'

Beza stooped to whisper in Calvin's ear. 'This is sheer madness.'

'Your *Blast* brings down calumny on our cause,' Calvin went on, 'which is to reveal the truth of Christ's teaching. Our campaign must show a united front. There are schisms aplenty within the reformed church without this. We cannot allow a stray cannon such as you to fire off random shots in all directions, to blast hither and yonder without hindrance and endanger lives. As Dr Beza has warned, your thoughtless arrogance may provoke another round of persecution in England.

'You're a man of action, Mr Knox. Leave the theological debates to scholars who are trained in the art of rhetoric. This tract must be banned from sale and all copies gathered up and burnt. Who knows the consequences if it falls into the wrong hands? You cry out for an avenging assassin to vindicate the liberty of your country. What if someone answers your call?'

VIII

Revelation

> Then the eyes of the blind will be opened
> And the ears of the deaf will be unstopped
> Isaiah XXXV: 5

Musselburgh, 10 August 1558

Early on the morning of St Laurence Day, the square at Musselburgh Mercat Cross was hoaching. Merrymakers keen to empty their pockets at the fair rubbed shoulders with pilgrims eager to witness Our Lady of Loretto's miracle. The briny air over the seaside town was clammy and close and the overpowering stench of fish made Elisabeth feel queasy. She mopped the sweat from her brow.

'Are you well?' Isabelle asked.

'Well enough, though I fain would rest my weary legs.'

Overhearing her plea, a gentleman jostled Elisabeth and Isabelle towards the bench at the front. 'Move up and make room for the holy sisters.'

His companion laughed. 'Staying true to your reputation, Squire Meldrum, by pandering to the ladies!'

Startled, Elisabeth whirled round. 'Squire Meldrum, is that truly your name?'

'Nay, Dame Prioress, my companion jests. I am Robert Colville of Cleish from the Kingdom of Fife.'

His friend winked. 'But because he's a chivalrous loun, we cry him after thon noble knight in Davie Lindsay's heroic romance.'

A shiver careened up Elisabeth's spine. Doubtless Davie was glowering down on – or perhaps up at – them in disapproval at this very minute. She raised her eyes heavenward.

'Like the great makar, I distrust miracles and pilgrimages,' Colville said. 'With all respect, Dame Prioress, I no longer have faith in the Roman Church but my wife does. Heavy with our first child, she's asked me to hang this on the Virgin's statue at the Loretto shrine.' From a velvet pouch he drew out a rosary. Beads of freshwater pearls and blue gemstones and a golden crucifix made it a costly offering. 'I doubt this will help in her travail – more likely it will line the hermit's pockets.'

His companion laughed. 'The squire is too gallant to gainsay his lady fair. Look, here comes the procession!'

Behind the monks and friars, Thomas Doughty guided a young lad tapping his way with a stick and helped him onto the stage from where he addressed the crowd.

'Tak tent! Tak tent and preen back your lugs! Are you good honest folk of

Musselburgh acquent with this young pauper?'

'Aye,' the crowd chorused in reply. 'For we've given him alms many a time,' someone added.

'Will you swear on oath he is stone blind?'

Satisfied with the mob's assent, the hermit raised his arms. 'Then behold! For today Our Blessed Lady of Loretto shall perform a miracle.'

When a monk swung a thurible to scent the air, Elisabeth pinched her nostrils to keep from sneezing: burning incense always had that effect on her. To the chanting of prayers, Doughty placed one hand on the kneeling lad's head and raised the other to heaven. After anointing the lad's eyelids with the consecrated oil of chrism and sprinkling him with blessed water from Our Lady's well, he asked him to open his eyes.

There was a collective intake of breath as the lad rubbed his eyes with his knuckles and blinked.

'I can see! I'm cured!' he cried and kissed the hem of the hermit's habit.

Doughty stretched his arms wide. 'Praise be to the Holy Virgin who's made a poor blind lad see again.'

'This miracle has certainly opened my eyes,' Elisabeth said.

Isabelle, meanwhile, was peering intently at the wondrous lad. 'That's no miracle, Dame Prioress,' she whispered, 'thon's a prank. For that's Cammie who used to herd at St Catherine's. Mind the knack he had of rolling his eyes?'

Elisabeth sucked in a breath. 'By the Blessed Virgin, so it is. He's grown a lot. I didn't recognise him.'

Doughty stepped forward to the edge of the platform. 'Will you good burghers of the Honest Toun be willing to testify that a miracle has taken place this very day?'

'Aye,' the awe-struck crowd chorused and surged forward to fill the miracle boy's pocket with alms.

Feeling a tap on her shoulder, Elisabeth turned round.

'Forgive me, sisters, but I must bid you farewell,' Robert Colville said. 'I fain would speak to this young lad.'

IX

St Giles's Day

A dead image carved of one tree
As it were holy should not honoured be
The Monarch
Sir David Lindsay, 16th Century

Edinburgh, 1st September 1558

Trotting up the brae of the Canongate towards the city of Edinburgh, Isabelle kept craning her neck. 'Will we see the fiery dragon? Folk say it's settled upon St David's Tower in Edinburgh Castle, spewing forth fire for days and nights on end.'

'I hope not. There have been enough portents this year,' Elisabeth replied. 'Since thon fiery besom blazed in the sky throughout January, rivers have dried up and then risen again to drown whole villages.'

'I wish I'd seen one of the huge whales cast up onto the banks of the River Forth, or the hailstone as big as a dove's eggs that fell on the fields and destroyed the corn harvest. Do these omens mean God is angry with us, Dame Prioress?'

Elisabeth shrugged. 'Who kens? The papal nuncio believes so. Dr Row says these direful signs portend great dangers for our Church. That's why he has called on all devout Catholics to come out in force for the annual St Giles's procession.'

'Who was St Giles?' Isabelle asked.

'A French hermit and patron saint of cripples and lepers. His arm bone will be on display but not his effigy. Last year the heretics stole the gilded statue and flung into the Nor' Loch. Afterwards they fished it out of the stinking sewer and burnt it.'

They were nearing the Netherbow Port where loud angry jeering brought them to a halt.

'Doun with popery! Doun with St Giles! Doun with the whores of Babylon!'

At the gatehouse, a bunch of lads were quarrelling with the guard who refused to let them pass through to the High Street.

'Not without paying the toll,' the guard insisted.

'But we maun stop thon papist parade,' a rough looking lad shouted. 'God has commanded all idols and graven images to be pulled down.'

Elisabeth leant towards Isabelle. 'Not all the citizens of Edinburgh are prepared to pay their respects to their patron saint, it seems. Keep your palfrey on a tight rein.'

Spotting the nuns, the guard shouted, 'Come away by, sisters.'

As they manoeuvred their palfreys through the gate, the protestors hissed and spat at them. 'Get back to your bordel hoose, ye wanton hizzies.'

'Pay them no heed, Isabelle,' Elisabeth said to reassure Isabelle, though she, too, was shaken by their insults. It was one thing to be cried a cow-klink in Lindsay's *Satire*, but quite another to be howled down by an irate mob. 'Keep an eye out for the unicorn and head for that.'

Close to the Mercat Cross a voice shouted, 'Dame Prioress!' Robert Colville pushed through the crowd, dragging a lad by the hand. 'Providence must have led to our meeting here for I've something to give the young sister.'

When he pressed the velvet pouch with the pearl rosary beads into Isabelle's palm she shook her head furiously. 'I cannot take such a valuable gift.'

'This is your wife's token. Did you not hang it on Our Lady's statue?' Elisabeth said.

'Nay, I did not. I don't believe in such superstitions. Forbye, this cult of Loretto is not only idolatry but chicanery. I've been investigating this so-called hermit. Doughty may have been an abbey laird but he was never a monk at Mount Sinai.'

Elisabeth was curious. 'An abbey laird?'

'It's what they cry a debtor who seeks sanctuary at Holyrood Abbey. Doughty took refuge there after running up gambling debts. Because he couldn't pay back the money he owed, he fooled the monks into thinking he was a holy man who could fast for thirty-two days by praying to the Virgin Mary. Then he pranced about half naked, claiming a voice was telling him to go to the Holy Land to rescue her statue. There are as many false prophets as true ones. The trouble is telling them apart.

'This Loretto miracle only confirmed my scepticism. You holy sisters deserve to have this as a token of my thanks for uncovering this wicked conspiracy wrought by the grasping friars.' Colville grinned. 'I strive to be like Lindsay's knight and show the right!'

Elisabeth bristled. 'What do you mean?'

'I overheard what you said about Cammie and lured him with the promise of recompense to wheedle the truth out of him.' Colville rubbed an imaginary coin between his thumb and forefinger. 'He was a poor herd boy at St Catherine's until the mendicant friars got wind of his knack. They spirited him away and lodged him in one of their cells, making him practise every day until the crafty lad became skilful at feigning blindness.'

Elisabeth fixed the lad with a fierce look. 'What? You ran away with the friars to set up this trumpery?'

Cammie's wind-burnt face flushed scarlet. He rolled his pupils down and cast a nervous glance around. 'Aye, well, what would you rather do? Chase after yammering yowes on a cauld, dreich winter's day?'

'After a few years they put him out to beg on the streets as a blind pauper and made him vow on pain of hellfire never to reveal his secret. But I've warned him he's bound for hellfire unless he confesses his fraud publicly at the Cross here. We must open the eyes of those blinded by false doctrine and fraudulent miracles.'

When Cammie's bottom lip quivered and tears welled in his eyes, Colville drew open his cloak. 'Never fear, to make sure the friars wreak no revenge, I shall protect you with my drawn sword. Then I'll take you back to Fife and into my service.' Addressing Elisabeth he said, 'A note of caution, Dame Prioress, for this revelation will set a wheen of wildcats amongst the doos.'

'It will that. Thanks for the warning, Squire Meldrum. Come, Isabelle, we must make haste.' Elisabeth mounted her palfrey.

'Should I keep these beads, Dame Prioress?' Isabelle asked.

'Aye, to pray that the friars' wicked souls burn in hell.'

In St Giles' Kirk, Elisabeth weaved her way through the crush of clergy in search of Archbishop Hamilton. Above their heads she spotted the square black cap of John Row, the papal nuncio, newly arrived from Rome. In contrast to the Scottish priests with their dowdy garb, Row stood out like a peacock amidst a flock of dunnocks. His purple double-breasted robe of brocaded velvet was lined with sable of richer quality than anything their archbishops could afford. In one hand he held a pair of soft leather gloves that he slapped against the other to hammer home the point he was making to Maitland.

'Sir William, I need to speak with the archbishop, have you seen him?'

'Unfortunately, he cannot be present today,' Maitland replied.

How fortuitous, Elisabeth thought. 'I sense a quarrelsome mood in the causeway and fain would warn him to cancel the procession before any blood is shed.'

'That may be a matter for Dr Row to decide,' Maitland replied. 'He is the papal nuncio after all.'

Row looked down his long nose and sneered. 'Nay, Dame Prioress, we shall carry on as usual. We cannot let a few rabble-rousers bully us.'

'From what I've seen at the Mercat Cross, it's more than a few and they're growing in number by the minute. Forbye, you're putting Queen Marie in grave danger.'

Row gave a supercilious snort. 'As head of state, the queen regent must lead the procession. Her presence will calm down the over-excited *hoi-polloi*.'

'But the Loretto miracle has incensed them. The young lad is about to …'

'That miracle was an inspiration, a triumph for the Church,' Row broke in. 'The monks are to be applauded. The queen regent's party has already left Edinburgh Castle, I hear. Sir William and I must be on our way.' Waving her away as if swatting a pesky fly, he turned his haughty back on her.

'Be it on your own head,' Elisabeth murmured. No doubt this Vatican vicar held women in contempt. That may be how thon arrogant Doctor of Letters behaved in the company of cardinals but a common causeywalker had more manners.

Elisabeth went in search of Isabelle and found her quizzing a monk who was laying the relic of St Giles in a portable shrine.

'A wealthy burgess paid for the arm bone to be mounted on a golden hand and donated the diamond ring on its finger,' the monk explained.

Isabelle pointed to another shrine containing a crude figurine clumsily nailed onto a block of wood. 'What's thon? Wasn't the statue burnt?'

'We borrowed this statue from the Grey Friars. Not so grand as the gilded statue but something for the folk to revere.'

Elisabeth scoffed. 'The sight of thon grotesque *marmoset* will further inflame the rabble's wrath. The Abbot of Unreason was never so foolish. Come, Isabelle, let's join this farce.'

To the sound of minstrels playing tabors, trumpets and bagpipes the procession set off down the High Street towards the Canongate. Flanked by Maitland and Dr Row, the queen regent looked uneasy as jeers rather than cheers rose from the crowd. Alarmed at her tense expression, Elisabeth feared the menacing mob would bring on a seizure: however brave the queen regent might be in spirit, her heart was weak.

When the procession halted to pass through the Netherbow Port, the jeering grew louder, increased by the taunts from Elisabeth's tormentors waiting on the other side. She rode up to Maitland and tugged his sleeve. 'The queen's safety may be of little concern to you but this rabble worries me. Let these friars process if they must, but advise the queen to turn back.'

'Ah, the meddling nun again.' Row's lips sneered, but his darting eyes looked uneasy.

'Doubtless in St Peter's holy city you've faced only adulation, but do these hoots of derision sound like applause to you?' Elisabeth said. 'The *hoi-polloi* have just found out the holy monks have fabricated a false miracle.'

'What do you mean?'

Hearing of Cammie's fraud, Row's haughty *hauteur* wilted. 'This is dreadful news! Why didn't you tell me before?'

'Because you steekit your lugs and turned your back on me, Dr Row,' Elisabeth retorted. 'Once the people hear Cammie's confession, they'll have your head.'

Row's snooty face turned as white as a winding sheet. 'What should we do?'

'I'll ask my nephew's advice,' Elisabeth said.

As Lord Provost of Edinburgh, George Seton, Abbess Joanna's son, was responsible for civil order. A riot must be avoided at all costs, he agreed and rode off.

After what seemed an eternity, Seton returned with an offer of shelter from a city burgess at his house in the Canongate. 'Sandy Carpenter would be greatly honoured if Her Grace would also partake of his humble board.'

While the queen graciously accepted the invitation, Dr Row rudely rebuffed the offer. Accustomed to a Vatican diet, his belly could not thole Scots fare, he said.

'A swig of Loretto water is said to ease the queasiest stomach,' Elisabeth replied, 'and fire up the faintest of hearts,' she added detecting his disquiet. 'But never fash, my nephew will soon disperse the mischief-makers. Once these scallywags have had their fun they'll move on.'

'I doubt it.' Dr Row paced the floor, slapping his gloves. 'This is the work of the English, paying Protestant preachers to stir up trouble.' The din from outside stopped him in his tracks. 'Look! They're desecrating the statue.'

Elisabeth gawped out of the window in horror. The rowdy rascals were shaking the shrine to dislodge the statue but firmly nailed to its perch, the *marmoset* would not budge. Frustrated, they struck it repeatedly against the cobblestones, knocking off its head and kicking it along the street.

'Doun with the idol! Droun the monkey! Droun the monks!' the crowd jeered.

When the friars made a half-hearted attempt to intervene, the lads chased them down the Canongate, spurred on by the taunting crowd. 'Look at the priests rowping like ravens! They're fleeing faster than they did at Pinkie Cleuch!'

Visibly shaken, Dr Row flapped his gloves at Seton. 'Civil disturbance is your responsibility, Lord Provost. Round up the miscreants forthwith and ensure they suffer the most severe punishment in law. For my part, I shall bid Archbishop Hamilton to put the strongest possible curse on their damned souls.'

'Aye, I'm sure such a jinx will work a miracle,' Elisabeth murmured to her nephew.

X

Birth and Death

Sing up, heart, sing up, heart,

Sing no more down!

But joy in Elisabeth

Who weareth the crown

Popular Song, 16th Century

Geneva, November 1558

In mid-November, the winter cold began to bite, but Anna Locke's frostiness was more cutting to Knox. She no longer helped him with his work. Why was she giving him the cold shoulder? With Marjory nearing childbed and Mrs Bowes looking after Nathaniel, he had no one to shoulder his heavy workload: forbye, the pitter-patter of tiny feet and the screeching of excited children disturbed his concentration.

Unable to thole it any longer, Knox flung open the study door and called for Mrs Bowes. 'I need peace to think, dear mother. Please keep the children quiet.'

She folded her arms defiantly. 'Nothing to do with me. You'd better speak to your lodgers. Mrs Hickman's bairns shriek like banshees whenever Harry Locke chases them. He's a naughty lad. Besides, I've my hands full looking after Nathaniel. Marjory is nearing her time and needs to rest.' Turning her broad back on him, she stomped off down the passage.

Knox's spirits sank. He should stand firm in his own home but her snapping and sniping sapped his resolve. The burden of domestic cares laid on his shoulders was dragging his spirit down. Domesticity was proving to be no quiet haven in which to shelter from the hurly-burly of life.

As he lifted the latch to enter his study, a strange squeaking sound distracted him. Seeing Anna trundling the birthing chair along the passage towards the bedchamber, he rushed to her aid.

'Do you think me too weak to manage this?' Her voice was sharp.

'Nay, of course not. A burden shared is a burden lightened,' he replied but his quip raised no smile from Anna. Tentatively he touched her arm. 'I've missed your company, dear sister.'

She threw him a look that would wither bramble blossom. He'd never seen her bonnie lips curl with disdain before.

'I'm only following your edict that woman should stay silent before man's superior wisdom. Besides, with two wise men, you've no need of me. While you argue about how many angels can dance on the head of a pin, your fickle and feeble women are working away quietly, their wonders to perform.'

'I know full well we men can be dull-witted ...' Knox began but her chilly tone and ice grey eyes cut him short. 'Come, we cannot bicker out here.'

In his study, Anna refused the conciliatory goblet of wine. 'I've read your blasted trumpet and I'm saddened to know you have such a low opinion of our sex. Your slanderous accusations have cut me to the quick. Again and again you insist that, even in her highest state, woman is man's humble servant. You seem to agree with those woman-hating antiquarians – Aristotle, Ambrose and Augustine – who claim our conduct to be full of every vice. Do you truly believe we're foolish, mad, and frenetic?'

Knox threw up his hands. 'My dear sister, I didn't mean to offend you. I do not hate women. My aim is to show how papist queens are unfit to rule and I've based my views firmly on scripture. The revealed will and word of God stands plain and evident on my side.'

Her lips tightened. 'Yet you ignore the example of Deborah, a strong woman who led the Israelites into battle and defeated the Canaanites.'

'She was indeed a godly woman possessing mercy, truth, justice and humility,' Knox grudgingly admitted, 'but she was a prophetess not a queen – very different from our mischievous Marys.'

Anna glowered. 'It saddens me that you insist on quoting Old Testament rabbis who declare women to be unclean and inferior to man in every way yet Christ called us not daughters of Eve but daughters of Abraham. He found fellowship with his female followers and even allowed a sinful woman to anoint his feet.

'Your Pharisees claim women are liars by nature and so may not bear witness. Yet whom did Christ choose to spread the word of his resurrection? Not the cowardly apostles cowering in upper rooms but his mother and sisters. Why do you pay heed to these priests rather than Jesus Christ? Men are liars and rogues who rob us of learning so we cannot read what lies they write about us. But at least one brave woman has a response to your *Blast*. I suggest you read this.' She drew out a book from her pocket and slapped it down onto his desk.

Knox glanced at the title: *The Book of the City of Ladies* by Christine de Pizan. It gave him a jolt. Was this not the book once praised by Prioress Elisabeth?

'I have heard of this book.'

'But clearly not read it otherwise you wouldn't have written with such vehemence. Your *Blast* is ridden with the type of slander she decries – spreading falsehoods and lies about women.' Tears sprung in her eyes but her lips squeezed into a scornful sneer. 'Why did God form such a vile creature in making woman? Or did he? I've marked some passages you and your wise men should take heed of.'

She thumbed through the pages. 'Here is one. Man was not *physically* made in

God's image – Madame de Pizan writes – we all share in God's essential *spiritual* nature. Nor does a person's gender determine their loftiness or lowliness but their conduct and virtues. She gives boundless examples of brave, doughty women: martyrs, who held to their faith despite torture and death, warrior queens who led their people out of tyranny. How can you consider us weak, silly creatures when the evidence contradicts you.'

Flummoxed by her arguments, Knox strove to vindicate himself. 'There are exceptional cases wherein we find the spirit of mercy, truth, justice, and of humility. Under these godly matrons God showed mercy to his people ...'

'Cease dredging ancient scripture for justification, John,' she interrupted. 'You needn't look far to see wives helping husbands in their daily business and mothers sacrificing their lives to deliver men such as you into the world. Would you call your mother a monstrosity of nature?'

Knox hung his head. 'My mother died when I was very young ...'

'Even so, soon your wife will labour long hours to deliver your child, yet you have scant regard for her sacrifice.'

'That's not true. I adore my beloved Marjory but God has allotted men and women different rôles. Bearing a child is an honour bestowed on womankind. Motherhood is a sacred state but Eve's disobedience has forever condemned mothers to suffer in childbirth.'

Anna puffed in scorn. 'That's another misconception. No doubt you accept the rendition *in dolour* shall thou bear children, whereas *in sorrow* is a more fitting translation. A sorrow that is soon overtaken by the joy of nurturing a new life.'

Before he could reply, the door scraped open and Marjory leant against the doorjamb, ashen-faced and clutching her belly.

'Oh, Anna, I feel the baby coming. But it's too soon. It's not my time.'

Anna sprang up. 'I must attend to Marjory. Her travail has begun.'

Feeling fushionless, Knox paced his study and resisted the temptation to close his ears to the screams of his wife's labour pains. Agonising hours later, Anna came to say that Marjory had been delivered of another son. He threw up his hands.

'Thanks be to God. How is Marjory? I must go to her.'

'She's very weak and asleep now. It would be best not to disturb her rest. The long labour has sapped her strength.' A look of innocent mischief crossed her face. 'Besides, since she is unclean, you may not see her until she is purified.'

Knox frowned. 'There shall be no such papist churching ritual for Marjory. Sprinkling mother and child with holy water to fend off the devil is as superstitious as a spaewife casting a spell to keep away the evil eye from a newborn bairn.'

'Is it not written in Leviticus? Which also commands the sacrifice of a year-old lamb as a burnt offering to the Lord. Failing that, two turtle doves or two pigeons will do.' Anna's lips twisted into a cruel sneer. 'As Madame de Pizan says, the fool sees his neighbour's peccadillo and fails to see his own enormous crime.'

Knox glowered. 'We shall indeed give thanks to the Lord – by offering prayers for the safe delivery of Eleazar.'

'Eleazar?' She arched a silky eyebrow. 'Is that a wise choice? As far as I recall, Eleazar was born in the wilderness to the high priest Aaron and destined never to see the Promised Land. It is a name tinged with despair.'

'Perhaps it does reflect my despondent mood,' Knox replied. 'But it means help of God – and I'm in need of all his divine help.'

The Auditory, 29 November 1558

When Goodman sprinkled the infant with water from the baptismal font, Knox beamed with paternal pride. Snoozing in his arms, Eleazar never even flickered an eyelid. Baptised in the sight of God and witnessed by Miles Coverdale and his wife, Elizabeth Macheson, his second son was now a member of the Christian flock. Before leaving The Auditory, Knox invited everyone home to wet the bairn's head.

'It's a Scottish custom,' Mrs Coverdale explained to her bemused English husband. 'We now wet our ain whistles with a christening cup.'

Upstairs, Marjory was resting in bed when Knox brought Eleazar to be nursed. He leant over and kissed her on the forehead.

'Unlike his noisy big brother who squawked in protest at his baptism, this wee lad uttered not a squeak,' Knox said.

Marjory attempted a smile. 'Signs perhaps that Nathaniel will be a preacher – and Eleazar a scholar.'

When the jubilant father rejoined his guests, he was distressed to observe Anna standing apart and aloof in the corner of the room. So she still had not forgiven him.

Knox handed her a goblet of wine. 'A peace offering, dear sister. On this happiest of days I hope you will forget our differences and drink to the good health of Eleazar and Marjory, if not mine.'

With a nod of thanks she took a sip. 'I'm sorry to cast a gloom on your joy but I've received a letter from Henry with news from England. Though it affects everyone here, I'm not sure if this is a good time to break it.'

'Let me be the judge of that,' Knox said. 'Forbye, a worry shared is a worry halved.'

Anna hesitated. 'Mary Tudor has breathed her last. She died believing she was giving birth when all the time she'd been fostering a malign growth in her stomach.'

Knox could hardly believe his ears. 'The Jezebel, Bloody Mary Tudor, is well and truly dead? Can this be true?'

Anna gave him a frosty stare. 'You may not take the word of this weak and silly woman but surely you will not question my husband's.'

'Nay, nay, of course not, it was just that ...' he faltered, chilled by her coldness. Despite his gift of prophecy, Knox had not foreseen the death of his nemesis. 'Surely this is a matter for rejoicing. I must let everyone know.'

Calling everyone to attention, he said, 'Having descended to the bottommost pit of hell, the light has broken at last. England has woken up from a sweating nightmare. Mary Tudor is dead.'

There was a stunned silence before Goodman raised his goblet. 'Let us give thanks that Mary Tudor has finally gone to meet her maker. She will now have to justify her bloody reign to Almighty God.'

'What happens now?' Whittingham asked.

Looking directly at Knox, Anna said, 'Before she died, Mary named Princess Elisabeth as her heir.'

Mrs Coverdale clapped her hands. 'She professes the Protestant faith. These are glad tidings indeed. Come, Miles, we must make preparations to return to England at once.'

The news of Elizabeth's accession did not delight Knox who waited until his guests had departed before venting his concerns.

'Another woman on the throne. And ill-begotten. How can this be?'

'Since she's a Protestant, we may overlook her accident of birth,' Whittingham said.

Goodman stroked his heavy jowls. 'But not the fact she's a woman. The same objections we raised against Mary still apply to her sister.'

'There's no rhyme nor reason in all this,' Knox said. 'Satan must be corrupting God's plan.'

Anna froze him with a glacial glare. 'Why do you imagine the devil has a hand in this? Perhaps God in his inscrutable wisdom has made Elizabeth an exception to his law to show men the error of their prejudices. Besides, she is a Tudor and may govern as well as any man. Henry and the others believe a Protestant queen will push through religious reform and bring peace prosperity and liberty to our troubled land.'

'But a queen cannot govern on her own – she must wed. Who shall she choose?' Knox retorted.

'She may already have found her champion,' Anna said, 'for Henry writes that Robert Dudley rode at the head of her cavalcade into London.'

Robert Dudley! Son of the notorious Duke of Northumberland! This was a bad omen. As his belly gripped with apprehension, Knox winced. John Dudley had paid dearly for his powermongering and ambitious Robin would be greedy to avenge his execution.

'Dudley's already married. Elizabeth will need to look abroad for a consort,' Goodman said. 'Once again we face the threat of being ruled by a foreign prince.'

Anna shrugged. 'Whatever happens, I'm going home.'

Knox gripped her arm. 'You cannot leave, dear sister. Not until the ash from the pyres cools down – it's too dangerous.'

Anna looked at him askance and gently but firmly removed his hand. 'Henry assures me it's safe to return now that our brothers have been released. Besides, he misses us dreadfully and Harry pines for his father. Anthony has arranged safe passage for us all on the *Mary Rose*. We plan to leave for Antwerp before the winter weather sets in.'

'Anthony and Thomas have been freed? Praise be to the Lord who has opened the gates of their cells.'

Anna's eyebrows twitched. 'Rose Hickman rather deserves praise for their release. She greased the wheels of justice with bribes of sugar and velvet to the Lord High Treasurer.' She turned to Whittingham and Goodman. 'What about you, brothers? Will you go back to England?'

Whittingham shook his head. 'My life is now here in Geneva with my family – Catherine and Zachary.'

Goodman's answer depended on Knox. 'I shall follow Brother John, wherever he decides to go.'

'My blasted trumpet has sounded out of season. I fear it has blown all my friends from me,' Knox said with a rueful glance at Anna. 'I shall await the Lord's instruction.'

Skittish with excitement, Harry Locke leapt over the chests and crates, baskets and bundles heaped on the street. When Jamie caught hold of the lad and birled him high in the air, Harry screamed with laughter.

'We're sailing home on the *Mary Rose*. It's a huge galleon, named for my aunts. Will you come with us, Jamie?'

'Not yet, wee laddie. But soon.'

Knox stole a glance at Anna standing aloof and distant. He cleared his throat. 'Your forlorn husband will be eager to see you again.'

'And I him. It has been too long.'

'I'm not only sorry to see you go, dear sister, but I rue the day our friendship was soured. It grieves me sorely to leave you with a bitter taste on your tongue.'

Anna turned to him. Tears glistened her dove grey eyes. 'I, too, am sorry, John. I was greatly winded by your *Blast*. Please forgive my blunt words.'

Knox gave a wry laugh. 'Not so much blunt as pointed. No doubt I deserved them, dear sister. By nature I am churlish: I have more need of my friends than any have need of me.'

She blinked to clear her tears. 'Swear you will write and tell me how it fares with you. Whatever happens, out of sight must not become out of mind.'

'Nay, dear sister, your absence will only intensify the fondness in my heart.'

'And look after Marjory. She is a precious jewel. Neither she nor her mother have read your *Blast* – I suggest they never do.' She gave a short laugh before adding, 'You'll never have a moment's peace if Mrs Bowes claps eyes on it.'

Feeling bereft after their departure, Knox wandered round the empty rooms, mulling over his situation. If his flock returned to England, as many of them were planning to do, he would have no one left to tend in Geneva – only his wee family. However deeply grateful he was to be blessed with a loving wife and children, he felt he still had to fulfil his destiny but when and how were in God's hands.

Stopping outside their door, Knox lifted the latch as quietly as he could and slipped into the candlelit chamber. Marjory looked up from her sewing and put a finger to her lips. She tilted her head at Nathaniel and Eleazar tucked up together in their cot.

'Did you make your peace with Anna?' Marjory kept her voice low. 'I sensed ill-feeling between you.'

'My treatise, *The First Blast of the Trumpet against the Monstrous Regiment of Women*, angered her.'

Marjory nodded. 'I'm not surprised. It does indeed sound … monstrous. Why did she take umbrage?'

'Because of my belief that, since God created man superior to woman, divine law must also apply to female monarchs. Why, in any family, man is the head and woman the limbs. It's the natural order. No man ever saw the lion make obedience and stoop before the lioness.'

Marjory looked pensive. 'Yet I disobeyed my father, John. Was that sinful?'

'It was your father who was sinful, my wee bird. He did not deserve your respect,' Knox replied. He let out a sigh. 'No doubt the force with which I express my views displeases Anna. But when I hear the voice of God, I cannot silence it. I must trumpet the truth to the world in the pulpit and on paper.'

Marjory held up the tiny hat she was sewing. 'God has given us all different talents, John. While I ply the needle you play the trumpet.'

'Your words greatly comfort me, my wee bird. I've never doubted the talents and abilities of modest women who know their place within the family and do not presume to govern a nation.' He kissed her gently on the forehead. 'You are the perfect wife, Marjory, on whom I can always depend to keep tryst.'

Lulled by the soft snuffling of his sleeping sons, Knox lay with his head in Marjory's lap. What greater bliss could he ask for? He was drifting off when Jamie rapped at the door. A visitor had arrived. Reluctantly, Knox shook himself out of his dwam.

'At this late hour?'

John Gray stamped his feet to shake the dust from his shoes. 'Fate plays merry japes, Mr Knox,' he said. 'I've been dispatched on a dual mission – to Rome on papist business – and to Geneva to give you this.'

As he read the missive, Knox rubbed his forehead. 'How can I believe this? What will I find in Scotland? Mary Tudor may be dead but Mary of Guise is still alive.'

'But neither hale nor hearty. Her weak heart may give out at any time. Forbye, the Lords of the Congregation are against the French alliance that threatens religious reform. Whatever you decide, Mr Knox, the lords are determined to go ahead without you.'

A reformation in Scotland without Knox at its head? That could never be.

'Your years in the wilderness are over, Mr Knox,' Gray said. 'It's time to come home.'

XI

In the End is my Beginning

I am the beginning and the end.
I will give to him that is athirst of the well of the water of life freely.
Revelation XXI: 6–8

Dieppe, February 1559

'*When I am dead and opened, you shall find Calais lying in my heart.*' Knox tugged his beard. 'Said to be Mary Tudor's dying words, but in my case it will be Dieppe.'

Jamie laughed. 'Aye, I've lost count of the number of times we've been stranded here.'

'Until granted safe passage, it looks as if we'll be biding a while.'

Auberge au Port was crammed with religious refugees negotiating with skippers and captains who could demand whatever price they wished for the short voyage across *La Manche.* The cost of the fare did not prevent Knox from sailing. John Wedderburn had kindly offered to arrange his passage to Dundee but Knox had applied to Queen Elizabeth for safe conduct to travel through England.

'Why not sail direct to Scotland where they keenly await you?' Wedderburn asked.

'Already the forces of evil are gathering in England: Satan has entered the sheepfold. Mrs Locke writes to say that my nemesis Richard Cox has already returned with his Frankfurt crew to grovel at the feet of the new queen. He even preached the sermon at her coronation.' He strove to quell his rising temper.

'These pompous prelates will now appoint themselves archbishops with bells and smells, cassocks and copes and bountiful benefices. I must warn my English flock to stand firm against those who desire to drag the Church of England downwards into the pit of papistry.'

Even greater was the fear that Cox would persecute those under his charge at Geneva. That thon demon would wreak revenge on Anna and her family enraged Knox. He must rescue her from Cox's clutches.

Knox kept personal heartache at bay by composing tracts and admonitions to the faithful. When he took the latest batch down to the laigh to be published, Wedderburn pointed an inky finger at a pile of letters.

'This waiting must be sheer purgatory for you, Brother John. Perhaps your torment is over. There's a letter from England for you. Let's hope it contains your safe conduct.'

Knox tore the letter open with clumsy fingers. His eyes alighted on the secretary

301

of state's signature. How had William Cecil risen so high so quickly? But then why was he surprised. Sir William was a true chameleon with the ability adapt to his surroundings, see in two directions at once and speak with a forked tongue. 'So the phoenix has risen from the ashes?' he muttered.

'Cecil is using my *First Blast* to stir up prejudice against me and making me *persona non grata* in royal eyes. Listen to this:

I must refuse your request for safe passage. As the author of the First Blast you are the last person Her Majesty will allow to travel through her realm, stirring up sedition. In fact she considers you to be the incarnation of everything in religion and politics that her soul most loathes.

Knox looked up. 'Has he forgotten I was Edward VI's chaplain? Is he sullying my reputation under thon godly monarch?'

'*You are a zealot, Mr Knox and, in her experience, zealotry can be troublesome. You may say that your Blast was written without reference to Queen Elizabeth but to her half-sister, but your principles still apply.*'

Knox jabbed a finger at the letter. 'How dare twa-fanglet Cecil fob me off! Thon two-faced Janus turns like a weathercock in the wind. He deserves to be hurled into hellfire for his silence during Bloody Mary's persecutions. The Scarlet Whore has fallen with all her Babylon around her, yet Cecil has survived and risen to a position of honour and dignity. Why?'

Wedderburn shrugged his huge shoulders. 'That's the way the world turns, brother. As the queen's secretary, Cecil must defend her against those who question her right to the throne – including you.'

Knox scowled. 'If Elizabeth openly confesses that God has given her an extraordinary dispensation to rule, I shall be more than willing to recognise her lawful authority. But if she insists the laws of men have crowned her queen, she will not long lack punishment. Such foolish presumption will greatly offend God.'

Equipped with writing paper and supplied with ink, Knox took up his pen to strike back at Cecil. *Unless you repent of your trumpery and trickery you, too will face divine retribution,* he finished off with a flourish.

March had come in like a lion and gone out like a lamb but Knox was still delayed in Dieppe. Throughout the weeks of restless waiting, Marjory's letters were a comfort being full of news about Nathaniel and Eleazar to cheer his spirits – her mother's, however, were replete with reproaches. Why did he not tell them his plans? When would he send for them? Had the flighty Scots lairds changed their mind again? If so, he should come back to Geneva. Spring had already sprung in the city of God: time for new beginnings. Though guilt seared his conscience, Knox could not abort his mission this time.

Amongst all his gude-mother's grumbles, one nugget of information caught his attention. The guard, Robert Stewart, had arrived in Geneva with another Scotsman – James Hamilton, Earl of Arran – to speak with Dr Calvin. After a few days they had left together. This aroused Knox's curiosity. Why would Arran consult Calvin? Was he planning to return to Scotland and spearhead reform? With Robert Stewart as his lieutenant? If so, this signalled an even greater urgency to return home.

Stuck in Dieppe, Knox was powerless to prevent the closet papists taking control in England. Meanwhile, in Scotland the lords were scheming a rebellion without him. But what kind of reformation would it be without his guidance? He felt as desperate as the prophet Mordecai who donned sackcloth and ashes to wail loudly and bitterly in mourning.

A dull thud at the door disturbed his thoughts. Wedderburn fell into the room, wheezing after climbing the steep stairs. He slumped onto the bench, 'Secret plans – de Guise brothers …'

Knox had to wait until he'd caught his breath to winkle the story out of him. The duke and cardinal were petitioning the pope to use canon law to expel Elizabeth from her throne on the grounds of being both illegitimate and a heretic and claim the crown in favour of their niece, Mary Stewart.

'This can never be,' Knox said. 'A woman wearing the crown is monstrous enough but at least she's Protestant. A Catholic queen on the English throne and married to a French king would spell disaster.'

'That's not all. With their sister's help, they plan to use Scotland as a base to attack England. But first they need to suppress the reforming lords.'

'That will not be hard,' Knox growled. 'The jingle of French gold and silver in front of their snouts will lure the rascal rogues. I maun let the English court know so they may thwart this deep-laid scheme of ruin.'

Alarmed, Wedderburn squealed, 'How will you do that? It would be most unwise to commit this knowledge to writing. Who could be trusted to deliver such a message?'

Knox stroked his beard. 'Perhaps I can fell two dogs with one bone. I'll write to Cecil telling him I wish to speak to him in private about matters of the greatest importance. That will itch his neb so much he'll grant my passage.'

By the end of April, Cecil had not risen to his bait. Knox was at a loss what to do: the guiding voice was silent. Should he return to Geneva or make his way directly to Scotland? He yanked at his beard until his chin smarted. Shooting pains pierced his brow like arrows. He wrestled with the demon of depression that threatened to suck him down into the darkest pit. The fiend throttled him in its terrifying grip, choking the breath out of him and torturing his brain with dreadful nightmares. However much he prayed, answer came there none. Had the Lord deserted him?

He lay on the bed drained and desperate until the thump of feet bounding up the stairs two steps at a time roused him. The door banged open.

'The *Saltire* has docked, master,' Jamie cried. 'Skipper Will's here to pick up some folk. Can we go home now?' He hopped from one foot to the other.

Knox raised his throbbing head. Had the Lord answered his prayers? Was this to be his deliverance?

He dragged his wasted carcase down to the quayside where his brother was loading up the boat. Jamie was already unwinding ropes on deck.

'After being so long land-bound Jamie is itching to set sail,' Knox said.

'What about you, brother? Are you ready to weigh anchor.'

Knox shivered in the spring breeze. 'What do you think, Will? Should I stay or go?'

'England may not want you, but Scotland does. The time is ripe for reformation and you'll no be wanting Errant Arran to lead it. Take the tide at the flood, Johnnie. There's nocht got by delay but dirt and lang nails.'

Knox glanced heavenwards. The morning mist was lifting and a ray of sun caught the *Saltire's* pennant – the blue and white cross of St Andrew. The sign he'd been waiting for. He bowed his head.

'So be it.'

As the time for departure approached, Skipper Will became increasingly agitated. The *Saltire* was set to sail before the tide turned but there was still no sign of the mysterious passengers. 'I've a mind to cast them adrift but my head would roll if I did.'

Darkness was falling when two cloaked figures emerged from the gloaming and scurried along the quayside towards the gangplank.

'I get seasick,' one of them whined.

'If you bide here you'll have no belly left to boak.' The second voice was a gruff growl. 'For they'll rip out your guts and wring them round your snivelling neck.'

On board, they flipped back their hoods. Both men were heavily bearded and unkempt, as if they'd been sleeping rough. Recognising one of the men, Knox and Jamie swapped worried glances.

Robert Stewart shoved his travelling companion forward. 'Meet my lord James Hamilton,' he said. 'Never fash, master prophet, the earl is a staunch Protestant and will aid our cause. Since her auld mother cannot live forever, Queen Mary will need a regent. Once we've dinged doun the French sow we'll put the earl in her place. But first we're stopping off at the English court for him to win Queen Elizabeth's hand.'

Grinning foolishly, Arran did a wee jig. 'Then I'll be King of England and

Scotland!'

Stewart grabbed his arm and hissed, 'Steek your gab, you daft gowk.' Swivelling round to face Knox he declared, 'And you, Master Knox, shall be prophet in our promised land.'

AUTHOR'S NOTE

However outstanding his achievements, the reputation of the Scottish Reformer, John Knox, has been overshadowed – some might say tarnished – by the opinions expressed in *The First Blast of the Trumpet against the Monstrous Regiment of Women,* that women being 'weak, frail, impatient, feeble, and foolish' made them unfit to rule.

Never mind that his sentiments were echoed to varying degree by most of the late medieval and Renaissance world, his polemical pamphlet has marked him out as a rampant misogynist. It may come as a surprise, therefore, that Knox did not hate women. On the contrary, he depended rather more than most men on the sympathy and affection of these 'frail, feeble, and foolish creatures' and, even more surprisingly perhaps, they reciprocated his feelings.

That the wiry, fiery Scottish preacher had charisma, the power to arouse fervent devotion and enthusiasm, is well documented but he must also have possessed a certain amount of personal charm to enchant women. Knox never lacked female admirers or female company. He was married twice – to much younger brides – and married women abandoned their husbands and family to follow him. Scandal was rife at the time – he was accused of using the black arts to steal men's wives from under their noses. Whenever he made a journey he took around with him a certain number of women whom he used to satisfy his lusts.

His torrid relationship with Elizabeth Bowes, mother of his first wife, seventeen-year-old Marjory, has been the subject of speculation over the centuries, causing tongues to wag about incest and adultery. Knox was a zealous correspondent carrying on regular correspondence with many women, not least Anna Locke whom he invited along with her sister-sin-law to join his ménage in Geneva.

These circumstances paint quite a different portrait from the caricature of Knox as the dour, pulpit-thumping Scottish Calvinist who hated women and made me curious to delve deeper into his friendships with women. By lifting the veil on his private life to reveal the man behind the myth, *The Second Blast of the Trumpet* seeks to give a more rounded picture of Knox as husband, lover, father and beloved friend.

Acknowledgements

Every writer of historical fiction stands on the shoulders of others – historians, academics, scholars and biographers – who have done the ground-breaking work, unearthing riches in archives and libraries for us to glean. While I mined countless books and articles, some only for a few nuggets – I admit to plundering from the following: Jane E. A. Dawson, *John Knox;* Pamela Ritchie, *Mary of Guise in Scotland;* Rosalind K Marshall's biographies of *John Knox* and *Mary of Guise; John Knox – Democrat* by Roderick Graham, and *The Swordbearer* by Stewart Lamont. For a more general history of Scotland during the early Reformation, *Court and Culture in Renaissance Scotland* by Carol Edington; *Scotland Re-formed 1488-1587* Jane E. A. Dawson; *The Rough Wooings* by Marcus Merriman proved invaluable. Diarmaid MacCulloch gives a comprehensive account of the European context in *Reformation: Europe's House Divided 1490-1700* while his study *Tudor Church Militant: Edward VI and the Protestant Reformation* sets the English scene. Robert M Kingdon, *Adultery and Divorce in Calvin's Geneva,* sheds light on the darker side of Calvin's exemplary city of God.

As well as published works, I'd like to acknowledge the countless web resources, especially blogs written by fellow writers and historians who freely and selflessly share their knowledge and research. Without having them literally at my fingertips, my novels would have taken so much longer to write.

I am especially indebted to fellow writer Kristin Gleeson for her perceptive insights and invaluable advice and to beta reader Altyn Bazarova for her sharp eyes and helpful suggestions.

Thanks also are due to the staff at the John Gray Centre in Haddington and to the team at Knox Robinson Publishing.

Last but not least, warm and grateful thanks to all the readers, friends and family whose humour, companionship and kindness have sustained me throughout the dark days.

Lightning Source UK Ltd.
Milton Keynes UK
UKOW02n0757101116

287158UK00002BA/4/P